Life, love & everything in between

A tale of heartfelt love,
callow emotions,
sensual romance
within a flicker of lifetime.

\- by K. Loma

Also available on Kindle, other devices and retailers.

ISBN:

Paperback -   978-0-9932263-2-8

Kindle -   978-0-9932263-1-1

ePub -   978-0-9932263-0-4

Dedicated to love –
in all its weird and wonderful forms
and pristine hallowed glory.

Preface

There are some gaps included in the narrative of certain situations and instances in the story, which is intentional. All characters are above 18 years of age and there is no implication of any of the characters or situations in the book to any real person, place or thing. Any similarity is purely coincidental. This is a work of fictional literature and should be enjoyed in the same light.

Some parts in the story depict moments of sexual nature and could be considered taboo in certain countries/cultures due to its storyline. The reader is advised to use their discretion. This story is especially for the open-minded, hopeful and dreamy romantic.

I have very much enjoyed writing this story as I have felt every emotion when I was writing it and I have tried my utmost to convey the feelings through these words although at times I may have failed miserably. At such times, I ask of you, kind reader, to overlook my shortfalls and fill the gaps appropriately. At the end of the day, I wish to convey nothing but heartfelt love through this story.

- K. Loma

Table of content

Acknowledgment

Chapter 1 – early days

Everyone was finished for the day and our parents had settled in front of the TV and were deciding to sleep early. My dad was beat after working all day. My mom had been busy in the kitchen making a wonderful meal after she had come home from work. Since mom had started working part-time, she said she never got a chance to cook us meals anymore and she missed that. That day, she had finished early so had time to cook. We were all waiting for Sam to get home. Earlier that afternoon, she had gone out with a friend but was expected any minute.

***

Sam and I, Alex, were fraternal twins – she was born minutes after me so she always called me 'bb' (short for big bro) and I used to tease her as 'baby'. Since we were fraternal twins, there were inherited similarities derived from the common genealogy for both of us. Although this was true in essence, we grew up to realise the differences – we had slightly different physique and body structure. We also had slightly different temperaments.

I was a typical male – big-boned, physical, and single minded while she was a typical female – slender, sensual and very creative and artistic. I am not stereotyping but I had recognised the differences between us far earlier than the similarities. As such, we did look different although I had heard people claim to spot our parents in our looks.

Although we were fraternal twins and as such there were few similarities between us, genetically, we often felt a connection between the two of us. She had reciprocated this just the same, as usual. Over the years, our parents, Stuart and Beverly, had simply come to accept it to be sibling love. For them it was good in one sense – we never fought with each other.

Sam had always been excellent at reciprocating my feelings. There was seldom a time when I had to elaborate anything to her – I guess you could attribute it to our 'link', of being twins. We understood each other implicitly. I always felt complete in her company and presence and so did she. We also found out that for some reason we missed each other when we were apart for long. A week had come to be long enough for us to go without seeing each other.

When we were growing up as kids, I do remember the very first few times when we had gone on separate school trips and by the time we had got back, we both had been 'miserable'. We had run into each other's arms when we had got back. After a few failed attempts, even the teachers had recommended our parents to just let us be together until we 'grew up' and 'grew out of it'. They just thought it was very sweet.

We grew up for sure but over the years, we just got closer and more comfortable with each other. Therefore, it comes as no surprise that we have been very different from other siblings – instead of fight, argue and bicker, we cared, collaborated and co-operated with each other all the time.

We had our 'tussles' occasionally but it was all a guise for a tease and to enjoy some closeness. She loved to tease me and over the years, she had sussed out some of my 'weaknesses'. I knew one of her biggest weakness – she was very ticklish. I used that as my personal defence shield when I needed to. Nonetheless, one rule, out of just a few in our house, laid down by my mom very early on was that under no circumstance was I allowed to physically hurt or hit Sam. I was meant to look after her well-being and likewise no matter what, she was supposed to respect my cautions and advice as an older brother.

I guess that was never really a bother because not only was I protective of her, I would always look out for her and likewise she always looked up to me for advice and guidance. We had developed a secret code for communicating urgency and we used those key words and cues at times. This always made me feel warm inside because no one knew the codes and no matter how many times others had tried, we had not divulged it to anyone. There was an unspoken language between us and we seemed to read each other's minds through our expressions, body language and glances.

We never really needed 'best friend' while we were growing up because we were very close. In fact we had developed such closeness and trust between us, we considered ourselves as best-buds. It used to be difficult to write essays in primary school about our sibling when we were very young kids. I used to see her as my other half, my best buddy, my soul-mate. For a long while when I was growing up, I thought 'sister' was just an 'official' name for such a person. In my mind, she was my life. Apparently, the same applied for her.

Over the years, we had developed the unspoken and implied restraint from divulging anything we shared between us – she and I never told anyone about what we spoke and did between us, not even to our parents. The secrecy sustained a rather unusual non-verbal intimacy between us and it provided the trust that made us both feel very confident together.

We grew up relying on each other and my mom always said how lucky she felt that she never had to worry about us growing up – we grew up without an urgent need for being looked-after. While we were growing up, mom had stayed home taking care of us and being a perfect homemaker. Therefore, it was a relief to her when we took care of each other and she did not had to watch our every move.

Apparently, when we were toddlers, we had been known to place dummies into each other's mouths, as kids we held the bottle for each other and even slept in a hug or while holding hands. We kissed and caressed each other a lot when we were kids. When we used to be playing out and about, people used to coo at our mutual love. "They do get along lovingly," my mom used to remark.

Over the years, as we realised that our special relationship was raising some eyebrows, we had decided to 'tone it down' by making friends and hanging out with others. Having grown up so close to each other, it was difficult for both of us to find good friends – Sam found it more difficult than me, although I was the one who spent more time alone. She found it difficult to relate to other male friends and her girl friends were very different from her. Although she was a very social and bubbly person, sometimes in the evening or after dinner, she would come around for a quiet hug and we used to talk while lying in bed.

I loved to talk to her about a lot of things – she was an ideal person to talk to. She would listen, question and somewhere in there, in her subtle ways, give me new thoughts and ideas, new perspectives on life. It comes without saying that we were good at consoling each other in the times of sadness too.

***

Sam came home after having gone out with her friends and went straight to her room in a hurry. While climbing the stairs mom and me had noticed that she had been crying and it was evident she was not in a good mood from the bang of her bedroom door as she shut it. Then we had heard sobbing coming from her room just before it was muffled.

Since Sam and I never really argued or fought, it was rare in our house to hear doors being slammed – our parents had a happy, contented marriage. Moreover, I had never ever hurt her or upset her. Needless to say, I was taken aback with this display. We had realised this was serious. I was in the lounge with mom and dad and they had just sat down in front of the TV waiting for dinnertime. My parents had stared at me with a big puzzled and alarmed question mark expression. I stared at them for a moment.

Then I got up mumbling, "I will see what the matter is."

"Good boy," mum mumbled. "Tell her dinner is ready." My parents never got involved between our personal affairs unless we asked for their advice – they left us to deal with each other's issues. Since I was so good at dealing with Sam about her issues, my parents just left me to it.

When I opened her bedroom door slowly, I peered in her room. She had buried her face in her pillow while lying on her tummy on her bed. Her arms were flung around the pillow and she was sobbing quietly still fully dressed. I gently closed the door and after walking slowly to the bed, I sat on it on her side and leaned on my elbow bringing my face close to her head. I started stroking her head gently, running my hand over her long light brown hair and on to her back. I did this several times. Her sobbing was slowing down and I felt she was calming down.

"Hey sweetie", I whispered gently in her ear. She turned her face toward me on the pillow and gazed at me, still tearful but had stopped sobbing.

I could hardly see her in such a state. It broke my heart to see her like that. When she looked at me after slowly composing herself, I caressed her face with my palm and lowered my face to her and asked, "What's the matter? Talk to me."

She stared at me with her tearful eyes. Her mascara had run. She had stopped sobbing but her eyes were still wet. She sat up slowly, turned around and sat on the edge of bed, dropping her feet to the floor and scooting next to me with a tissue in her hand. As I wrapped my arms around her gently stroking her back, I said softly, "Nothing in the world is worth so much heart-ache." I really did not know how I came up with that but something was telling me she was distraught over someone. I had never seen her cry like this before. This was her first.

She wrapped her hands around me tightly and sobbed for a few moments. I rubbed her back and tried to calm her down. As I pressed my cheek on her cheek, I ran my hand over her head down her hair. Without shushing her, I tried to calm her sobbing. After a while, she pulled out from the hug and looked at me in my eyes. She just stared at me for a few seconds.

I quietly whispered again, "What's the matter, hon?" I was still stroking her back slowly and gently but now I cupped her cheek in my palm. Seeing her in tears had made me tearful too.

She lowered her gaze and lowering her hands from my hug turned away and softly said, "I've split up with Billy. He dumped me," and sobbed again in her tissue.

I threw my arms around her and she hugged me while starting to sob again.

"Oooo." I sighed relief and sympathised while pulling her in my arms again trying to console her. I had feared something worse.

I smiled and exclaimed, "Well it's his loss. I never really understood what you saw in that douche bag in the first place. Never liked him. You deserve a lot better."

She just giggled under her tearful sobs and again calmed down before she stopped sobbing.

She poked her elbow in my stomach and muttered, "You are just saying that."

"I'm not." I protested. "You know how much I adore you. You certainly deserve a lot better. I don't know who, but certainly not that douche bag." I tried to make light of the situation.

She had been going out with Billy for a while and I thought it was going ok. He was her first real 'boyfriend'. I did not really appreciate him much as her choice, but I had thought that was down to my possessive jealousy and eventually had come to accept their friendship.

While she was turned on her side in my hug and still in my arms, I pulled her close and planted a few kisses on her forehead.

She kept glancing at me while I consoled her.

"It's your fault," she said abruptly looking straight at me in a girly whinge.

"My fault?" I was shocked and surprised as I stared at her. She grinned and so I laughed out. "How is it MY fault?" I was trying to contain my giggling. Now she was giggling from under her tears too.

"You have spoilt me by being so nice. I was wrong to assume he would be like you."

"Well sweetheart, you just made an ass of u and me", I giggled again.

She giggled too. "Stop making me smile. I feel like crying." She whinged in a girly manner.

She was good at relating to my twisted sense of humour.

"Sweetheart, you cannot compare me to him." My ego had received the biggest boost. "And moreover, you and I are different from everyone else. What you and I have is very special and unique. And yes I do adore you but that's because I do feel you are special and deserve a lot more."

I pulled her in my arms again and hugged her tightly. I gently rocked her. I planted a soft kiss deep in her neck just below her ear. That must have sent tingles in her body because I knew it was her weak spot.

She quivered slightly. "I'm just so glad to have you in my life." She said softly. "I adore you too, you know."

"I know, hon." I whispered softly as I pressed her into my hug in acknowledgment. She loved it when I called her that. She used to call me that too.

"Not as much as I adore you." I remarked teasingly.

She punched her elbow in my stomach again jokingly and gave me a stern look. I chuckled.

She was much composed now as she wiped her eyes and tears.

"Hungry?" I looked at her.

She just nodded after a momentary glance.

"I'm starving. I was waiting for you. Mom asked me to get you down for the dinner. Come on." I cocked my head in the direction of the door.

"Go on. I will be there in a minute", she spoke looking at me with a gentle smile.

"You are going to be ok?" I tilted her face toward me with my curled finger under her chin.

She nodded in a shy grin, dimming her eyes slightly to acknowledge her composure.

"Ok." I gave her a soft quick kiss on the cheek, stood up and walked to the door. I glanced at her back, and saw her looking at me. I smiled at her warmly, and stepped out the door and gently closed it behind me. Then I walked down the stairs and sat at the dinner table. Mom and dad were already at the table.

"You guys can start. I will wait for her. She is coming in a minute." I suggested.

"Everything ok?" Mom inquired caringly.

"Yep. All ok now." I nodded reassuringly. "She said she will talk to me later. Man trouble." I grinned.

"Oh dear." Mom exclaimed with a sigh.

"Good lad." Dad thanked me for caring for her. "Let's tuck in. I'm starving."

That evening after the dinner, Sam had cuddled next to me on the couch as mom and dad were relaxing in front of the TV. After a while, she looked at me and signalled to go with her.

"Good night mom and dad. I'm going upstairs to bed. I had a long day." She had waived good night.

She gave me one of her cues as she trotted upstairs to her bedroom.

I waited for about 10-15 minutes before I got up, waived goodnight myself and went upstairs. I went into the bathroom, freshened up for the night and then slowly and quietly tiptoed to my bedroom.

***

Sam and my bedrooms were in a corner adjacent to each other at one end of the house while the master bedroom was on the opposite side. In the middle was our common bathroom. Mom and dad had on-suite bathroom. We only had two bedrooms as such with a smaller study. For that reason, it was decided that when it was time for me and Sam to sleep in separate beds, as space was limited, one of us would take the study room while the other would get the bedroom and would have to share the shelves – the bedroom was more spacious and the study was a smaller room in comparison. Mom left us two to decide who took which room. As usual, Sam wasn't fussed and she looked at me and I wanted her to make the choice and we had just looked at each other for a while.

"Oh sort it out you two", mom had said exasperatedly and left it to us.

I had told Sam she could have the main bedroom if I could have access to it as and when. She was more than pleased to do so and had agreed and from then on, she had permitted me to use her room. There was more. Among the few rules that we had in our house, mom and dad both knocked and waited for 'come in' before entering our rooms if the door was closed. They treated us as proper adults from the very beginning. They never barged in if the door was closed but unlocked even after knocking. They always said, "A closed door needs to be treated as locked; else it could have been left open."

However, due to my arrangement with Sam, she had granted me 'special privilege' to access her room without knocking. She never required me to knock and just the same, she never knocked before entering my room. As such because both our parents knocked and waited before they opened closed doors even if they were unlocked, Sam and I fell into a habit of never locking our doors; just closing them shut when we needed some privacy. Nonetheless, the privacy applied only to our parents – never between us. That arrangement between us had always made me feel very special and close to her. It had also boosted our non-verbal intimacy.

***

While I dwindled the time waiting to hear my mom and dad get to bed, I waited patiently in my room. Once I heard the house become quiet, I went out my door closing it quietly behind and opened Sam's bedroom door and closed it behind me quietly. As I entered her room, she was in her bed curled up facing the door on her side under the duvet. It seemed like she was in her nightshirt.

When she saw me enter her room, she turned her table lamp on and raised the duvet to let me in the bed. As I got in her bed, she snuggled next to me and I wrapped my arm around her and lay on my back. She lay her head on my shoulder as she flung her arm around my chest and hugged me. As we settled in the bed, she shuffled close to me. After we had stayed like that for a while, she quietly started the conversation.

"I never really thought other guys would be so different from you." She spoke softly.

"In what way?" I stroked her back.

"Most of them seem to be just horny jerks." She spoke angrily. "No one really has the genteel heart as you."

"Well not all are horny jerks." I tried to justify calmly.

"I did see one today," she exclaimed. "He made me feel so smug just because I did not want to get physical."

"Was that the reason for today's heartache?" I inquired.

She nodded looking up at me. I felt her cheek move against my chest.

"Did he hurt you?" I asked her with straight voice.

"No." She shook her head as we looked at each other. "He just wouldn't take a 'no' for an answer."

"Now that is not news to me." I said nonchalantly. "There are a lot of guys who get worked up when they are in the mood and don't know how to be respectful."

"I just said to him I was not ready for a physical relationship and he kept pushing me. When I said I needed time, that's when he said I could have all the time I wanted and dumped me."

I just hugged her close to me while stroking her arm. "Forget him and put this behind you. Clearly he was not worth it."

"I just did not want to get physical with him that's all. He was nice enough to go out but I did not want to get physical with him. I did like him you know." Her voice suggested she was tearful.

"Don't worry about him now. Have you guys broken up officially or will you think of patching things with him?"

"No thanx. He is history." She said with a strong conviction. "Even if he begs, I ain't giving him a second chance."

"Ok. Then if he bothers you, let me know." I assured her in a big-brother kind of way.

She giggled with a girly smile. "Thanks hon. I don't think he will after the way he treated me today."

After a moment of silence, she spoke softly, a little hesitation and dismay was in her voice, "Do you think I might be lousy at being a girlfriend?"

"Don't you dare talk like that." I said sternly. She could tell from my voice I wasn't impressed about what she had said.

After a moment of silence she spoke, "I just wanted to see how it feels to be in a relationship. I didn't want it to end up like this, a failure."

"It's not your fault." I urged.

"Somehow it does feel like that, particularly since it was my first." She sighed despondently.

"You need to set high standards." I nudged her. "You are an angel and you need to choose more carefully." I complimented her.

"So what about you? Why aren't you in a relationship?" She asked me.

"No thank you." I replied. "I ain't interested."

"Why not?" She was puzzled. "Quite a few of my friends fancy the hot pants of you."

"Nah. I'm ok." I just shrugged it off.

She was looking at me quietly, expecting me to elaborate. Between us, we never stopped before completing our conversations. Phrases like 'forget it' or 'it doesn't matter' didn't exist between us. She stared at me and I looked at her. We had turned on our sides and were gazing at each other. I decided to open up.

"For me trust is a big thing and I need to be sure I am going to be handled with good care and sincerity. Promise should mean something, you know." I looked at her. "I don't like girls who change their mind. Most of your friends don't know what they want." I was sincere in my comments.

"True." She said softly. "I understand what you are saying."

"Even Jennifer?" she gazed at me. "She likes you a lot. What happened?"

I had gone out with Jennifer for a while. But things had fizzled out – rather I had slowed things and calmed them. I knew Sam was very close friends with Jennifer and I didn't want to ruin things between them because of me.

"She didn't live up to the promises she made." I looked at her. "I know she is your best friend so I didn't want to ruin things for you two, but I didn't want to get hurt either."

"What do you mean?" she asked being puzzled.

"Although she said she liked me and all, I never felt it with her. She seemed to just say it without actually showing it." I tried to elaborate. "For me, actions speak louder than words and I know real feelings cannot stay hidden from me for long." I looked at her and caressed her cheek as I smiled. "I've been with you for long, so I know when I'm loved."

She looked at me and smiled back as I shrugged my shoulders and grinned. She realised I had implied about her.

Then she hugged me and we lay there in silence for a while. I cuddled her in my arms.

She spoke softly again after a while. "Can I ask you something?"

"Anything hon. You know that." I nudged her. We were allowed to ask anything between us. Nothing was off-limits.

"I know." She smiled. "I just wanted to know if you had been physical with anyone yet." She remained quiet for a moment before looking at me.

"Like just playing or actually...?"

"Well either." She waited anxiously for my response.

"I have been physical a bit with Jen when we were going out, and Sara before her. They kissed and caressed me but nothing past that."

"Oh. That's all." She noted.

"Why do you ask?" I was being genuine. "Are you jealous?" I smiled.

"That's a mild word for me tonight because of how nice you have been to me." She said softly. "But I just wanted to know."

We lay there for a while in each other's arms. After I felt her nod away, I helped her roll away on her side and slowly sat up in the bed. I kissed her cheek and tucked her under the duvet. I got up from the bed and stepped out of her bedroom.

Next day, I gave her a big 4-foot tall stuffed toy teddy bear as a gift. I left it plonked in her bedroom when she was out. I had left a greeting card stuck to its hand. The card had a picture of a white swan taking flight over a lake with its wings stretched wide.

I had hand-written a verse inside the card:

> *Water runs dry from a swan's feather,*
> *as it has to fly higher and farther.*
> *Spread your wings and take flight,*
> *to new pastures and horizon in sight.*

When she came home, I was purposely sitting in the lounge. We were all waiting for her to get home so we could have the dinner together. When she came downstairs from her bedroom after freshening and changing into her nightwear, I looked at her but she just gazed at me with a grin and she did not say anything. I did not know if she liked her gift. After the meal, I stayed back helping mom to clear the table but Sam went to her room. Then I sat on the couch watching TV for a while. Sam never came downstairs.

When I went upstairs to kiss her good night, she was in her bed, curled up on her side facing the door. When she saw me pop into her room, she looked at me and gestured me to come in and sit next to her. She held out the card and asked me its significance.

"What does it mean?" she asked me. "What are you trying to imply?"

"Swans don't care about getting wet because water runs dry from their feathers. They shake it off like nothing happened and fly away without giving it a second thought, because there are a lot of wonderful places they have to get to, and see bigger and better things to enjoy."

"Thought so." She murmured, and then stared at the picture in the front of the card for a while. "Don't they mate for life?" She asked me gazing in my eyes.

I nodded and smiled. "You are not just a pretty face, are you?" I teased her.

She just grinned.

I looked at her deep in her eyes for a moment, with a warm gaze and said, "You need to find a swan because you are one too; I'm sure you don't realise it. The quicker you accept it, the quicker you will realise you can never be happy among poultry."

She took my hand in her hand, pulled it close to her face and kissed my palm gently. Then tucking it around her chest, she turned around on her side to face the other way and pulled my arm indicating she wanted to be spooned. I cuddled her as she lay there quietly and silently.

"Thank you for being you." She whispered softly.

"It's my pleasure as always." I whispered in her ear. I lay there for a while and as she loosened her grip on my hand, I got up propping on my hand and looked down across at her face. She had her eyes closed. I lowered my lips and planted a soft kiss on her cheek.

"Sweet dreams, hon," I whispered. I tucked her under the duvet and I caressed her hair as I ran my hand over her head. Then I caressed her cheek with my knuckles gently. Then I kissed her cheek and slowly got off her bed. I closed her door softly behind me as I stepped out of the room.

I was unable to fall asleep even after about half an hour of lying in my bed. Just when I was feeling sleepy after about an hour or so, I thought I had heard my door open and close slowly and quietly. I continued drifting to sleep. The room was illuminated with streaks of soft light from outside and was otherwise dark.

It must have been Sam as no one else walked in like that. I was sleepy anyway and I continued drifting to sleep. If she wanted me, she would usually wake me up so there was no reason for me to wake up. I was sleeping on my back with my face turned toward the door.

Sam just stood there and I heard sound of her walking toward me. I pretended to be asleep. She then seemed to have kneeled next to my bed. A whiff of her fragrance gave her closeness away – I could never miss recognising that sweetness. After a moment or so, I felt and heard her hair rustle as she lowered her face to mine and I felt her lips on mine as she planted a soft kiss. She must have done that very gently and softly so as not to wake me. I wanted to let her think that so I continued to pretend to be asleep.

There was moment of silence. I think she wanted to make sure I was still asleep and the short sensual demonstration of her admiration for me had not stirred me up. Then I heard a rustle that indicated she had stood up and walked away from the bed. Then I heard her mummer, "I love you." I heard the door open and close quietly behind her.

I had many mixed feelings that night. I knew we were close but that was the first time I had truly realised her feelings about me and it made me feel very happy. She really loved me deeply.

Chapter 2 – something special

For our 18th birthday, I had been wrecking my brains to think of something nice to gift Sam. I had asked her what she wanted. After a moment of contemplation, she softly said, "The fact that you are in my life, I have had the best present ever already."

That had made me so warm inside. "Come on hon. please give me some idea sweetheart." I had begged her again after I had hugged her in appreciation to what she had said. "Please." I looked in her eyes, nearly begging.

She looked at me with her deep warm eyes then said something that stayed with me forever. "Hon, whenever you feel you wish to gift me something special, let it be your own creation, one of its kind so it can become truly mine." She had said it calmly and gently. "That would always be special to me just as you are." She cupped my cheek and looked at me with warm eyes and a loving grin.

Therefore, I had presented her something truly unique on our 18th. It was a half-opened oyster shell with a pearl inside, resting on a proportional wooden pedestal. On the front face of the pedestal were the words inscribed on a small plaque "*you are more precious that any pearl*". When she saw it first, she was perplexed. "It is beautiful. I'm sure there is more to it than meets the eye." She had smiled while inspecting it.

I explained to her how I had found the shell on a holiday in the sea. I had cleaned it and painted it with resin, and stuck inside it a single natural pearl I bought from the mall. I had made the wooden stand in our garage and hand written the plaque on it.

On hearing all this, she looked at it again, placed it gently on her table next to her bed, and then opened her arms wide and just scooped me into a tight hug. She held me like that for what seemed hours.

"I adore you so much", she whispered in my ear still hugging me.

When she came out of the hug, I saw tears welled up in her warm eyes.

"Hey baby." I took her in my arms and kissed her cheek. "Didn't you like it?" I was trying to make her smile.

"Don't be silly." She punched me jokingly on my shoulder. "I love it. It is the most wonderful gift I've ever received," she said softly. "I'm just overwhelmed by the love you show me at times."

"You did say it had to be special." I smiled.

"I know. This is very special indeed," she said softly pushing herself into my arms.

I hugged her tenderly taking her in my arms and kissing her on her neck. She had melted in my arms as we hugged for a while. All the while, I could feel her hand stroking and running through the hair on the back of my head. She loved to play with my hair as I loved to play with hers. I kissed her gently on the cheek with a soft quick kiss just before we came out of the hug. Her soft curvy torso had melted into my arms.

"I have something for you too," she said excitedly.

She handed me a wrapped box with nice ribbon and a heart sticker. Talk about putting sensual touch on something as bland as a gift box. That was my little sister.

When I opened it, there was a 100ml eau de toilette bottle. There was the letter X inscribed on it with gold coloured resin like an insignia. I just looked at her. She used to call me 'X' quite many times. It was short for Alex. When she was little, she could not pronounce my name and used to call me that. It just stayed with her like that even after she grew up.

"Go on, try it." She was waiting with baited breath.

I sprayed it on my arm, rubbed it in and let it mature. As I took a sniff, I realised it was very classy and refreshing fragrance. I could smell some citrus fruits, a small hint of flowers and a very classy after-note. It matured into a very refreshing fragrance. Clearly, it was blend of many different fragrances. It was a pleasantly complex fragrance.

"Nice." I smiled as I looked at her, inspecting the bottle and the box. "I like it; very interesting fragrance."

"Oh good." She jumped with excitement. "I was not sure if you would like it. But by now I think I have sussed your taste."

"Go on. Tell me more about it." I was curious to know. It was apparent that this was not an off-the-shelf purchase.

She smiled coyly. "Remember the trip I went last month with my friends. Well it was not quite what I made it out to be. I had visited a perfume factory. They provide factory tours and after the tour, you can make a personalised custom fragrance of your own. They usually only do 30ml bottles but I paid extra to get me a 100ml."

"So you created this perfume?" I was curious, now that I had realised what the gift was.

She nodded. "They taught us the basics of fragrance and how the perfume is made. Then they gave us about 15 minutes to make up our own collation. From what I had researched and understood there, I came up with 3 different ones and then finalised this one."

"Why this one then?" I looked at her inquisitively.

"This reminds me of you." She said softly. "We were told that perfume has individuality and personality and this is just you. When I smelled it, it made me think of you." She was very sultry and sensual in her voice.

"Thanks." I smiled and hugged her. "May be YOU should use it then rather than me," I teased her.

"Then I would be loopy all the time and won't get anything done." She blushed. She nudged my arm in a tease.

After our birthday, I felt Sam and I had begun to come closer. I realised it later but she had started to let her hair grow just because I liked long hair. She started asking me to take her shopping, just so that she could ask my opinion on the clothes she chose. She would ask me to choose her perfume for her. I used to do the same – let her choose for me. I started letting her shop my clothes for me – just because she complained that I had no taste in fashion. I had figured it was her way of suggesting that I wear her choice of clothes. She never wore anything that I had not chosen.

"I need you to take me shopping," was her code for asking me indirectly to choose for her. When I realised that, I started selecting her clothes and she would try them for me.

She had a lovely figure, just a little shorter than me and although she was not athletic, she kept her figure in a good shape. She had curves all at the right places, and as she was not skinny, I loved cuddling her in bear hugs. I felt her soft torso melt in my arms every time. She had long thick straight light brown hair that she kept letting grow. She did not have a fringe, just because I did not like it. Instead, she parted her hair sometimes in the middle, and sometimes on the side, and let the bangs flow past her ears. Her sweet oval face looked good with a nice forehead. She never wore makeup just because I always encouraged and complimented her natural beauty. She even used the mascara sparingly. However, she always smelled lovely. One whiff of her fragrance as she strolled past me or hugged me would get me sighing.

Her fragrance is what I could never forget. "You chose it remember?" She used to remind me always. It was the second reason I kept finding excuses to get close to her always, apart from the fact that she was a very tactile person. She had magic in her fingertips and her touch was sensual yet electric – it used to raise goose bumps in me all the time. Yet she did it so casually and without any real intention. I could feel the love in her heart through her touch just as much as she would melt mine with her warm piercing gaze every time she looked at me.

She loved me to hold her tenderly at her waist. When we were home alone, she would love to feel my arms wrapped around her tummy holding her from behind. I would snake my arms around her tummy from the back and she would place her hands over mine. I would pull her in my hug, and she would press into my arms. I would nuzzle my face over her shoulder and press my cheek on her cheek. That made her feel very warm and loved inside. She would place her hands on mine and stay in the hug for a long while. At times, she would turn and press herself face to face and let me give her one of my bear hugs, squeezing her at her waist, while she wrapped her arms around my neck. She would always press herself deep in my hug, our torsos pressed against each other.

I could tell when she wanted to feel my hand around her as she used to get close and gently nudge me or wrap my arm around her back as she pushed herself into me. It used to be so natural and innocent that no one really took notice. She loved taking my arm when we walked together. She used to put her arm around mine and hold my hand at times.

No matter what favours she asked me, I could never say no to her. Whenever she asked me for a favour, all I could say is "and in return…" teasingly. Every time her 'compensation' is what I used to look forward for doing her favours. Just as she did me favours, I used to return in kind.

As she was very feminine and artistic, her hobbies and interests would not really interest a guy. Nonetheless, I used to either tag along or ferry her about for it when she needed me to give her company because never once did she turn down an opportunity to spend time with me, no matter what I was planning on doing.

Theatre, symphonies and movies were her thing. I loved movies too. So there we had something in common. The choices were where the favours would usually start. I liked action, thriller and murder mystery. She preferred romance, comedy and chic-flicks. We both loved sci-fi and drama. Nonetheless, we always had a lovely time after the movie discussing it over dinner. That was the part I loved the most. After watching a good thoughtful movie, even she used to get into the discussion. We used to spend long hours critically analysing some good ones we had seen over the years. As she was creative and artistic, she used to interpret things very differently which always made me smile at her lateral outlook in life. It also taught me the subtle wisdom that I had come to appreciate from her so much.

Our sense of humour was quiet compatible. Although she thought I would die of starvation if I ever decided to be a stand-up comedian, I did manage to make her roll in laughter at times. Once you started Sam giggling on something, it would take a while for her to stop giggling, and I would giggle just looking at her. Mom and Dad used to roll their eyes and just leave us be, "oh here they go again."

Sam jack-jumped in conversations a lot – where I was logical and would hold a conversation for some time, she used to go off on a tangent very quickly and then make a comment where I used be like "huh? Where did that come from?" and then we used to laugh. It used to be interesting to figure out how she had landed on that topic from what was in discussion at the time.

I did not drink alcohol in our family that much, just because I never enjoyed the taste for it. Sam used to enjoy white wine and sometimes rosé. Our parents had not encouraged drinking wine at home as a habit. Although they had some, Sam was allowed only a glass occasionally; she and I enjoyed good food. Mom was an excellent cook and homemaker. She took care of us with all the love in the world.

Although we were raised with reasonable amount of discipline, we had open-minded parents who encouraged us to think big and beyond. That was also the reason why they rarely frowned on the closeness me and Sam shared between us. In their minds, we were close because we were twins and fencing it with rules would had just aggravated the situation.

I remember one afternoon, Sam and mom had spent hours in the kitchen cooking something. Apparently, it was a surprise for me that Sam was learning to make. Sam had discussed with mom what she wanted to cook and mom had asked her to create a list of ingredients.

"X, could you get me some stuff from the store please?" Sam yelled out from bottom end of the stairs in the lounge.

"What do you need?" I popped my head on the landing.

"Here's the list," she smiled as usual. "I need it soon." Those eyes, that smile, those looks. I had died.

"How soon?" I was in the middle of a game.

"Now." She exclaimed. "Mom and I need it now so we can cook it."

"Talk about last minute preparation." I exclaimed and got changed and came downstairs.

"Ok. Where's the list?" I said.

As she handed me the list, she started elaborating me the amounts and varieties as substitutes if they did not have her sort of ingredients.

I just looked at mom totally confused. She just shrugged her shoulders and smiled.

"Why don't you just come with me?" I looked at Sam with one of our visual cues. "That would make it so much easier."

Sam looked at mom. "Can I?"

"Might as well. If he cocks up the list, it will take twice as long to fix it. Anyway, until you get these things, we can't make a head start." Mom looked at her nonchalantly.

"Ok. Give me one minute." Sam ran upstairs and got changed. When she came down, my eyes lit up. She had changed into a casual sleeveless shirt with a discreet yet seductive V-neckline, which hugged her waist and was tucked inside a slender, figure-hugging pair of jeans. She had done her hair in one of her unique styles. She put on boots and she looked gorgeous. She smelled heavenly and she had a smile that lit up like sunshine.

"Come on then." She took my arm and we headed out.

"Bye mom. See you soon." I flew her a kiss.

"Don't be late. I have dinner to sort too." Mom warned us.

"Don't worry." Sam shouted her confirmation as we stepped out.

Sam never gave up an opportunity to spend time with me, staying in or going out, and neither did I.

That night when we were enjoying our dinner, dad made a comment about the fine dessert. "What's the occasion?"

"Sam made it for Alex because he likes it." Mom said to dad with a sly smile.

Sam just looked at me coyly while eating the chocolate cake she had made that evening along with the piña colada cocktail. She had made a special 'virgin' batch for me, as I liked the non-alcoholic cocktails better.

"What about the icing? That's the best part," dad exclaimed while enjoying the cake.

"Alex doesn't like icing." Sam said.

"So? We do." Dad looked at mom then her.

"Next time." Sam agreed.

Dad just looked at me then Sam, then mom, then smiled, shook his head and finished his dessert.

"I thought it wouldn't taste nice. It doesn't look as good as it should." Sam said while gently stroking my thigh under the table. She always sat scooted up next to me. She was trying to be humble about her cooking.

"It tastes lovely." I looked up and looked at our parents and then her, trying to be encouraging. "It's meant to be eaten not looked at. And it tastes heavenly." I tried to be complimentary.

"Thanks hon." She was glad that I had loved it. "You are always an easy pleaser."

Dad cleared his throat.

"And both of you too." She giggled. We all just laughed.

My closeness with Sam was developing steadily and consistently. We used to spend quite some time playing our video games on our console in her room. The cabinet was just next to the door and in front of the bed, against the wall. At times, we used to sit in the bed. She used to recline on my chest and sometimes she used to sit between my legs. We had gotten a beanbag and a large soft cushion that we usually used, to make it comfy to sit on the wooden floor at other times. Then Sam suggested we could make things interesting.

She suggested that we play the game in single-player mode but each one of us would use only one side of game pad. She would sit in my lap on the cushion, between my crossed legs, with her back pressed on my chest. I would cuddle her slightly in my arms and one of us would use their left hand to use the left controls while the other used their right hand to use the right controls on the game pad. When we tried it the first time, all we did was giggle and fall about laughing, seeing just how confusing the whole thing had gotten.

Once mom came up to see what the whole racket was about. When we explained her what we were doing, she just shook her head, smiled and told us to keep it down.

This new way of playing games was rather sensual. It meant that we had to place our other hand somewhere as it was not being used. I usually hugged her around her tummy and she placed her hand on my thigh.

When that way got boring, we decided to turn it into a 2-player mode. Now, each one of us used alternate sides on the two pads. Therefore, within the two of us and two pairs of hands, no single person controlled one game pad fully. Sam would use the left controls on one and right on the other. I would use exactly the opposite. We used to laugh our asses off at times while playing games like these. We called them 'mixed singles' and 'mixed doubles' in our coded way.

This new way also meant that we had increased the closeness even when playing games on our consoles. It provided me with a warm glow inside and I loved to play like that.

We used to share the beanbag and the cushion at times. She used to press herself back on to my chest and I used to cuddle her deep in my arms. Our cheeks would brush at times depending on how we sat and then I would plant kisses on her cheek. She used to have her hair in a loose bun or in a rubber band so it would not cover her cheeks. We loved pressing our cheeks together and she would caress her palm on my cheek sometimes. She used to run her fingertips over and under my thighs gently. It sent shivers through my body. When I quivered, she used to giggle with laughter.

"Stop it. You are doing this just to tease me." I used to nudge her without much intention for her to stop. She used to turn her head and plant soft kisses on my cheek occasionally, or raise her palm and gently place it on my cheek. That used to be a cue for me to know when she wanted me to turn my face and kiss her cheek.

Chapter 3 – project makeover

The school was ending in few months time. We both had decided to continue our diplomas in the local college after summer. It sounded prudent in many aspects rather than make a big move to university. Financially it would give us the breather we needed.

Sam came to my room one evening. As she lay on my bed, I continued working at my desk.

"X", she called out to me softly.

"Yes hon." I replied without looking toward her, continuing with my work.

"What have you thought about doing this summer?"

I put my work aside and looked at her. She turned in the bed, propped her head on her hand and while resting on her elbow she looked at me.

"Nothing much. I have been looking for some work but none so far." I replied.

"Me neither." She replied. "I have tried but everywhere it's dry."

I looked at her. Usually she had something floating in her mind when she asked such dead-end questions.

"I was thinking,..." she continued, "...instead of wasting the opportunity for some work experience, and feeling disappointed about job market, why not we collaborate and do something together?"

I was intrigued. "What do you have in mind?" I turned to her with keen interest.

"Hear me out." She continued. "Why not invest our time in getting our house renovated?"

"In what sense?" I was perplexed.

"Well this place has not been redecorated for a few years now. We both have developed sufficient skills to be able to paint, wall-paper or redecorate simple areas like the lounge or our bedrooms."

"Sure." I acknowledged. "But that's going to cost money."

"Eureka, Archie." Sam chuckled with sarcasm.

I smiled realising her twisted humour.

"We will put forward a proposal with a plan and a budget to our parents." She continued to elaborate. "Then if they agree, we will buy the stuff and redecorate it ourselves. Two months of solid work should be able to sort this place. There are two of us. That's a lot of man-woman hours."

Now I chuckled at her political correctness. "Sounds possible. I'm assuming you already have sorted some plan out."

"You aren't just a pretty face are you?" she teased me again. "Well I was thinking why not start with re-arranging of the lounge, re-painting the house, say select rooms for now, and then see if we could have some of the carpets replaced."

"I'm in." I agreed. "When do we tell mom and dad?"

"Let's broach the topic at dinner tonight." She suggested winking at me.

"Deal."

After a moment of silence, she put forward another question to me, "Will you be ok spending time working with me?"

I looked around to her. "I would love to. Why wouldn't I be?"

"I don't know; just asking if you would rather do something else with your friends."

"I would be more than happy spending time with you." I said. "I mean working with you."

She smiled at me with a twinkle. "I was thinking, let's make it a standard 40 hrs-a-week routine. Evenings and weekends are ours to enjoy. That way we will get a feel of what a full time job feels like."

"Good idea." I nodded. "That doesn't sound too hectic."

Then as she lay there, for a moment, she murmured quietly, "Don't worry I will make it worthwhile. It will be fun working together."

I stood up from my desk, turned around, went close to her and lay down next to her in the bed. She rolled on her back, threw her hands over her head and looked at me. I lowered myself on her and hugged her tenderly.

"Every minute I spend with you is full of bliss." I whispered in her ear.

She wrapped her hands around my neck and hugged me with warmth. "I'm glad you think that. I love to spend time with you too."

I sat up and rested my elbow on the bed. "Even if this plan does not shape up, we will find something else to do together, how about that?"

She smiled in acknowledgement. Her eyes glowed with excitement. I lowered my lips, kissed her cheek and hugged her for a while. She ran her hands over my back wrapping her arms around my neck.

In the evening, after the dinner, Sam and I broached the topic to our parents. After listening to us carefully, dad looked at mom.

Then looking at us, he spoke with appreciation, "Kids, this house is yours too. If you feel you wish to make home improvements, I am all for it. However, I would like to see some budget and some plans so I know what I am getting myself into. Not that I don't trust you, but at the end of the day, the buck stops with us." He looked at mom. "So you understand when I say this, as long as it will be a good investment, we are all for it. What do you say?" he looked at mom.

"I'm fine with it too." Mom nodded.

"Then in a week's time, we will provide you with a plan and a rough budget." Sam suggested.

"How about I give you a budget right now, and you make it fit inside it? I ain't no president or prime minister to work forward." He chuckled.

Sam and I looked at each other. "Sure."

So dad gave us a rough budget.

"Is that maximum or there is a leeway?" Sam asked.

"There is a leeway but not too much. Work with the figure as max because I know you will go over that definitely anyway. I'm already assuming a surplus in the figure I have given you." He smiled looking at mom.

"Ok." Sam and I looked at each other. "We have our project."

"So is this your idea for the summer?" Dad asked.

"Yep." Sam replied. "Rather than waste time looking for jobs and getting depressed, we thought it would be nice to invest some time and resources in our own home."

"Great idea." Dad looked at mom with admiration.

"Plus we were thinking, we would like to start doing groceries for us." Sam added looking at me. I just nodded.

"Mom, you don't have to worry about getting it anymore. We will get it every week." Sam said squeezing my hand.

"That would be kind of you." Mom smiled.

"What magic mushrooms did you have for breakfast today?" dad giggled looking at mom and then us both.

"Oh dad. Stop teasing us. We are trying to contribute to the family and we realise we could make a start somewhere." Sam was girlish.

"I'm just pulling your leg, sweetheart." Dad leaned forward on the table. "Your consideration and help is always appreciated. You know that. It is nice to see you kids taking responsibility in the house, and without our prompts. That is something."

After the meals, Sam and I went upstairs to discuss about our project. We spent the majority of a week looking at ideas and calculating costs for them. Sam was always the creative one so she came up with a ton of ideas for the makeover. I got the maths sorted and the different options and combinations. It was fun working with her. I saw a very different side to her personality. Sam was a bright and inspiring person to work with. She had a very calm and relaxed approach to work. May be she enjoyed working with me since we were close to each other anyway, but the time we spent together was always full of excitement.

She took every opportunity to touch and hug me, get close and hold me. She ran her fingers though my hair, held my hand while walking, wrapped my arm around her and hugged me sometimes. It was all very warm and loving.

We had realised that we ended up using many skills to create the plan from the given budget. It helped us develop and strengthen our technical and personal skills. I had begun to realise the significance of such in-house projects as good substitutes for work placements.

Where Sam fell short, I would help her out. When my abilities fell short, she filled the gap. We made a good team and we loved working together. Apart from the learning we were gaining, we were also getting closer together.

When we were presenting the plan one evening, dad just stopped us and looked at the maths. "I trust you guys to make good decisions about the colours and aesthetic. I just want to make sure you have not missed anything critical in your consideration. That is all. So far, it looks good. Go ahead." He approved with confidence. "And remember, we are in this together. If you hit a wall, so as to speak (he air quoted 'wall') do not think it is your problem to solve alone. We will solve it together. You are never alone. This is not a test. It is an exercise to develop and learn." He smiled at us.

Sam hugged him. "Thanks dad."

The weeks that followed were really good. During the summer, Sam and I worked on our project every day. We had created daily and weekly planner so we had a target to reach every day. The first week proved challenging. We were falling behind by the end of the second week. Therefore, we sat down and re-did the schedule with some additional buffers. What seemed like an easy 5-week project now looked more like a 7-week one. Moreover, we had to scale a few bits down and reduce the scope slightly. Since this was not a test, Sam just smiled and said, "More quality time together." She hugged me and we both smiled at each other.

During work, we listened to our favourite music and took time to dance to some tunes. Occasionally, we used to chat about different things. I would watch her every gesture, her every expression and her every movement. She would enjoy my gazes, encourage my closeness and hugs and touch me at every opportunity. By the time we had finished the makeover, I had lost touch of time. I would look forward to spending time with Sam everyday without really paying much attention to what we were doing. She had a very unusual way to take the chore out of work and instead make it enjoyable.

When we were painting Sam's bedroom, I left a small kiss mark of my lips on the wall very close to her bed when the glossy paint had half-dried. It was placed so that when she lay in her bed on her side facing the door, she would notice it directly in front of her sight. I did not tell her about it. Two days later, Sam came into my room at dawn and climbed into my bed under the duvet. She kissed me softly on my cheek and said, "Thank you for the kiss."

I had just smiled. "You noticed it then huh."

The next time I had seen it, she had painted red outline of a perfect heart around the kiss mark, with the kiss mark just on the bottom right corner inside the heart.

While I was standing there admiring her idea, she came and stood by me, hugging me with her arms from behind me. "You kissed my heart," she said softly.

"You felt it then." I whispered, kissing her forehead as I pulled her by her waist by my side.

"uh huh." She nodded. "Deep inside."

When we had completed the work, we showed it to our parents, not that they did not see it being completed every day. The final amount did go a tad bit over, but dad actually smiled. "You have done extremely well I must say. This is not too over the budget. I had anticipated a lot more extra expense." He smiled. "And it does look professional, not just good and new. Well done guys." Our parents looked at us with pride.

We both were chuffed. We were thrilled about our success with our first real project. There were lessons we had learned in hindsight. Nevertheless, the most important thing that had happened was Sam and I had gotten closer to each other.

We got one more surprise – dad decided to 'pay' us our labour charge for the makeover. "You did it out of the goodness of your heart, without being prompted and without any expectation of reimbursement. I feel you deserve some remuneration for your hard work."

He had paid us both full-time wages for the hours we had spent working on the project. In addition, he gave a generous 'tip' for being such good kids. Mom and dad looked at us with complete admiration and we both were thrilled beyond words.

"This is way better than any work placement." I exclaimed. "We enjoyed the work and got paid for it." I laughed.

Sam and I hugged dad and mom and we enjoyed a lovely meal that evening.

We had installed an audio surround system for the TV with built in USB audio player in the receiver. I had purchased the speakers on the internet. Sam had selected a nice unit to house the entire media centre. We had digitised all of mom and dad's CD collection. The bookshelf was redecorated with glass doors. We had also managed to change the sofa to an L-shaped corner unit stretching the entire width of the lounge in front of the TV. There were two recliners built-in the sofa and Sam had loved the lounger-style end corner unit. We could seat five people in the lounge now.

Once the makeover was done, we all loved enjoying the new sofa. Sam would love to sit with me reclined in the lounger and then plonk herself in front of me reclining back on my chest. Dad loved his recliner and mom got used to it soon enough. "This is the life." Dad remarked occasionally when he relaxed after meals.

"It is really comfortable, isn't it?" Mom agreed with him. "Nice work you two."

Sam would feel chuffed and I would snuggle her while she cuddled close to me on the lounger.

Occasionally Sam had fallen asleep lying on me – sometimes on her back with my arms around her tummy, her hands pressed on my hands, or sometimes she would turn and lie on my chest, her head on my shoulder or nuzzled in my neck, her feet intertwined in mine and I would be holding her in a soft embrace. Her tender warmth would feel so loving against me at such times. I would not want to move all night. Seeing her sleep so peacefully in my arms would be such a complacent moment.

Mom would often throw a blanket on us before she and dad went to bed.

"I will carry her up later," I used to quietly whisper to mom.

I used to stay there for a while until such time I could feel Sam stir up. Sometimes she did not, so then I carried her in my arms to her bed.

Chapter 4 – first time for bedtime

Our 19th birthday was approaching soon. We had decided that we would exchange our gifts at midnight on the eve of our birthday that time. We were in her room playing games and then watching TV waiting for midnight. By then our parents would had been in bed fast asleep anyway. Just before midnight, we decided to exchange out gifts.

She presented her gift first. It was a rather big, tall and slightly heavy box. When I unwrapped it, it was encased in a transparent hard glass cylindrical cover and had a wooden circular base. It stood about 6 inches tall and 4 inches in diameter and was a pure white figurine; it looked like something from the Circle of Life™ collection. I just looked at her and went back to examining it in detail. She stood there looking at me patiently but anxiously. "Go on." I urged her to explain the gift. She elaborated the detail slowly.

It was a figurine of a young couple – a male and a female, although the facial features were generic – in a sort of detached embrace, like a stance in a ballroom dance. The woman had her hair in a loose bun hanging over the back of her neck (like Sam sometimes did) and they were of the similar height with the woman slightly shorter than the man. They were little less than arms length from each other. Each had their left hand placed just at the waist, and the right hand placed on the left shoulder (closer to the neck) of the other. They seemed to be looking into each other, the heads tilted just slightly toward the right, and although they were not kissing, on prolonged look it felt that in the next moment they would move in for a kiss. The subtlety of this dual expression and impending possibility was very intriguing. Each of their torsos from hip down morphed into a circular column and each appeared to be part of the double helix of the DNA strand, appearing to be burying into the base. The two pairs of hands crisscrossed when seen as 3D and that resembled the base pairs in the DNA strand. On the base of the wooden stand was inscribed a note, "You complete me".

For a moment I was just standing there appreciating the figurine holding it carefully so as not to drop it. The whole thing was just out of this world with so many scientific and artistic connotations and analogies.

As I stood there admiring it, I said in complete surprise, "and you made it from scratch!?" I was taken aback with the profound nature of the gift.

She nodded. "It has taken me few months to make this. I had to start from a drawing, then create a mould and then create a cast. I had to seek some professional help to create the mould and cast. It was challenging but I think I have managed it well given that it is my first."

This was my time to well up in tears. As I looked at her while being speechless, she saw the tear and slowly and gently took me in her arms and hugged me deeply. I was still holding the figurine in one arm so I could only pull her using my other arm. She planted a deep sensual and wet kiss on my neck below the ear and sighed in my ear, "I feel lost without you, you know." She broke away from the hug to look deep into my eyes. "That is the truth." She just gazed at me for a while to let me soak in the sincerity in that statement.

I just stared at her speechless with my eyes welled up. I planted a deep long kiss on her cheek, and this time I felt her pull me into her arms. I felt the warmth in her heart through her firm hands wrapping me in her hug. When we broke out of the hug, she brushed away the tear on my cheek with a grin. Then I presented her with my gift.

I had used Sam's last year's idea and created a perfume for her, just as she had done the previous year. It reminded me of her – sensual, tantalising and tender. It was a very feminine, floral yet organic fragrance that left a very classy after-note when it matured. It was very light fragrance.

When I presented it to her, she tried it on her arm and then just sprayed it all over her skin under her top. "I love it hon." she exclaimed with wide eyes. "It is such a light fragrance."

"One would have to get pretty close to you to smell it on you. That is what it represents – closeness, apart from the fact that the fragrance reminds me of you; as you would say." I smiled with a slight blush.

She slowly wrapped her arm around my neck, moved into my arms gently and planted a wet kiss on my neck under my ear.

"No one gets closer than you." She sighed in my ear. "I will use this to remind you of our closeness."

I wrapped my arms around her waist and back, and held her in a tight hug as she melted. She was holding my cheek in her palm and when she moved out of the hug, she looked very sensual and deep in my eyes.

Then as she was putting it aside, I gave her another gift – a card in an envelope. "Awe what's this?" she exclaimed.

"I stole your idea from last year and so I did not think it was genuinely original of me. So I have created this as a second present for you."

"You did not have to. The perfume is very original anyway." She tried to appease me.

The card had a photo of young couple from behind holding each other, like we often used to. As she gently opened the card, she read the poetry written inside.

I had handwritten inside the card:

With you

In your eyes, I see the visions I have never thought.
In your voice, I hear the wisdom I have always sought.

In your touch, I feel the desire I have craved.
In your hug, I gain the certitude I never had.

In your company, I realise the experiences I have missed.
In your smile, I see the hope I have always wished.

With your memories, I go to places I have never been.
With your love, I live a dream I have never seen.

X

Then she welled up and melted in my hug again.

"I think we are hopeless at exchanging gifts. We should stop giving them from next year," I said with a teasing giggle.

"No. Don't say that." She punched my arm gently in protest. "I love it. Makes me realise just how wonderful you are and how lucky I am to have you in my life."

"It can't be good if it makes both of us tearful." I was trying to make light of the situation.

"Stop being silly" She giggled. "These are happy tears. Nothing wrong with them"

"Oh my. Then what is sad laughter?!" I smiled.

She just looked at me with puzzled face. Then realising I was pulling her leg with one of my twisted humour she punched my arm gently and shook her head with a smile. I giggled.

Then she sat on the side of the bed turned around facing toward me with one leg folded at the knee under her bum and one on the floor. She held out her hand beckoning me to walk to her. She patted on the bed to indicate to sit next to her.

"I love and adore you so very much, hon," she whispered staring deep in my eyes.

"Me too hon." I replied.

"Without questioning the request I am about to make, will you just go along with it? Just for my sake?" She spoke softly lowering her gaze just for a quick second.

"Sure hon. You know me, I'm always game for anything you say."

"Sleep here tonight with me. I want to feel you close to me." She sighed. "Don't ask me why I want you to. I just do." She shrugged her shoulders. "Like old time when we were young."

I moved up close to her and hugged her gently. "Of course I will. But what about mom and dad?"

She just looked at me perplexed.

"What if anyone of them wakes up and happens to knock on your door while I'm here?" I looked at her for a resolution.

"They won't. Tomorrow is a working day." She tried to rationalise it. "It will be ok. Don't worry." She sighed. Her eyes were very warm and hungry for love. "If anyone does knock, I will make an excuse and we will see through it."

"Ok. Let's try this once this time."

Her eyes lit up just as her heart skipped a beat.

As we got into the bed under the duvet, she turned off the table light and the room was flooded with darkness. As usual, the faint streetlights poured in without much help in illuminating the room.

As we lay in bed, letting our pupils dilate to adjust to the darkness in the room, I spooned her tenderly. She pushed herself into my arm as I let it travel around her tummy and waist. As she felt my face close to her neck, she moved her hand gently and wrapped her hair away under her neck toward the front, exposing her neck above. I felt she wanted me to get closer, as she held my arms and pushed herself closer to me. I bent my knees and pressed my thighs on her as I cocooned her in my hug.

I heard her sigh softly as she felt the warm closeness melt her. We lay there for a while enjoying the warmth we were sharing between us. As she melted, I planted a few soft wet long kisses on her neck, just below her ear.

She moaned sensually and gently threw her hand up over the back and held my head as she ran her fingers through my hair. As she turned her head slightly, I kissed her cheek. As she continued to turn her face toward me, the next kiss was planted very close to her lips, accidently. Therefore, I paused and I looked at her. She lay still for a while gazing at me. Our pupils had adjusted to the darkness and we were able to make out each other's expressions through the streetlight that poured through the window.

She turned and rolled slowly around on to her side and faced me. As we fumbled to adjust in the bed, we shuffled and turned over on to our sides facing each other. She shifted closer to me, trying to snuggle deeper into my hug as I wrapped my arm around her. I shuffled closer to her in the bed. I slid one arm under her pillow and wrapped her in my arms. Her face was nuzzled on my neck below my cheek.

"This feels so good." She sighed in my ear. "This is the first time we are sleeping in the same bed together, after such a long time." I felt the excitement in her voice. "I missed this so much all this time."

As I hugged her, she buried and pushed herself into my arms. Our knees knocked about so I shifted and she took the cue and we intertwined our legs. Now we were snaked into each other's arms and I wrapped her tightly in my arms. We lay there in silence for a while. We both enjoyed the closeness because we both truly had not felt it in a long time since we started sleeping in separate beds.

She moved away slightly and lay on the pillow on her cheek, facing me. Her lips were inches away. Now the street lights from outside were slowly brightening the room as our eyes adjusted to the darkness. I could make out her face and her hair gently flowing over her cheek and ear. I gently stroked and caressed it, sliding it behind her ear as I let it cascade on her neck. She pressed her hand over mine and taking it in her hand moved it to her lips and planted kisses on my palm.

"Thank you for the gifts," she sighed. "You made me feel very special."

"That's because you are. I'm just glad you liked them, hon." I was trying to make no big deal out of it.

"I loved them, just as much as I love all the other things you do for me." She caressed my face gently.

We lay there quietly for a while, trying to see through the darkness, tracing the contours of our faces. Her fragrance was now seducing me with sensuality.

"You smell divine." I remarked.

"It's one you just gave me." She flicked her hair back from her neck exposing her neck for me to smell the fragrance. Rising on her elbow, she moved herself and slowly lowered her neck to let me smell it. Propping herself on one hand across on my other side, she held her neck on my face while I took in her fragrance. I took in a deep and slow breath and it hit me, sending sensual glow in my body. I raised my hand over the back of her head instinctively and pressed my lips on the neck planting many wet kisses on her spot.

She sighed deeply and moved down to meet my eyes. She pushed me back gently with her hand on my chest, rolled me on my back and she stretched over my chest. She gently shifted and aligned herself so she could wrap her arm around me and let me hug her. She kissed me on my cheek a few times and then broke out of the hug and she rested on her elbow with her head propped in her hand. She stared at me for a while, trying to understand the emotions going through my head.

Then she slowly leaned over my face, without losing her sight on my eyes, and kissed my forehead. Then she kissed my eyelids one by one and then my nose. Then she lay back and gazed at me. I caressed her back and appreciated her sweet gesture.

"Shall I tie my hair back?" she asked me while I ran my fingers through her hair.

"No. I like it like this." I said. "I like to play with it and run my fingers through it."

"You can play with me too, you know." She said softly and slowly lowered her face on my lips.

Then she moved her face around placing her cheeks on my lips and then her chin and then her eyelids one by one. I realised what she wanted so I kissed her face back as she moved it on my lips. Then she brushed her cheeks on mine nudging her nose against mine, pressing her cheek on mine. She kept doing this sensually, all the while her hair cascading around on my face and I could smell the fragrance arousing me.

When she paused, she looked straight in my eyes trying to gauge my reactions. Then she leaned in and laid her hand on my chest as she rested next to me, slightly climbing on my shoulder along my side. She slid her leg between my legs. She was still propped up on her elbow so she was looking down at me while I lay on my back.

Then she started kissing me in soft gentle short pecks. She started at the forehead. Then she laid soft pecks all over my forehead and then kissed my eyelids. She continued kissing my cheeks one by one, laying soft pecks as she travelled along. Then she kissed my nose. As she went past on to the other cheek, she pecked softly on my jaw line, and travelled along it kissing her way gently to my chin. As she went past it, she kissed my cheek that was closer to her. Then she circled back and pecked close to the tips of my lips. With every peck, she paused and looked at me, gauging my eyes and my reactions. All the while, she kissed me with pecks she stared deep in my eyes.

She kept planting soft pecks along the base of my lower lip and the chin and circled around my lips.

As I placed my hand on the back of her head, it must have moved her lips as a peck landed on my lips gently. She paused for just a moment and planted a second and a third very close on the lips.

When she paused, she was looking deep in my eyes. She caressed my cheek in her palm and ran her fingers through my hair. Her face was very close to mine and I could feel her warm breath on my face. Her lips were hovering on my lips waiting to land.

She pressed her cheek on my cheek and whispered in my ear, "I love you so very much." Her hair was tickling my face as I caressed it away.

"Me too hon." I replied with assurance. "Just as much."

She grazed her lips on my cheeks again as she raised her face and then planed soft kisses all over my cheeks. She stopped and stared at me for a long while. I looked at her as our eyes locked.

"Spoon me." She whispered. "I want to feel you wrapped all over me as we sleep."

"Ok." I whispered.

As she turned over on her side, I shuffled to make space and get into position. I lifted the duvet, and after letting her lie on her side first, I cuddled and spooned her from behind.

We settled under the duvet and we lay still for a while. She moved her hair from behind and wrapped it to the front so I could get close to her neck. I nuzzled and planted wet kisses on her neck as I hugged, cuddled and spooned her in my arms tightly.

"You have no idea just how happy you have made me feel today." She whispered.

"That is all I always hope for." I whispered pressing her into my hug to reciprocate the love.

Taking my hand and stroking it with her hand, she whispered sensually, "Good night hon, sweet dreams. I know I will."

"Good night hon." I kissed her neck again.

"I love you." She said as she quivered.

Taking my hand in hers, she brought it to her lips and kissed it couple of times. Then we lay still and the night grew quiet as we drifted to sleep.

I had enjoyed all her sensual warmth without really figuring out where this was leading and why she had started or stopped the way she did. There were questions in my mind, but neither did I doubt or question her motives, nor was I pushy to make moves myself. I had realised from her past disappointing experience she liked to take her time. Whether it was that or she was sussing me out, I was not sure. No matter what, in her company I never worried much about anything. I always knew I was in safe hands. No matter what, I was always game. That is what she loved about me.

Chapter 5 – changing landscapes

One morning I saw Sam in the kitchen, staring out into the garden while sipping on her hot cocoa. I went close to her and hugged her gently from the back. I slowly and gently snaked my arms around her tummy and while pulling her in my arms, pressed myself on her back pulling her in my hug and pressed my cheek on her cheek. She loved these hugs. She smiled, melted in my arms and leaned back pressing against me.

"Good morning gorgeous." I whispered to her.

"Good morning sunshine." She smiled as she caressed my cheek with her palm fondly. She continued feeling my cheek press on her cheek as I brushed her cheek with mine. She melted in my arms and stroked my hands encouraging me to hug her. We both loved cuddling like that.

"I have a penny." I said to her planting a kiss on her cheek.

"Huh?" She just turned partially and looked toward me over her shoulder being perplexed.

"For your thoughts." I smiled, hinting to her.

"Ah." She giggled. Then she turned and looked at the garden again. "I think you will need the whole jar this time."

"Really?" I was surprised. "Go on."

"What are your plans for this summer?" She spoke half expectedly.

"Nothing as usual." I replied. "I think it is going to be occupied in a minute." I nudged her.

She giggled. "I was thinking, this time around, IF you wish to...", she turned slightly to look in my direction over her shoulder, "...why not landscape our garden? We have such a big garden, and mom and dad have not had time to look at it for a while now. Let's see what we can do."

"That's a big project hon." I pointed out. I continued holding her in my arms.

"Yeah. But with the two of us, we would be able to deal with it." She turned slightly and looked at me. "Right?"

"I'm game as usual." I concurred. "I don't know anything about gardening and landscaping so you will have to tell me and I will just do it." I hugged her at her tummy pulling her close to me. She had placed her hand on mine and caressed it a few times.

"As if I am a gardener by profession." She chuckled with some sarcasm. "We will just figure it out together. It's not rocket science after all."

After a moment of silence, she remarked, "It will be hard labour, much more than the last project." She sighed. "But I think it will be very rewarding." She turned and hugged me.

"Anything you say." I kissed her cheek as she cupped my face. "And anyway, it always is." I looked at her straight in her eyes and she smiled back cupping my cheek.

That evening, she broached the subject and dad took a moment to think it over.

"That will be a big project." He acknowledged.

"He said the same thing." Sam looked at me and smiled. "But I think it is possible. We will do it in stages. That way if we run out of steam, at least things will not be left half-done."

"Interesting method." Dad looked at Sam. "She isn't just a pretty face you know." He looked at me and smiled.

"Don't I know it!" I smiled looking at Sam.

"So what do you say?" We both looked at mom and dad.

"Landscaping is expensive stuff. Nevertheless, if you are doing the manual labour, I guess I just have to pay for the material. Even then you are looking at a bigger budget than last time, aren't you?"

Sam nodded.

After a moment dad gave us a budget. "This is a very rough ballpark figure. As usual, I am considering all kinds of contingencies and buffers. But stay within the limit if you can."

Sam nearly jumped out of her chair. "You are kidding me!"

Dad looked at her puzzled. "Why?"

"That's way more than what I thought you were ready for. We could do so much more with that amount." Sam exclaimed.

"Well then. Get to work." He looked at us and then back to mom. "This is turning out to be a fine investment already – we created a hell of a pair eh?" Dad looked at mom and smiled.

"Oh stop it. Don't say it like that." Mom dusted him off.

Dad just laughed.

"We are going to need a lot of material. As usual, I will give you a breakdown of the plan in a few weeks time. How about that?" Sam suggested.

"Sure sweetheart." He squeezed her hand. "Can't wait to see the end result."

Although the front of the house had some small bushes and greenery with most of the space for driveway parking, we had a rather big garden at the back of our house. It ran east-west so it benefitted with a lot of sunshine year round. Moreover, as our house was situated uphill and away from other properties, the garden had a lot of privacy. In the past few years, it was left untended mostly because mom and dad had gotten busy with work. Sam and I had helped to clear the weeds a few times and trim the so called 'grass' that was growing wild.

A few weeks later Sam called me into her room. She showed me some sketches on her pc about the garden landscape. She had used some software to design different landscapes for our garden. They looked beautiful. They were rather elaborate and provided prices for the finished outcome.

"You are brilliant hon." I hugged her and kissed her forehead. "This is amazing. How long did it take you for all this?"

"The first one took longer as I had to understand how it all works. But then once I got into it, the others were easy."

I looked at them. They looked like professional designs.

"So what's next?" I asked her.

"Which one do you like the best?" She asked me. "We need to make a decision and choose one."

"They all look beautiful to me." I remarked. "Which one do you like?"

"Honey, please." She pleaded. "You do this all the time. I want you to choose this time. I've created the designs so I need a third-person unbiased view. Please tell me, which one do you like?"

I stared at them for a while. "What's this?" I pointed something in the drawing.

"A hammock." She smiled.

"Isn't it big for a hammock? Or is it not to scale?" I inquired.

"It is big – meant to be for two people." She smiled with bright eyes.

"Really?" I realised what she was hinting at.

"I want one for us." She smiled coyly. I stared at her with delight.

"What's this then?"

"A couch swing – for mom and dad." She clarified. "This is standalone so it depends IF they want one."

"And what's this here?" I pointed out. "Looks massive."

"It's a gazebo." She said. "For us to have meals in the garden in the summer."

"It looks so romantic." I exclaimed. "And it is massive."

"It's meant for us four but it can take up to 6." She smiled. "I will be looking for some nice big extending table if I can get some."

"You do have a good eye for design and creativity." I caressed her hair and stroked her shoulder. "I would not have seen this for the life of me."

"You say that, but you are very imaginative." She said. "You just don't realise it."

"Well whatever you say baby, but that is good work." I was about to leave.

"Hold on mister." She pulled me back. "You still haven't told me which one you like best?" She reminded me.

I smiled at her.

"Come on. Just point one and that is it. I like them all. Therefore, you will not be upsetting me. Just choose one." She looked at me. "It is important for me to know your choice." She whispered sensually.

"That one." I pointed to one that I liked best.

She looked at the one I picked. "OK." She smiled. "There. See it wasn't that difficult was it?"

"I wanted you to choose it." I nagged.

"Why can't you do that once in a while?" She hugged my waist and leaned on me. "You always let me choose everything, every time."

"I like to please you." I said caressing her face while looking down at her.

"And you think I don't?" She smiled.

"You are just too sweet." I flicked my nose and then lowered my face and kissed her cheek with a quick smooch.

"This summer is going to be great." She said loudly as I went into my room.

"Not to mention laborious." I shouted back.

"And fun while we are working together." She added.

"Can't deny that." I replied. "A lot of fun."

"All worthwhile. You will see." She added.

"As usual." I replied. "Can't wait."

For the first day of our project, we had made a good start. After finishing a good breakfast Sam had prepared, we uprooted weeds together after I loosened the soil. Then she handed me the hedge trimmer and told me to go crazy on the garden, trimming everything down.

"Take everything out. It's annihilation time." She laughed.

While I swept through with my trimmer, she collected and raked everything on one side. By lunchtime, we were sweating and hungry.

When we were sitting down for light lunch, I noticed Sam was flush red from heat. Her cheeks had gone red and she looked 'hot'. I stared at her for a while and just smiled.

"You keep gazing at me like that and I'm gonna do things to you in a minute." She gazed back with a very blushed look.

"What!" I laughed. "I'm just looking."

"Yeah. Right." She smiled. "You know exactly what you are doing to me. Stop it." She looked away coyly.

I just smiled back and continued gazing at her fondly.

"In the evening, we will go out for a drive." She said softly. "How about that?" She looked at me intently.

"I'd love that." I smiled.

"Come on then. Let's get cracking."

It took us two full days to strip the garden bare. On the third day, I was stripping the top soil while she was on her knees collecting the crumbles away. I glanced at her, in her short sleeveless top and khaki shorts. She had done her hair in a loose bun on the top. I knew she was aware of my gazes as she looked at me occasionally and smiled. I kept smiling back. We had the stereo blasting our favourite music out in the patio.

Once the top soil was peeled, she asked me to poke and loosen some areas so she could even the surface out. She went through every square feet of the entire garden, making sure the top layer was even and horizontal. That took an entire day.

"We cannot rush this part otherwise the garden won't be levelled properly." She cautioned.

It was later than we had planned but we finally got the whole garden bare to its skin. When mom and dad came home, dad exclaimed, "Whoa, what happened here."

Sam just chuckled. "Don't worry dad. It has to get worse before it gets better."

"Hope so." He just smiled.

After Sam and I had our showers that day, she asked me to get changed to go out for a nibble.

"Mom can we borrow your car for the evening?" Sam asked her. "Me and X want to go out for a bite."

"Ok." Mom replied. "Don't be late."

Sam handed me the keys and we drove out and picked up a meal to go from a fast food joint. Then she showed me a place out in the countryside where there was a small lake. We parked there and had our meals.

Then she pushed the front passenger seat all the way back, reclined it a bit and asked me to lay on it. Leaving the door ajar, she walked around toward the passenger side and lay on me, reclining on her chest. I hugged her in my arms. She was facing the door as she lay there in my arms.

"I was waiting to be here like this all day." She said.

"Why?" I did not realise her desire.

"I feel close like this. I love to lie in your arms like this, watching the sun go down, feeling the evening breeze. Most importantly, I like to feel you close to me and you hold me so lovingly."

She had nuzzled her face in my neck. I held her and kissed her forehead as I stroked her hair. She had put her hair in a simple ponytail. She raised her hand and cupped my cheek. After a while, she looked up and scooted a bit higher up. She lay on top, sprawling on my chest to face me. She crossed her arms on my chest and rested her chin on her hand. We stared at each other for a while. Her face was up close to mine. We both just stared into each other's eyes for a while. I caressed her hair as I played with her loose ponytail.

"We did good work so far." She spoke looking up at me.

"You think?" I asked.

"Uh huh." She hummed lowering her face in my neck and kissing my cheek.

"Tomorrow we dig holes and lay the new plantations." She whispered. "We will be working closer together."

"I like that." I whispered. I kissed her forehead.

"You will get to glance a lot at me." She said with a smile.

She lifted her face and ran her fingers in my hair. Then she pulled my face toward her and while looking deep in my eyes, planted a long kiss on my cheek.

"That was for making me all hot and bothered all day with your eyes." She smiled coyly and nuzzled her face back in my neck.

As the sun dipped below the horizon, the red hue it splashed all over the sky looked amazing.

"Tomorrow is going to be a good day for gardening." She smiled gazing at the horizon. "Red sky at night..." she whispered.

"Hon. We need to be getting back home now." I urged her.

"OK." She nodded.

I cuddled and rocked her in my arms for a few moments.

We drove back home and spent time having a nice chat with mom and dad in the lounge, until our bedtime.

The following day, Sam gave me the printout of the plantation arrangements she had prepared. All along the north side of the garden she had identified various plants and shrubs, bulbs and flowering varieties. On the south side was going to be the gazebo, the hammock and the optional swing if my parents wanted it.

I looked at the layout and figured out a way to mark the edgings. She wanted them in arcs rather than straight lines. Therefore, I made use of two wooden stakes, and a rope and marked the arcs for her. She smiled at the smart and easy way of working them out.

"Show off." She narrowed her eyes and stuck her tongue at me. Her lips looked so enticing.

We drove to the nursery and got the plants that she had identified. It was lunchtime when we had finished there so we stopped on our way to a fast food joint to pick up a quick meal.

Back home, after our meal, she placed each plant carefully at the specific places and showed me where and how deep to dig.

"This needs to be planted in the ground, the top needs to be level with the ground. No higher."

"Yes ma'm," I smiled at her.

"Come here you tease." She pulled me and pecked me on my lips.

"mmm. I should do this full time, do you think?" I smirked.

"You can only work for me though." She hissed possessively. "You won't get a good reference if you leave." She giggled.

"If I'm kept well, why would I need to?" I continued to play along.

"I would also give you incentives." She teased me running her hands on my bum.

"Now you are talking missy." I laughed. "Do I have to do overtime?"

"Well not really, but I might need you to give me hand elsewhere, you know, odd jobs here and there." She stared at me with a naughty glance and winked.

"Ou." I sucked my teeth. "That's gonna cost you a bit more."

She paused giggling at my comment. "Oh. This is making me all hot again." She tried to fan herself to calm down. "You are such a naughty little tease. Naughty, naughty, naughty."

She waved her finger at me and poked my nose. She shook her head with a smile and let me pull her into my hug. As she came out of the hug, she planted a quick smooch on my cheeks and handed me the spade, still smiling coyly.

I started at one end of the line. As I dug each hole, she planted the pot with all kinds of fertilizers and growth enhancers. Then for each plant, she dug out a small trench along the edging line and laid the edging blocks. By evening, the garden was shaping up nicely. At least one side seemed civilised as opposed to the total annihilation we had seen until the day before.

That night, the weather forecast spoke about impending rain within a day or so. Sam and I looked at each other with a panic.

"We will need to amend our schedule then." She suggested.

"OK. We will see what happens." I calmly responded.

"Mind you, we have achieved a big milestone to date." She lay back on my chest with sigh of relief. "The plants have been put in and the top soil has been done. If we have to wait a day now, it won't make much of a dent to our work completed so far."

"A break would be nice." I whimpered.

"Ou. You are tired hon." She caressed my face. "Well if it rains tomorrow, we will take a break. How about that?"

"Mom, you can take your car tomorrow if it rains." She told mom.

"OK dear." Mom replied without looking at her.

"Shall we go and see how to rearrange our schedule?" Sam winked at me.

"Come on then." I smiled.

"We are going up stairs and then to bed." She waved good night.

"Good night." I waved too.

"Good night." Mom and dad waved us back.

It was not too late so I think they were going to stay up a little anyway.

I went into Sam's bedroom. She pulled out the schedule.

"Let's see what we need to change." She sat down in the chair in front of the PC and turned it on.

I bent down from behind the chair and hugged her pressing my cheek on to her cheek. She cupped my other cheek as I rocked her gently. I turned and planted a soft kiss on her cheek and continued pressing my cheek on her cheek. She kept looking at the monitor screen as it booted, tenderly caressing my face.

"Ok. Let's see." She clicked open the files.

As we went through the schedule, it appeared that our timeline would be delayed by a few days depending on the rain. Other than that, we were ok.

"Holiday tomorrow?" she asked me.

"uh huh." I nodded, still nuzzling my face in her neck.

"At least we get to lie in tomorrow." She smiled.

"Good." I sighed a relief.

The next morning, I woke up and found her snuggled next to me in my bed. When I stirred, she was looking at me, her eyes locked on mine, a small sweet grin on her lips, waiting for me to wake up.

"Good morning sleepyhead. I missed you so I decided to join you." She said. "Slept ok?"

"I'm sorry but I'm still sleepy." I said smiling.

"Oh come on. The sun's up." She ruffled my hair. "I feel so lonely without you."

I was lying on my chest, face turned towards her, hands under the pillow.

She decided to straddle me on my hips.

"Shall I massage you?" she suggested.

"No. Thanx." I mumbled. "I'm ok."

She whispered in my ear lowering her mouth to my face. "It won't be a bother. I know you don't like to impose on me."

"Nah." I shook my head. "I'm ok really." I was still sleepy.

"Ok then. I will just lie on you." So saying she stretched and lay on top of me full length, her chest pressed down on my back. As I felt her weight press me in the bed, I moaned gently, "Oh. That feels good."

"See. I know you would have liked a massage but you don't wish to trouble me." She iterated.

"Just lie like that. It feels good." I spoke under my compressed breath.

"With pleasure." She whispered.

She pushed her hands under my pillow placing them over mine and intertwined her fingers in mine.

"This feels so different." She said.

We lay there for a while like that.

"I could spend all day like this with you." She said.

As we lay in silence for a moment or so, she spoke quietly, "Is your heart beating faster because of me?" She had her ear pressed on my shoulder.

"Bingo." I smiled.

"Aw. I like that." She said. "I wonder if it skips a beat too."

"Now that won't be cute." I remarked with an alarm.

After a moment of silence, I asked her, "Can I take a bathroom break?"

"Sure." She rolled off me. "Don't take too long."

"O man." I shook my head smiling helplessly.

She giggled.

When I got back after freshening up, she was lying on her back under the duvet waiting for me to return. She wanted me to lie on top of her now so I got under the duvet, stretched myself along her entire length and lay on her, pressed her in the bed under my weight slowly and gently. She wrapped her arms encouraging me to lie on her. I nuzzled my face in her neck and dug my hands under the pillow. She smelled divine. I was glad I had just freshened up.

I felt her tender bosoms press on my chest. This was the first time we had been close this way. It did feel very sensual indeed. I always went along with whatever she suggested.

As she felt me get hard from the warmth and closeness, she ran her hands over my back and her fingers through my hair very fondly, kissing me on my cheek and neck. I could hear her moan softly. She intertwined her legs with mine. I placed soft wet kisses on her neck. She gasped a deep moan and quivered all over. As she felt my arms hug her shoulders and waist and press her bosoms into my chest, she melted in my arms.

"This feels so good." She sighed deeply as she wrapped herself tightly in my hug. "I want to stay like this as long as we can." She said.

"I ain't moving if that is what you mean." I whispered.

"Good, because I love this feeling of closeness." She sighed. "It is so reassuring."

After about 10 minutes, I grew concerned about crushing her. "Shall I at least roll over on your side?" I looked at her with slight concern.

"I'm fine honey, but I understand your concern. You can, only if you hold me just as tightly." She said.

I rolled off her and lay on my side facing her, and took her in my arms as she turned to hug me. Her face was pressed on my neck. I wrapped my arms around her head and waist, snaking my legs around hers. I pulled her in my hug.

"Ooh. This is what arms were made for, so I could get bear-hugs from you." She sighed. "You know just how to melt me."

While I hugged and caressed her back and waist, I seemed to have slipped my hands under her t-shirt and caressed her back. I could feel her bare skin on my fingertips. She brushed her face on my lips encouraging me to kiss all over her face. Her lips were grazing very close around mine.

"I need to calm down otherwise I won't be able to stop." I sighed trying to calm down.

"You don't have to." She whispered looking at me with trepidation.

"Trust me hon. I do." I grinned.

"OK." She looked deep in my eyes with a touch of dismay but complete consideration as she loosened her hug.

I rolled on my back and tried calming myself. All the closeness, the caressing and kissing had aroused me to no end. She just stared at me. I was staring at the ceiling. After a few moments, I glanced at her and got up to take a shower.

When I walked back in my room after my shower, Sam was in her room. I changed and popped in her room. "The bathroom is all yours," I said.

"Uh. OK." She replied. She seemed far away.

She took some clothes and walked into the bathroom. She was gone for a while. I was downstairs relaxing on the sofa lounger.

When she came downstairs, I beckoned her to sit in my lap and I wrapped her in my arms. She still seemed quiet.

"Are you ok?" I asked her.

"Uh huh." She nodded.

"If there was something on your mind, you would tell me, right?" I asked her.

"Yes." She nodded again.

"Sure?" I confirmed. "You don't seem yourself."

After a moment of silent embrace, she spoke softly, "Can I ask you something?"

"Yes." I hugged her to reassure.

"Have I done anything to upset you?"

I pushed her out of the hug slightly to look at her. "Why would you think that?" I was genuinely puzzled about her comment.

"I just wanted to check. I thought I had." She looked at me with serene eyes.

"Of course not honey. Whatever gave you that idea?" I tried to shake it off. I caressed her. "I'm fine. Are YOU fine?"

"I don't know." She lowered her gaze.

"Honey!" I sat up facing her. I saw her eyes were wet. "What is the matter? Have I upset you in anyway?"

She welled up. Then brushing her tears away, she tried to compose herself.

"Talk to me. Please." I encouraged her to speak, caressing her hand and cheek.

"While we were in your bed just now, you stopped. I said you did not need to, but you said you wanted to." She spoke calmly.

Then she looked at me. "You don't like the closeness between us?"

"I do." I said softly caressing her. "I had to stop for a different reason."

"You don't like the intimacy between us?" She asked me.

"I do. I think it is very sweet and tender." I replied.

"Then what made you want to stop? Is it me?" She welled up in tears again.

I couldn't see her in tears anymore so I took her in my arms and hugged her.

"Honey. I need to tell you something." I whispered softly. "But I will only tell you if you promise me you won't get upset with me." I looked at her.

"I won't get upset." She shook her head trying to compose herself. She seemed nervous.

"Promise?" I wanted her assurance. "I won't be able to deal with it if you got upset over this."

"Promise." She nodded. "Whatever it is just tell me." Her impatience was growing.

I collected my thoughts and spoke slowly.

"We were so close and intimate earlier in bed that I was drifting into a different territory in my mind. If I hadn't stopped, I would have ended up...." I stopped and I looked at her deep in her eyes.

"What?" she asked me urgently. "Ended up what?"

I lowered my gaze and continued, "...kissing you...." I looked at her again.

She did not understand the big deal. "We have kissed each other a lot of the times." There was an expression of perplexed puzzlement on her face.

"...on the lips." I elaborated. "I'm sorry for saying that but I would have ended up kissing you on the lips."

"But I told you, you did not need to stop." She said looking at me. Her anxiety was slowly fading.

"I thought you implied it for something else. I did not want to lose control over myself and end up doing something I or we regretted later. That's why I had to stop."

"You don't want to kiss me on the lips?" She asked me with dismay.

"I do." I looked at her with sincerity. "I did not think you wanted me to ...."

"Why would I not want you to kiss me? I love you..." she looked at me with a mix of ridicule, sarcasm and puzzlement.

She stared at me for a while, scanning my eyes, trying to gauge the feelings I harboured in my heart. Then without saying anything, she moved slowly closer pausing slightly to gauge my reaction and seeing if I would pull back. Seeing as I didn't move, she tilted her face and planted her lips on mine softly. She kissed me on my lips for a moment without moving them much, staring at me all the while. Then she moved away. As she stared at me, our hearts had made it clear.

Then she moved in slowly and cupping my cheek in her palm, planted soft pecks on my lips, all the while looking into my eyes. I could barely feel her lips for the first few kisses. As she felt me kiss her back, she planted few more, gradually increasing the duration and the pressure.

Then she pushed on my shoulder gently to encourage me to slide on my back on the lounger and she lay on top of me. As she lowered her face to mine, she matched our lips and landed her lips on mine to kiss me.

First, I could feel only her lips – soft, warm and sensual. Her hands wrapped around my head as she kissed me, her fingers running through my hair. My arms were caressing and hugging her back pulling her closer to me.

She was being very gentle and sensual with her kisses. She pressed the lips on mine slowly and every time she kissed me, the duration for the kiss lengthened. All the while, each kiss was soft and she did not move her lips once they were planted.

Then she started moving them slowly as she caressed her lips with mine. Then she started planting small soft kisses like smooches. Then she stopped and looked at me with deep inquisitive gaze.

Then she lowered her lips again and this time I felt them part gently but slightly. I could feel them caressing and licking mine as she moved her head around. I felt wetness on my lips. When she felt my wet lips, she moaned and sighed. She moved and adjusted her position so her leg was over my thigh in between my legs and she was now straddling half way on my chest.

Her arms were wrapped around my neck under the pillow, she was kissing me with her parted lips while running her fingers through and pulling on my hair on the back of my head.

I let my tongue slide between her lips. As soon as she felt it in her mouth, it was like I had lit the touch paper. Her passion went up a few notches. She let her tongue loose in my mouth and we French kissed each other for while. I could feel the hunger in her lips.

She stopped and looked at me. She stood up slowly, took my hand, and beckoned me to follow her. We walked upstairs to her room.

Once in there, she got in the bed and held out her hand to indicate for me to join her. As I got under the duvet, she got on her knees, held the duvet around her shoulder and shuffled a bit to make room for me to shift in the middle of the bed and straddled me with her knees on either side of my legs. Then after adjusting the duvet and pulling it over us with her hands, she lay on top of me slowly, our legs locked and her arms now sliding down under my neck wrapping around it. She eased herself on my chest gently and slowly.

"You comfy?" She whispered. "I'm not too heavy, am I?" She was always considerate and caring.

"You are like a feather." I whispered and smiled.

As she settled on top of me, she tilted her face slightly to align her lips, and then lowered them on mine with passionate hunger.

As she met my lips, she parted them wide and slid her tongue into my mouth. I slid my tongue in her mouth and the dance of our lips and tongues generated enough passion to boil our blood.

"How will I ever live without kissing your lips now," she exclaimed while stopping for a breath.

"You can kiss them anytime you like hon. They are all yours." I said softly.

"Oh I know." She expressed her right over them. "And I will never stop kissing you ever." She hissed. "You have the most sexy lips and mouth I have ever kissed, sweetheart. I love kissing you so much." She said with a deep sigh. "It is a pity I waited this long."

I just wrapped my arms around her back and neck and offered her my lips and mouth again so she could quench her thirst.

As I caressed her head, her silky smooth hair cascaded like waterfall and danced around between my fingers. I played with her hair, gathering it in my hand, running my hands all over its length. As I ran my hands all over her back, I could feel her curves and I kept pulling her in my hug. She kept pulling on my arm and burying herself deeper into my hug.

Her bosoms had been pressing against my chest. I could feel their tenderness as she moved and writhed in passion while licking, sucking and kissing my lips. Her nightshirt was thin enough for me to feel her skin through it. She felt my hands all over her. She stopped kissing for a while and looked deep in my eyes, inspecting my expressions. She raised and supported herself on an elbow as she paused for a while.

I pulled her head closer to me and her lips on mine and sucked her tongue in my mouth as I planted a few more kisses and licks on her lips. She melted and stroked her hands all over my arms and neck. Then when we paused for breath again, she was supporting herself on her side, with her face propped on her hand over her elbow. She was doodling circles on my chest lost in imagination. Her leg was playing footie with mine as she moved it gently.

"I agree with you about what you said in the past." She spoke softly.

"Like what?" I was puzzled.

"You like to take things slowly and not rush them." She whispered. "I like that too; it makes the relationship strong and sustainable." She rationalised.

"I was talking in general." I tried to clarify myself. "I did not think you were implying about you and I."

"No. But you are right. I like taking things slow. Let's me enjoy every moment and really savour it." She doodled a few more circles with her fingertips on my chest as she spoke.

"It is just nice to know you have a strong foundation." I stated. "Anytime you are in doubt, you can stop, rectify the bumps and carry on. If you rush things, you may leave behind weak foundations and then unexpectedly things collapse one day." I was trying to use a metaphor.

"I know what you mean." she sighed softly, still doodling on my chest.

We were quiet for a while.

"Jen's brother drove his car over a pothole the other day; wrecked the suspension apparently. Cost him an earth to get it fixed." she trailed off.

"Huh?" I did not know what she was on about.

We both just looked at each other. Then she suddenly realised that she had jack-jumped as usual. "Oh sorry. You were talking about foundation and bumps and I recalled a conversation I had with Jen the other day." She giggled sheepishly. "Sorry."

I just shook my head and smiled. "Ok."

As she lowered her face back on mine, she slowly planted kisses on my lips again. As she continued to kiss me, her lips parted and our tongues touched each other inside our hungry mouths again. As we kissed more, our lips and tongues continued licking and sucking our lips.

When we paused for breath, she slid herself a bit lower and pulled me on my side. Then she pushed herself into my arms and I wrapped her in a tight hug as we lay there facing each other. I could feel her warm breath on my chest and neck and it drove me wild.

We lay there in each other's arms for a long while, without saying much. I cuddled her in my arms and she pressed herself in my bear hug. She kept running her hands over mine, occasionally kissing them and brushing her cheek on my shoulder. Her hair kept getting in between, running on her cheek. She kept brushing it past running her hands over it.

"It's a pity we have to get up for lunch." I murmured.

It had been pouring all morning and it had not eased.

"There is very little point going out." She remarked. "Why don't I fix something at home?"

"I will help you." I said.

"That would be nice." She sighed as she turned to look at me. "You hungry?"

"Umm, always." I smiled.

"What would you like?" She stared at me not realising my pun.

"Breasts and thighs." I giggled.

"I mean for lunch." She laughed coyly, realising I was implying innuendos.

"Well. You did not say." I remarked. "I don't mind. I am not fussed."

"Shall we go downstairs and see what you fancy?" She suggested innocently.

"We don't have to go downstairs for that." My eyes glowed with naughty suggestion.

"I am trying to calm down here, and you ain't making this easy on me." She whispered helplessly, dropping her face in shyness against my chest.

"OK. OK." I giggled. "Sorry. Let's go downstairs then." I kissed her cheek and caressed her face.

She turned around and looked at me with her face turned to me. She was blushing red in her face.

"Don't tease me. I already have trouble dealing with myself when you are around me as it is." She pleaded.

"I will try to behave." I said. "But I cannot promise anything." I smiled.

"You are so naughty." She rolled away and murmured. "I never knew you had such naughty streak in you."

We got out of bed and went downstairs in the kitchen.

After thinking of a few options, she put some sausages for herself, veg burger and potato wedges for me in the oven and added some mixed vegetables for boil in a saucepan. While we waited in the kitchen for it to cook, I stared at her as she took my hands in her's and came close to me.

I hugged her and she wrapped her hands around my neck. While I kissed her, I snaked my hands all over back, waist and hips. She kept pressing herself in my arms trying to feel closer to me. After a few minutes of kissing me, she moved out of the hug and took my hand in hers. She walked to the lounger and let me lay on it. Then as she lay on top of me full length wrapping her arms around my neck, she planted her wet kisses on my lips.

"I hope this doesn't ruin my appetite." I smiled at her. "Desserts are usually after main meal."

She just blushed and continued kissing.

When the meal was ready, we sat at the dinner table enjoying our hot meal, watching the rain drizzle away in our garden.

"We will need to even those out tomorrow." She spoke while staring at the garden. She had been gazing in the distance at the garden for a while.

"Huh?" I tried to catch up with her thoughts.

"Oh." She realised she was not just jack-jumping but day-dreaming too. "I was looking at those puddles and we will have to level them tomorrow before we finish the top layer." There were small puddles of rainwater forming on the top soil in certain areas.

"Were you thinking this all in your mind then?" I asked her.

"Yes." She giggled. "Sorry." She smiled at me.

We fed each other spoonfuls from our plates. When we were done, we cleared the table and loaded the dishwasher.

"Would you like some dessert?" she asked me innocently.

My eyes glowed with a big ear-to-ear smile. She realised the pun and blushed.

"Oh don't do this to me." She blushed deep red with a smile.

I laughed out loudly. "You have gone completely red in your face. I don't believe it." She hid her face in her palm, letting her hair fall around to cover it. I fell about laughing. "Man o man. That was first time I've seen that."

"Behave." She tried to sound strict as she tried to compose herself and stood up brushing her hair back over her shoulders.

I was still giggling.

"Now you know what you do to me." She said coyly slapping me tenderly to make me compose myself.

"Oh honey. You are so sweet." I hugged her tenderly in my arms.

"It's you, making me all hot and bothered." She nudged me with her elbow. She slapped me tenderly on my arm.

Then she looked at me lovingly.

"Now be serious for a moment. Do you want any dessert?" She gazed at me caressing my cheek.

"No thanx. When I have you I don't need any desserts." I whispered seductively.

"You just cannot help it can you." She shook her head.

"What?!" I smiled at her. "I did say no."

"You sweet devil." She poked my nose with her finger tenderly and hugged me.

When the rain had subsided for a while, we went out in the garden and she drew edging lines around the puddles to mark them. "Tomorrow we will need some soil to fill them in."

"Shall we go in and order the hammock and the gazebo? Tomorrow it will be easy to install them." She suggested.

"We will also need some patio slabs." I suggested.

"You are right; for the gazebo." She looked at the area where it was meant to be placed. "This area will need some hard stone layering too."

We went in her room and checked a few things on the pc.

After a bit of deliberation, we placed an order for a hammock and the gazebo to be delivered at our place the next day.

"Can you do the maths and tell me how much stone and sand we need to create a patio area for the gazebo?" She looked at me.

I sat down at the pc and spent time getting some figures and information together.

"There." I showed her the calculations. "That's how much we need."

"That's a significant amount." She spoke reviewing the figures. "We will have to order that to be delivered too. They look heavy." She pointed to the patio slabs.

"They ARE very heavy." I said looking at the weights of each as mentioned on the website.

"You will see when we have to place them tomorrow." I looked at her with a smile.

"That is going to be a major milestone." I pointed out. "It is not as simple as it seems."

"Well we will take it one step at a time, kiddo." She ruffled my hair.

Over the next week or so, we were able to install the hammock. It was loads of fun, trying to get on it. We laughed and giggled and she screamed and shrieked. When we finally managed to learn how to get on and off without falling over, we lay in it for a while.

"Oh this is pure bliss." We both agreed. We stayed in the hammock cuddling each other. The summer breeze was keeping things cool while the sun was warm on the skin.

After a few days, we levelled the top soil, and laid the patio slabs for the gazebo. When things were completed, the garden was looking very nice indeed. The last to be planted was the new lush green turf lawn. The garden looked brand new!

After a week of putting final touches, Sam and I arranged a quiet dinner in the garden on the Friday evening for all of us as a surprise. We had ordered a delivery and we both helped arrange and serve the meal out in the gazebo.

Both our parents were over the moon on how much the garden had been transformed. Particularly dad was very touched with our abilities and creativity. "You guys are something." He admired our motivation and commitment. "We feel so proud today." He looked at mom. He gave us both a big hug.

While we were having our meal, dad suggested he would invite his boss round for a nice dinner, just to show him the new garden. "It would be nice."

"How about you invite someone from work too?" he suggested my mom.

"I suppose so." Mom smiled.

"Great. That looks like a good date."

"Dad, we still need some time to sort some lights in the garden." Sam reminded him. "But I guess we can sort that in a week I think."

"That's excellent. I will get some dates and we will arrange." He looked at mom.

"Do we have to be there?" Sam queried quietly.

Dad and mom looked at her perplexed. She looked at me.

"I mean you all are going to be adults from work. We would feel like gooseberries. Can't we go out that night?" She looked at me again and back to our parents.

I looked at them with a nod.

"We will set everything for the dinner so mom has some help and you can leave the clearing for us to get done when we get back. But if we go out that night, then that would work best."

Dad and mom thought about it and agreed.

"I see what you mean." Dad acknowledged. "I guess it would be ok if you went out. At least wait until they arrive. I would like them to meet you so I can tell them about your excellent work here." He said proudly.

"No worries at all." Sam was delighted about the arrangement.

She cocked her shoulders with a beaming smile as she looked at me.

In a week, we had contacted an electrician and sorted out a mains adaptor for the garden. Sam and I had lit up the garden with LED lights all over so it now looked amazing.

Although she had to ask a bit more money for that, Dad was more than pleased to see the result. Mom and dad stood in the garden marvelling at the place and the way it had transformed over the period of weeks.

One day while we were having dinner, dad looked at mom and started speaking to us.

"You know last time I decided to pay you for your hard labour." He looked at Sam and me. "Well this time I am not going to." He looked at mom.

He waited for a while to see our expressions. We just shrugged our shoulders. "We did not do it for that dad." Sam said. "You already know that I assume."

"Yes. I know." Dad smirked. "See that is the thing. Now that you are confident you can pull off something like this I was hoping you would be a bit forthright asking for it." He looked at our puzzled looks.

"You cannot let anyone take you for a ride." He smiled. "I have a surprise for you." So saying he put an envelope in front of us.

Sam and I looked at each other.

"Go on open it." Dad gestured.

I let Sam open it. When she read the piece of paper inside it, her eyes blew up with excitement.

"You are kidding me!" She looked at him with excitement. Then she looked at mom who was softly grinning.

She looked at me and flipped the piece of paper to show me.

It read "3K deposit toward an urban car of your choice."

"I recon the landscaping you have done is worth more than I could have afforded. I owe you at least this to say thank you."

He smiled at both of us looking at mom.

"There is a condition – we will sign you up on our insurance for now, but you will maintain it and service it out of your pocket. And another thing, you will take mom when you make the purchase."

Sam shot off from her chair and ran around to hug dad. "Thank you so much. This is just too much."

Then she ran and hugged mom. "Thank you."

"Thank you." I was speechless.

"You deserve it sweethearts." Mom agreed with proud appreciation.

"Why an urban car?" Sam asked.

"Well I have the SUV, mom drives the small family one so we thought it would be perfect if we added a micro or as you guys call it urban to our collection. That way if we need to swap cars on any occasion, we would have the appropriate lot."

"True." Sam agreed. "It's plenty for us for now anyway."

"Exactly." Dad agreed. "Your mom likes the idea too. She is keen to drive it to work sometimes. That's why she wants to be there for the selection and purchase." Dad smiled.

"Don't just bring my name into it. I know, once you drive it, you will hijack it for your own good. Then we will be stuck with your tank." Mom laughed.

"Well aren't you so clever." Dad smiled. "So it is settled then."

"You made us so happy today. Thank you." We both nodded and looked at them.

"That's what parents are for – to spoil such good kids like you." Dad looked at mom and smiled. "Well done though."

"Talking about which, I was speaking to my boss, and he has agreed to come over on Sunday in 2 weeks. Does that work with you?" he looked at mom.

"Sure, I will ask at my work place too. Don't worry about me, if I cannot arrange on the same day. We will set that date anyhow."

Sam looked at them. "So can we arrange something for that day then, for us?"

"Sure." Dad said. "But make sure you don't plan to leave before 7pm. They will arrive at about 6:30pm. I want you to sit with them for a while."

"No problem", Sam nodded. She smiled at me.

"This evening keeps getting better by the minute." She smiled excitedly.

"That means we can sort things on Saturday for the dinner." She looked at mom.

"Thanks sweetheart." Mom smiled at her.

"I will help you. Do not start doing everything alone. X will sort out the shopping for us." She looked at me and I nodded.

After the dinner was over and the table was cleared, Sam indicated me to get upstairs rather than wait in the lounge.

When I was in her room, she asked me to close the door.

"We can go out for once, officially." She smiled with excitement.

I looked at her with some hesitation on my face. "I want to ask you something."

"What is it?" She asked. "Go on."

"I know you are excited to go out that day." I looked at her. "Can I ask you out..." I looked at her, "... on a date?"

She looked at me with a surprise. "Really?"

I nodded. "I would love to take you out on a date. A real, rather fancy date." I said. "I have always wanted to and never really had a chance."

"I guess I will just have to wait for another time then." She smiled.

I looked at her perplexed.

"I was going to ask you out." She smiled coyly. "May be some other time." She blew an air kiss at me.

"If you had already planned something, I don't mind going along with your plans." I said. "I will take you out sometime later."

"I would rather you take me out. I would like that better." She looked at me coyly.

"I am not sure what it would be like yet. I will need to plan, but I wanted to take you out that's for sure."

Sam laughed. "You aren't supposed to say that to the girl you are asking out, silly."

"Well I am sorry." I blushed at my embarrassment.

"Don't worry. I know as long as I am with you, I will love every minute of it. In fact, I do not want you to go through too much hassle. Keep it simple."

"OK." I said. "It is set then. It's a date."

"All I need now is to fall asleep in your arms and I would be ready for heaven tonight." Sam fell back in her bed with her arms flung open.

"Your wish will be done." I got into the bed.

"Ooh." She giggled as she quivered.

"What's the matter?" I looked at her with amazement.

"Just recalled our experience from the other day when it was raining." Then she smiled sensually looking deep in my eyes.

"Really?" I looked at her with surprise.

"If only I could show you how you make me tingle and smile, and how much warmth I feel because of you." She sighed while looking deep in my eyes.

"I'm glad I have such good effect on you." I just smiled as I got under the duvet and spooned her.

In the following days, we did not waste time in finding a car for us. Sam and I were on the internet all the time window-shopping and checking out deals. She was looking for the 'looks and feels' while I was checking out the 'specs and functions'. Within days, we had narrowed the list and then invited mom to get in our search.

When we had selected the make and the model of the car, she called dad one afternoon and got contact details for the dealer.

"Come on kids. Let's get us a new car." She said.

We drove to the dealership and they showed us the used car under 1 year warranty in excellent condition – complete service history, low miles and single owner. It looked like a great deal. We left the negotiations for mom to handle. She got the dealer to speak to my dad and it got sorted.

The dealer shook our hands and handed me the keys with a smile. "Go take a test drive while I get the paperwork sorted."

I looked at Sam and mom nodded to us. "Go on. I will be driving it later anyway." She smiled.

Sam and I took a small test run in the car. I drove going out and she drove coming into the dealership. We were both pleased and glad about the good deal we got.

When we got back, mom smiled and asked, "Like it?"

Sam exclaimed, "Love it!" I nodded in appreciation.

"Dad is sorting the insurance as we speak." Mom told us.

"When do we come back to fetch it?" Sam asked looking at the dealer. I looked at mom and then at the dealer who was busy completing paperwork still.

"Now. Once I get this sorted." He looked at us while busily completing the documents. "If it hadn't been for this, you could have driven away half an hour ago."

Sam was thrilled that we were going to be driving home in that car.

"We will have to fill her up." I mentioned to Sam.

"Yes." She now realised the extra expense.

"I will drive behind you." Mom suggested.

"OK." Sam looked at me. "You can drive on the way home."

"Don't you want to drive?" I asked her.

"No. You can drive home. I will drive from tomorrow." She smiled being complacent.

All the while as we drove home, she was smiling, excitedly looking around checking all sorts of knobs and controls.

"We should have brought our playlist." She remarked.

"Let's get home first." I told her to relax and enjoy the ride.

"Do you know what this means?" She asked me. "We can drive anywhere we want, together." She smiled winking at me.

Our newfound vehicle of freedom had provided a new wave of excitement in our lives.

Chapter 6 – the first date

The Saturday before the dinner party, Sam helped mom get the food sorted. She came with me to get the groceries. Then she spent all of Sunday in the kitchen to help mom.

"Can I help?" I inquired trying to make myself useful.

Both the women looked at each other and smiled. "Keep us company." Sam suggested.

"OK." I pouted.

"Honey, there is not much to be done now. We are nearly finished. You helped with a big part of getting the groceries." Sam caressed my face.

"You can get the dinner set ready if you want." Mom suggested.

"That's right." Sam suggested. "Get the crockery and cutlery and set the table under the gazebo."

"Good." I smiled trying to be useful as I went to the cabinet in the lounge.

"Be careful with the china." Mom yelled out.

"I will. Don't worry." I yelled back in compliance.

"I do worry." Mom murmured. I heard Sam laugh aloud.

By Sunday evening, Sam had arranged the gazebo and laid out the table. She had put out meal-warming trays and placed candles in them ready for the evening.

Mom went to get changed and dad was getting ready. Sam was in the kitchen preparing starters and cocktails. I was helping her by keeping her company, rendering what little help she asked. Occasionally she would pull me and wrap my arms around her to feel my hug.

By evening, the first couple had arrived. Mom introduced them as her supervisor and her husband. We shook hands and invited them to sit in the garden under the gazebo. Mom showed them around the garden.

In a short while, dad was at the door welcoming his boss and his wife. They seemed pleased about the invitation. He ushered them into the garden and all the guests introduced themselves.

When they had settled, Sam and I brought out the cocktails and wine. I got the men some spirits. The allocated drivers opted for pop so Sam offered them virgin cocktails.

"Wonderful." One of the guests appreciated the efforts.

After a while, we brought in the starters when they had all seated in the gazebo.

Dad's boss appreciated our efforts. "Seems like you two have really pleased your dad." He remarked. "I can see why he is so proud of you."

"He is too generous with his appreciation." Sam tried to be humble and hugged dad wrapping her hands around his neck from behind him. "We just did it for our home." She looked at me and held my hand.

"Oh she is such a sweet girl." He appreciated Sam's humility. "You are lucky to have such mature kids." He nodded to our parents.

Sam went around the table and refilled the cocktails and drinks. She lit the candles in the warmers and placed the meals in ceramic casseroles on them. Then softly, she reminded mom and dad that the bowls would get hot and remain warm for a while, and so they needed to be careful while serving.

"Honey, you have done enough. Now go and enjoy yourselves." Mom asked her to go on our night out.

"Sure?" Sam inquired.

"Yes honey. Hope you have a good night." Dad elaborated that Sam and I carry on with our plans.

"Leave everything for us to clear tomorrow." Sam whispered to mom and reminded her not to clear after the dinner. "Me and X will sort it tomorrow morning."

"Ok. Now go. Have fun." Mom caressed her cheek lovingly.

We both went upstairs and took turns to shower and change. I wore a dark maroon full shirt with soft feel, dark brown trousers and a tie. I waited for Sam in the lounge.

As I saw her step down the stairs, I could not take my eyes off her. She was wearing a long cream flared dress with thin shoulder straps and pleated design that accentuated her bosoms. She had done her hair with one of her amazing hairstyles. She looked gorgeous. I looked at her with complete awe and warmth. Her eyes were running all over my face to see herself in my expressions. As she slowly walked downstairs and stood in front of me, I was still appreciating her beauty.

"I'm speechless." I admired her beauty the only way I could.

"That's exactly what I was hoping for." She smiled at me. She held out her hand and curled her fingers around mine. "Thank you." Her eyes filled with warm glow after seeing the thrill in my eyes.

"I have something for you." I brought forward the box I was holding behind me.

I opened it to unhide a necklace with zircon diamonds set in studs all around the front half.

"Oh my!" She gasped. "Hon, that's too much."

"Nothing is too much." I brushed her off. "Go on. Wear it."

She gently took it out of the box and inspected it lightly.

"Would you mind helping me put it on?" She handed it to me and turned around.

As I undid the clasp on the necklace, she pushed her hair aside for me to place it around her neck and I clipped it in place.

Then she turned and faced me, inspecting my expressions again.

"It looks beautiful on you." I remarked. "Just as I had imagined." I could not take my eyes of her beauty. Her eyes seemed to be glittering more than those diamonds.

She held out her hands and held mine.

"Do you not want to check it out in the mirror?" I asked.

"I can see myself in your eyes. I don't need mirrors." She said with warm loving gaze.

I hugged her gently and felt her arms around me.

As we broke off the hug, I took my jacket and her coat and carried them on my arm. The evenings used to get a bit chilly and I did not want her feeling cold. I took the keys and we stepped out.

We drove for a while toward the city. I was playing some of our favourite songs. She kept gazing at me with loving eyes. I smiled at her a number of times. I took her hand, placed it on my thigh and caressed it.

We drove to a theatre and I ushered her in. I had luckily gotten hold of some good tickets for a stand-up show. She particularly liked this comedian.

We had a great time laughing through the entire show. She kept touching my arm and we held hands a few times. I loved to see her laugh out loudly. She thoroughly enjoyed the show. Later, when we stepped out, she was still giggling at some jokes she kept recalling. It was so nice to see her laugh and smile.

Then we drove to a very fancy Thai restaurant in the town centre. I parked close by in a multi-storey car park. I carried our jacket and coat in my arm as it was not that cool yet. She had her hand in mine. I stole glances at her beauty at every opportunity. She just blushed and squeezed my arm in appreciation.

"You do spoil me so much." She sighed coyly.

"That's because you deserve every bit." I said.

While we were walking, as she was holding on my arm and walking very close to me, I could smell her perfume. "You smell gorgeous." I remarked.

"Thank you." She came close and squeezed herself to me. "It's one you gave me on our birthday. Don't you recognise?"

"You still have it?" I was surprised.

"I use it only on special occasions." She sighed seductively.

I had already made reservations at the restaurant, so we were ushered to an aloof corner. Sam asked me where I was going to sit. She sat next to me at an angle as usual. The ambience in the restaurant clearly suggested it was a very classy place.

The waiter took our orders for drinks. I mentioned the wine I had already selected. I asked for a large glass for Sam. I asked the waiter to choose a large non-alcoholic cocktail for me. "Surprise me." I had suggested.

"You will love this wine." I suggested to Sam. "I have specially ordered it for you."

She smiled at me in reciprocation.

While the waiter had left us to look through the menu, Sam gasped looking at the menu.

"Hon." She had gazed at the right hand column with numbers. It was a very pricy place indeed but I wanted her to enjoy it for that night.

"I want you to know how much I love you and how precious you are to me. So just order what you like without thinking too much of anything else." I suggested her very politely. "Please. This is my treat."

After taking a moment while looking through the menu, she tried to compose herself. "I'm sorry. It's just a bit overwhelming that's all." She tried to grin through her wet eyes. "And it's not even a birthday." She tried to hide the tears in her eyes. I squeezed her curled fingers in my hand. She smiled at me with warm appreciation.

When the waiter came to take our orders, we ordered the starters and the main meal.

As usual, we were going to share our meals. In fact, this was the ideal setup for Sam to do so.

While we waited, she had a sip on her wine. She took a few sips more and then took a big gulp.

"This is good." She exclaimed softly. "When did you become a wine expert?" She was surprised.

"I do my research." I smiled at her. "It's Moscato wine."

"This is going to go straight to my head." She smiled.

"Don't worry. Just take it easy as the night is going to be long." I smiled to her.

"As long as I am with you, I know I will enjoy every moment." She tilted her head and said sensually.

"So did you like the stand-up?" I asked her.

"I loved it." She giggled. "I liked the idea. It made the mood so much lighter."

"I'm glad you liked it." I smiled. "Were you anxious before?" I inquired with some concern.

"A little." She blushed. "I was so looking forward to tonight and I wanted for things to be perfect." She looked at me with warmth. "I want us to remember this for a long time."

As we stared at each other, she held out her hand and I held her hand in mine. I leaned forward on the table and we curled our fingers in each other's hands.

"This is a lovely place. Quite classy." She looked around to check the surrounding decor.

I kept gazing at her beauty. She just blushed coyly.

"You look heavenly." I sighed.

"Thank you." She dimmed her eyes in appreciation, squeezing my hand in hers. "You look delicious." She twitched her nose at me and smiled in her eyes.

"I want to thank you for coming into my life and loving me the way you do." I whispered.

"The pleasure is all mine." She sighed as she dimmed her eyes at me.

Just then, the starters arrived. After the waiter dished them out for each other and wished us to enjoy the starters, we helped ourselves. We took turns feeding each other spoonfuls of each starter. Each starter we had ordered was exquisite and tasty.

"Wow." Sam exclaimed. "This is awesome."

"It is." I agreed. "I'm glad you like it."

"This is absolutely delicious."

She took some more sips of her wine. "Um. This is lovely wine."

I asked our waiter for another large refill of the wine.

"I already feel light headed hon." Sam smiled.

"Don't worry you are in safe hands tonight." I assured her. "Just pace yourself, that's all."

When we had finished the starters, Sam sat up and looked at me deeply.

"You look particularly sexy tonight." She hissed looking at me and smiled.

"Do I?" I smiled at her tipsy state slowly developing on her mind. Usually I did not hear her say things like that.

"I could have had you as a starter." She said.

I giggled.

She realised she was feeling tipsy. "Oh that wine has gone to my head." She giggled. "See now look what you have done, naughty." Then she giggled more.

"I think you need to drink some water." I called the waiter to get us some water.

"I think so too." Sam spoke a bit tipsy.

When the main meals arrived, she was not in a state of helping herself so I dished out some food for her. As she slowly took bites of her meal, she seemed to recover.

"Eat something so the effect will die down." I suggested. "You had the wine on empty stomach."

"I'm always drunk over you." She said while looking at me.

I tried to feed her some spoonfuls. She loved being fed by me and enjoyed the meal.

"This feels so good." She moaned softly in a state of trance.

"I just hope you are sober when we have to walk out." I smiled.

"I will be ok. I am always ok when I'm with you." She smiled.

I could see her face flush red from the wine. She was trying to cool herself by drinking the cold water.

"See what you do to me." She looked at me all hot and bothered.

I just smiled at her warmly.

"Stop looking at me with those eyes. You are making me worse." She lowered her gaze coyly.

"I'm just appreciating what I see." I smiled at her lovingly.

We ate through our meal enjoying every spoonful.

After a while, her colour had come back and she was feeling better.

"That wine is dangerous." She remarked.

"No it is not. In fact, it is only 7%. You had it on empty stomach that's why it went to your head." I tried to explain.

"Something surely did." She giggled and winked.

When the waiter cleared the table, I thanked her for the good food.

"It was lovely." Sam spoke with admiration.

"Shall I get you some more drinks?" The waiter asked us.

"No." Sam exclaimed with a smile.

I just smiled and said we were ok.

"Any desserts?" she inquired.

I looked at Sam.

"I can only share." She seemed to be full-up.

We ordered a dessert to share between us.

"Surely sir. One coming up right away." She went away with our order.

"If I forget to tell you this later, I want to say it now. Thank you for everything." Sam spoke softly. "And I mean EVERYTHING."

"Honey you shouldn't mention it." I caressed her hand squeezing it gently.

"This has been the best date ever." She gazed at me with love and warmth.

"It's not over yet." I smiled.

"Then it is the best ever." She repeated.

She looked at me. "I love you so much." She whispered softly.

"I love you too." I whispered back.

We enjoyed the dessert between us. I fed her spoonfuls and she was just enjoying herself and the beautiful feeling she had experienced with the wine. All the while, she had her eyes locked on me and she gazed at me with a sultry sensual look.

"I'm full up now. You finish it." She urged me to finish the dessert.

When we were done, we decided to wait for a few more minutes until she felt a bit more sober.

After a few gulps of water, she was ready to leave.

"Can I visit the ladies room before we leave?" She asked me.

"Sure. Take your time." I gazed at her while she walked slowly to the ladies room. 'She IS absolutely gorgeous' I thought to myself.

I paid the bill while I waited for Sam. When I saw her walk to the table, I gazed at her from head to toe. I nodded to make sure she was ok to leave. She smiled and took my arm.

"Thank you." The waiter appreciated the tip I left behind.

"Thank you for the excellent evening." I thanked our waiter.

"Hope you enjoy the rest of the night. Good night and hope to see you again sometime." The waiter wished us good night as we walked out of the restaurant.

I asked Sam to put on her coat. "It is going to feel cold."

She stood there gazing fondly at me as I buttoned it up for her. She stared at me all the while with loving warmth in her eyes.

She then unexpectedly, came closer, pulled on my neck to lower my face close to her, pressed her lips on mine, and planted a soft kiss.

"Thank you." She sighed.

"My pleasure." I sighed back hugging her.

I took her hand and slowly we made it past the restaurant.

As we walked down the town centre, we came across a sitting area where there were benches, greenery and some nice soft fountains with cascading waterfalls.

"Would you like to sit her for a while?" I asked her.

She nodded with a girly smile.

I located a nice wooden bench and making sure it was dry and clean, sat on it. Then I asked her to unbutton her coat and hand it to me. Then I asked her to sit on my lap, with her legs straddled on one side. As she sat, I flung the coat over her shoulders and wrapped her in it. She then flung her arms around my neck and I rested back hugging her into my arms.

She looked at me with deep gaze and lowered her lips on mine. As she took my face in her palms, she kissed me tenderly for a while.

When she paused for breath, she looked at me and said, "You are my angel from heaven."

I just hugged her and cuddled her in my arms. She felt warm and cosy.

We looked at the people around us – some were just sitting chatting, some were walking slowly hand in hand. Some had decided to sit in the turf lawn. There were friends, couples young and old, and families with kids running around in the fountains. The night summer breeze was flowing through Sam's hair and teasing my senses with the tickles. The cool temperature was gently caressing her, making her feel rather pleasant.

She sat up, closed her eyes, let her head fall back a bit and took in a deep breath of the cool breeze. When she exhaled, she opened her eyes and turning her head to me looked at me with a smile. She leaned into me and pressed herself into my arms as she wrapped her arms around my neck. Occasionally, our eyes would meet and she would plant a kiss.

"Shall we play a game?" I broke the silence.

"Go on." She became inquisitive.

"You know the 20 questions. Well we both get 5 questions each to ask anything about each other." I suggested.

"That sounds exciting." She smiled.

"Ok I will go first. What is the most favourite part you like about our relationship?" I asked her.

She looked at me. Then with a thoughtful pause, she said, "The way you accept and love me."

I looked at her puzzled, waiting for some elaboration.

"I have never had anyone love me like you love me. You are not just one thing, you are everything rolled into one." She looked deep in my eyes as she caressed my cheek with her knuckles and cupped my face.

I tried to take in what she had said. "OK." I nodded in reciprocation.

"Can I ask now?" She asked.

I nodded with a smile.

After a slight pause she asked, "If there is one thing you would like to do for me, what would that be?"

I contemplated the response and simply said, "to make you utterly and deeply happy."

She smiled. "That is a cop-out answer."

I smiled back with surprise. "It is a valid answer."

"You are so sneaky." She shook her head. Then she looked at me deep in my eyes and kissed my lips.

"Were you expecting some other response?" I gazed at her with a raised eyebrow.

She just smiled. "It doesn't matter now. I like your response anyway."

I asked her my next one. "Ok. What is your most favourite way you feel loved by me?"

She exclaimed without much thought, "That's easy. Your bear hugs. I love them. That is why I cannot get enough of them."

"Really?" I was surprised. "Just hugs?"

"Well hugs and what follows with them...the kissing and cuddling..." She tried to imply with a 'duh' expression on her face. "But yeah. Your cuddles and hugs are the best. I feel so warm and loved when you take me into your arms. It feels like I am in a love cocoon." She wrapped herself with her arms to gesture her feelings.

I smiled at her expressions and gestures. I took her in my arms and wrapped her tightly against my chest. She melted and said. "Umm. Best thing in the whole world."

"Ok my turn." She said. Then after careful pause, she asked me, "If there is anything you could do with me, what would it be? WITH me." She reminded me the word this time.

I thought carefully and said, "Be with you by your side for life."

She looked at me for a long moment and kissed me with wet lips. Then when we broke our kiss, she squeezed my face in her bosoms and wrapped her arms around my head. "I want that too, so much." She sighed as she ran her fingers through my hair.

When we paused for breath, she looked deep in my eyes with a sultry look. As I gazed at her, our conversation had become telepathic for a moment.

"Ok now my turn." I broke the silence. "What is the most annoying thing about me?" I asked her softly.

"There is none." She shrugged her shoulders looking at me.

"You have to think of one, even the most silliest or insignificant if it has to be."

She just looked at me with a puzzled face. "I cannot think of any."

"You have to." I urged her. "There ought to be at least one. Come on!" I smiled at her.

Then after a while of encouraging her, she looked at me and asked if I would get upset.

"This is just a game. You just need to answer it." I smiled.

"Promise?" She looked at me.

"Honey." I shook her in my arms. "Just tell me."

She spoke slowly. "Sometimes it feels like you are holding back your feelings for me. I might be wrong but that is how it feels sometimes."

"Ok. See no worries." I assured her.

She looked at my expression. Then she caressed my face and pressed my face in her bosoms.

"I love you, you know that." She said to me.

"I know honey." I replied. "And I love you too."

"Ok. My turn. Same question." She asked me.

"You cannot ask me the same question." I tried to evade it.

"You never said I couldn't." She argued. "Stop wiggling out."

I smiled realising fully well she was much smarter than I was.

"You know I am right. You are wiggling out now." She looked straight in my eyes.

"You are perfect." I replied smiling at her warmly.

"Bull shit." She held my face in her palms and was very insistent. "Come on tell me."

After careful thought, I worded my response. "You are related to me in such a way that puts social confines on the way I would like to express my love for you."

She became sombre and held me for a while in silence, staring deep in my eyes, looking inside me as though she was trying to read the feelings in my heart. "I wish things were different too honey." Then she took my face and kissed me softly and tenderly. I could feel her eyes well up.

"Hey, shh." I tried to console her. "We will work things out. Don't worry." I took her face and kissed her lips.

"We shouldn't need to." She tried brushing her tears.

"It will be ok. Don't worry." I consoled her.

"Hope so." She sighed.

Then she reminded me, "You avoided answering that question very cleverly mister." She looked at me with stern eyes. "You haven't really said any attributes about me that annoy you."

"I have." I said trying to wiggle out again. "That is the annoying thing ABOUT you."

"Not me per say." She reminded me. "It's about our relationship actually."

"Hon, you are perfect." I tried to wiggle out again.

"Bull shit." She took my face in her palms and pushed me to be tell her one annoying thing about her. "Come on." She urged me. "Please." She looked deep in my eyes.

After a moment of contemplation, I said, "I think sometimes you don't feel deserving of the love you are shown – by me or others. That really gets to me very strongly. You don't realise or accept just how special you are." I said with a serious tone.

She quietly took in what I had said. Then she kissed my lips tenderly.

"How come you are so sweet?" She looked at me deep in my eyes. "Even when you are criticising me, you make me go weak in my knees." She just shook her head and planted another kiss on my lips.

"Ok my turn. What turns you on the most?" I asked looking very sensually in her eyes.

"You." She nearly yelled without much thought. "Everything about you, all of you." And then she giggled.

"Really?" I asked to confirm.

"You have doubts?!" Her surprise at my query had a hint of ridicule. "Do you know how wet....I mean how you give me goose bumps all the time?" She pressed her lips between her teeth at her slipup. "I'm sure it's that wine." She giggled again turning her face away coyly.

"Really?" I smiled and noticed the slip up there. "Wet did you say."

She blushed and buried her face in my neck. "Oh god." She felt really embarrassed.

"That's ok. I will take that as a compliment." I held her as I enjoyed her blushing.

"You should. I enjoy my effect on you, so you should take your effects on me as compliments." She whispered still pressed in my neck.

"What effects on me?" I asked her with a smile.

She sat up, looked at me with a 'duh' expression full of 'are you serious' ridicule and wiggled her bum discreetly on my lap making me aware of my erection poking into her thighs.

Now I blushed and pressed my face into her bosom. "Is it that obvious?"

"Duh. Hello!" She made an ironical sound. "That answers MY question too then huh!" She looked with a smiley face.

I smiled with embarrassment. "Well if you weren't so hot may be I wouldn't feel this way. It's your fault."

"Ah. No one was asking about whose faults they were mister, just about the effects." She giggled again.

"Ok so does that mean it's my turn again?" I asked.

"No. I want to ask my question." She protested.

"You already asked it." I protested back.

"I did not. You just volunteered an unsolicited answer." She giggled.

"You are so sneaky." I nudged her and tried to tickle her.

"No please." She tried to control her shrieks. "I beg of you, not here." She pleaded to me with the most sensual eyes.

"I would have so pounced on you right now if only we were at home alone. The look you just gave me; oh!" I sighed.

"Really?" she smiled. "I was just being genuine. Don't tickle me here, I would be so embarrassed."

"As if I would ever embarrass you at all." I replied hugging her in my arms, looking deeply and earnestly in her eyes.

"So my question." She smiled. "What SPECIFIC things about me turn you on?"

"That is a trick question." I complained. "You are asking me many items."

"You are saying there aren't?" She glared at me with a stern face and a raised eyebrow. She had trapped me in my argument.

"No. There are, tons." I said sheepishly. I realised I had walked into that one blindfolded.

"Go on then." She smiled. "Reel them off one by one."

"O man." I blushed and pressed my face in her bosoms.

"Is that one of them?" she giggled.

I nodded simply.

"Ok. Next?" She smiled.

"Your hair." I said in an exclaimed voice. "I love your long hair."

"Really?" She was surprised. She ran her hands through it.

"Oh yes." I exclaimed even more. "And what adds to it is that I know you let it grow for me."

"That's true about everything I do, Einstein." She looked me deep in the eyes and stuck her tongue out at me. "OK. Next?"

"Your eyes." I looked at her. "I see them looking at me, and I melt."

"Melt or solidify?!" She giggled.

I let out a hearty laugh. "That is true." I acknowledged.

She just looked at me and smiled in unison watching me laugh out heartily.

"I melt, but you solidify." She reminded me looking at me and smiling.

I laughed again at her crude analogy. "You are so clever at this."

She just smiled and reiterated. "That's true isn't it?"

I nodded in acknowledgement still recovering from my laugh.

"Ok what next?" she reminded me of the question list.

"Your touch." I said looking at her, interlocking her fingers with mine. "It is very sensual and electric."

"So it charges you up." She smiled and raised her eyebrow.

I smiled and nodded again at her attempt to create another personified analogy.

"I'm loving this." She smiled as she swung her feet.

I hid my face in her bosom trying to hide my embarrassment.

"Go on." She smiled getting excited. All my appreciation was boosting her self-esteem.

"Every time you come close to me, your fragrance drives me wild." I said to her.

She leaned closer and I pressed my face on her neck and I smelled her perfume.

"That's one reason I put it on, hoping to bring the moth to the flame." She cuddled me in her bosom and let me hug her tightly for a while, running her fingers in my hair.

"I need some more." She said breaking out of the hug and grinning at me.

"O man." I tried to think. "Your kisses." I suggested. "Now talk about solidification. O wow!" I exclaimed.

"Really?" She was surprised.

"Hon. You have no idea how hard... I mean what you do to me when you plant your lips on me." I tried to hide my slip up.

She just let out a girly laugh. I hugged her close in embarrassment as she realised my slip up.

"That's plenty now." I tried to protest.

"Ok." She giggled and hugged me in appreciation of my truthfulness.

"My turn now." I tried to divert the topic. "What could you not live without in our relation or regarding me?"

She could not understand the double negative.

"What is the most critical thing about us or me for you that you can't live without?"

"Your physical presence in my life, your closeness, your touch." She held my face in her palm. "I couldn't live without holding you, touching you or kissing you, having you in my life physically."

"So the memory or feeling is not enough. You need me in body too, not just mind or heart." I surmised.

"I am afraid so. Just your thoughts are no good for me. I have you in my thoughts all the time anyway. Whoopee do." She shrugged nonchalantly. "I need you in flesh and blood. Imagining your hugs is lot less rewarding than actually feeling them."

"Ok." I looked at her trying to empathise with her need.

"Does that make me superficial?" She paused while looking at me anxiously.

"Hey." I hugged her. "Nobody said anything about judgements here." I kissed her lips. "We are just chatting."

"OK. Then my turn. Same question."

I looked at her. "I guess my most critical thing would be your love for me. I cannot live without knowing you love me. As long as I have your love, I am ok."

"So the physical side is not critical?"

I thought for a while and then spoke, "I don't know. I have not missed you physically because you have always been around me. So I wouldn't know. I guess not. But all the time, what really is essential to me is knowing that at any moment you love me. If ever I lost your love, I would not be able to live on."

"You mean like if I died?" She tried to clarify.

"No. In fact that won't upset me as much since I would know you died while still loving me. What would kill me the most is if I did something to lose your love for me, or if you drifted away from me and did not love me anymore or over time stopped loving me for whatever reason."

"I would never stop loving you. Ever." She kissed me with deep sensuality. "There is nothing you would do that would make me stop loving you. I know you and I know you would not do anything that would hurt me like that. So I would never stop loving you. That is a promise."

"Thanx honey." We looked into each other's eyes.

After a long moment of sombre silence, I suggested we start heading back home. I glanced at my watch as it was getting late.

She looked at me deep in my eyes and then cupping my face in her palms planted her lips on mine for a long sensual wet kiss. As she felt my erection poke her, she grinned slightly as she wrapped her arms around my neck and ran her fingers in my hair. I squeezed her in my hug as I kissed her back tenderly.

I let her stand up while holding on to my hand. Then I stood up and I wrapped her in her coat, buttoning it up properly. She kept gazing at me warmly all the while. Then she wrapped me in my jacket. We walked to the car park holding hands. She kept pressing herself close to me, and we held each other around our back at the waist. She was dragging her feet and I knew the reason. So I didn't rush her.

Before I paid for the parking, she held me in her arms, looked me deep in my eyes and kissed me one last time knowing that we would be returning to the confines, not being able to be ourselves. She hugged me and kissed me with wet lips and we sucked each other's tongues. I held her and kissed her back softly. I felt her melt in my arms. She had wet eyes and said, "I had the most wonderful night. Thank you for everything."

"It has been my long standing pleasure." I smiled.

After paying for the parking, we left the place and headed home.

When we got home, the lights in the house were turned off with only the landing light left on behind for us.

We went upstairs quietly. She took my hand and led me to her bedroom.

Once inside she asked me to close the door.

"I want you to sleep here tonight." She looked straight in my eyes. "Don't worry. Tomorrow is a working day."

"Ok. I will freshen up and come in." I whispered with a smile.

"I will be waiting." She smiled at me sensually.

I stepped out of her bedroom quietly and we both freshened up for bedtime.

When we got in the bed, she asked me to spoon her tightly. I wrapped her in my hug pulling my knees closer so I created a love-cocoon as she liked it. We drifted to sleep soon enough.

In the night, I must have drifted in and out of sleep for some reason. Visions of me in her bed and her closeness kept gliding in and out of my senses.

I stirred sometime around 3 am I think. I looked across lifting my head very slowly over her shoulder and she seemed fast asleep. At least she had not moved and was breathing slowly. As I lay back slowly, I tried to lie on my back. I must have shifted the duvet. I noticed her turning around and she glanced at me.

"Sorry hon. I seemed to have woken you up." I apologised.

"No. I was awake. I did not know if you were and did not want to wake you so I was lying still."

She then turned and climbed half way over my chest, leg locked in between my legs, her arm swung over my chest and her head nestled on my shoulder. I wrapped my arm around her back and waist.

We lay still for a while.

"Did you sleep well?" She whispered.

"On and off." I replied. "It is difficult sleeping with you next to me." I said softly with a smile.

She turned toward me a bit concerned at my comment.

"You are too tempting." I smiled trying to calm her anxiety.

When I said that, she looked at me quietly for a while and then slowly withdrew her arms and sat up in bed. Then she lifted her nightshirt in one quick sweep and let it drop on the side of the bed. She wasn't wearing any bra but had a laced panty. Then she looked at me, propped herself on her hand next to my pillow. Lowering her face, she whispered to me. "Would you like to get your shirt off?"

"Sure." I sat up slowly and she helped me pull it over my head. She gently dropped it on the floor over her nightshirt.

She gently pushed me down in bed on my back with her hand on my chest. Then she got on her knees, pulled the duvet aside from over me, swung her one leg across, and straddled me over my waist, her each knee on either side of my waist. Then she pulled the duvet over her back and gently lowered herself on my chest as she lay on top of me. Pulling and wrapping us under the duvet, she wrapped her arms around my neck under the pillow, and with her legs straddled on my waist on either side, she pressed her naked bosoms on my chest as she pressed herself deep in my hug while melting away.

"You don't have to hold back your desires for me, you know." She said very sensually in my ear. "I hunger for you just as much if not more."

With that, she planted her lips on mine and we spent a long time licking, sucking and kissing each other's mouths. I kept caressing her back and she kept tugging and hugging me pressing herself into my arms.

"I said that I like to take it slow like you." She sighed as she paused for breath. "But that doesn't mean we have to deprive ourselves of pleasure when both of us want it."

When she paused for a breath, she sighed sensually, "You make me feel so loved. I'm never going to stop loving you."

"I do love you very much," I whispered in her ear. "You drive me wild."

"Oh so do you, hon." She said sighing deeply. "You do, so very much. I'm just trying hard to take it slow so I savour these moments with you. I don't want this to stop."

As I kissed her, I played around her back, tracing my fingertips letting them caress her skin all over her back along the spine from top all the way to the bottom and back again. I caressed her sides and waist wrapping it tightly as I pushed her pelvis deep on my crotch. Her breathing got intense when she felt my bulge on her pelvis. Her lips got hungrier and devoured my lips and tongue. We kissed and licked each other's lips for a long while.

Her hair felt silkier against her soft back. It slipped and glided through my fingers as I ran my hands all over her back. I loved to feel her hair. I gathered it in my palm and stroked its length, then ran my fingers through it and bunched it together in my hands as I kissed her. 'She lets it grow long just for me' I thought delightfully. We were both lit up with deep passion. Our breathing was very deep and we had been kissing for a while now.

She paused for a breath and gasped, "I feel so drunk from your love." She exhaled deeply.

She let her head drop and nuzzle her face deep under my chin on my neck while she slowly slid down. She felt drunk, never mind talk like one too.

"I can't take this anymore." She was panting heavily. "I need to calm down."

"Now you know what I felt that day when I wanted to stop and calm down." I spoke to her. "Remember the day when we took a day off during our garden landscaping?"

She just looked at me, nodded and grinned coyly and kissed me.

I was still hugging her as she lay there on top of me. "Hold on to me tightly and stretch your legs out," I whispered to her.

Holding her firmly with both arms, one wrapped around her neck and the other around her waist, I rolled on my side on my elbow, rolled us gently but quickly and laid her down on her back next to me. As I slowly unwrapped her from my hug, she looked up at my eyes, still panting but now easing away slowly. I kissed her on her forehead and let her catch her breath. I was breathing heavy too and found myself warm against her soft body.

As I was propping myself on my elbow with my arm under her pillow, I looked at her and her bare bosoms. She let me gaze her naked beauty. I lowered my lips on hers when her breathing had calmed down and planted kisses.

Then I looked at her and started kissing her chin, then her neck, moving lower with every kiss all the way to her chest. She arched and threw her head back, pushing her chest up. Then I started kissing all over her bosoms.

When I landed on one of the nipples, I gently placed my lips around it, licked it with my tongue and sucked it gently. She pulled on the hair on the back of my head pressing my lips on her boob and letting out a deep moan. "Oh hon. That's not going to help me calm down. You are firing me up again."

She kept caressing and running her fingers through my hair as I continued kissing her boobs.

Then going lower, I kissed and licked her tummy and she flinched a bit at the quiver it sent out all over her body. I planted wet kisses all over her tummy and then propped myself up again on my arm. I gazed at her deeply again and gently lowered myself next to her on my side. As I lay my head on the pillow next to her, she turned and faced me. We were lying there, face to face looking at each other, admiring the beautiful and sensual moments we had just enjoyed.

She raised her palm, cupped my cheek, and said softly looking deep in my eyes, "Now I know. This is what heaven feels like."

"And now I know this is how an angel feels like." I whispered back.

"Spoon me." She sighed softly. "Hold me tight"

I lay down behind her on my side as she turned on her side. We were both lying on our right side. I slipped my right arm below her pillow and under her neck. She raised her head slightly letting my arm through. Then as we shuffled close to each other, I gently placed my left arm on her hip and let it slid on her tummy.

She took both my hands and interlocked her fingers through mine from above my hands. She took my right hand from below her neck, wrapped it round her neck and pressed it on her left boob. The other over her hips she wrapped it around her hip and pressed it on her right boob. Then she pushed herself in my arms melting slowly and purring like a kitten as she bent and pushed her bum into my crotch.

Our body heat was tantalising and her fragrance was acting like fuel on an open flame. She gently let her fingers loose from mine and she pressed my open palms on her boobs. I cupped them gently as I pulled her deep in my hug, wrapping her tightly. She kept her hands pressed on mine as she continued to wrap herself in my tight warm embrace. My lips planted wet kisses on her neck, just below the neck, on her back and under her ear. She was tingling and quivering all over at every kiss.

"Umm," She said every time she quivered. "The things you do to me and the pleasures you make me feel. Oh my." She sighed.

When I stopped kissing her, I raised myself, looked over her shoulder and she turned slightly to meet my gaze. I planted a soft kiss on her cheek. She turned her head to meet my lips and I planted long sensual kiss on her lips. She stayed like that in my hug, all the while I was kissing her. When I had kissed her to my heart's content, I paused for breath. Then as I lay back down and spooned her, she sighed quietly "I will never ever stop loving you."

We lay there like that quietly until we drifted to sleep.

The next day when I had got to my room from my shower I saw Sam had left her phone on my desk with a sticky note with a heart drawn on it, with the words 'Play me' on the note. The phone had headphones already connected. I got dressed and then I put the headphones and pressed play.

The song started to play. The display indicated that it was 'Things you are to me' by Secret Garden sung by Elaine Paige. One of my favourite groups but I had not heard of this one before. Therefore, I listened to it intently.

If I held in my hand, every grain of sand since time first began to be, still I could never count, measure the amount of all the things you are to me.
If I could paint the sky hang it out to dry, I would want the sky to be oh such a grand design, an everlasting sign of all the things you are to me.

[chorus]
You are the sun that comes on summer winds.
You are the falling year that autumn brings.
You are the wonder and the mystery in everything I see the things you are to me.

Sometimes I wake at night and suddenly take fright, you might be just fantasy. But then you reach for me, and once again I see all the things you are to me.

[repeat chorus]

(music interlude)

[repeat chorus]

All the things you are... to me.

Goosebumps were running all over my skin to the point I could feel nothing but tingles all over; my eyes had welled up from the overwhelming emotions the song had conveyed to me – Sam's feelings for me.

I took off the headphones and slowly walked to her bedroom. As I peered in, she was sitting on the bed waiting, anticipating. When she saw me in her doorway, she stood up slowly. My wet eyes said everything she wanted to know. I walked to her and wrapped her in my arms tightly. She hugged me back tightly, wrapping her arms around my neck. I whispered in her ear, "I don't think I deserve so much." My throat has choked up with emotions.

She whispered back, "I'm sorry, I wish I could give you more, much more than I have to offer."

We kissed each other on our necks and cheek and held each other in our hug for a while. It felt we were hugging for eternity. When we came out of our hug, we stared into each other's eyes. Although she had welled up too, she tried to brush my tears. "Now you know." She smiled at me.

I took her face in my palms and planted a soft gentle kiss on her lips. She kissed me back for a long while melting in my arms.

Chapter 7 – the romance

After our date, our relationship had developed through leaps and bound. We were a lot more comfortable with each other. As we were growing up, our parents had realised we had grown closer to each other. I think they were concerned about our closeness but for some reason had not raised an issue.

Sam and I used to be tactile around each other and since we had become so comfortable, we sometimes did not realise it. Although we were careful, a slipup would raise a few eyebrows particularly when we were out. Most of the times, mom did not say much even though she had noticed we had gotten tactile. Nevertheless, it was instinctive rather than intentional, sensual rather than erotic. The one thing that could not be missed was the mutual love we had developed – it was evident even to the blind.

When we ate our dinners, Sam pulled her chair and sat close to me. I could feel our knees touch particularly when she wore shorts and folded her leg under her bum when she sat. She placed her hand casually sometimes on my thigh. At times, when she grinned, she would wink or raise her eyebrow at me seductively. She knew I used to find that very enticing – she loved to see me blush red.

We had started sharing our meals. We used to sneak opportunity to feed each other spoonfuls from our plates when we used to eat together. When we visited restaurants, she and I shared platters willingly. One large drink with 2 straws was the most favourite thing for us when we ate fast-food. She left out the crust off pizzas and I loved to finish them. She started drinking lemonade just because I drank it. She once asked for Lime Lemon for a change and we both loved it.

We used to share a large cup of 3-scoop ice cream rather than get our separate cups. We each would choose one scoop of the flavour we liked individually, and one scoop of the flavour we wanted between us. Thus, every time we would sample different ice creams so both of us had something each liked and tried.

Once she dared to feed me the ice cream using her finger rather than the spoon. "Just once," she begged. "I wanna see how it feels." We were at the cinema, sitting in the back row away from prying eyes, so it was rather discreet affair. She licked her finger and then scooped some ice cream, and then offered for me to lick it off. The experience proved very warming and sensual indeed. She cooed at my lips licking her finger. She giggled softly and the warmth could be seen in her eyes. I attempted to lick her finger gently as I sucked the ice cream off them – I didn't want to bite into her fingers. I smiled at her expressions. Moreover, she asked me to feed it to her in the same way and so we ended up eating it that way. Her lips on my fingertip made me all warm inside. She added a gentle soft lick with her lips in addition to her tongue playing around on my fingertip.

When we were not hungry enough for a 3-scoop tub, we used to buy one cone with one or two scoops and then spend time taking turns licking it slowly, trying to tease each other. We both used to stare at each other intentionally as each of us licked it slowly and sensually in turns. However, we only did this when no one was around because this used to get very sensual very quickly.

When we used to hang around in the kitchen at home, she loved to hug me from behind me while we were casually talking or clearing things in the kitchen. A gentle tight squeeze of her arms around my chest, a brief moment with her cheek pressed against my shoulder from the back. She loved hearing my heartbeat and holding herself against me as I caressed and held her arms and stroked them with mine. When we used to be alone in the house, she would then give me a peck on the cheek when she made me turn just after breaking out of the hug.

Ever since mom had started working, there were times when we were home just the two of us. On these occasions, we used to go the extra miles of kissing each other for a long while. When the passions used to burn our skins we used to ask the other to stop and help calm down. We both had agreed to take things slowly. But every single day it seemed we were inching closer. All this just meant we were savouring and enjoying every moment we spent with each other. I do not remember any day that we did not spend where we did not touch each other on some pretext.

When sitting on the couch watching TV, she would prefer if I had one of my arms around her waist at the back, hidden behind her back. She used to sit so that I could wrap it around her back, and rest it just between her arm and waist. That way it was not obvious and she had the closeness she could enjoy. When she needed to caress my thigh, she would use a soft throw or blanket over us. Her most favourite way was to lay her legs across mine. That way I could run my fingers on her thighs occasionally. Her way of appreciating my touch was to lean against me and kiss my cheek, without looking at me.

The easiest way was when she used to sit reclining on the lounger along my side, her chest pressed against my side. In that way, if she wanted, she could move forward, recline on my chest, and place her head on my shoulder and have a arm hug. She once fell asleep like that. When mom and dad were ready to go to bed, they turned the TV off. It had made me stir up but I was sleepy too. When they noticed us on the couch, mom sighed to dad looking at us, "Just like when they were kids."

"Shall we wake them?" dad suggested.

"No. Leave them." Mom whispered. "They will wake up on their own and go to bed. I'll throw a blanket on them."

In my sleepy state, I had seemed to hear bits of that conversation. In our house, our parents did not wake us if we were asleep. They let us wake up on our own.

I loved playing with her hair. It had now grown long enough to stop just at the hips – thick, silky, straight and light brown. Similarly, she loved to run her fingers through my hair. She liked it if she could pinch it in between her fingers as she would scissor her fingers through the hair. If she could not do that, it was too short.

Since she had long hair, I bought her a ton of hair accessories. We used to sit for hours where she would show me how to do her hair with all those accessories. I would love to brush and plat it for her, particularly when she wanted to feel close. She would sit between my thighs with my legs spread out when we sat on the couch while I slowly brushed her hair.

She did her hair in a different style every day just to see my smile and amazement. I used to look at her and her beauty used to ooze when she got dressed and ready for the day; essentially, she dressed to please me. Her creativity knew no bounds as she came up with some really cool hairstyles each time. Even when she used to just gather it in a loose bun, it used to look so sensual.

"You are just too easy to please hon," she used to cup my cheek gently and smile. "It's nice to be loved so much." She would kiss me a 'thank you' when I appreciated her like that.

Once when we were out in the mall, she was dressed rather simple but looked absolutely gorgeous. On an impulse, I used my phone and asked her to give me a pose and clicked a picture. When I reviewed it, I realised she was truly photogenic. Since then I did not hesitate to click away at her beauty. She loved to pose for me and never once shied away. I must have clicked a million pictures. I had created a slideshow and a photomontage of some of my most favourite ones.

I had enlarged one picture as a poster and stuck it on my wall opposite my bed. I had clicked it on a cloudy day, in our garden when we were just relaxing. We were chatting and she seemed in a rather sensual mood that day. For a moment, I asked her to give me a pose and I clicked a few dozen pictures in rapid successions. One such picture came out to be my favourite – a close-up of her face from the right side, down to her shoulders, her ear covered with her waving cascading hair, her contoured face partially covered behind the hair to reveal a feminine beauty, her eyelashes in a lowered gaze oozing coy and blush, and a soft grin highlighting the curved red lips full of bliss. Every time I gazed at it, I used to feel warm inside and would melt. That picture had captured all her essence in its entirely purest form and it illustrated my definition of a perfect woman.

She had presented to me a voucher for professional makeover photo session, as she did not have any good pictures of me. Since she wasn't so good with photography, she had paid for a professional photo session especially for me. I was never a poser so I had finally agreed on the condition that she accompanied me and she would participate at least for some shots.

That day the session had turned out to be so loving, tender and fun. The pictures had turned out fabulous and she had purchased twice as many as she had previously planned. She was over the moon because since then she had a picture of me that she loved to gaze just as I had one of her on my wall.

Feeding popcorn to each other in the movies was casual fun for us just the same. She used to lean on my shoulder at times or lean across my chest with the hand-rest between us lifted away into the backrest. When we used to be at home and particularly in her bedroom, watching TV in bed, she used to love to play the 'kiss and get' game of feeding me the popcorn – she used to hold a popcorn in between her lips gently and then let me fetch it using my tongue or lips. Sometimes, she used to cheat by sucking it into her mouth just as I went to retrieve it, getting me to French kiss her in order to get the corn. It used to feel so sensual. Sometimes I used to forget about the corn and just end up sucking the life out of her lips.

"Stick a fork in me, I'm done." She used to melt in the bed breathless.

Although I seldom danced, I had watched her dance at home many times. When we used to play music, she used to sway to it countless times. Her moves used to reflect exactly the emotions she would be feeling at that time. Her interpretations would be a vision to behold. Every time I saw her dance, I used to feel nothing but sensual pleasure oozing out of her. For that reason, in my mind, dancing was associated with making love – if she urged me to join her, it would feel we were making love.

Once she asked me, "Why don't you dance?"

I had just smiled in embarrassment, "I can't, so I get very anxious and so I don't."

"What if I taught you?" she asked me inquisitively.

"Then I would definitely not dance." I exclaimed.

"Why not?" She was saddened.

"You make me feel all gooey inside when you dance with me." I giggled. "Because I love you so much, I get very aroused and I feel we are being intimate together. I end up associating dancing with making love."

"Does that bother you?" she asked me gazing at my eyes.

"What?" I was not clear what she wanted to ask.

"Developing intimacy between us." She asked me. "Does that bother you?"

"No. I love to feel close to you, and dancing with you makes me feel rather intimate. But then I lose track of everything and then all I'm thinking of is you and..." I confessed, stopping short.

"That's because you don't and have never danced." She smiled to me. "Once you learn how to dance, you will feel ok expressing yourself in that way and it won't make you feel gooey." She giggled while imitating me. "You will just be able to enjoy everything about the dance, including the intimacy and still feel ok about it."

"You think?" I was sceptical. "I'm not sure about that." I was being shy again.

"If you learn with me, I will take care of you. And if we danced together, you don't have to be anxious."

She studied my face and suggested, "Would you mind taking dance lessons with me?" Her looks were very inviting and pleading. "Please. I know you will love it once you get used to us dancing together and when you develop some moves in you. Trust me hon." She encouraged me.

I had just looked at her with hesitation. "When I see you dance, I want to do things just while watching you dance. That is how much you turn me on. Can you imagine if I dance with you?!"

"Please. For me?" she had pleaded.

I paused and then said, "On one condition." I had proposed.

"Go on." she had smiled.

"You will learn to swim." I suggested.

"No. please no." She had pleaded. "You can't do that."

"There is nothing to be worried about, I will teach you. You will be in safe hands." I had assured her.

"I want you in the pool with me. If you aren't entering I won't either." She had urged.

"I don't need to be in if only you do what I ask you to do." I told her. "Babe you know why I am asking you to learn to swim." I had tried pleading with her.

"I know. But you do know why I hate the pool." She whined.

When she was about 7, she had fallen in the pool over some kid-fight when one of the kids had pushed another and she was tripped and had fallen into the water, just because she was around the kids when they were pushing each other. At that time, she did not know how to swim and had nearly drowned. Ever since then she was scared of pools or swimming in general.

She would be learning to swim in about 15 days with about an hour every day if I could get her to follow my lead correctly. The dancing sessions were for a whole month and twice a week.

"You can use a 'voucher' if you wish," she had suggested. We used to create a yearly booklet of custom vouchers for all kinds of activities that the other person usually did not appreciate. We used them as vouchers every time we had to ask for a favour from one another. Although these vouchers were for activities either of us would generally find boring and so whinged about participating in them when redeeming a voucher, the fact that we used to be together ended up making the whole experience that much fun. In the end, the whinging was just a 'drama'; in our hearts, we knew we were going to be together feeling the closeness we enjoyed so much. As we grew up, we eventually just forgot about creating the vouchers; we just ended up doing favours for each other.

When she urged me to be her dance partner, I was very hesitant. However, given how much I loved her, I gave into her pleading. I could never say 'no' to her anyway.

"I promise you I will take full care of you at all times." She had promised me.

When I did start participating, I realised the change it had made to my self-confidence and my inhibited personality. During the dance class, she loved the closeness and made full use of the time to soak in the love. Her subtle ways were so good that no one knew or batted an eyelid. When we danced, it was as if she was dancing for me. All the sensual moves that she did were moves she would make to tease and arouse me. That way she helped me relax by distracting me. "Keep your eyes on me," she used to say. She used to be very gentle and patient with me for every minute and every mistake I made.

Moreover, I could never deny, seeing her dance would be like the feast for all the senses and the mind all at once. Her fragrance, her touch, her sensual and seductive smile, graceful movements, and her whispers when we used to get close – all made me insane. After the dance sessions, I would love to kiss her for a long while before we got home. She used to love seducing me throughout the session just for that reason. She had a sensual seductive pair of eyes – I could never tell their colour as I could see them in different colours every time. Her lips curved up all the time when she used to be with me. They were deep red, full of life and hungry for my lips.

Pairing up with her during those sessions taught me some nifty abilities that increased my list of skills. I did come out of my shell, gathered appreciation to a very unusual new form of self-expression, and I could enjoy dancing without feeling anxious. In fact, it provided me with yet another form of expressing my feelings, especially to her, through the different forms of dance moves I got to learn. We used to spend quite a while dancing together at home in the lounge to my favourite music when we used to be on our own. We both had made a dance routine for the song 'Remember this' by Blue Stone. I had associated it with her. Every time I heard that song, I imagined her, smiling, teasing, enticing and dancing.

Although we had slightly different tastes for music, she loved all of my collection and found it very emotional. I liked New Age, Contemporary Electronic and Ambient genre along with Pop, Slow Rock and Dance with some eclectic singles from Jazz, Opera and R&B. I was also very keen on World music compilations by artists from at least a dozen different countries. I had collated my music into separate playlists based on the moods it brought out in me.

I used to love waking up to my music in the morning. Ever since I had purchased my audio surround system, I used to wake up to my soft music in the morning instead of an alarm. She used to love that. She used to say, it was like waking to a thousand kisses. There were times when she used to wake up and dance to the tunes, particularly some that were upbeat. Seeing her dance, I used to feel 'high' and she used to encourage me to join in. If my parents were still in getting ready for work, especially my dad, he used to smile at us watching us dance around and shake his head in disbelief, "What did you two smoke this early in the morning?"

"Join in and find out," Sam used to giggle. Her moods used to be infectious, particularly when she was happy; she used to be happy most of the time anyway. She would get everyone to join in eventually.

"I have a long day ahead of me." Dad used to throw his hands up walking away after joining for a few minutes. "You two ain't real."

Once Sam woke up early one morning and came and sat on my bed waiting for me to wake up. She was watching me sleep. When I felt her sit by me, I stirred and saw her warm eyes grin at me lovingly. I lifted the duvet and let her in beside me. She slid under the duvet and I wrapped her in my arm as I spooned her. We lay there quietly for a while enjoying the warmth and closeness. Her hair was splayed all over my chest and covered her face like a veil. I planted soft kisses on her cheek.

After this episode, she came by, often sporadically, slipped in my bed some mornings and held me in her arms to feel the closeness. We used to spoon each other depending on our moods. Waking up to the soft music and her warmth in the morning was heavenly bliss.

"This is way better than any alarm." I murmured in sleep while I cuddled her.

At times, I planted wet kisses on her neck and sent her quivering all over the body.

"The day hasn't even begun and you are sending me loopy already." She said caressing my face with her palm.

"Stop being so wonderful then." I used to charm her.

On one particular morning, she had stayed in bed for longer so I had gone to her bedroom closing the door behind me and sat in her bed. She was still asleep – at least her eyes were shut and her breathing was slow. I lowered my lips on her cheek and planted a soft kiss, trying not to wake her up. Without opening her eyes, she took my hand in her and flipped the duvet to let me in her bed. As I got under the duvet, she scooted into my arms and pushed herself into my hug. I wrapped her in my arms throwing my leg over her and snaking myself around her in a warm snug embrace. She moaned as she planted a kiss on my chest and melted. We remained motionless for a while, enjoying the warm closeness.

"What's the matter?" I whispered stroking her hair and her back.

After a moment of silence, she sighed without moving, "Can you tell?"

"I know you better than you give me credit for." I cuddled her for assurance.

After a moment of silence, she sighed, "I had a rather bad dream, just when I was waking up."

"Do you want to talk?" I stroked her hair again.

She pulled out of the hug slowly and looked deep in my eyes running the gaze around my face. Then she shook her head and pressed herself into my hug.

"I won't push you, you know that. But I think it would help if you shared." I spoke trying to encourage her.

"It was just a dream." She murmured. "I just need to feel your love for a while."

"So it was about me, then." I suggested.

"I don't want to be reminded of it please." She said pleading.

"OK OK." I hugged her and kissed her cheek. I pulled her close into my arms as I rocked her gently.

While we were lying in bed, the morning alarm on the stereo had been playing. Now a song had started playing and it was one of my favourite world artists. We lay quiet as the song played along. It was one of my favourites so I was enjoying it thoroughly. Seeing me so pleased, she whispered to me, "Do you even know what she is singing about?" The song being sung was in Mali language.

"With such deep beautiful voice and such emotions how could it not be talking about love?" I hypothesised. "And even if she were cursing, it does sound so beautiful; so does it matter?" I giggled.

Sam giggled with me. "No but seriously now, as you like it so much it must have good lyrics. Do you know what she is saying or singing about?" Sam was lying facing away from me, our fingers were intertwined in each other's hands as we lay there spooning.

I got up from the bed, releasing myself from her hug slowly. I got to my CD collection and got the album cover out of its sleeve. Then climbing back into bed I read the lyrics of the song. She rolled on her back intently listening to what I had to say.

"Ne bi fe." I said. "That's the song. It means 'I love you'." I stared at her as she gazed at me.

Then I read out the description about the song provided by the artist.

"It's a happy song about passionate love when you are lying in bed caressing each other while the dawn is breaking and the cocks are crowing outside. You love that person so much that you don't want to imagine being without them."

I looked at her. She was welling up slowly. I held her hand and I continued to read.

"The chorus translates to *'I am in love with you, the passion is so strong, don't shame me'.*"

"Set that to play again and come spoon me." She urged me. After I reset it to play again, I spooned her tightly. We lay still and heard the song without saying much, trying to soak all the love it had in itself.

She quivered while listening to the song and this time I had not even kissed her. She was very emotional.

"That is exactly how I feel right now. I can actually feel the emotions in the song." She sighed.

I held her close and she whispered still facing away from me, "You have enriched my life in so many different ways. Now I cannot even dream on how it would have been if you hadn't been in my life."

"You have enriched my life too." I tried to console her. "I do hope I am able to show that to you in everything I do for you."

She turned around and looked at me. "You are very special person; so deep and full of substance." She looked deep into my eyes and peered deep into my soul with her piercing gaze.

After a moment of silent embrace, I suggested, "I have an idea. If you give me 5 minutes, I will show you what it is."

"OK." She released her arms from the hug and looked at me with a slight grin. "5 minutes. Don't take too long." She looked at me with warm eyes.

"5 minutes." I gestured her using my fingers.

I gently got up from her bed, tucked her in the duvet, sprinted out and closed her bedroom door as I stepped out.

Few minutes later, I returned to her bedroom carrying a breakfast tray with scrambled eggs, toast with jam and some hot cocoa with cream. I laid it on her lap as she sat up bright eyed. "Breakfast in bed," she exclaimed. "Awe sweetheart." She smiled with a warm glow.

"That's more like it." I settled beside her and caressed her hair, brushing it away from her cheek. I looked lovingly in her eyes, now glowing bright.

"These babies were meant to sparkle." I looked at her eyes and caressed her cheek.

"All I need is you and I'm always over the moon." She murmured as she bit into the toast.

On one occasion, out of curiosity, she had listened to one of my playlist one afternoon. By the time she was done, she was in tears. I went to see her, a bit concerned seeing why she was so tearful. When I spoke to her, she mentioned she had been listening to the playlist called 'Corticotrophin'.

"It is so sad and humbling list." She said looking at me through her tears. "Why do you even have it?"

"That hormone is released when one cries. I had created it to help me cry. I have now created a new list called Endorphin. It now helps me to rise above when I'm feeling blue." I had elaborated.

"When do you feel like that?" she was perplexed and concerned. "And more importantly, why would you want to listen to music to make you cry?" She was speechless.

"Not so much now, but there used to be times when I felt like crying and that list helped me open my floodgates." I said with a slight grin, acknowledging the power of the music.

"Like when?" She was very curious to know. She took her headphones away and took my hand to sit me next to her.

"Well this is going back before we actually got close like we are now. I used to feel alone and solitary sometimes and there used to be times when I did not handle it very well." I confessed.

"Why did you never tell me?" She asked becoming very concerned, while caressing my cheeks feeling sad.

"I did not want to drag you down with me. You used to be with your friends at those times." I smiled. "And at other times we did hang out together anyway." I shrugged my shoulders. "It was only when I went through some depression phases at times through loneliness." I confessed. "I can't help it." I shrugged again.

"I can." She looked me with love in her eyes. "You will tell me the next time you feel like that."

I just nodded with a smile. "I don't remember feeling like that ever since we have become close." I smiled to her.

"Good. Let's keep it that way." She smiled warmly.

Without any surprise, her favourite playlists were Serotonin, Adrenalin, and Oxytocin.

"Why that name? Oxytocin?" She asked me.

"That is the hormone that represents love, affection and bonding." I smiled at her.

"Our kind of music." She had smiled, winking at me. "I felt that when I was listening to it. You have included one of my songs in there too." She smiled.

I smiled at her. "It is now one of my favourites."

"You also have another folder like that with the same names." She pointed it out to me.

"Yes. This one is only music and no lyrics. That one is with lyrics – the normal pop songs. This has new age and instrumental. Very little or no words, just emotions." I elaborated.

"I get it now." She had wondered with big bright eyes.

"So what's Leptin?" She inquired. "I never heard that word before. Is that a hormone too?"

I nodded. "It is the hormone that is released to trigger satiety, particularly when you are eating. It tells the brain that you are full up." I smiled as I tried to explain to her.

She looked perplexed still. "How does that work here?"

"Those songs give me so much peace that I feel fully complacent with life. I feel so much peace that I am ready to give up this body and rise above, to become non-corporal in fact. After I've listened to even a few songs in that list, if He came to take me away I would go with Him without batting an eyelid. That is how complacent and peaceful those songs make me feel."

"Whoa. That's heavy." She exclaimed. "You are not going anywhere without me."

I laughed. "I am just trying to explain hon."

She just stared at me for a while. "You are very deep." She looked at me with admiration.

"Am I?" I just smiled nonchalantly.

"You are. Very deep and thoughtful. I like that about you." She spoke softly. "You don't do anything without thinking through do you?"

"No." I smiled. "I like to make decisions after careful thought and analysis. So I don't have regrets."

"None what so ever?" she was curious.

"None." I was confident.

"I like that." She had hugged me.

In the pool, I did help her learn to swim in record 10 days. The only two things I had asked her to follow – 'trust me implicitly and follow what I tell you to do to the dot, nothing more nothing less'.

"I trust you with my life," she had said looking straight in my eyes with a sincere look.

I had started by helping her wade in the shallow end first until she was comfortable with water. Then I had explained to her the deep breathing cycle and why it is so important to get it right. Then I had encouraged her to breathe while dipping her head under the water on and off in rhythm. Once she was comfortable breathing like that, the rest followed very smoothly. I encouraged her to swim underwater and practice deep breathing. In fact, I had helped her gain the confidence she lacked all this time. She loved getting into the water with me after that. I even taught her diving. She used to try the lower boards only but enjoyed plunging in the water together with me.

We used to swim underwater rather than at the surface. I would love to take her all the way down in the deep end. We used to swim together along the floor of the pool from the shallow end, and get to the depths at the deep end of the pool. Then we would stand on the floor, float about in an embrace and pretend to be dancing for a while in suspended animation.

At times, we would hug each other and just float there in the deep underwater, trying to feel our tactile senses come alive. Her hair would glide around in the deep and she would look like a heavenly mermaid. Wrapped in each other's arms, touching gently, eyes closed, the world shut out from our perceptions, we used to feel so much calm and peace together like that. We would be like dolphins, swimming together intertwined without even making any ripples on the surface.

She hated sitting across me at restaurants because she could never feel the closeness that way. Usually when we went out with our parents, she loved to sit on the inside of the couch next to me. The only time she sat opposite me would be if only the two of us were out together and there were only two chairs at the table and she did not want to make it obvious by moving the chair closer to me. At such times, we used to tangle our legs under the table.

During these times that I used to sit facing her, I used to eat my heart out looking at her beauty. For a long time, we used to stare at each other without saying much, just admiring each other, our conversations purely telepathic. She used to say that I had the warmest eyes she had ever seen and that by looking at them she would go weak in the knees. That is why she rarely stared into my eyes for long. "They make me do things," she used to say.

I used to look at her and take in every little detail of her beauty — the curved long thick eyelashes that tickled my face when she pressed her cheek against mine, the lips that sucked the life out of me every time they touched my lips, the tips at the corner of her lips that brightened my day every time they curved up because she had seen me or been with me, the thick hair cascading and flowing all over her shoulders and back with soft waves that invited me to spend eternity getting lost in them, her fragrance that ignited passions in my mind.

She never wore any makeup. I loved to see her natural beauty and encouraged her to be comfortable in her own skin. Because we kissed often, she did not get into the habit of putting on lipstick either.

"As much as I would love to mark my territory, I don't want to call for unnecessary attention," she had said once. When she saw my expression of perplexity, she had signed about the lipstick mark left behind. "Anyway, with the number of times I need your lips on mine, I would end up putting lipstick all day."

"I fancy tasting YOU on my lips and the wax ruins it." I had remarked.

While we would be in the garden chilling out in the afternoon on the lawn during some days, she used to lie on her back perpendicular to me, with her head resting on my chest close to my heart. I would lie on my back, listening to music or just staring into eternity in quiet contemplation. Her hair used to dance and flow around in the soft breeze and I could smell its fragrance and feel the soft magic on my neck and chin.

We used to lie there like that for hours, at times chatting, at times listening to our music or at times doing our own things while being close. Then sometimes she would roll on to her side, and hear my heartbeats with her ear pressed on my chest. Apparently it made her feel warm – "It beats for me," she started mimicking me.

Occasionally, she would roll over on to her tummy and plant soft kisses on my lips, particularly when we were alone in the house. She would lie like that, with her face close to mine, running her fingers in my hair. While we chatted for hours, occasionally she would close in and plant kisses on my lips, cheek, chin, nose, forehead on and off during the entire time, randomly.

Sometimes she would just press her forehead and nose on my cheek and hold it there for a while, or sink her forehead under my chin and press her face on my neck, planting soft kisses on my neck. She loved nuzzling her face on mine, letting my lips caress her face as she moved and grazed it over my lips lazily. She would love to brush her eyes on my cheeks, letting her eyelashes tickle my cheeks and lips as she planted kisses on my chin and neck. All the while, her hair would cascade and flow all over my face, tickling and teasing me. All this was done with casual sensuality.

Our parents used to say to us, "What in the world is there to talk about so much," because they said we never shut up. They found us always chatting about things, giggling or in each other's arms. Nonetheless, they did appreciate that never once had they seen us fall out with each other, let alone hurt or hit each other or yell, shout or curse each other. We were the most well behaved siblings they had ever seen. For that one reason alone, they never really questioned us about our closeness.

There were times when Sam used to beckon me in our coded signals to accompany her on a quiet evening walk or a drive. Without a word, she used to gesture, stare or vocalise her need for spending some quiet 'us' time together. She loved to take my arm and walk next to me touching my hand and pressing her cheek against my shoulder, hands around waists, without saying much.

At other times, she would just toss the car keys to me, and tell me to drive for some time out of the town and park somewhere quiet. We used to drive to our lake outside the town that we used to love spending such quiet quality time together. I used to lie on the passenger seat reclined back, and she would recline on my chest.

Sometimes she would lie on me with her back pressed on my chest so I could hug her around as if I was spooning her. She would urge me to place my legs on the dashboard so she could feel my thighs as she rested her legs on mine. At other times, she would lie on her chest and I would wrap her around her back. She would have her cheek pressed against mine, or nuzzle her face in my neck. Seeing the evening sunset without saying much, while gently kissing each other's cheek or caressing each other while hugging tightly, would be her ideal way to recuperate all the loving she had missed throughout the day.

We loved relaxing in the hammock in the garden. We spent quite a few summer days just lying in it together. I found it very relaxing to listen to my music through headphones lying in the hammock. At times, when she was able to join me, she used to let me know. She would stand next to me. If I had my eyes closed, she would caress me gently by running her fingers through my hair or caress my face. If we were alone in the house, she would plant soft kisses on my lips to attract my attention. If I had nodded off, she would kiss me softly to wake me up. If I saw her walking toward me, I used to ask her, "Wish to join me?" and she would nod with a smile. Then I would ask her how she wanted to lie with me. If she wanted to read while I listened to my music, she used to lie on top with her back pressed on my chest, slightly shifted over me. I used to let her rest her head on my arm and fold it at the elbow creating a pillow for her. We used to lie like that for hours, without saying much, each doing our own thing. The closeness was enough to convey the conversation.

Sometimes, when she wanted to be closer, she would bring along her headphones and we would listen to the songs together. She used to lie on top of me with her chest pressed on mine, sprawled half across my chest alongside me. I used to hug her with my arm and she used to place her head on my shoulder. She used to find this a rather warm and loving closeness.

Sometimes, she would just lie like that without the need to listen to the music. "I love to hear your heart beat." She used to say at such times. "Makes me feel so special and warm to be so close to you."

We often sent each other SMS messages telling how we missed one another during the day. When it was possible, we used to catch a meal together. Her friends used to tag along sometimes. "They are really keen to go out with you, you know." She used to say to me looking deep in my eyes.

"OK." I used to reply back. "Make sure it doesn't go any further." I used to say to her.

"You don't want to go out with anyone of them?" She used to question.

I used to just shake my head and refrain. "Not interested."

"What am I supposed to tell them if they ask me?" She used to ask. I used to shrug my shoulders.

Once I gazed at her and smiled. "Tell them, I am already with someone." Then I planted a soft kiss on her forehead and had waved goodbye to go for my class. She had bit her lip with warm reciprocation when I had turned to wave at her before turning a corner.

We used to spend time in the library studying together, or helping each other with our homework or research. She would spend time just sitting by me and I would accompany her during her study time. We helped each other with our work and she used to love to distract me and tease me with her tantalising looks. At times, when I gazed at her while explaining something, she used to forget her studies or even my explanation, and just gaze deep in my eyes. Her lips would curl up slowly and her eyes would fill with sensuality. I used to stop in my explanation, stare at her square in her eyes, and then for a few moments our conversation would be telepathic. Seeing just how much she admired, adored and loved me would melt me to my core.

"Now that you have had your 'break', can we get back on track?" I used to tease her suggestively.

"I wish I had a longer break." She would smile seductively.

"Focus, please." I would plead.

"Only if you become invisible, and then you can touch me and kiss me all over and no one would know." Her eyes glowed when she suggested that once.

"O man." I just shook my head.

She just giggled. "Or better still, if I could become invisible, that would be better still." Her eyes used to glow with excitement. I used to blush red, trying to imagine what was on her mind.

In spite of all this closeness and sensuality that grew between us, I never found her dressed provocatively. Every time she wore anything, it was sensual, classy and enticing but never provocative or erotic. I think that is why our parents never laid down rules – no matter how close we were and how we expressed it, there was little or no vulgarity in it. It could have been seen simply as love between siblings. We never made it obvious or concerning. What they did not know was what happened when no one was looking. At such times we used to express our love lot more physically.

One of my pet hates was doing the laundry. My mom had made us responsible for our own laundry ever since we were old enough to do it. We were taught to become independent and self-aware. Sam used to be very particular about doing her laundry; me, not so much. I used to find excuses to get her to do my laundry, when she used to ask me for favours. Later she just started doing my laundry along with her own.

"He will never learn to do it on his own if you keep doing it for him." My mom used to whinge at her.

Sam used to just smile looking at me, shrug her shoulders and carry on. "It's ok ma. He does things for me too."

"You should be so thankful." Mom used to shake her head at me.

Sam once asked me, "Don't get me wrong hon, but why don't you like doing your laundry?"

"It's a chore." I shrugged my shoulders. "I hate it when I have to do chores. It is boring."

"OK." Sam paused to ponder for a while. "How about we make it interesting?"

I looked at her. "How?"

"You do my laundry and I will do yours."

"You like doing my laundry?" I was perplexed.

She nodded. "It's called pheromones." She had smiled with a glee in her eyes. "Have you ever done my laundry?" she grinned at me.

I shook my head.

She smiled looking at me. "Try it once and you will see what I mean."

The next time we had to do laundry, I did try and sure enough found it very arousing indeed; handling her clothes and underwear, taking her intoxicating scent and of course the 'pheromones'. I used to feel her soft night wear on my fingertips when it used to dry.

She instructed me how she liked them washed and what temperature and what softener. Then when we used to shop, she used to pick her softener and I used to pick mine. I used to ask her to try different fragrances just to make some change. I used to beckon her to try and smell the fragrance of a new softener in the store if I found any and she would tell me if she fancied it. My mom used to find that so very odd. Sam used to whisper to her, "at least he is doing laundry. Look on the positive side."

We had started surprising each other with unexpected snippets. I used to leave kiss mark on the mirror in the bathroom, or leave love notes on the mirror, or she would leave behind her bra and panties in the shower if I were going to shower after her. I used to spray my perfume on her sleepwear to remind her of me and she used to use my shirts secretly for a while and put them back on the hangers. I used to smell her on me all day at such times, going completely loopy.

I had messaged her once.

'tonight – u & me, in ur bed.'

'why wait? ;-)'

'don't dare me'

'promises promises'

'what am I allowed?'

'anything goes =D, try me'

'don't tempt me'

'don't resist me then'

'I need to behave'

'not with me you don't! xxx'

'don't talk like that. I won't
be able to stand up
after my class!'

'I need to see proof =P'

'You will get it later, just you wait'

'I am wet ;-)'

When we cooked each other anything, we put smilies, kisses and hearts on the dishes or on our spreads. She used to draw heart with ketchup; I used to spread jam on her toast to make a heart. Once I cut her toasts in heart shapes. She smiled and hugged me. She had made me heart shaped cookies. My drinking glass at dinner table most often had her lip marks on it. Sometimes she used to leave bookmarks in my notebooks with her photographs that I had taken. We selected each other's clothes when we changed to go out.

On seldom occasion, we had taken a chance and slept in the same bed in the night. Although we used to love to crawl into each other's bed in the morning for a hug, only on rare occasion had we slept together in the same bed all night.

One day we were in the garden lying in the lawn. Sam was resting her head on my chest while stretched out perpendicular to me. For a while, we had chatted and laughed. Then she had rolled around so she was now looking down on my face. She pressed her face on my lips and she played around like that for a while. She spread her hair and let it fall all over my face and let it tickle me. She gathered it all and spread it over her head covering and hiding our faces underneath it as she pressed her lips on mine. She left her lips planted on mine like that for a while, soaking the love.

***

Beverly and Stuart gazed out into the garden while they were in the kitchen. They saw Alex and Sam lying on the lawn.

"There is trouble brewing in paradise." Stuart said.

"Is there anything you suggest we do?" Beverly asked him.

"Intervention now will hopefully stop it getting worse."

"Do you think this is capable of being stopped?" She asked him. "Look at them. Every year they get closer and fall deeper."

"Are you saying you are ok with this?" Stuart was shocked.

"No. But I know there is little we can do about it." Beverly answered calmly.

"We are their parents. We CAN do something about it." Stuart was stern and forceful.

"Although they are our kids, they are adults now. They have the right to make their choices. What happens when you confront them and they decide, choose or feel forced to walk out of our lives? Will you be ok deserting your own kids?"

He remained silent.

"They are our kids." She said to him calmly. "We have loved them. They would not do anything bad."

"This isn't right."

"That doesn't make it wrong either. It is just different, different from the norm, from what we understand. Just because we may not understand it, does not make it wrong. Norms change over time. Therefore, who are we to challenge this? All they have expressed toward each other is love. It is not happened just now, they have been loving each other for all their lives. How can that be ugly?"

"I'm not saying it's ugly. It's just wrong."

"I'm saying it's not wrong, it just ain't right. There is a difference." She argued. "You push them and they will end up doing something we will both feel sorry about, and it would simply be over nothing more than love. There is a lot worse some other parents have to accept and live with regarding their kids."

He had gone silent for a while knowing full well what she had said. "Doing nothing is just going to let this tornado build up." He argued.

"If there is nothing we can do to stop the build-up, we will just have to brace when it makes landfall."

Both just stood there in silence.

"Leave it with me. I will deal with this." She suggested him.

***

Chapter 8 – crash, bang, whollup

One day when we were driving to one of our activities, I had stopped at the lights waiting for them to turn green. We were the first at the lights. We had been chatting and teasing each other just as normal and I was enjoying her sensuality while she tingled and teased me. As the lights turned green, I slowly pulled out and I was still glancing at her as I was driving.

Just as I was pulling into the crossing, I noticed from behind Sam, a car was speeding toward us on her side and had jumped the lights and coming straight for us. Just when I realised what was going to happen, I turned the steering away from the speeding car and slammed my breaks. I shouted "Sam, duck." She just instinctively curled her head in her hands and leaned close to me. The speeding car crashed into our front passenger-side wheel, swerved us to a side, banged against our entire length of the passenger side sideways, and I slammed into a car on the corner.

By the time I had gained composure, I realised I had pain shooting through my leg, I had bruising on my head with some blood, a bad whiplash but otherwise I was ok. I looked over to Sam. Her door had been smashed and glass had shattered all over her. I could see some blood on her side arm and leg and she was unconscious.

"Sam, Sam" I cried out. She was leaning over toward me but I could see she was bleeding on her side and her arm. I could not see if she was hurt on her leg but I feared she was.

By the time I had gained composure, the police had arrived on the scene and the area had been cordoned off. One police officer instructed me to stay put. He said he had called the emergency service and for me not to move.

It took a few minutes more for the ambulance to arrive. Until then, I was checking for Sam's pulse making sure she was still alive. She was breathing and I could feel her pulse but was still unconscious.

"Sam. Open your eyes." I kept caressing her cheek. I did not dare move her neck.

When the emergency crew lifted her out on a stretcher, I could see she was in a bad shape but apparently, she was breathing.

We were rushed to the nearest hospital. They tended to my wounds but they were not as serious. After I was patched up, they allowed me to see her. She was still unconscious. I was told about her injuries. Apparently, she had a lucky escape with only some bruised rib on her side, a hairline fracture to her arm, elbow and her leg. But with good care and rest she could pull through.

"Why is she still unconscious?" I asked the doctor.

"She has a concussion on her head otherwise she should come around soon. But don't worry, she does not seem to have any internal bleeding. Her situation is stable for the moment, although we will have to keep her under observation. If you wish you can sit with her."

I sat down beside her. "Can I hold her hand?" I asked the doctor.

"Sure. Talk to her. She may respond to your voice. I will be back later." The doctor said.

"Thank you doctor." I shook his hand gently. I was aching all over myself.

"You two have had a lucky escape." The doctor nodded to me.

As he left, I looked over to Sam. She had a neck brace and cast on her arm and leg. I couldn't hold back my tears.

"Sam. Honey. I am right here baby. You are all right. You have had some injuries but you are ok. You will make a good recovery. Everything will be fine. I'm right her for you." I kept talking to her and stroking her hand trying to see if I could get her to open her eyes.

I kept kissing her hand. While I was doing that, I saw her eyelids move and quiver. I could see the bumps on her eyelids move slowly. She was gaining consciousness.

"Sam honey. It's me, Alex. Open your eyes baby. I'm right here."

She took a few more minutes before I saw her eyes open slightly.

"Yes sweetheart. I'm right her." I went up close so she could hear me. "I'm right her baby." I kissed her forehead and caressed it, holding her hand in mine.

She looked at me with drowsy eyes. She was struggling to keep her eyes open.

"It's ok baby. Take your time. I am right here." I kept talking to her. "You are ok and safe with me now." I spoke to her.

I felt her fingers move and try to squeeze my hand as she looked at me. "Good. See I am right here. You are doing just fine. Everything is going to be ok." I said to her.

"Do you recall what happened to you?" I tried to see if she remembered anything.

She nodded slowly and suddenly paused realising the pain in her neck, and then blinked her eyes.

"Good. You are safe now. You have just had some bruising. No permanent damage. With good rest doc said you will recover fully. So don't worry at all."

She looked at me and tried to run her eyes all over me seeing my bandages.

"I'm fine too. See I am talking to you. It just looks worse that it is." I tried to tell her that I was fine too. "I'm ok. Don't worry about me baby."

I could see tear run down her eye.

"Hey honey, don't worry about me. Everything will be ok." I tried to calm her down. "I just look worse than I am. I promise I'm ok."

Just then a nurse rushed in and checked Sam's stats on the monitor. She checked her pulse and her blood pressure.

"There, everything seems fine. How you doing sweetheart?" she asked in a pedantic manner. "Don't move your neck as yet ok? We want to make sure there is no damage first. I will remove it in a few hours."

Sam slowly blinked.

The nurse looked at me and smiled. "She is out of the woods. I will be around but you can sit with her now. She should be ok."

"I have given you pain medication." She whispered to Sam. "You should not feel much pain. If you think it is getting unbearable, let me know. You have taken a considerable beating so it will hurt a bit. OK?" Then the nurse left.

I sat down next to Sam and took her hand. She looked at me and whispered to me, "Are you ok?" and welled up again.

"Hey baby. Look. I'm better than you; just some bruising. In fact I should be crying about you." I tried to smile. "You took the major brunt of the beating."

"I love you." she mimed at me squeezing my fingers in her curled hand.

"I love you too hon." I kissed her hand. Then I lowered my lips and kissed her gently on the cheek.

"All will be fine. You will see." I caressed her face.

She blinked her eyes to reciprocate.

"Mom and dad?" she mimed.

"I haven't told them yet. I was waiting for you to come around first. I will give them a call now if you want."

She blinked again. She squeezed my hand.

"I am right here. I ain't going anywhere. Don't worry."

I made a phone call and let our parents know. Within half an hour, they were there. When they saw her, mom was tearful. However, I consoled her and told her that with some rest Sam would recover fully. "No permanent damage done."

She felt relieved.

I spent the night with Sam. My body was hurting like hell. However, I did not care. I wanted to make sure she knew I was there beside her.

Next morning when the doctor came around for the visit, he was more than pleased about her stable condition. "I think she is ok to be discharged."

"I would like to take her home if that's ok." I said.

"Ok then. I will get the paperwork and medication written up." He looked at me.

"You have been very lucky sweetheart. Now you need a lot of rest so if you promise me, I will let you go. How about that?" The doctor spoke to Sam.

Sam nodded. Her neck brace had gone. She was talking slowly in a low volume.

"Can you sit up for me please?" the doctor urged her.

He asked me to give her a hand. Sam sat up slowly in the bed whimpering at every motion. She must had been in a lot of pain.

"Good. Excellent." He made notes. "Any pain?" he smiled.

Sam nodded emphatically.

He smiled. "OK. That's normal. We just want to make sure you are not too drugged up. You understand." He commented. "I will write some more pain killer and you will feel better in a few days."

"You will need to use wheelchair for now because you have a cast on and you should not move or put strain on it yet. It needs to heal so you won't be able to move that leg." He tried to explain to her.

"Good. If you have some mode of transport, I will clear you to leave in about a few hrs. How about that?" He said to me.

"I will call my dad to pick us up." I said to him.

"Good. Do that." He agreed.

"You will be just fine. Don't worry. Your brother has my number if you need to call." He winked at Sam with a broad smile and left.

"Thank you doctor." I thanked him.

Sam lay back in the bed. She took my hand and asked me to sit with her.

"What happened...?" She asked me. "...about the accident?"

"A car ran a red light. It was being chased by police." I spoke. "It hit your side head on and that's why you were hurt pretty bad." I started to well up.

She held my hand and shook her head. "It wasn't your fault." She spoke softly. "You told me to duck." She said softly. "I remember."

"Yes but I was driving." I said to her. "I should have been more careful."

"Thanx to you I am her talking to you now." She said. "Thank you my angel for looking after me." She kissed my hand.

I lowered my lips and kissed her forehead.

"You will make a full recovery. You will see." I promised her.

"Where did you sleep last night?" She asked me.

I looked at the couch next to her.

"Oh baby. You must feel shattered." She sighed and welled up. "Why did not you go home?"

"I will be ok. Don't worry about me." I said. "We are going home now anyway."

When dad arrived, we helped Sam into the back seat and I got in through the other side and let her rest leaning against me. We drove back home with mom waiting to help her settle in.

By the time Sam had settled in it was evening. Mom made us some dinner and Sam ate it lying across on the couch in the lounge. I fed her gently. Her arm was strapped in a sleeve and her leg was in a cast all the way up to her hip.

Then we helped her up the stairs into her bed.

"Rest for a while. I will be right back. Do you need anything for now?" I asked her.

"Don't be too long." She made a puppy face.

"I just have to sort a few things for you for the night, hon. Then I will be right her." I smiled at her.

I went downstairs and collected a big bottle of water, some tissues, towels and went back up into her room.

"There. See? I think we are set for the night." I said to her. "Now I will be here taking care of you till you are 100% original," I smiled.

I sat down beside her and caressed her face.

Mom and dad popped in to kiss her good night before they retired to bed.

"Let us know if you need anything." Dad said to me.

"We will be fine dad. Don't worry." I assured him.

"Of course you will." They waived good night.

"You are her knight in shining armour." Dad said with a smile.

Chapter 9 – helping hands

Sam wanted me to sleep in her room for the first few nights. I had slept the first night on a mattress on the floor so as not to accidently roll over her in the night; I rolled in my sleep a lot, and I'm not just talking about tossing and turning.

She hardly had any sleep for the first hour. I had woken up many times to hold her hand. She must have been in a lot of pain. The doctor had said that her wounds would look very bad in a few days time but that would be expected as she had been bruised pretty badly. Eventually sometime in the night she had asked me to sleep beside her. She could not bear the pain 'alone' she had said tearfully.

In the morning, mom and dad came in and tended to her for a while. There was no need for them to take leave from work when I was around to take care of her anyway. With me around, they had realised they would be redundant as usual. After they kissed her goodbye, mom told me she had laid some breakfast for us and some meals were in the fridge if I needed them. "I will be home in the evening. If you need me, call me." She said to me.

"We will be fine." I looked at Sam and smiled. "Won't we hon?"

"Don't worry mom. I am fine. I will see you in the evening." She reassured mom.

After our parents had left, I asked Sam if she needed some breakfast. "Hungry?"

She nodded.

"Ok what do you fancy?" I looked at her.

She just looked at me for a while with piercing eyes and smiled with a sensual teasing look.

"O man." I giggled. "Seems like you have recovered already." I laughed out loud.

"What?" She made an innocent face.

"Do you want some eggs, or just some cereal?" I looked at her.

"Cereal is fine." She said.

"I don't mind cooking you some eggs. Don't hesitate. It's not a bother." I tried to convince her.

"Only if you will have some too." She said to me in a girly tone.

"Ok give me a minute and I will be right back. Do you need anything before I prepare breakfast?"

She shook her head. Then she paused and held her hand out beckoning me to come close.

"I know I must stink but I need a kiss." She said softly.

I lowered my lips on hers and gave a soft kiss. I caressed her face. "You always smell divine. I know you want to freshen up. I will help you after breakfast how about that?"

She nodded with feminine compliance.

When I returned to her room, I laid down the breakfast tray in bed across her lap. I had made some scrambled eggs, toast with strawberry jam and some cereal with milk. "If you want juice I will get some. But I thought it would be too sharp for now." I spoke softly.

As one of her arm was strapped up, I sat on the other side. "If you wish, you can try eating with your other hand but if it gets too difficult, I would love to feed you." I suggested.

She looked at me and smiled. "Let me try first." She tried with some difficulty.

"Not bad. You are good with both hands." I smiled.

"I still would like you to feed me" She said. "It feels nice." She smiled.

"I'd love to." I smiled.

After we had finished breakfast, I took the tray away and came back into Sam's bedroom.

"When is your class?" She asked me.

"What class?" I dismissed her.

"Don't miss your class hon." She pleaded.

"I'm not leaving you today." I wouldn't listen.

"I will be fine." She tried to convince me.

"Definitely not today." I reiterated. "I ain't going anywhere leaving you her alone for today. Nope. Not happening."

"Would you like to help me up? I need to freshen up." She extended her hands at me to help her out of bed.

I got the crunches and helped her out of bed. "I need to brush my teeth first," she indicated as we walked slowly to the bathroom. I supported her on one side while she used her crutches. I laid out some paste on the brush and handed it to her.

It was very clumsy at first but soon she got the hang of it.

"It's amazing isn't it?" I spoke softly looking at her struggle to brush her teeth. "We take so much for granted that we realise its importance only when we lose it." I muttered.

She paused and looked at me in the mirror. "I know exactly what I have and I'm always more than grateful." She spoke with sincerity.

"Hon." I stroked her back gently. "I was just saying because of how we take our hands and legs for granted and only when we can't use them do we realise how important they are for us."

"I know what you meant but you are right in that." She acknowledged.

After she had brushed, she washed her face.

"Can you excuse me for a few minutes?" she coyly said to me. "I need the loo."

"Sure." I turned to leave.

"Hon." She called out for me.

I turned and looked at her. "Yes sweetheart?"

She stood there and looked at me shyly. Then she lowered her gaze to her panties. "I need some help." She whispered and gestured.

"Oh sorry." I gently pulled her panties down and helped her sit on the loo.

She looked at me and smiled.

I stepped out and closed the door. After a while, I heard the flush and after a few moments later I stepped in.

"That nearly killed me. I must be really bruised up because I couldn't bend." She said.

She looked at the shower-bath.

"There is no way you will be able to get in there for at least a month." I said to her looking at her gaze. "You will need bed baths till then." I said.

I could see her eyes gleaming gently at the thought of it. "Would you be giving me bed bath?" she exclaimed, slightly surprised, sceptical and excited at the same time.

I looked at her face, glowing with smile. "I would if you'd be ok with that." I sounded sincere.

"I would love that, only if you are ok with it." She looked at me hesitantly for my reaction.

"I'd love to. You should know that by now." I looked sincerely. "I'd do anything for you."

"Wow. I don't mind getting hurt then. Would be totally worth it." She giggled.

"You are so naughty." I shook my head in amazement and smiled. "Even in this state."

I helped her to her bedroom. "Come on in here and I will help you for a bed bath."

I walked her to the bed. Before getting in, I helped her to strip. She kept looking at me all the while. She asked me to take her bra and panties off too. I paused in case she wanted to reconsider.

"I cannot leave them on." She shrugged nonchalantly.

"Lie down and I will get the bowl." I helped her to get in the bed.

I got a bowl of hot water, a towel and her sponge with some of her favourite liquid soap.

"Would it be a standard bed bath or a special one?" she smiled coyly as she looked at me.

"For you it is always extra special, hon" I replied smiling. "Would you like that?"

"Go crazy." She smiled. "Or best of all, make me crazy!" She giggled.

"Ok. Let me see what we can do." I whispered softly. "It's my first and I want to be gentle anyway as you would be really sore from the wounds."

"With your touch, I will heal in a minute." She smiled.

I made her lay on the towel so as not to get her bed wet.

As she rolled and lay on her back, I started to sponge her gently. I could now see the bruising on her. It had turned purple, dark blue and black and it certainly looked worse today.

"I'm so sorry." I welled up seeing her in that state.

"Hey hon." She reached out and held my hand squeezing it gently. "Don't do this to yourself. Please. I told you it's not your fault. In fact you have saved me." She whispered lovingly.

I tried to compose myself with difficulty.

She held on to my hand and brushed her thumb over my fingers. "I need you to be strong, ok?" She pleaded with me with another squeeze on my hand. "I won't be able to get through this without you." She sighed welling up.

I looked at her and composed myself nodding my head. After she realised I would be ok, she let me start with the bed bath.

I gently started sponging her starting from her foot. As I ran the sponge over her leg, she parted her leg to expose her thighs. I gently sponged her thighs and her inner thighs. As I sponged her close to her mound, she took my other hand in her hand and squeezed it. She closed her eyes and tossed her head back in the pillow. As I rubbed and sponged her vulva gently, it must have sent waves of pleasure as she sighed deeply.

She moved her good leg apart and bent it at the knee, opening it slightly. I sponged deeper between the thighs. Every rub I made sent her sighing and I could feel the squeeze on my hand.

Then I gently straightened her leg down on the bed and continued sponging her tummy. Then I did her hands and then came up to her chest.

"Pity you can't use your hands instead of the sponge." She suggested with a sultry smile.

"Better still. How about my lips?" I whispered back teasing her.

"Oooo," she closed her eyes and tilted her head back in the pillow with a deep sigh. "You are such a tease, hon" she smiled coyly.

"I'm not." I protested smiling. "Would you like that?"

Her lips curved in a brilliant shiny smile. "I'd love it."

After I had carefully sponged her neck, chest and bosoms, I was careful to inspect and gently clean the bruised areas on her sides and ribs. She whimpered a bit and I pulled back sharply for a moment but continued gently after she gazed at me with a comforting smile. When I had sponged her chest, I lowered my lips and gently kissed her starting from her tummy and navel, coming up slowly around the boobs and then the nipples.

Her breathing was deep and she sighed heavily. She had closed her eyes tilting her head back in her pillow, turning it to one side, enjoying the bliss while running her fingers through my hair.

When I stopped, I looked at her and she opened her eyes and looked at me, her hand cupping my face.

"I'm sorry you are in this mess." I sighed.

"Shh. Stop it silly." She caressed my cheek cupping it gently. "If it hadn't been for you, I wouldn't had been so lucky." She sighed. "I get to be kissed all over for my bed baths for a whole month or so. Are you kidding me?" She exclaimed. "I would gladly ram into a truck again," she smiled.

"You are something you know that." I laughed out loudly.

"Wouldn't you?" She smiled at me. "And this is just the start of the day. Wow."

"Everyone should get hurt like this, shouldn't they?" I remarked sarcastically.

"Umm. Now now. No use getting carried away. Not everyone has an angel to look after them do they?" She looked at me and took my hand in her.

I stroked her hair and her forehead and planted a kiss there.

Then I asked her to turn over on her tummy. She whimpered slightly as she rolled slowly. She stopping rolling all the way on her chest as one of her arm was strapped. She used her other leg in cast to stretch out and prop her up.

I sponged her back. I made note of all the bruised areas she had. When I sponged her bum, I squeezed the sponge and let the hot water run down between her cheeks. She moaned deeply squeezing my hand in response. She scissored her legs to encourage me to sponge between her bum cheeks. I sponged her bum cheeks and pressed deep between the gap and I ran the sponge all the way down to her vulva.

"For a man, you have such gentle hands," she purred.

"I don't know how bad your injuries are," I said to her. "I don't want to hurt you."

After I had sponged her bum, I planted soft kisses on it. She lowered her hand on my head and ran her fingers through my hair sighing.

After doing her bum, I sponged her back and the neck. She lifted her hair away so I could sponge her neck. Then I sponged her shoulders and arms. I was careful to sponge her bruises lightly. She whimpered slightly.

When I had sponged her back, I planted kisses all over it, starting all the way from the bum, I kissed all of her spine and then I planted kisses deep in her neck on her weak spot. She quivered a few times sighing and moaning.

Then I saw her lie there with her eyes closed for a while, enjoying the bliss she had experienced just then.

As she turned around and looked at me, she smiled. "That was brilliant."

"I'm glad you liked it." I whispered with a smile.

"If I have to look forward to this every day in the morning, I won't sleep at night." She sighed sarcastically.

"Anything that pleases you." I smiled and caressed her hair.

"Oh. Don't talk like that. It makes me so wet." She moaned.

As she sat up in the bed, I gave her the sponge to rub down more if she wanted. She took it and sponged a bit more. Then handing it back to me, she gazed at me expectantly.

I handed her deodorant and perfume. She handed them back after using them.

"I feel so much better now." She smiled.

"Good." I smiled back.

She opened her arms and beckoned me to hug her. I scooted next to her and gave her a hug gently wrapping my arms around her. As I hugged her, she let out a small whimper and then melted in my arms. She tugged on my t-shirt to get it off. I slipped it over my head and then hugged her again. I could feel her warm skin on me. She ran her fingers slowly on my shoulder, back and arms. She rested her cheek on my shoulder as she sat there hugging me gently, her arm around my neck, her fingers running through my hair.

We sat there hugging each other in silence. I tilted my head and planted kisses on her cheek. As she slowly tilted her head, she offered her lips as she turned and looked at me, her head still on my shoulder, her arm holding my arm.

"You have no idea how much I love you." She said.

"I do hon." I hugged her in acknowledgment. "And I hope you know how much I love you too."

"I do." She gently moved her lips and planted a soft kiss on my lips.

I stopped and looked at her. "You must be feeling cold." I looked at her and noticed her goose bumps on her arm as I ran my fingers over them.

"That's all you my dear, not the cold." she smiled at me with a slow blink of her eyelids. "That is what you do to me," smiling coyly again.

"Really? Wow." I looked at her goose bumps and couldn't believe my eyes.

"Now you know what I keep telling you." She smiled at me.

I kissed her and got up to clear the bed. I asked her what she wanted to wear. She smiled sensually and said coyly, "You choose."

I smiled and then I got her a long nightshirt to put on and some soft lose pants. I helped her into her pants sliding them slowly up her long slender legs. She gently raised her bum to help me pull them on. As she lay down, she had her hands on my shoulder and partly around my neck. She was looking deep in my eyes. We stared at each other for a while and then she pulled me closer for a kiss, wrapping her arm around my neck and pulling me into her hug. I lowered my lips and planted kisses on her lips. She whimpered a bit as she stretched and her bruises on the side reminded her of her unwell body. I gently kissed her back, caressing gently, making sure I did not hug her tightly.

"Hold me tight." She said. "I want to feel your closeness."

"I'm just worried about your bruises hon." I voiced my concern.

"Never mind them. Just squeeze me for a while. It makes me feel close and loved. As such I can only use one arm and I can't pull you close enough."

I lay on her, while supporting myself so I didn't press her with my weight. I tried hugging her, slowly squeezing her in my arms as she kissed me back, running her hand through my hair on the back of my head.

She kept looking at me, gazing deep in my eyes while she kissed me.

Then she opened her arm and lay there in complacent bliss with her eyes closed.

When she opened her eyes, she looked at me and smiled.

"What a morning." She sighed.

I got up and put the bowl and sponge away.

"What do you wish to do?" I asked her.

"Don't ask silly questions" She smiled at me. "If I had my way I wouldn't waste time talking about it. I'd just do it." She looked at me.

"You can, you know that." I said to her with a straight face.

"No not like this." She shook her head and looked away. "Stop talking like that. I've told you, it makes me worse." She kissed me.

"How about we go downstairs and watch some TV?" I suggested.

"We can do that here." She looked at me with surprise. I realised my dumb thinking. "Sorry." I smiled sheepishly.

"How about watching all your favourite movies?" I suggested.

"All MY favourite?" She exclaimed. "Was that your concussion talking?"

"Stop it," I smiled at her sarcasm. "I think it will make you feel good."

"I know what will, but we will keep it for when I AM well." She smiled coyly.

I searched for a movie. "Which one baby?" I asked.

"I would like a nice romance drama." She smiled.

"O man." I muttered. She giggled. "You choose and then come and cuddle me under the duvet."

I started the movie and got under the duvet cuddling her on one side.

"Wow. Movie in bed with my angel. I did not know the doctor ordered such special care." She giggled.

"It was not optional. For you only special is allowed." I kissed her forehead.

She cuddled on my chest letting me wrap her in my arm. She was still moving slowly due to her bruises.

After the first half hour through the movie I realised she had dozed off in my arms with her head on my shoulder. I was in quandary. I wanted her to sleep properly but did not want to disturb her sleep.

I waited for a few minutes. Then I decided to move myself slowly and gently every few times to let her adjust her sleeping posture. Finally, I was lying back in the bed, I had slid a fair amount and she was nearly horizontal on the bed. I pulled the duvet over her, turned the TV off and became motionless. She seemed to stir once she heard the TV shut off.

"Shh..." I slowly stroked her face and forced her eyes to shut again and I lulled her to sleep.

I waited for her to slip into deeper sleep and then I slowly got out of the bed and closed the curtains on the window to darken the room. Then I left her to sleep while I continued watching some channels on the mute TV.

She must have been asleep for nearly half an hour. When she stirred, she was aching and wanted to turn over. I gently rolled her on her side and laid her on her back. I let her doze off again but I felt her hold my hand tightly and she wanted me to stay with her.

"I'm right her. Don't worry. I ain't going anywhere hon." I stroked her hand to assure her.

She let my hand loose and dozed off slowly.

I got my laptop from my room and sat at her desk trying to see what I could be working for my class that I had missed that day. I turned my chair so I could sit facing toward her bed while I was working at her desk, in case she stirred. I tried to work quietly, not making a lot of tip-tap on the keyboard.

I worked for while, watching her occasionally, making sure she was asleep. She slept like a baby for nearly another hour and a half.

The following day I got her an electric toothbrush. In the morning, I showed it to her and she just looked at me with a coy grin while I opened the packaging.

Looking at her gaze at me, I tried elaborating the reason why I had bought it. She heard me explain how it would help her brush in her situation and she just smiled coyly.

"I realise all that," she sighed grinning at me softly, "but what I am trying to figure out is if there is any limit to your sweet thoughtfulness." She gazed at me deep in my eyes and offered a kiss on my lips. Then looked deep in my eyes again and caressed my cheek.

A few days went by like this with me taking care of her during the day. In the evening, she used to spend time with me in her bed, either on my lap or on my chest.

It had never occurred to me, but mom offered her bed baths in the evening and Sam in her wisdom had accepted them, just to curb any raised eyebrows. So in the mornings I only spent time making her tingle and give her goose bumps.

After the first few days, I asked if I could wash her hair. She agreed as she knew I loved to play with her hair anyway.

I propped her on her back against the edge of the wash basin in the bathroom while she sat reclined in a chair. I let her hair gather into the bowl. I filled it with hot water and then spent at least 15 minutes washing her hair slowly. I let her relax so I could talk to her all the while. I gave her some glasses to wear so as I did not splash water or shampoo in her eyes.

I ran my fingers through her hair, shampooed and caressed it a lot. After I washed it, I put conditioner that she liked. After that, I gently rinsed and dried it with a towel, wrapped it around and left it to soak up the moisture. I always considered the image of her hair wrapped in a towel, and she in a bathrobe to be very sexy.

After a while, I dried her hair with her hair drier. I teased and played with the hair drier blowing it on her face and neck. Then when she was sitting up, I held her hair loose in my hands and pressed my face all over it. I let it caress my cheek and I took in a deep breath of its fragrance.

"I love your hair. It is so long, silky and lovely." I turned around and looked at her. She was looking at me with very sympathetic eyes to realise how I was pleased about such simple things.

"Go on. I know you want to plat it." She suggested.

Then I combed her hair for a few more minutes and then tried platting it in a nice French plat.

"Happy?" She asked me after I was done.

I nodded. "Very. How about you?"

"Are you kidding me! I am over the moon." She exclaimed.

After a week, we took her for her first follow-up. Dad drove us in his car. I helped her to the waiting room and we waited. When she was seen, the doctor was amazed at the recovery she had made.

"Excellent." He exclaimed. "How do you feel?" he asked Sam.

"Fine. But I still ache at some places." She whinged. "And when will this come off?" she pointed at her cast on the leg.

"Soon, provided you continue to heal at this rate." The doctor smiled. "How about if you come back in another week and we'll decide then?"

"Sounds good to me." Sam smiled looking at me.

When we drove back home, Sam urged me to start attending my classes. "I'm fine now, hon," she urged me.

"I won't go away more than a class at a stretch." I warned her. "I will pop in between my breaks."

"Ok." She had agreed.

"And I want you to message me every 15 minutes." I asked her.

"Ok I will. Now please go." She smiled and asked me to leave her with the TV remote, her mobile and the cordless handset next to her. I also left her with a bottle of water and some fruits to eat.

In the class, I could hardly focus. I sent her a message on the cell phone.

'How are you?'

'Im fine. Where r u? x'

'In stupid class where
u banished me. ='('

'then pay attention and
stop msging me. =P '

'cant. Miss u =('

'yes u can. I ain't
replying now. =S '

'don't do that. I need
to know u r ok. =* '

'I always am, hon,
as long as I have u xxxx'

'luv u xxxx'

'me 2. So very much.
Now get back to the class
and focus =D '

'M'am yes m'am =P '

'hahahaha. Whateva xxx'

Next day I decided to cheer her up. So on the way back home I stopped by a superstore and collected a huge bouquet of peach coloured roses.

When I got home, I entered the door and saw her lying on the couch watching TV. As she realised I was home she yelled out 'hon' and she flung her arms up to get a big hug from me.

I lowered the bouquet, hid it away and then ran to her to give her a big hug and kiss.

"Missed you so much." She sighed.

"I know. I just had to pop into the store to get something."

"Like what?" Her eyes now gazing at me with curiosity.

"It's for you. Give me a minute." I ran and fetched the bouquet. Then I handed it to her.

She urged me to help her sit up.

"Awe. What's this for?" She was all warm inside.

"I wanted to give you this for a while now. I thought today would be a nice opportunity."

"But why? What's the occasion?" She was perplexed about my idea to give her flowers.

"I just wanted to see a smile on your face. You have been cooped up all this time and I know how hard it must be." I said kneeling down in front of her at the couch.

She just looked at the flowers and then she looked at me. My face was close to her and she held out her palm and caressed my face, looking deep in my eyes.

"My first gift of flowers." She sighed. "No one has ever given me flowers."

"Really?" I was surprised and saddened.

"Really!" she exclaimed. "You are my first, as usual." She took my face in her hand, lowered her lips, and kissed me on my lips softly.

"I will remember this." She said.

"Well. At least it served its purpose." I smiled shrugging my shoulders. "At least they made you smile." I wasn't sure why it was a big deal.

"They have made me more than smile. It's just that I cannot tell you in my current state. You will get to know it later when I'm all myself." She smiled at me with deep sensual gaze.

"If you say so." I gave her a quick peck and stood up.

"Can you be a gentleman and put them in a vase for me please?" she sighed coyly.

"I was thinking of the bin actually." I smiled sarcastically.

"And could you put them where I can see them", she continued.

"Anything more?" I looked at her with a smile.

"Oh. Don't look at me like that." She looked away. "Those looks usually kill." She giggled. "I'm already half dead here at the moment with all the love you have just showered on me." She giggled teasingly. "I was hoping if you could give me CPR?!" She winked at me.

"Sure. How many times do I zap your heart before I wait for your breathing to start?" I joked.

"Zero times!" she laughed aloud.

I bashed her gently while play-fighting with a pillow.

"Come on then." She urged me to fight back after taking a pillow in her hands. "You think I can't fight with you at the moment." She swung her pillow at me. "Come on give it to me, tiger."

I just paused and looked at her with exclamation on my face and a bright-eyed smile.

"Yeah anything you can." She stuck her tongue at me, raised her eyebrow seductively and continued swinging her pillow.

I was just being careful and I kept pushing her in the couch with her pillow in between us.

"Is that all you got?" she kept taunting me giggling all the while.

"You want to be careful how much you ask for." I said to her.

"Ooo. Promises promises." She teased me wiggling her waist.

Then after a few swings of the pillows, we fell about laughing as I pushed her in the lounger and fell on her.

"That felt great." She exclaimed in excitement. "We haven't done that in years." She giggled.

After we had stopped for a breath, we just looked at each other and gave each other a long and gentle kiss as she kept caressing my cheek, looking deep in my eyes.

"Love you." She whispered while gazing deep in my eyes. "Thanx for the flowers, hon. They are beautiful."

"Always as usual, it was my pleasure." I smiled back at her.

While Sam was still recovering, she made sure I did not miss any classes. I was beginning to feel guilty that she was missing hers and I was catching up on mine.

"Hon, could you stop by Jen's place on your way back and pick up some of her notes for me please?" She asked me one day before I left for my class. "She called me yesterday on how I was doing and we spoke for a while. It was nice to hear from her."

"Sure." I complied. "I have been collating some notes for you anyway." I showed her the photocopies I had been compiling from her friends. "I just did not know if you wanted to get into this yet."

She glanced through them. "Wow. There is quite a bit in here," she muttered while flicking through the pages. She looked at me. "You are so thoughtful."

She held out her hand to get me close to her. As I held her hand, she kissed it gently, thanking me for the work I had done to get her the notes. Then she intertwined our fingers and pulled me closer to her. "What would I do without you." She gazed deep in my eyes and planted a kiss on my lips.

After another week of good recovery, Sam could walk around without the cast, but still had to use elbow crutches for a few days until she got her strength back. I was so pleased to see her walk again and make a full recovery. I gave her a big hug.

"Thanx hon, as usual, for being there for me." She thanked me with a warm kiss. "I am gonna have to think very carefully on how to return this in kind."

"Oh don't be silly. It was my pleasure." I laughed it off. "And anyway, I did owe you this, you know." I shrugged my shoulders with guilt.

"Na na. Don't even go there. For the last time, I am warning you. If you say things like that again, I will break your leg with this, I promise you." She raised her elbow crutch at me. "I've told you to stop thinking like that." She was very serious. "I'm not kidding you."

"Ok." I gave in sheepishly. "Sorry."

"You better be." She smiled sarcastically. "Else, I will make you into a sorry ass."

We both laughed.

After Sam had recovered in about a month, my dad broached the subject about the car. It had been a write-off and we had received some money toward it. I had been shaken pretty badly and I did not feel like getting one right away. I was lucky I had postponed it until then.

As Sam was recovering, she did not have time to be driving anywhere. But when dad brought the topic up one evening at the dinner table, mom looked at him and let him carry on the conversation.

"I was thinking what you wish to do about a new car?" he asked me looking at mom.

"I don't know." I replied. "I have gotten used to getting by on the bus." I shrugged my shoulders. "The money we got paid from the write-off isn't much to get a new one." I sighed. "I don't have much saved." I made up a lie.

"Why are you being reluctant?" Sam quizzed me.

I looked at her and did not say much.

She leaned forward, took my hand and caressed it gently. I was just looking down trying to make feeble attempts to eat.

She scooted closer to me, placed her hand on my back and gently caressed my back.

Mom and dad looked at me while I continued pretending to eat in silence. Then gazing at Sam for a moment, I just lowered my gaze and flooded into tears, "I could have lost you in that accident."

Sam realised my loss of confidence and scooted close to me and hugged me, "Oh hon. I understand." She hugged me and kissed my cheek slowly caressing it while consoling me. My mom and dad looked at each other and then mom tried to console me, "Alex, we know it was awful but it wasn't your fault, sweetheart. You got to get past it somehow."

Dad joined in, "Hell you have even helped your sister recover all on your own." He tried to make light of it. "She is brand new."

Sam giggled.

"Come on now." Dad dusted off the conversation with a spark. "I was thinking it would be ok if you had a better car this time. So how about we add some contribution from us." He looked at mom. She squeezed his hand in acknowledgment. "You deserve a break." He looked at me and patted my shoulder. "We couldn't have been luckier to have such wonderful kids as you. I think we should treat you this time."

"Thanx dad." I smiled at him brushing off my tears.

Sam kept running her hand over my shoulder and back. "And if it hadn't been for you, I wouldn't be here." She nuzzled close to my neck. "You saved me. Think it like that."

"I'm sorry. I think I need to think of my responsibilities too I guess." I grinned.

"Of course." Dad spoke out. "I can't be driving these ladies around on my own. They would drive me around the bend." Then he laughed out loudly. "Soon I would want to plough into a wall myself."

We all fell about laughing.

In a few weeks dad had paid out a handsome contribution and Sam and I looked around for a good deal. This time I had paid careful attention to the airbags and the side door protection. It took me a while to start driving again. With her persistence, Sam asked me for a lift on every excuse.

"When can I start touching you while we drive?" she asked me once while we were driving to do our groceries. "I did not want to distract you, and make you anxious or stressed."

I looked at her when we had stopped at the lights.

"I miss the closeness." She acknowledged with a warm gaze.

"You never distracted me." I took her hand and placed it on my thigh, gently caressing it. "You are a temptation, not a distraction." I smiled at her.

She leaned toward me slightly and placed her head on my shoulder. "I love getting close to you." She said.

I caressed her cheek and then as the lights changed to green, I slowly pulled out looking around all the four streets as I drove off.

"I don't think you are ever going to get past it", she sighed. "Even now, you keep looking around when you drive."

One day I got an email from Sam with an audio track attached to it. The email read 'for your ears only....'

It was 'Falling for you' by Colbie Caillat.

I put on the headphones, listened to it and the lyrics filled me with emotions.

'I don't know but I think I may be fallin' for you,
dropping so quickly.
Maybe I should keep this to myself,
waiting 'til I know you better.'

[chorus:]
'I am trying not to tell you, but I want to.
I'm scared of what you'll say.
So I'm hiding what I'm feeling.
But I'm tired of holding this inside my head.
I've been spending all my time, just thinking about you.
I don't know what to do. I think I'm fallin' for you.
I've been waiting all my life and now I found you.
I don't know what to do. I think I'm falling for you.
I'm falling for you.'

'As I'm standing here and you hold my hand,
pull me towards you and we start to dance.
All around us, I see nobody.
Here in silence, it's just you and me.'

[repeat chorus]

'Oh, I just can't take it. My heart is racing.
Emotions keep spinning out.'

[repeat chorus]

'Oh. Oh no no. Oh.
Oh, I'm falling for you.'

It took me a long time to take in the words as I listened to it again, let alone the emotions that went with them. I loved Sam very much and seemed like she loved me too but as usual we both were unsure in what way and how deep.

I was warm with emotions for her all through the night. In the night, I thought of something that I could say or do in return. Nothing seemed to come to mind. I did not want her to get the wrong end of the stick. I usually over-complicated things in attempt to be elaborate and I did not want to do that with this opportunity.

When I got up in the morning, I heard Sam get ready for the college. I waited until she was in the shower. Then I quickly left my phone on her desk. I placed my phone next to her and left a sticky note on mine with a heart.

I had set a song on my phone to play – 'I don't know much (but I know I love you)' by Aaron Neville and Linda Ronstadt.

Then I got changed quickly and when she had come out of the bathroom I got in and showered.

When I was getting ready in my room, I saw her step in, close the door and she handed me my phone. Then she just looked at me and slowly getting close to me, wrapped her arms around my waist and hugged me firmly and then slowly melted in my arms. She did not say anything and stayed in my hug for a while. I just held her close to me.

When she pulled away, she gazed at me deeply, smiled warmly in her eyes, and spoke softly, "Can I ask you out for lunch this afternoon?" She looked at me for an answer.

"Of course." I replied. "I will message you when I'm out of the class."

"Deal." She smiled and gave me a quick peck and left the room. "I will wait downstairs." She smiled.

That lecture at the college could as well had been given in a foreign language because I just couldn't get her out of my thoughts. All I kept waiting for was the stupid time to speed up fast so I could meet her for lunch.

When we met up, she was smiling with glittering eyes. We decided to eat at a quiet place so we chose a restaurant. When we had ordered, she looked at me and taking a sip from the glass, softly asked me with a smile, "Slept well?"

"Umm," I rocked my hand with my fingers spread out. "OK I guess." I grinned.

She smiled back. "I couldn't focus on my lecture." She confessed.

"Me too. All I wanted was to see you for lunch." I confessed too.

She leaned forward and touched my hand gently running her finger slowly on my skin. "Why didn't you message me?" She gazed with a question on her face.

"I did not want to disturb you in your class." I said.

"Can I ask you something?" she looked a bit anxious while her gaze wandered around.

I leaned forward and curled her fingers on my hand. "Anything hon."

She looked at me. "Do you consider yourself to be a tactile person?" She looked at me and then went on to elaborate, "You know like I am very tactile, especially with you."

"Yes. I think so." I replied.

"I've not felt your hands all over me though." She said softly. "Aren't you 'grabby'?" She made gesture and smiled.

I made a perplexed expression on my face. "Hold on. You were on about being tactile, like you are. You aren't grabby. That's totally different." I remarked. Just then we were served our meal.

We paused our conversation and waited for the waiter to leave. Then we just smiled and carried on talking while we started eating.

"Well I think some would think I was, particularly with you. I know, sometimes, I can't keep my hands off you so I like to reach out and touch you or hug you." She spoke softly.

"All in good taste. You do it so sensually, I would not call that grabby at all. No way. I love it in fact."

"You like me being grabby then?" she was surprised. "I mean tactile." She corrected herself when I stared at her. She smiled. We continued eating our meal. We fed each other spoonfuls as usual.

"Yeah. I love the fact that you like me and miss me so much." I said between spoonfuls.

"Do you miss me physically?" she gazed for my response, becoming shy.

"Always. God, if only you knew." I tossed my head around in obvious exclamation.

"Then why don't you show it?" she inquired. "I have never seen you get tactile with me. I always think I am pushing myself on you." Her eyes were saddened a bit.

I took her hand and squeezed it gently. "I just don't want to fall off from the pedestal." I sighed. "It will be a rather long fall down to earth, you realise." I took a bite and looked at her.

She put her spoon down, dabbed her lips and looked at me while leaning forward. "The pedestal is fixed with concrete blocks, reinforced with steel girders and founded with stone blocks on the base. And you are strapped tight, your feet nailed and cast in it." She smiled and nodded. "No chance in hell are you coming down off it EVER!" she smiled.

I laughed at her metaphor.

"I'm serious." She looked at me with surprise. "Don't know what you are laughing for."

"You know what I mean." I pleaded.

"I don't." She shrugged her shoulders.

"I know you don't like horny jerks." I smiled at her. "Remember Billy?" I tried to help her recall.

"You are comparing yourself to that jerk?" she stopped and leaned forward almost in a crazy fit.

"Shh." I tried to shush her looking around. Then smiling at her I quietly said, "No. I'm not comparing myself to him, but I thought you did not like those kind of people."

"If you put it that way of course no girl would!" She made an expression of ridicule. "But I could never dream of you ever behaving like that. You are the most decent guy I've known. Your touch melts me every time." She acknowledged quietly. "It's just that I don't seem to be melting as often as I would like to."

"You like me being tactile with you?" I was doubtful.

"I love it." She gasped while taking a sip. "Need more." She flicked her fingers gesturing teasingly.

"Ok. I will keep that in mind." I smiled at her. "I just did not want to come across as disrespectful, unpleasant, 'horny jerk'." I air quoted too.

"Do you even know what those terms mean?" she looked at me sarcastically sipping on her glass.

"I'm guessing from your expressions, I don't." I sheepishly agreed.

"Then just forget about holding back so much." She narrowed her eyes at me. "You are such a control freak. Why are you in such control of yourself all the time?" She asked me leaning forward. "I really want to know now because to tell the truth, I have never seen you lose your inhibitions or controls."

"Only control makes us human – else we would be no different from animals." I spoke quietly.

She just looked at me. "Don't get me wrong. I love it that you are so restrained and disciplined." She gazed at me. "But I want to see you lose it. Especially with me." Her eyes gleamed with delight as she looked at me.

"O man." I smiled feeling a bit warm inside and shook my head. "You are something you know that."

"So what do you say, hon?" she looked at me in anticipation. "Starting from tonight?"

I simply nodded. "I just love you too much you know. I would hate to upset you by being disrespectful."

"You are upsetting me right now...." She glared at me. "...by holding yourself back so much. It is very hurtful and disrespectful." She stared at me.

"Ok." I lowered my gaze sheepishly. "I get the message."

"Great." She smiled. "There goes another lecture today."

We both giggled as we ate our meal. As we ate happily, I kept gazing at her warm eyes, looking at me throughout the meal. After paying the bill, we stood up and she took my arm. As we walked out of there, she held my arm close to her, wrapping her hand in mine.

When I was in the next class, my cell phone buzzed in silent mode in my pocket. As I clicked it awake, I saw Sam had messaged me.

'I enjoyed lunch. xxx'

'me 2 x'

'im missing u =*'

'me 2. Luv ur hands ova me when u do.'

'I want to feel urs from now on, when u miss me '

'that wud be all the time'

'wud luv it =D'

'sure?'

'bring it on hon. Cant wait'

'=) ok'

'how about movie later tonight, my bed?'

'not a chick flick, please!'

'u choose it, I will enjoy it ;-) '

'=D ok its a date'

'no, a sleepover!'

'ok. =)'

'u r my angel. Luv u ciao xxx'

My heart skipped a beat. She had recovered just fine for my liking.

Chapter 10 – growing out of teens

Our 20th birthday was approaching fast. With everything that had happened with the accident and Sam's recovery, I had not had time to look around or think of it. A few months before our birthday, Sam surprised all of us with something. At the dinner table, after we had finished our meal and were just sitting chatting, she took out an envelope and placed it in front of our parents.

"Mom and dad. This is for you."

They both were surprised. Dad indicated mom to open it. When she opened it, she looked at dad with astonishment.

"These are return flight tickets for 2 – you and I." She looked at him and then Sam. Dad looked at Sam astonished.

"And there is a hotel booking for two for an all-inclusive extended weekend at the beach." Mom looked at Sam and then me.

"Did you know of this?" she asked me.

I was surprised at this as everyone. "Nope. That is all her."

Sam spoke slowly. "I was thinking, with everything that we have been through this year, I wanted to thank you all for being so nice and taking care of the family. Mom and dad, I, or rather we...", she looked at me and squeezed my hand, "...couldn't had asked for more from you as parents. You have been the best. And I wanted to thank you in my own limited way toward that."

Mom and dad were dumbstruck. "We have raised a hell of a pair here, eh?!" dad exclaimed. "They are making us tearful now." He tried making a joke of it looking at mom.

"The only snag is you guys will need to take the Friday off to make this work. Hope that is not too much inconvenience." Sam pleaded.

"My dear." My dad spoke out authoritatively. "I mean do you know what a hassle it is to take a holiday these days? And I mean 1 whole day. That will kill me," and fell about laughing. "Of course sweetheart. Don't you worry. Thanks but I don't know what to say."

Mom hugged her gently. "You shouldn't have."

"You both deserve a nice chill out time alone together." Sam said excitedly. "I will just need to confirm the arrangements again so they know the booking is confirmed. I had told them about the possibility that you may not be able to make it."

"We will be more than pleased sweetheart." Dad spoke in gratitude looking at mom.

"That is sweet." I spoke to her. She looked at me and just smiled with excitement.

Mom and dad had arranged to fly and I was going to drop them off at the airport in the morning. They would be gone Fri early morning and arrive back late evening on Sunday.

One night Sam came to my room and got in bed next to me.

"You know the Fri that you drop off mom and dad," she spoke softly. "Do you have any plans for that weekend?"

I paused and shook my head. "Nope. Why?"

"I was thinking of planning something for us two together as we would be home anyway." She spoke.

"A trip to the moon?" I giggled.

"No silly." She slapped my arm tenderly, trying to tell me off while giggling. "Just something I was thinking to do." She gazed at me. "It would be nice if you did not make any plans."

"All yours." I smiled.

She blushed at those words. "Oh you are such a pleaser." She hugged me, kissed my cheek and stood up.

"If you are planning to exchange gifts, I suggest we do them either before or after the weekend mom and dad go away." She suggested. "Just something I am planning." She said. "It would make it clumsy to exchange gifts during that weekend."

I was wondering what was cooking in her mind.

A few days before my parents were going away, I decided to surprise Sam with her gifts. That year had been tough for me and I had not had time to arrange anything fancy.

One day, I had asked her to get home late in the evening and not enter her bedroom. I was going to take her there later in the night after we had our meals and were ready to exchange our gifts. I had put her nightwear in my room for her to change and relax. As usual, she had smiled and agreed.

After the meals when I finally took her upstairs, I asked her to wait in my room. I closed the door and she sat on my bed. Then I gave her the first gift – it was a crystal glass cube with a shape of rounded 3D heart, laser-cut inside it. On one side of the cube, were words inscribed in laser above the heart 'I bleed when I miss u' and on the opposite side, below the heart were the words 'I beat when I kiss u.'

She looked at it in amazement and just threw her arms around me and hugged me. Then she kissed me deeply and tenderly.

"I love it so much." She softly spoke. She looked at it again. Then she kissed me again on my lips.

I was glad she liked it.

Then I gave her another gift – it was a rounded heart shaped amber pendant about just under an inch wide. It was relatively clear and with only one or two inclusions. There was a very fine, small hairline crack inside it. She looked at me with anticipated looks. "Go on." She smiled waiting for my elaboration.

"As you know," I began explaining to her, "Amber is one of the most ancient resins that hardens and traps all kinds of wonders inside it. No two pieces are identical and it seals in itself a time capsule, perfectly preserving it inside. That is my heart, I'm giving to you." I smiled at her. "The hairline crack is to indicate the bruises I may have had in the past and now it's all yours for keeps."

She just looked at me while listening intently. Then she kissed it in her palm, gently hugged me and asked me to put it around her neck. She then looked at it and pressed it on her chest.

"It will be safe and warm with me." She sighed sensually, looking deep in my eyes. "It's at home now."

"It is not something I have created, but I thought it is original and one of its kind." I confessed.

"It is your heart." She kissed my lips. "It will always be special to me."

I smiled at her.

Then I handed her a small envelope. As she opened it, she took out a small card. It had a picture of a lamp on the front (as in Aladdin's lamp) and inside it read 'You did not have to rub a stupid dusty lamp to get this free wish, so use it wisely.' She smiled while she read the card.

Inside she found one of our 'voucher'. It had my blood-stained thumbprint on it on the bottom right corner and the words 'I promise to honour my word to....' written on the top left.

"It is blank." She looked at me puzzled.

I simply grinned. "I owe you one completely open favour." I said softly. "Consider it as a blank cheque."

"I can ask for ANY favour?" she looked at me with surprised but sceptical eyes.

"Umm yes." I nodded and affirmed with certitude. I did not want to reduce the significance of the gift I was giving her by being reluctant or conditional. "I will trust you to use your judgement to ask whatever you see fit. I promise to stay true to my word and honour it."

"Why?" she was puzzled.

"I have not had a chance to give a very special gift this year with everything that has happened. And I couldn't think of anything more special than an open favour for you to use."

"I will use this wisely." She sighed with delighted eyes. She looked straight in my eyes for a while. "Does it have expiry?" she inquired with a sly grin.

"Valid for 1 year - until our 21st birthday."

"Ok." She nodded taking that information in.

I smiled and she hugged me.

"This blood thumbprint." She pointed to it as she showed me the voucher. "It is yours I presume?"

I nodded. "I wanted to show you just how sincere I am to keep my word of honour."

She was serene and just looked at me. "You didn't have to do that. Your word was more than enough."

I just smiled and shrugged my shoulder.

"You won't change your mind about this later when I finally ask for my favour?" she wanted to make sure.

"No. I trust you implicitly." I smiled. "There is one more gift for you." I looked at her.

"One more?!" She looked at me with anticipation.

"It's in your room but you need to close your eyes and not peek." She agreed with excitement.

I took her hand and I guided her to her bedroom slowly. I gently closed the door behind me and turned the lights on.

"Ok. Now you can look." I said softly.

There were rose bouquets placed all over the room – all colours and shades. I had placed roses in vases all around the room. She gasped audibly and her eyes could not contain the happiness as she welled up. For a while she could not believe what she was seeing. Her dropped jaw was still open as she looked around the entire room.

Then I took her hand and slowly walked her to the bed. Then gently rolling the duvet down, I peeled it away to reveal what lay under it. I had layered the bed under the duvet with rose petals – all over the bed. There was a sweet and sober tiara on the pillow. She gently peeled the covers further out and looked at the bed, fully sprinkled with thick layer of rose petals.

"A bed of roses, for my lovely princess." I whispered softly.

She just looked at me and slowly wrapped herself into my arms now tears running down her eyes as I could hear her sniff.

She had wrapped her arms around my neck and she did not let go for a long while. All the while, she just kept kissing my neck and cheek. I could hear sniffs. I just held her in my arms and caressed her back. I kissed her cheek and neck under her ear on her weak spot. She just wrapped me tightly in her arms.

"This is for someone who was never given flowers before." I said to her. "Now you get to sleep in them."

Slowly breaking out from the hug, she composed herself. I brushed her tears and smiled at her. She grinned back at me.

"You are the most thoughtful person I have met." She whispered, while shaking her head failing for words. "Thank you." She looked at me and kissed my lips again. "I love you so much."

I tried to brush her tearful cheeks. "All I want is to see you smile." I grinned gazing at her. She gazed at me lovingly.

"I ain't sleeping there without you." She indicated to the bed and shook her head.

"Ok." I smiled. "Give me a minute and I will be back."

"Quick." She urged. "Don't keep a princess waiting." She smiled.

I smiled. "I will be back in a minute."

When I got back, I gently closed and locked the door behind me. She was still waiting, sitting on the corner of the bed. As I entered wearing my sleepwear, I asked her why she wasn't changed. She stood up, pulled her top over her head and dropped it to the floor.

"There." She said to me with a smile. "After all I'm sleeping on a bed of rose petals."

She undid her bra while gazing square in my eyes and left her panties on as she walked to her bed. I lost my t-shirt and we got in under the duvet gently rolling it back over us as we lay under it.

"With you, there is always a first for everything." She said.

"You suggested that I be original." I sighed. "This year, with everything happening with us, I could only manage this." I confessed.

"ONLY?" She giggled sarcastically. "ONLY! Wow. If this is your humble modesty, god help me with your eager exuberance." We both curled in each other's arms and hugged tightly.

"Every year you manage to make it so memorable." She whispered as we lay close to each other looking deep into each other's eyes.

"You make the rest of the year memorable by being you." I whispered. "It's the least I can do."

"I hope I get a chance to show you, just how much I love you." She sighed.

"You do that every moment I spend time with you." I caressed her cheek, slowly running my fingers on the hair resting on it, slowly brushing it at the back.

"I am glad you feel that way." She sighed. "I want to feel your warmth all night." She turned on her side, pressed her back against my chest and let me wrap her in my arms. She lifted her head to let my arm slide under her neck and she wrapped my hands around her, my palms cupping her bosoms.

"This is how a princess sleeps best." She said.

I felt her hair brush against my face and I buried my nose and smelled its fragrance. As I shuffled my face in it, she gently brushed her hair past under her neck and between the pillow and exposed her neck for me. I planted soft wet deep kisses on her neck just under her ear. She quivered throughout her body and giggled. "You have all night to stop," she said with a moan.

As we lay there, she softly whispered to me without looking back, "I will give you your special gift on Friday night."

"Ok, hon." I kissed her on her shoulder.

"I am not sure if I will be able to sleep tonight." She whispered. "Would you mind if I woke you up with kisses and hugs in the night when I miss you?"

"Be yourself, hon." I sighed to her in her ear.

"O god", she moaned. "I'm already wet."

Chapter 11 – the dinner

One early Friday morning, we dropped our parents at the airport and waved goodbye to them while they walked through the departure gates. Sam and I went out for the morning and had some lunch in the afternoon. All the while, she seemed in a rather 'high' mood that day. Her lips curved up constantly. She gazed at me all the time; it seemed like she was trying to read my thoughts. Occasionally she would turn serene and then sigh.

"What's the matter?" I asked her a few times.

"Nothing." She sighed and lowered her gaze giving out a smile.

I realised there was something up but did not know quite what it was. Something was cooking in that pot of hers.

When I dropped Sam home in the afternoon, she kissed me goodbye. "No earlier than 9pm." She warned me.

I was meant to stay out all afternoon until about 9pm.

"What is it that you are planning?" I was very curious.

"You will soon find out." She just looked at me with deep gaze and caressed my cheek. "I just hope it works out like I have imagined," she muttered under her breath as she stepped out of the car.

"What was that?" I asked, having missed what she said.

"Nothing." She brushed it off.

I did not know how to kill all that time. "What am I supposed to do?" I asked.

"What do you normally do when you have time to kill?" She asked me perplexed.

"I spend it with you." I replied as a matter-of-fact.

She smiled. "Well, today make it first and spend it doing something different. Just don't be earlier than 9pm." She waved her sensual goodbye.

I decided to visit the library to browse some books and later stop at the mall for some window-shopping. After a long time, it was truly my first to be spending time on my own leaving Sam at home on her own.

***

Sam was standing next to the kitchen worktop, looking into the distance through the window. The meals were all ready and dished out in carousels and she had finished clearing the work surface. It was few minutes before 9pm.

'You still have time.' A voice in her head spoke. 'You can still turn this around and not go through with it.'

'But I want to. I so want to. I will suffocate if I don't come out with it now.' She thought to herself.

'There is a big risk for what you are trying to pursue. Do you really wish to take that chance?'

Sam stood there as her imaginations ran wild and into a dark downward spiral. Images came to her mind of the despair and sorrow, of life without Alex's love, her soul mate. She was overcome with grief and gasped at the images and thoughts she experienced. 'No. That cannot happen. Not under any circumstance.' She gasped breathlessly. 'I would rather die.' She was tearful from the emotions.

'That's why you have to think rationally.' The voice kept pressuring her.

'I cannot live on like this. I need to know. I would rather know than just live in uncertainty.' She told herself. 'I need to know where I stand. I know there may be a heavy price to pay, but that is my cross to bear.'

Sam took a deep breath, brushed her cheeks and composed herself.

"Remember he has loved you till now. Just be yourself and he will understand." She encouraged herself as she peered through the window and saw Alex come driving up the road.

"Here goes nothing." Sam walked into the lounge, straightened her dress, looked in the mirror and stood waiting for the door to open.

***

In the attempt of providing the true ambience for the remainder of the chapter, it is the author's intention that the reader listen to the playlist chronologically before, during or after the read so as to recognise the emotions that the author wishes to convey in the story through the music and the songs. Granted, it is a very unusual request for a rather unorthodox way of experiencing emotions in literature.

Playlist

Sarah McLachlan	I love you	4:44
Jessie Ware	Running	4:29
Anita Baker	Caught up in the rapture of love	5:21
Richard Hawley	Open up our door	4:43
Ten sharp	You	4:28
Bread	Baby I'm a want you	2:26
Carpenters	touch me when we're dancing	3:21
Yanni feat. Leslie Mills	The keeper	3:28
Kylie Minogue	come into my world	4:03
Shania Twain	I'm gonna getcha good	4:29
Ewan McGregor & Nicole Kidman	Come what may	4:02
Take that	Rule the world	4:00
Celine Dion	Falling into you	4:18
Bread	Make it with you	3:11
Selena	I could fall in love	4:42
Conjure one	Sleep	5:00
Celine Dion	Halfway to heaven	5:05
Shania Twain	Thank you baby	4:00

When I got home it was about 9:10pm, just the time she had mentioned I be back. As I entered the house, Sam was in the lounge waiting for me. I saw her standing in the lounge, dressed in a peach coloured bandeau-style midi dress with pleats that stopped a few inches above her ankles. I could see her bare shoulders and her bosoms pushed up showing her beautiful curves. Her hair had a French plat starting high up at the back, but then it was pinned loose in a small glitter clip at the neck and the hair let loose ending in soft curls on her back. She had some small flowers in the plat and some glitter on the clips that pinned the hair on the sides. She was not wearing any shoes, so I guessed we were staying in. I noticed she was wearing my amber heart pendant; the only piece of jewellery on her.

The ambience of the lounge had been lowered, illuminated by only candle light and I could see the table was laid out with prepared meal in casserole, tablecloth laid out very neatly, cutlery and candles to go along side the plates. There was a bottle of champagne on ice. The dinner was ready to be served. I took a deep breath, as I really did not know what the whole setup was for. It seemed like I was going to get a cooked meal as a birthday present.

As I looked at her mesmerising beauty, without speaking, she held out her hand standing in the middle of the lounge and asked me to come closer. She had one hand behind her back. When I got close to her, she smiled and handed me an envelope without speaking. I opened it slowly glancing at her.

Inside I saw a voucher. It was the blank voucher I had handed her the other day as her special gift. On the voucher, she had filled in the blank after the phrase:

'I promise to honour my word to....*not speak, not question and not refuse to accept or participate in anything that is offered to me for the whole night.*'

I was speechless. She had used my 'blank voucher' to get me to enjoy this evening that she had planned. My heart was beating fast. I did not know what I had gotten myself into. Nevertheless, I knew she would use her judgement to be reasonable. I took a deep breath.

I looked at her with anticipation. She nodded to ask if I was ok with that voucher. I nodded in acknowledgement and a grin. Then she cocked her head at the table and gazed at my eyes to ask if I was ready to eat. I nodded again.

She then grinned softly, took my hand, led me to my chair and helped me sit down. Then she moved around to my right and poured us both some champagne.

Then she walked briskly and sat down on my left side at the corner of the table so we were sitting at angles at the table. I could see her fully, from head to toe from where I was sitting. She was at arm's reach from me and as I waited for her, she adjusted herself in the chair and raised her glass. I raised mine and we clicked them and had a sip. She offered me some strawberries.

Then she served us both our starters in our plates and sat down again.

Then she nodded me to start and waited for me to have my first spoonful.

As I had my first bite, I realised they were my favourite starters. It must have taken her a while as they all tasted delicious. I smiled and indicated with a 'thumbs up'. She then took her spoonfuls feeling gratified and settled to eat.

Then she clicked 'play' on the stereo that was placed close to her on her left on the table. It was connected into the surround system we had in the lounge for the TV. Then she looked at me and grinned with a deep warm gaze.

I heard the music play and the opening bars rolled on.

Sarah McLachlan – I love you

I could recognise the song; it was from one of my playlists. One of my favourites.

'I have a smile stretched from ear to ear to see you walking down the road. We meet at the lights. I stare for a while. The world around us disappears.'
She stared at me while we slowly had our spoonfuls.

'It's just you and me on my island of hope;
a breath between us could be miles.'
I was attentively listening to the song, now in a very different
context. We took a few more mouthfuls looking at each other.

'Let me surround you, my sea to your shore. Let me be the calm
you seek.'
I looked at her glancing at me deeply.

[chorus]
'Oh and every time I'm close to you there's too much I can't say
and you just walk away.'
I looked at her warmly as she gazed at me.
'And I forgot to tell you I love you,...', she looked at me with warm
eyes, *'...and the night's too long and cold here without you.'*
I was looking at her as she gazed at me deep into my eyes.
'I grieve in my condition for I cannot find the words to say I need
you so.'
I stared at her with solemn expression. She kept gazing at me with
deep stare, a slight grin that showed how she was bearing her
heart to me.

(music interlude)

I moved my hand slowly, trying to judge if she would move her
hand away or if I was allowed to 'participate'. I curled her fingers
in mine and slowly stroked my thumb on her fingers curled in my
hand. I stopped eating and just sat there listening to the song,
trying not to choke on the emotions the song was building inside
me.

[repeat chorus]

All the while, she was sitting calmly looking at me, her eyes
pouring out her emotions through the song.

Once the song faded she gave me a sensual glance and continued
eating her meal. I was speechless, and carried on eating slowly.

Jessie Ware – Running

When the opening bars rolled on for the next song, she slowly moved and swayed her shoulders to the beat and moved to the rhythm. She was now having some spoonfuls and had some sips of her champagne. I continued eating while looking at her, anticipating the lyrics to start rolling. I recognised these songs – they were from my favourite collection.

'Your words alone could drive me to a thousand tears,' I was looking at her puzzled. She nodded her head with a slight grin and narrowed eyes, while taking some more mouthfuls, staring back at me.

'all the same words that kept me here for all the years.' She then grinned slightly staring with her eyes warmly at me.

[chorus:]
'I'm lost again, it's happening. When you're around I just go weak. All I wanna know, is it mutual?
Then I never want to leave. Then I'm ready to run, ready to fall; think I'm ready to lose it all.
And I'm ready to run, ready to fall, think I'm ready to lose it all. Keep me running, you keep me running. You keep me, keep me running.'

All the while she was slowly swaying to the music, intently looking at me.

She slowly looked at me with piercing gaze, now she was just swaying her shoulders to the rhythm very gently looking deep in my eyes. I was trying to read the thoughts flowing through her mind.

(music interlude)

We started eating again and had some more mouthfuls. I was a bit sombre. I did not want her to think I had played around with her emotions. I was perplexed. I gulped some champagne.

'Oooh..'
'Ohh, would you hold my hand like the air was so gently here; never give up, never give up.
Ohh, would you pull me close so nobody knows we're there. No one can find us.'

She was swaying in her seat to the rhythm so slightly and sensually, I was trying to keep my mind on the lyrics than her soft tender movements.

(music interlude)

We continued eating our spoonfuls, constantly gazing at each other. She was swaying gently from her hips upwards, like the kelp forests in the ocean waters, her hair flowing around softly, her back arched whenever she tilted her head back closing her eyes into her trance.

[repeat chorus]

We continued eating. I could see her lose herself in the song, as she let her head tilt back, her hair flowing on her neck. She kept softly swaying in her seat from the waist up. Whenever she sat upright, she glanced at me with piercing warm and sensual eyes.

(music interlude)

We had our last spoonfuls. She dished out some meal in my plate. Then she started having her meal and asked me to try it. All the while, I was slowly taking in my spoonfuls and the powerful emotions that were rolling over to me through the song.

I was a bit serious after that song. I looked at her trying to show her my emotions, my sincerity. She just grinned and gently dimmed her eyes in acknowledgement.

Anita Baker – Caught up in the rapture

The next song rolled with the lyrics and I recognised it immediately.

'When we met, I always knew, I would feel the magic for you. On my mind constantly, in my arms is where you should be. I love you here by me, baby. You let my love fly free. I want you in my life for all time.'
As the music progressed, she swayed to the beat gently, looking at me.

[Chorus 1:]
'Caught up in the rapture of love. Nothing else can compare, when I feel the magic of you.'

She gazed at me with piercing eyes and gently shook her head to match the lyrics. Then she took some mouthfuls.

*'We stand side by side, till the storms of life pass us by.
Light my life, warm my heart, say tonight will be just the start.'*
She looked at me intently.
'I love you here by me, baby. You let my love fly free. I want you in my life for all time.'
I tried eating but the emotions were getting the best of me now.

[Chorus 2:]
*'Caught up in the rapture of love. Nothing else can compare, when I feel the magic of you.
The feeling's always new;
caught up in the rapture of you.'*

(music interlude)

I tried taking some sips from my glass. She filled our glasses again.

*'I love you here by me, baby. You let my love fly free.
I want you in my life for all time.'*
She again stared right at me.

[repeat chorus 2]

I just ate helplessly taking small mouthfuls. I glanced at her throughout.

*'Caught up in the rapture of love.
Caught up in the rapture of love.'*

(music interlude)

She swayed slowly as the music faded out.

She stopped eating and took a sip. Then as the opening bars slowly rolled in, she placed her elbow on the table, rested her chin in her palm and she looked at me with deep gaze. I paused and looked back at her.

Richard Hawley – Open up your door

As the song rolled on I realised this was one of my most favourite songs. She knew that anyway. On a normal day, it gave me goose bumps all over my spine. Tonight she was playing it for me, to portray her feelings. I quivered with a deep sigh.

'Open up your door. I can't see your face no more.
Love is so hard to find, and even harder to define.
Oh, open up your door, 'cos we've time to give
and I'm feeling it so much more.
Open up the door. Open up your door.'

(music interlude)

I took the words in quietly in a totally new context tonight. All the while, she was staring at me, deep into my eyes, showing the warmth in her eyes. I was so breathless with emotions, I thought I was going to die.

She looked at me with very warm eyes. I was sitting back looking at her intently. Then she slowly leaned forward on the table, still looking deeply in my eyes. Then I leaned forward in reciprocation, and I held out my hand to hold her hand. She gently and slowly turned in her chair, let out her hand and let me hold it, her fingers curling in my palms around my fingers. I gently stroked her fingers with my thumb gazing at her deeply in her warm wet eyes. They shimmered like diamonds in the candlelight.

'Open up the door. I can't hear your voice no more.' Her eyes were singing out the words.

'I just want to make you smile. Maybe stay with you awhile.' I could see her eyes becoming wet as she gazed at me with loving warmth.

'Oh, open up your door, 'cos we've time to give and my feelings aren't so obscure.
Open up the door. Open up your door.'

I felt a quiver rise up to my head.

(music interlude)

As the crescendo rolled, I could see a tear running down her cheek. Then I saw another roll on the other cheek. All the while, her warm eyes fixated on my eyes, were telling me how deeply she loved and wanted me. I felt my throat choke up and I welled up at her emotions. I squeezed her fingers gently trying to assure her. She just kept swaying gently to the music, her head swinging side to side slowly and a soft gentle grin on her face acknowledging her bare heart. She never shifted her gaze from my eyes.

'So open up the door 'cos we've time to give and I'm feeling it so much more.
Open up your door. Oh, open up your door.'
She swayed gently sitting in the chair gently rocking at the rhythm.

'Love is so hard to find and even harder to define.' As the music built on, her tears were rolling down her cheeks now, full flow as she gasped for air.

'Oh, open up your door and I've never been so sure.
Oh, open up your door. Open up your door.'
She gently let her hand free out of my fingers, brushed the tears aside trying to catch a breath, still grinning softly at me. She took a sip and tried to compose herself. I was beside myself with emotions.

When the music faded out, I was still staring at her, while she was still gazing with a soft grin. She looked at me coyly. I did not have the stomach to eat anymore after my throat had choked my life out with that outpour of emotions.

Ten sharp – You

As the opening bars for the next song rolled out, the tempo shifted to a bit more positive. I could see she was smiling trying to finish her last few spoonfuls. This again was one of my favourites. I used to imagine singing it to her whenever I heard it on my own. Tonight, she was singing it to me through her wet warm sensual eyes.

'It's all right with me, as long as you are by my side. Talk or just say nothing. I don't mind your looks never lie.'
She shook her head coordinated to the lyrics and I grinned at her.

'I was always on the run finding out what I was looking for. And I was always insecure just until I found...'

She was slowly swaying to the music.

'Words often don't come easy. I never learned to show you the inside of me, I know my baby.
You were always patient, dragging out what I try to hide.' She was 'singing' the lyrics with her eyes.

'I was always on the run, finding out what I was looking for and I was always insecure until I found you.'
She tossed her head back, closed her eyes and swayed her shoulders to the music gently. Then she looked at me still swinging, trying to say the words through her gaze. She went back to having some mouthfuls. She gestured me to have some too.

[chorus]
'You were always on my mind.
You; you're the one I've been living for.
You; you're my everlasting fire.
You're my always shining star.'
She nodded to me gently indicating the lyrics.

(music interlude)

I looked at her with a small grin trying to match her glowing face now grinning. As the music rolled on, I stretched out my hand and she held out her, letting me hold her fingers in mine.

I tried to have some mouthfuls.

'The night's always a good friend;
a glass of wine, and the lights are low.'
She smiled suggestively raising her glass to me.

'You, lying beside me;
me, full of love and filled with hope.'

(music interlude)

She slowly swayed still rooted in the chair. Since she was sitting close to me, I could see her hair gliding around as she enjoyed the music, occasionally closing her eyes in trance and then gazing at me intently. She looked so sensual.

[repeat chorus]

She again started to sway slowly to the rhythm enjoying the words and the music, gazing at me deeply, implying everything being said in the lyrics.

When the closing bars started to fade out, she slowed down and squeezed my fingers in her palm as she withdrew her hand to take a sip from her glass. She filled our glasses with more champagne.

Bread – Baby I'm a want you

As the next song rolled into the lyrics, I did not get a moment to catch my thoughts. I recognised it again. She was on a roll tonight.

'Baby I'm-a want you, Baby I'm-a need you.
You're the only one I care enough to hurt about.'
She grinned at me coyly. I was filled with warmth.

'Maybe I'm-a crazy. But I just can't live without your lovin' and affection givin' me direction like a guiding light to help me through my darkest hour.'
She grinned at me with deep sensual look. The words filled me with warm love.

[chorus:]
'Lately I'm a-prayin' that you'll always be a-stayin' beside me.'
She tilted her head in acceptance.

'Used to be my life was just emotions passing by;
feeling all the while and never really knowing why.'

(Music interlude)

Her soft grin and warm eyes melted me inside. She gently got up and cleared a few things from the table. I pushed my chair back waiting to get up. She gestured me to sit and enjoy the song.

'Lately I'm a-prayin' that you'll always be a-stayin' beside me.
Used to be my life was just emotions passing by. Then you came along and made me laugh and made me cry. You taught me why.'

She had cleared the plates in front and sat down again, looking at me with her sensual grin.

'Baby I'm-a want you. Baby I'm-a need you.
Oh, it took so long to find you, baby.
Baby I'm-a want you Baby I'm-a need you.'
As the song faded out she stood up and faced me. Then with her hand held out inviting me for a dance, she led me to the centre of the room.

Carpenters – touch me when we're dancing

As the opening bars rolled in, she slowly gazed at me and started slowly swaying to the music. She had her fingers of her one hand intertwined gently in mine, the other arm around my neck, her cheek pressed gently on mine, and she had her hip pressed on mine, slightly on the side. I could smell her mind-blowing sensual perfume. I wrapped my arm gently around her waist and held her close to me.

'Play us a song we can slow dance on; we wanna hold each other.'
She was swaying her hips slowly.
'Play us a groove so we hardly move; just let our hearts beat together.
Oh, baby, 'cause it feel so good, when we're close like this.
Whisper in my ear and let me steal a kiss.'
She quickly planted a kiss on my cheek.

She was slowly swinging her hips to the music. Now she moved her arm from my hand, wrapped it around my neck and pressed herself into my arms, urging me to hug her close. As we danced slowly, she melted.

[Chorus:]
'Come on and touch me when we're dancing. You know you've got that loving touch.
Touch me when we're dancing. I want to feel you when I'm falling in love.'
She planted a soft kiss on my neck. She looked at me with warm sensual gaze.

'Tonight's the night and it feels so right. My heart is saying it to me.
You're the one I've waited for so long. So let your love flow through me.' She looked at me intently with warm sensual gaze. I looked at her with deep emotions.

'Oh, baby, 'cause it feels so good just to be this close. You've got me up so high I could fly coast to coast.'

As I was holding her at the waist, she leaned back, spread out her arms and while swaying gently she tilted her head back and arched her back. She was lost in her emotional trance while I was holding her at the waist. She enjoyed the crescendo and then pulled herself into my arms standing upright back into my arms.

[repeat Chorus]

She wrapped her arms gently around me, touching her cheek on mine and melting in my arms as her swayed slowly to the music.

(Music interlude)

She gently moved her face and she kissed me on my lips gently staring me with deep piercing eyes.

[repeat chorus]

She continued to sway as the song faded out.

Yanni feat. Leslie Mills – The keeper

As the next song rolled on, she took the beat and started slow dancing the basic ballroom steps with our hands curled in one another. She encouraged me to take the lead. All those dance lessons suddenly felt very relevant.

'I've been like a bird without song for awhile, dry like a lake without rain for awhile. You suddenly stepped in my life, and made me cry, like an angel.
Ooh, you're something else, like a smile without an end
Come into my life, go a little deeper. Come into my life, you could be the keeper.'

I tried to take the lead and did some moves I recalled; nothing very complicated. Seeing me take the lead, she smiled and happily complied. This was the time I had seen her not in tears so I wanted to keep the mood upbeat.

[chorus]

'You're pulling me closer and you're flowin' in with every emotion that rushes me on to your love, light me up. Oh, you could be the keeper.'

I danced and we swung around in some smooth ballroom steps. Then as she picked up the rhythm and she moved to the beat, I let her improvise on her own.

'I've been like a home without people for awhile, empty like a poem without words for awhile.
You suddenly stepped in my life, and made me shine, like a diamond.
Ooh, you're something else, like a dream without an end
Come into my life, go a little deeper. Come into my life, you could be the keeper.'

[repeat chorus]

I took the lead and did some moves I recalled for all the sessions I did with her. She smiled and followed my lead happily.

(music interlude)

We improvised and I was taking the lead while she was helping me lead by suggesting the moves. I seemed to find it difficult to focus with all the emotional outpour that had happened.

'Ooh, you're something else, like a dream without an end
Come into my life, go a little deeper. Come into my life, you could be the keeper.'

[repeat chorus]

She slow danced with me for the last chorus. Her cheek was pressed on mine as she pressed into me and she was enjoying the closeness. I was just worried she would well up again due to the emotional lyrics. She let me soak the lyrics of the song.

'All I have. All I have
Turn me on to your love, light me up
Oh, you could be the keeper.'

As the closing bars faded out, she stepped back away from me and she did a deep curtsy while going down on one knee, lowering her head fully for a few seconds. I was completely taken aback with her humble graciousness. I bowed to her with gratitude. Then offering my hand I helped her to stand up. As she stood up taking my hand, she grinned seeing me bow to her. She had welled up, just as I had feared. She took my hand and walked me to the table and sat me down.

Kylie Minogue – come into my world

As the next song started playing, she served me a bowl with some dessert. I looked at her with delight looking at the dessert; my favourite. She just grinned back, caressed my face and acknowledged my gratitude.

'Come, come, come into my world.
Won't you lift me up, up, high upon your love?'
Slowly swinging to the music, she sat down and continued eating the dessert.

'Take these arms that were made for lovin', and this heart that will beat for two.
Take these eyes that were meant for watching over you.
And I've been such a long time waiting, for someone I can call my own.
I've been chasing the life I'm dreaming. Now I'm home.'
She was grinning and in a jolly mood.

[chorus:]
'I need your love, like night needs morning. Come, come, come into my world.'
She was tilting her head back in a trance again, stopping to look deep in my eyes with deep warmth.
'Won't you lift me up, up, high upon your love?'
I saw her tuck into the dessert and so I had some mouthfuls.

'Take these lips that were made for kissing, and this heart that will see you through, and these hands that were made to touch and feel you.'
She gently touched my hand and caressed it.

'So free your love. Hear me, I'm calling.
Oh won't you come, come, come into my world? Won't you lift me up, up, high upon your love?'

[repeat chorus]

All the while, she was swaying to the music and finishing her dessert. I was just glad she was in a happy mood now, as I ate my portion of the dessert.

'I need your love, like night needs morning. Come, come, come into my world.'
She was tilting her head back in a trance again, stopping to look deep in my eyes with deep warmth. She again had a soft sensual grin on her face.

'Won't you lift me up, up, high upon your love?'

She was swaying slowly and sensually to the music. I could see the bliss in her as the song faded.

Shania Twain – Im gonna getcha good

Her mood had become a bit jovial. She was smiling wider and had a glitter in her eye. Before the lyrics started playing, she got up, put our plates aside, took the stereo, unplugged it from the surround system and handed me a big bottle of water. Then she held out her hand, and cocked her head indicating I needed to follow her.

The song continued playing through the stereo now. She took my hand and led me upstairs into her bedroom.

'Don't wantcha for the weekend, don't wantcha for a night. I'm only interested if I can have you for life, yeah.
Uh, I know I sound serious and baby I am. You're a fine piece of real estate, and I'm gonna get me some land. Oh, yeah.'
On the stairs, she turned around briefly and looked at me while still climbing the stairs.

[Chorus:]
*'So, don't try to run honey, love can be fun. There's no need to be
alone when you find that someone.
I'm gonna getcha while I gotcha in sight. I'm gonna getcha if it
takes all night.
You can betcha by the time I say "go," you'll never say "no".
I'm gonna getcha, it's a matter of fact. I'm gonna getcha,
don'tcha worry 'bout that.
You can bet your bottom dollar, in time you're gonna be mine.
Just like I should, I'll getcha good.'*

When we got to her bedroom, she placed the stereo on her desk
and plugged it in her audio system. The room flooded with the
music. She shook her head smiling slyly.

'I've already planned it.'
She nodded.
*'Here's how it's gonna be: I'm gonna love you and you're gonna
fall in love with me. Yeah, yeah.'*
She pointed at me and then herself.

*'So, don't try to run honey, love can be fun. There's no need to be
alone when you find that someone.'*

She took the bottle from me and walked to the bed, still holding
my hand. Then placing the bottle on the side table, she cocked her
head toward the bed and got underneath the covers.

[Repeat Chorus]

I followed her cue and got under the covers.

We lay on our sides staring at each other.

*'Yeah, I'm gonna getcha baby. I'm gonna knock on wood. I'm
gonna getcha somehow honey yeah, I'm gonna make it good.
Yeah, yeah, yeah, yeah.
So, don't try to run honey, love can be fun. There's no need to be
alone when you find that someone.'*

The room was lit with scented candles. It looked sensual with her
eyes glittering in their light.

[Repeat Chorus]

We lay there looking at each other while the closing bars faded.

Ewan McGregor & Nicole Kidman – come what may (Josh remix)

Then as the opening bars of the next song starting playing, she held out her hand and took my hand in hers. After kissing my palm gently, she placed it between her cheek and the pillow.

'Never knew I could feel like this, like I've never seen the sky before. Want to vanish inside your kiss; every day I love you more and more. Listen to my heart. Can you hear it sing, telling me to give you everything?'
She stared straight at me with piercing eyes.

'Seasons may change, winter to spring. But I love you, until the end of time.'
She gazed at me with deep sensual eyes.

[Chorus:]
'Come what may. Come what may. I will love you until my dying day.'
I could see her welling up again. I took her hand in mine and caressed it gently.
'Suddenly the world seems such a perfect place. Suddenly it moves with such a perfect grace.
Suddenly my life doesn't seem such a waste.
It all revolves around you.'
She looked at me now with tearful eyes.

'And there's no mountain too high, no river too wide. Sing out this song and I'll be there by your side.
Storm clouds may gather, and stars may collide.'
The tears started rolling down her cheek again.

[Ewan:]*'But I love you.'*

[Nicole:]*'I love you'*. She mimed the words through her sweet lips.

'Until the end of time.'
I brushed away the tears from her cheek.

[repeat chorus]

She rolled on her back for a moment trying to compose through the tears.

As the song faded out, I couldn't take this anymore. I was feeling my throat choke with emotions again.

Take that – rule the world

As the next song starting playing, she composed herself again and brushed her tears with a soft grin.

'You light, the skies up above me. A star, so bright you blind me.'
A quiver ran through my spine.

'Don't close your eyes. Don't fade away.'
She closed her eyes and swayed to the music.

[chorus:]
'Yeah you and me we can ride on a star;
if you stay with me girl, we can rule the world.
Yeah you and me we can light up the sky;
if you stay by my side, we can rule the world.'
She stared straight into my eyes.

'If walls break down, I will comfort you.
If angels cry, oh I'll be there for you.'
She nodded to me signing with her hands, "I love you" using sign gesture.
'You've saved my soul, Don't leave me now. Don't leave me now.'

She shook her head at me and then she rolled over on her back and tears rolled down her eyes. She stared straight to the ceiling, trying to calm herself. They rolled on for a few moments. She gasped for breath as she tried composing herself.

[repeat chorus]

I scooted over to her and gently caressed her cheek. She pulled me in her arms and I lowered myself in her hug, gently lying beside her. I cuddled her and kissed her forehead.

(music interlude)

I gestured back to her in sign "You, me, together, forever." She welled up again with tears and hugged me tightly.

'All the stars are coming out tonight.
They're lighting up the sky tonight for you.'
I kissed her gently on her lips.

[repeat chorus]

All through the song, tears kept running down her cheeks and I was tearful seeing how emotional she was.

Celine Dion – falling into you

As she dried her tears gently, she pushed her palm on my chest to indicate me to lie down next to her. She rolled on her side and faced me as I lay beside her. I wanted this to end, because I couldn't take any more of this.

The opening bars rolled in and I gasped for breath.

'And in your eyes I see ribbons of colour.
I see us inside of each other.
I feel my unconscious merge with yours and I hear a voice say,
"What's his is hers".'
She gently caressed my cheek cupping her palm on it.

'I'm falling into you. This dream could come true and it feels so good, falling into you.'
She stared at me with piercing straight gaze.

'I was afraid to let you in here.'
She grinned shyly lowering her gaze for a moment.

'Now I have learned, love can't be made in fear. The walls begin to tumble down and I can't even see the ground.'
She stared at me deeply.

'I'm falling into you.'
She gave me a slight node looking to me.

*'This dream could come true and it feels so good...',*she curled up her shoulders to make a 'cosy warm' sign, gesturing the love she felt, *'...falling into you'.*

'Falling like a leaf, falling like a star, finding a belief, falling where you are.'

I took her hand that was caressing my cheek, and gently kissed it. Curling her fingers below my chin gently, she caressed my lips with her thumb, running it gently on my lips while gazing deeply in my eyes.

'Catch me, don't let me drop! Love me, don't ever stop!'

Tears ran down her cheeks as she shook her head with pleading eyes. I couldn't hold it together anymore and let my eyes flood with tears. I took her hand and kissed it gently.

'So close your eyes and let me kiss you.
And while you sleep I will miss you.'
She grinned warmly seeing my tears, and gently reached out and dusted my tears away and kissed my hand.

'Oh I'm falling into you. This dream could come true and it feels so good, falling into you.
Falling like a leaf, falling like a star; finding a belief, falling where you are.
Falling into you.'

She swayed her head sensually, all the while gazing at me with warm wet eyes.

Bread – Make it with you

As the next song started rolling, she rolled on her back, composed herself and looked at me turning her head, while still lying on her back.

'Hey, have you ever tried really reaching out for the other side? I may be climbing on rainbows.
But baby, here goes.'
Very slowly she sat up in the bed and turned to sit looking at me.

[chorus]
'Dreams, they're for those who sleep.
Life is for us to keep.
And if you're wondering what this song is leading to,
I want to make it with you.
I really think that we could make it, girl.'

She unzipped her dress at the back and slipped it slowly down her legs. She lay down, lifted her bum, pushed it past her hips and then slipped it past her legs while she bent them at the knees. Then she looked at me. She was completely naked and wasn't wearing any underwear.

'No, you don't know me well in every little thing. Only time will tell.'
She slowly rolled the duvet away from me and gestured for me to sit up.
'But you believe the things that I do, and we'll see it through.'

I sat up and crossed my legs to face her. She looked at me, and gently unbuttoned my shirt and lifted it over my head. All the while, she was gazing at me trying to read my eyes and my expressions.

'Life can be short or long. Love can be right or wrong.
And if I chose the one I'd like to help me through,
I'd like to make it with you.'
She looked at me with deep intent.

'I really think that we could make it, girl.'

She helped me undress fully. Then looking at me straight in my eyes she gently lay down again on her side, under the covers and lay her head on the pillow looking and waiting for me.

(music interlude)

I gently shuffled and she raised the duvet to help me get under it. When we were under the covers, I lay close to her on my side, my head in the pillow looking at her deeply.

'Baby you know that...'

[repeat chorus]

She kept caressing my lips with her fingers gently. When the song was fading, she gently shuffled closer to me and planted a kiss on my lips and then lay back down, very close to me. She never took her eyes off me, all the while gazing at me with warmth and sensuality, all the while assessing my responses.

Selena – I could fall in love

As the next song rolled on with its opening bars, she scooted close to me and pressed herself into my arms. She slid her arm around my back and cuddled in my arms. I slipped one arm under her neck and she gently raised her neck to let my arm slide under her pillow. When she settled in my hug, I wrapped her and I could feel she wanted me to hug her snugly.

I took in the lyrics as the song progressed. It was again my favourite, a rather sensual one. She gazed at me deep into my eyes through the lyrics.

'I could lose my heart tonight, if you don't turn and walk away; 'cause the way I feel I might lose control and let you stay; 'cause I could take you in my arms and never let go.'
She held me close into her arms.

[Chorus:]
'I could fall in love with you, (baby).'
I had goose bumps all over my body.

'I can only wonder, how, touching you would make me feel.'
She gently ran her fingers down my thighs and gently grazed my erection as she traced her hand upwards to my chest.
'But if I take that chance right now tomorrow will you want me still.'
She came in close and quickly planted a kiss on my lips, gazing me squarely in my eyes.
'So I should keep this to myself and never let you know.'
Then she moved away again and looked at me deep in my eyes.
'I could fall in love with you, (baby)'.
She looked deep into my eyes.
'And I know it's not right, and I guess I should try to do what I should do. But I could fall in love, fall in love with you. I could fall in love with you.'

She was again tearful as she hugged me, as she melted and gave into my arms.

Siempre estoy soñando en ti   *I'm always dreaming of you*
besando mis labios,   *kissing my lips,*
acariciando mi piel,   *caressing my skin,*
abrazandome con ansias   *hugging me forward,*
imaginando que me amas   *imagining that you love me*
como yo podria amarte.   *as I could love you.*

'So I should keep this to myself and never let you know.'

[repeat chorus]

'I could fall in love, I could fall in love, with you!'
'I could fall in love, fall in love with you! (baby)...'

She kept kissing me through the closing bars. Then we both came out of the hug and lay there looking at each other.

She grinned at me through her wet eyes. I was lying there totally perplexed of all her emotions.

Conjure one – Sleep

As the next song rolled its opening bars, she looked me straight in my eyes. I was lying on my side very close to her. Her tears had stopped and she was looking straight and deep into my eyes with a straight face.

'I know it's late. I shouldn't call at this hour. But yet, my fate, I need lips to devour.'
She moved closer to me and put her arms out to hug me around my neck. I wrapped her in my hug.

'My nervous system is shot alright. I won't sleep unless you sleep with me tonight, deep with me tonight.'

She gently rolled me over on my back and climbed partially on top, her leg in between my legs and she was kissing my lips. Her bosoms were pressed on my chest, as she was partially on the side, and her hand was wrapped around my waist.

'I know it's late. We've known each other a while. I can't wait to see your twisted smile.'

She pushed herself more over me, as she straddled me, and pushed herself in my arms. I hugged her tightly, trying to press her against me, as she melted in my arms, our naked warmth fuelling our desires. She was making every move very slowly and gently, never once taking her eyes off me, gauging my expressions all the while.

'Kindred spirit of candle light, I won't sleep unless you sleep with me tonight, deep with me tonight.'
As she kissed me, she propped her bum in my hands letting me caress it as we kissed. She bobbed it on my erection and gently grazed it a few time as she slowly positioned her vulva over its head, looking at me with intentional eyes. I held her bum and waited, gazing deep in her eyes.

'And my thoughts to my sight. I'm so tired but I fight. Sleep with me tonight. Sleep with me tonight'
She kept gazing deep in my eyes, looking at my expressions, as she slowly lowered herself on my erection, without taking her eyes off my face. I could feel her ecstatic pleasure build in her eyes, while they closed slowly like blinds, as she took me in, her head tilting back in deep pleasure. She sank into my hug, planted kisses on my lips, and licked my tongue as she gently lowered herself on my hardness.

'Drown out the machinery in my head. Bring your peace of mind to my bed.'
She kissed all over my neck and cheeks as she gently and slowly rocked her bum up and down on my prick, letting her wetness glide on my erection slowly, giving her deep pleasure.

'Without sleep, there are no dreams. Without dreams, we fall apart at the seams.'
I held her bum as she gently rocked her bum, taking me deeper insider her, slowly, pulling my erection all the way out before it slid back in again.

(music interlude)

As she continued to kiss, I could feel wetness inside her labia and her moans relayed her passion and hunger for me. I was stroking her back and bum. This was very unusual and different for me; actually my first. Then she pulled me and indicated me to roll her on her back.

'Kindred spirit of candle light, I won't sleep unless you sleep with me tonight, deep with me tonight.'
As I held her firmly, she stretched her legs and I rolled her on to her back and rolled on top of her in one smooth rollover.

'And my thought to my saint I'm so tired but I faint. Sleep with me tonight. Sleep with me tonight.'

As I laid her on her back, she parted her legs to let me in between them and I lay on top. She was staring me deep in my eyes.

(music interlude)

She encouraged me to slide inside her. I wanted to be gentle so I lowered myself slowly on her and she felt me slide inside her slowly. She gasped and wrapped herself tightly in appreciation and encouragement, kissing me all over wrapping her arms around my neck and pulling me close to her. She was moving her hips to pump her wetness on my erection. I was synchronising with her movements.

'Sleep ...' The song faded out.

Celine Dion – Halfway to heaven

As she kissed me, I felt her warm juicy labia milking me with passion. She was wet and hungry for me. As the opening bars of the next song rolled, I was all into her passion, and we both had lost all inhibitions.

'Come and go with me. Wherever I am, I want you to be walking with your hand in mine; feel so fine.'
We continued to kiss with passion. I kept throbbing inside her. She could feel it slide all the way in.

'When I'm close to you, I know what it means to want to be true; never felt this way before. Is there more?'
I paused for breath and she looked at me. Her eyes were now pouring with passion and lust for me. The sensuality had been overcome with deep desire for me, desires that she had been hiding inside her, bottled for all this while.

'Are you feeling the same as me? Honestly? Don't you think it's surreal?'

As we looked at each other, our eyes recognised our thoughts and read each other's minds.

'I'm not dealing in fairy tales. If this fails, I don't know what on earth I will do 'cause I'm halfway to heaven. Let's go all the way. I don't want to give it up 'cause I'm already falling in love.'
She wrapped her legs around my waist and encouraged me to fuck her. I gently slid inside her and I saw her moan as she pleaded me to fuck her deep and hard by tugging on my bum and pulling me down. I drove myself deep inside her and she moaned in my ear.

'When we reach that place, I'm dying to see the smile on your face. I'm so sure you'll want to stay. That's okay.'
She ran her hands through my hair and kissed me on my neck and cheek. I could feel her warm breath on my skin. It was adding fuel to the fire inside me. I kept pounding and sliding inside her, getting deeper with every push.

'I have so many dreams to share; please be there. Let me share them with you.'
She came intensely, dug her fingers in my back, ran her fingers and pulled my hair on the back of my head as she held me tightly. I hugged her as I slowed my pace. Then when she had calmed, I started sliding inside her again.

'If you're looking for happiness, nothing less, come with me, baby I'm looking too. And I'm halfway to heaven. Let's go all the way.'
She kept kissing me, licking my tongue and lips. She kept encouraging me to slide in her deeper and harder. All this while she was coming and I could feel the wetness inside her very complimentary.

'I don't want to give it up 'cause I'm already falling now halfway to heaven.
Let's go all the way. I don't want to give it up 'cause I'm already falling in love.'
I continued to slide inside her as she came a few more time. Then when I thrust hard and deep she held on me and gave out a short cry. As she dug fingers in my back, she bit into my arm and she pulled my bum as she wrapped her legs around my waist. I paused and when I glanced at her for a quick moment, she looked at me with wet pleasured eyes and sighed slowly shaking her face sideways encouraging me to continue and not to stop. She pulled me back on top of her wrapping my neck. I carried on thrusting harder and deeper and she encouraged through her kisses.

'I don't want to give my life in moderation (baby now). I'm prepared to give myself up to temptation; it's time. I could use a little love and inspiration (baby now). Come and share the joy and join the celebration; It's time.'
She had stopped kissing me and I could feel one of her hand was grasping the pillow as she dug her face and mouth in it on the side to stop her from saying anything. I had buried my face in her neck, gently kissing her there all over, planting wet kisses. She had one hand over my head running through my hair.

'Hoping and praying that soon you'll be saying be mine.'
As I got closer, she must have realised my quickening pace. She held me around my waist with her legs. She did not want me to pull out. She wrapped her arms and legs tightly to encourage me to cum inside her.

(music interlude)

I came inside her with deep intensity. I felt the most wonderful feeling – it felt like all my life energy was being drained out through my erection, which was buried deep inside her.

'I don't want to give it up. I don't want to give it up 'cause I'm already falling in love. You're makin' all my senses come alive.'
As I came, she felt it inside her and she wrapped her arms around my neck, squeezed me in her hug, and came hard and deep with me, moaning loudly.

As we collapsed in each other's arms, the closing bars of the song faded out. We lay there as the song faded. I was still on top of her.

Shania Twain – Thank you baby

As the opening bars rolled up, I slid on her side and lay beside her. Exhausted, we looked at each other.

'Oh, thank you baby for lovin' me like you do.'
She kissed me.

'I did not like datin' and trying to find someone. I gave up waitin' for love to come along. There had to be some way, I knew I'd find it someday.'
She looked at me with complacency and gratitude.

[Chorus:]

'Yeah, thank you baby for makin' someday come so soon!'
She kissed my fingers and then caressed my lips.

'Yeah, thank you baby for lovin' me the way you do!'
She grinned very slightly. I just looked at her with perplexed emotions.

'So many numbers so many guys to call. Is it any wonder I got nowhere at all? Oh, well it had to be some way. I knew I'd find it someday.'
She looked at me and stared.

[Repeat Chorus]

'Thank you baby.'
She looked at me with a soft grin.

'There had to be some way. I knew I'd find it someday.'
She came closer to me and hugged me, gazing deep in my eyes, her eyes now glittering as diamonds.

[Repeat Chorus]

'Baby someway, someday, somewhere'
We lay there kissing and holding each other for a long while as the song faded out. We could now hear our hearts beat together, slowly calming down.

The silence gave a very unreal feel compared to what the evening had been so far – full of emotions, sensuality and now deep desire, strung with implied music. As we turned over to look at each other, she looked deeply in my eyes, with a straight face and apprehensive expression.

The moment she realised I was about to say something, she pressed a finger gently on my lips, rushed in closer and planted a long deep wet kiss on my lips, sealing them with her warm wet mouth. Then opening her eyes, still kissing me she looked at me shaking her head slowly from side to side and pressed my lips shut again, putting her finger gently on my lips. She shook your head gently to indicate that I shouldn't say anything. Then when she had realised I had understood her, she slowly lay down on her side facing me and continued looking at me deep in my eyes.

After a while, she sat up in bed, took a sip of water from the bottle and handed it to me for a sip. After I sipped it, I handed it back to her and she placed it on the side table. Then she got in under the duvet and lay down on her side, her cheek pressed softly on her pillow, eyes staring, gazing all over my face. I just looked at her.

There were a million things I wanted to say to her, tell her, ask her, as usual. However, I wanted to respect her wishes; I wanted to keep my word of honour when I handed her the blank voucher – the one she had used for something so sensual that night.

After a while, she closed her eyes and dozed off to sleep. Whether she was sleepy or was just trying to avoid eye contact with me, I don't know. It wasn't like we were going to talk anyway so she might had thought it was better to just sleep for the night.

Because she had fallen asleep, curled on her side facing me, I did not want to wake her up, even to hug and cuddle her. I couldn't spoon her either. I just looked at her peaceful face while she slept.

Then I got up, blew the candles and went back to sleep in her bed. I gently pulled the duvet and lay on my back, trying not to disturb her sleep. It felt very weird to be sleeping 'alone' like that when we had the most sensual night of all. Nonetheless, tonight I was going to honour her wishes. Hence, I just lay there, looking at the ceiling, wondering all the things I would be saying to her the next morning.

Every now and then, I turned my head and looked at the silhouette of her lovely face now in deep sleep, remembering all the tears that rolled over those soft pink cheeks. How her heart must have writhed in pain! I wondered why she put herself through so much tonight. May be that would be my first question for the following morning.

Chapter 12 – morning after

I must have had the worst night as I didn't sleep. I remember waking throughout the night, on and off. There were lots of things that kept me up and the million questions about the whole night that had unfolded were just a few among many.

When I opened my eyes the following morning, the dawn was just creeping in. The room that was lit with candles the previous night and then bathed with darkness after, was being flooded with sunlight trying to seep through the partially closed curtains. I looked at her and she was still asleep.

She apparently must have turned in bed in the night as she was on her chest and was now facing away from me. I could not see her face, just the soft sensual cascade of her long beautiful hair hiding her face beneath. The French plat was still just as sensual although the pretty flowers had disappeared. Some hair had come loose, but that usually was the most sensual part of hairdo for me. I gazed at her sleeping torso for a while. I tried to make conscious effort to shuffle the duvet, only slightly though, to see if she was awake. She did not stir. She must have been tired.

After staring out the window for a while, I decided to get out of bed. I gently moved my legs to the floor getting out of bed, slipped into my shorts, walked to the door, and stepped out, closing the bedroom door quietly behind me. I walked to the bathroom, and freshened up. Then I walked downstairs into the lounge.

I looked around and saw the dinner table – still left from our dinner from the previous night. The champagne bottle reminded me of the efforts she had gone to make all this happen. Her lip marks on the flute looked so sensual; it reminded me of all the kisses she had planted on my lips, cheeks, face and neck throughout the night. I quivered at the thought of the sensual bliss it had left behind in my mind. The audio surround system was still on from last night. I got up from the table and turned it off.

I walked back to the table. I stood there, leaning on the chair, looking at the corner where she sat. I sat there for a while, looking at the lounge, trying to see it from her eyes. I could not bring to my mind what had made her to orchestrate the evening in the way she did.

I dusted off the questions, and stood up. 'It would be a lot easier just to ask her when she wakes up,' I thought to myself.

Trying to get some distance away from my thoughts, I went into the kitchen, put a frying pan on the stove and turned it on low. I cracked some eggs, added some milk and beat them in a bowl. Then I added a couple of bread slices into the toaster and adjusted the setting for a golden crisp finish.

I got two cereal bowls and filled them with her and my favourite cereals individually. I tossed a dollop of butter into the pan and stirred the egg batter into the pan. Then I gently stirred it around for a nice soft moist scramble – she liked her scrambled eggs moist and she used to say I knew exactly how to make it moist.

I dished it out on two plates. By then the toasts had popped up in the toaster but I had let them sit for a while. I buttered one toast and I spread strawberry jam on one, her favourite. Then I poured some milk in a small jug and quickly grilled some hash browns, again her favourite. I laid it all out on a tray, added some cutlery and slowly climbed back upstairs to her bedroom. When I was trying to open the door quietly, the tray nearly slipped and in the haste to recover, I made a thud on the door.

I paused for a while, knowing what a lucky break I had just then. I slowly opened the door, and left it ajar. I walked in with the tray and seeing her still asleep in bed, I was trying to decide where I was going to lay it down. While I was deciding, I say movement and she stirred around slowly, looking around trying to find me. When she looked back and saw me stand there, I think it startled her a bit. She went back to her pose and laid her face in the bed.

I slowly walked to the bed, laid the tray down on the floor and pulled the duvet down on my side. Then I laid the tray out on my side gently. I placed the milk jug on my side-table and propping my pillow up against the headboard, I sat in the bed pressed against it. Then I held the tray up, pulled the duvet over my legs and settled the tray on my lap. Then I waited motionless for her to turn around. The warm fresh smell of scrambled eggs and hash browns could not let her sleep even if she wanted to; I knew that.

She slowly moved around and turned her head to face me, still lying on her chest, her face still buried in the pillow, her eyes closed. Then she slowly opened her eyes and gazed at me in my direction and when she met my gaze on her, her gaze and head moved slowly in retreat and she dug her face in the pillow for a while. I just stayed there waiting for her to get up.

After a further few minutes, she moved and this time, she rolled over on her back. Then she looked around slowly, making a very feeble attempt of pretending to be still sleepy. She sat up, now conscious that she was naked under the sheet. She pulled the duvet to her bosoms and sat up tucking it around her chest while she rested on the headboard next to me.

When I noticed she had sat up, I stared at her weird behaviour. After the night we had had, this seemed to be a little weird. My expression must have said it as she looked at me and looked away. I slowly handed her the tray and placed it between us on our thighs. She looked at it, and without looking at me, took the cutlery and started eating slowly. I started eating out of my plate and we did not speak while we ate our breakfast. That was so weird. She neither looked at me nor spoke. I think the silence was very awkward so she started gulping her breakfast in big mouthfuls; may be that was her way to avoid speaking.

I had no idea what the hell was up with her. But damn I was going to honour what I had promised her – my silence as she had requested last night. I just looked at her while we ate and still did not say anything. She never spoke a single word while she gobbled her breakfast down. I actually had to pour the milk in her cereal myself without being asked for it. When she had finished the breakfast, she looked around and slowly got out of the bed, and walked briskly out and I heard the bathroom door open and close.

I heard running water and then a flush. Then all went quiet again. Then I saw her slowly walk into her bedroom. She had put on a long nightdress. As she slowly entered the room, she looked at the bed and tried making eye contact with me. I was still staring straight at her with a rather straight face.

It seemed like she had wet eyes. She was hesitating to look at me for some reason. I had put away the tray and I was still sitting on the bed, with my arms crossed, looking straight at her with a very straight face. She slowly and hesitantly walked to the bed, as she realised standing away at the desk would make things more uncomfortable. She sat on the other side of the bed from me with her legs on the floor.

After a moment of silence and what seemed like at least a millennia of lowered gaze, she finally tried to make small talk, "Did you sleep well?" Her voice was groggy and she tried to clear her throat. "Sorry. Did you sleep well?" she repeated her question, trying to avoid eye contact.

"Oh and it's nice to finally hear you speak." I said. "Am I allowed to talk?" I was trying to be sarcastic. "You see, I did not know how long you were going to keep me bound in that spell." There probably was a very dry sarcastic tone in my voice.

Her eyes were wet, I could tell. She lowered her gaze as soon as she saw me stare at her.

I just looked at her and said with some puzzled gaze, "What's going on?"

At that, her eyes wandered aimlessly around on the bed, around the room away from me and I could see tear rolling down her cheek. "I'm sorry."

She lowered her eyes to her lap, her hands clasped together, fingers loosely intertwined.

"Sorry?!" I exclaimed. "You are sorry?" I was perplexed beyond belief. "Really? About what exactly?"

She tried brushing her tears away as she whispered under her sniffs, "About last night. Everything I did."

"Well I gave you the voucher. So you cannot be blamed for that." I replied. "I did promise you I would keep my word of honour about it." I replied calmly.

"And I'm sorry." She tried to calm down, trying to come to terms. "I did not think it would turn out like this." She sniffed and tried getting up from the bed and leaving the room.

"Sit down." I nearly yelled at her. I just looked at her. "You ain't going anywhere until you explain to me what is going on."

She looked at me briefly. She was shocked. There had been very rare occasions when I had yelled at her. That was why when I did yell at that moment, she knew it was serious. From the right mom had given me as her older brother, Sam had come to respect me and my inquiries. After all, I was her elder brother and I was responsible for her wellbeing. She was not allowed to walk away when I wanted her to clarify anything; that was our deal. The same went for me too. Today she knew I was being very serious.

She sat on the corner of the bed, with her side toward me.

"How did you hope it would turn out?" I asked her. "What did you expect?"

"I'm sorry it happened." She muttered looking down to the floor.

"You are regretting it?" I exclaimed. "So had you smoked something last night then? 'cause I sure as hell did not load up on that champagne so much as not to know what I was doing." I was trying to understand where she was coming from. Hearing her regret it really upset me to my core.

Her tears started rolling again.

"I knew what I was doing and I was fully aware." She tried to mutter under her sniffs.

"So why are you regretting it now?" I was perplexed.

"I did not think you would get so upset." She spoke softly.

"Really?!" I sounded sarcastic.

"I said I'm sorry." Tears were rolling down her cheek. This was tearing me apart.

"Will you just tell me in simple terms something I am trying to understand here please?" I tried to clarify something with her calmly. "Why are you crying, regretting and apologising all at the same time?"

"I don't want to lose you." She softly acknowledged. "That's why I am crying."

"Then what are you regretting? And why?" I asked.

"What I did last night. What I made you do." She murmured.

"Is that why you are apologising?" I asked.

She nodded slowly without looking at me.

"So you did not want to do what you did last night?" I was trying to clear my confusion.

She stopped sniffling. "I did. But not at the cost of losing you." She sighed. "I did not think I would lose you."

"Why would you think you would lose me?" I asked with a big surprise.

"Because of what I have done." She muttered to herself.

"And what is that?" I wanted to know.

"I crossed a delicate line." She sighed.

"What line is that?" I questioned her. I wanted her to clarify seeing her perplexed expression.

"I made love to you." She acknowledged with some shame. When she realised I did not know what she was on about, she said, "What we ended up doing, what I made you do."

"So?" I exclaimed with confusion in my head. I was staring at her for some elaboration.

She paused as if she had frozen in time. She looked at me with a mix of confusion and shock. She had stopped sobbing and her voice was calm and perplexed.

"Did you not like what we did?" I was perplexed and looked at her with a big question mark on my face.

"I loved it. It was my idea." She said with perplexed thoughts in her expression. "But it is clear you did not like it, that's why I regret it and that's why I am apologising to you, 'cause I really don't want to lose you." Tears started flowing down on her cheeks again.

"Oh God." I opened my arms and scooted close to her. I took her in my arms because this was killing me. She just looked at me.

"You made an assumption that I did not like last night." I said to her with ridicule.

"You seem so upset with me." She sighed being perplexed.

"I am upset with you because of how you did not let me say anything all night." I said to her.

"What?!" She just sat back and jolted.

"You did not let me say, speak or ask you anything all night." I said. "And today in the morning you were weirder than last night. That is what freaked me out."

"So ... wait. Hold on." She was trying to get something straight in her head. "You aren't upset about last night and what we did. You were upset you did not get to speak?" She was not sure what had hit her and if she had heard me correct.

I nodded. "I loved every bit of last night." I spoke excitedly.

"You do know what we ended up doing." She wanted to check if I had smoked something.

I spoke in a long drawn out tone, nodding my head slowly once. "Y-e-a-h."

"And you are ok with that?" She asked me again completely puzzled.

"Why wouldn't I be? Aren't you?" I questioned her not understanding where her doubts were coming from.

"Yes but that is because that's me." She said looking at me to say as if she was from Venus and I was from Mars.

"And I am different from you how? Apart from the obvious." I looked at her bosoms and then started at her lap.

"You mean to say you are ok with all this?" She asked me to confirm again. She didn't believe her ears, or rather her luck.

"Again, why wouldn't I be?" I spoke every word slowly and softly. I did not understand her point.

"I never really thought you loved me as I loved you." She acknowledged.

"Really?!" I exclaimed. "Well now you know, genius!" I smirked. "Took you this long to figure it out!" I could not believe what I had heard. "I have reciprocated virtually every single emotion you have projected to me. I have reciprocated every single gesture you made toward me. Tell me when have I EVER turned down you or anything that you have done or suggested?! Shouldn't that had given you a clue that no matter what it is and what you ask of me, I'm game?" I looked at her. I was fuming.

"That's true. I don't remember you ever saying 'no' to my requests." She agreed trying to remember. "How come? Why?"

"You understand me, you accept me, you like me and you love me, unconditionally." I looked at her with warm eyes. "How can I not give you all that you offer me? I love you, just as much as you love me." I tried to justify my feelings to her. "There is nothing I would not give you, if you were to just ask. No questions asked." I looked at her with a simple glance.

"So why the hell have you made me cry all this time for nothing?" she shrieked.

"Me? I made you cry?" I yelled back. "All I wanted to know is what the hell was going on. Why was I not allowed to say anything all night, and then all morning."

"Really?" she exclaimed.

"Y-e-s." I again spoke slowly. "What did you think I was mad about?"

"I thought you did not like it and you were upset with me and were going to finish with me." She confessed.

"Why the hell would I not like it? Have YOU smoked something?" I ridiculed her. "And why the hell would I leave you about something so wonderful?"

"I thought you felt I had ruined our relationship." She proposed trying to be logical.

"Why would anything we have done so far ruin anything between us? If anything, I think it has brought us closer, don't you think?" I had a big question mark on my face. "We have been getting closer for a long while now. You never felt this upset about any of that. Did you think it would just come to an abrupt halt one day?" I was perplexed.

She did not say anything.

I looked at her with a questionable doubt. "Now THAT would have definitely ruined it for me!" I exclaimed feeing upset.

She just looked at me. "I think we have got our wires crossed, haven't we?" She just broke out in a soft grin with a warm look on her face.

"You are right for once. You got me so cross all evening and night and I couldn't even tell you how much I loved you." I protested. "Every time you shed a tear it burned a hole in my heart."

"And all this while I thought you wanted to end it with me." She giggled.

"Really?" I laughed. "Is that what you thought?"

She nodded. "I thought you did not like what we did and were so upset with me for making you sleep with me."

"Really?" I fell about laughing on the bed. "You are seriously kidding me."

"No I'm not, you idiot." She smacked my arm as I fell about laughing in her lap. She started giggling too.

"O man. I should have pretended for a bit more then. I would have seen what more crap you came out with." I laughed my ass off.

"Shut up." She slapped me playfully on my arm again. "It nearly killed me."

When I had composed myself again, I sat up, held my tummy from the pain of laughing so much and looked at her.

"What made you think about all this nonsense?" I looked at her.

"People are weird about this stuff." She spoke squeamishly. "This is not normal is it?"

"What stuff?" I was unimpressed. "And what is normal?"

"This stuff – between you and me." She pointed at each other. "We aren't supposed to be together like this."

"And you figured it out now, genius!?" I exclaimed. "Did you or did you not see the train pull out of the station like a million years ago." I said sarcastically. "Man, you are special." I made a gesture indicating she was a retard. "And what about all the stuff we have been doing till now? Was that ok? Is any of that 'normal'?" I air quoted and shook my head in ridicule about her worries to raise such a question.

She realised my point. "Shut up." She slapped me one jokingly on my arm and started giggling shyly. "Well do you think people would agree about us?" She pulled a straight face and stared at me.

"We are two consenting adults, capable of making our own decisions. Why should anyone want to be interested in what we do or don't do?" I said calmly.

"What we did is considered illegal." She said calmly.

"Society has a very relative reference on what it considers legal and illegal." I said. "It's all a matter of time."

"Our parents will take offence to it." She sighed.

"So are YOU going to tell them?" I asked her.

She looked at me and shook her head.

"Good. Then forget it." I looked at her reassuringly. "I ain't going to either. So why worry? And anyway, have you told them anything that has happened between us till now?"

She shook her head being sarcastic, narrowed her eyes and stuck her tongue out. "Einstein!"

"So why now, why tell about this? Genius!" I narrowed my eyes now sarcastically.

"They are going to find out some day." She confessed. "We keep getting closer to each other every time." She said. "And now this."

"What if they never find out?" I spoke calmly.

She went quiet for a while. "I just did not expect such reaction from you." She confessed. "I wanted you to accept my feelings, don't get me wrong. But the way you think about this is quiet unexpectedly reassuring."

"Good to have such high esteem in the eyes of one's twin sister as always." I was sarcastic.

"Stop it." She nudged me with a big apologetic face. "You know what I mean."

"Yeah." I remarked. "You did not have the courage or confidence to think I might have the same feelings as you and that I may be confident enough to reciprocate them."

"Don't make me feel bad." She pleaded. "I feel sad as it is."

"You should be." I said sternly.

"I love you." She nudged me.

"Apparently not as much as I love you." I replied making a strong case.

"That is horrible and mean." She looked at me with wet eyes.

"Oh don't start." I warned her. "I had to bear like a gallon of those tears all last night and not be able to do anything about it." I took her into my arms. "Do you even know how it killed me to see you in tears, all night?!"

"All night, I kept thinking how I was 'forcing' you to participate."
She air quoted.

"And little did you realise, you were making me so blissfully
happy." I said. "In fact it was way better than a dream. It was real."
I looked at her with deep gaze.

"Every once in a while, I kept imagining you discarding my
feelings 'cause you did not approve of it." She said softly with a
heavy heart. "That was what was killing me inside and making me
tearful every time, when I imagined you breaking up with me
'cause you did not like how I showed you my true feelings for you."

"Hon. You got to do a lot worse than this for me to even think of
such crazy thoughts as leaving you." I softly spoke to her, looking
deep in her eyes. "If you continue taking me down this road of
bliss, you will just take me deeper with you. Nothing more." I
assured her. "I will just follow where you go."

She looked at me, caressed my hand and cupped my cheek.

"I love you." I said to her. "That's all I have ever done for you. And
there is nothing, absolutely NOTHING you would do that would
make me want to leave you." I said to her taking her face in my
hands. "I know you would never want to hurt me knowingly." I
said. "So I will always love you."

She just looked at me, shifted closer and planted a long soft kiss on
my lips.

"I love you more than you will ever know." She sighed, as she
looked deep in my eyes.

"Are you done crying over imaginary spilt milk?" I giggled.

She giggled and nudged me in my arm.

"Come here." I made a gesture for her to cuddle in my arms. I
wrapped her in my arms and she hugged me tightly, pulling me in
her arms.

As we slid under the duvet, she cuddled in my arms and we
hugged each other lovingly.

"I always hoped and wished that you would accept me like this and be ok with it. Somewhere deep down however, I had a shadow of doubt though and that tore through my heart when I imagined my life without you." She sighed softly kissing my chest. Then she became tearful again.

"Are you assured now?" I asked her trying to keep her from welling up.

She nodded. I felt her cheek graze against my shoulder.

After a moment of silence, she asked, "How come this doesn't bother you?"

"What?"

"Us, how we have come this far and now we are more than just siblings?" she said without looking at me.

"You do approve, don't you?" I asked her.

"Yes." She replied.

"So do I." I replied in a matter of fact manner. "Why should I be bothered?"

"Isn't this frowned upon?" she asked me.

"What if it is?" I asked her. "Is it love? Do you love me?"

"Yes most certainly." She said. "I know I do."

"Me too." I said. "So what is the problem?"

"People." She sighed. "Society."

"If we can enjoy each other's love without ruining anyone's lives, does it really matter in the bigger scheme of things? And people will come into question IF they got to know. Till then, no one is any wiser."

She went quiet for a moment.

"What about mom and dad?" she asked after a moment of silence.

"What they don't know, won't hurt them." I said. "I don't think they would understand."

"Aren't you making an assumption?" she was trying to be optimistic.

"Would you like to take the chance?" I asked her.

She was silent for a while. "I think mom would understand me if I explained it to her."

"Imagine the pain you felt about me not reciprocating to you and times that by 100 and add a pinch more certainty of it happening." I remarked. "That is what it may turn out to be if it does go south, against your better judgement."

"I think our parents are a lot wiser than you give them credit." She whispered. "I think if we explained to them in a rational and sensible way, they would understand."

"I ain't taking that risk." I said. "I don't know if this will destroy them, but what I do know is that I love them to bits. I wouldn't want them going through pain unnecessarily, if there was even a slightest possibility."

"So do I." She said.

"Then, for now, let's just keep this to ourselves." I tried to suggest her. "In time we will know when it becomes appropriate to disclose."

"Things will be difficult for us together like this." She whispered softly.

"If I had to, I would walk to the ends of the earth with you." I spoke quietly.

She raised her face and looked at me. I looked back at her with a gentle nod to reassure her.

"I am more anxious than surprised about that, you know," she said to me. "I know you would, without batting an eye. That is what scares me the most."

"What do you mean? Why would it scare you?" I was puzzled as she laid her head on my shoulder and I hugged her while we spoke softly.

"I get so overwhelmed with your love for me most of the times because I know how much you love me. That is why I am so head-over-heels fallen for you big time. But then, I am overcome with the sense of responsibility to safeguard your well-being and I question myself and my intentions, if I am being selfish, and somehow leading you to your downfall."

"Don't even think of being a martyr." I said to her sternly. "I hate that. Don't even think of doing that for me. You just do what you wish to do. Let me decide my life for myself."

She just nodded. "At times, I am unsure if I deserve you or so much of your love."

"What the fuck?" I just exclaimed jolting around and looking at her straight in the eye. "What the fuck?" I repeated each word slowly.

She realised she had said something she shouldn't had.

"The world is full of people waiting in a queue to push and kick you down all the time. If you are going to start doing their work for them, why bother even staying alive?" I was very upset on so many levels at what she had said.

"I am not saying this just because you are my sister and I've known you the longest, but I know what a wonderful person you are. I have seen your friends enough to know that you deserve a lot more than you get for your share of appreciation. So have SOME confidence in yourself hon." I gently squeezed her in my hug.

I wanted to give her some assurance. "I'm not talking about being vain, trust me. However, you need to have strength and courage to know you are very special, and not just in my eyes but in everyone's eyes. Anyone who doesn't see that is definitely undeserving."

After a moment of just gazing at me she spoke. "Do me a favour and don't ever ask me why I love you." She said softly. "I would need a lifetime to make that list." I think she had welled up.

I spoke softly, "And as for me, I have never let myself be as vulnerable as I am with you right now. You have my heart. Love it, caress it, cut it, kick it; your choice. I will take anything and everything that you give me from here and now even if it kills me. And trust me when I say it, it kills me sometimes."

She was alarmed. "When? What have I done?" she propped herself on the elbow looking at me.

"No." I smiled. "You haven't done anything. It's just that when I miss you, it really kills. Our times together, when we are close and I can feel your touch, are the best. When I miss you I go through 'withdrawal' and that is when it kills me." I air quoted with a smile.

"You need to let me know when that happens. I would run to you anytime." She softly caressed my face and kissed me. "You have no idea how it kills me to be away from you. That's why I am always touching you."

"I love that so very much." I sighed. "You set my body alight with your touch."

"And you do too." She giggled. "You give me goose bumps."

We both giggled and kissed each other.

I looked at her deep in her eyes and said softly, "I would not know what I would do without you now." I was welling up, the feeling making me realise the precious gift I had with her. "And I'm not just saying that. If you stopped loving me for ANY reason, I would want to die."

"I know exactly what you mean, hon." She whispered and kissed me with a long soft kiss on my lips. "Now you know how I feel too and why I kept welling up during the dinner. Losing you was never an option but the fear was constantly there."

She raised herself on her elbow and turning my face to stare into her eyes, she looked deep into my eyes and said to me, "trust me when I say this, I will NEVER stop loving you, EVER." Then she planted a deep long kiss on my lips.

As we lay there in each other's arms, I reflected back to the last night.

"So why did you make me promise not to speak all night last night?" I asked her.

"Actually, you walked right into it." She smiled. "You gave me the voucher and I had an idea of using it. Before that, I was in two minds about the whole thing. I did not know if you would approve. I wanted to do this desperately, to show you what I felt for you, hoping you felt the same for me too. I did not want you stopping me in the middle and we ending up in an argument. That would have ruined everything I had planned. I needed you to experience the full thing before you said anything. I wanted you to see my bare heart placed in front of you begging you not to judge me harshly and to consider my feelings."

"And now?" I asked. "Now do you think I do?"

She nodded. "I know how much you love me."

"I'm glad." I pulled her into my arms. "I must say, your choice of music was impeccable."

"It was all from your favourite collection." She said. "I just took what I thought was appropriate for my cause."

"I know. I could recognise all the songs. Which is why it was rather amazing because I had never heard them in that context before. I will always think of you when I listen to them again now." I sighed.

"I love all your songs." She said. "They give me goose bumps every time, which is why I decided to use them to convey my feelings."

"You must have gone to so much length to arrange all this." I sighed.

She nodded. "It was all to make you mine, hon."

"I was always yours, sweetheart." I smiled.

"It took me a long time to plan it." She giggled. "That's what I kept doing when I lay here with that stupid cast on."

"Awe." I made a soft sigh.

"I had to make it perfect."

"Is that why you gave mom and dad their holiday?" I suddenly exclaimed.

"The eagle has landed." She giggled.

"Shut up." I slapped her bum jokingly. "Awe. That is so sweet. It must cost you so much to arrange that though."

She nodded. "It was all part of the bigger scheme." She giggled imitating me. "I wanted to give the most precious gift I had to you in a rather special way and I needed complete privacy." She said.

"What do you mean?" I asked. "You mean the dinner?"

"You are my first." She said shyly.

I looked at her as she lifted her face to look at me. Then I slowly moved and planted a long wet kiss on her lips.

"I am touched." I sighed. "Why me?"

"You are the love of my life." She exclaimed in ridicule. "Hello!"

"When did you decide or realise you loved me so much?"

"I don't know. I think it just grew on me slowly as we have gotten closer." She sighed. "The first time I noticed you as someone other than my brother was when you consoled me after my breakup. Then you showered me will all those special gifts. And then you seemed to get closer to me without any hang-ups. You love me unconditionally. And now I cannot find a sane reason for not being with you as your partner, your lover."

"You are my first too." I whispered.

"Really?" she was surprised. "What about...?"

"Just kissing and cuddling." I said. "I never let anyone past the 'first base'. I wanted it to be you the first time. I was not sure it would be, but surely hoped. Since your break up you never really dated anyone so I kept the hope alive. I did not know if I had a chance, it was a remote possibility. But I wanted to take a chance and save myself for you, just in case."

"I'm glad we think so much alike." She said.

"Is that why last night you felt the sharp pain...?" I recalled.

She nodded coyly. "I was expecting some pain, but that was a bit more than I had expected. Fortunately I haven't bled much."

"I'm sorry. If only you had told me, I would have been gentler." I apologised.

"You can't rip it by being gentle." She giggled. "There has to be some pain to get some gain silly. And now it is done, I can look forward to more loving times with you."

"I would have preferred you had the pleasure without the pain." I murmured.

"For us women, some pain is pleasurable." She winked at me.

"So you won't feel pain now that is over and done with?"

"Well, it will need a few days to heal." She said very coyly. "It is still sore."

"Awe. I wish I could kiss it better." I said nudging her innocently (no pun intended).

"You can if you want to," came her delighted reply.

I realised what I had said. "Really?" I was surprised.

"Baby it's a whole new future for us now."

"What do you mean?" I was perplexed.

"Rather than me explain it to you, why don't we just explore it together and find out. Now we don't have to hold back or take things slowly, just take them one at a time." She grinned raising her eyebrow at me.

"Uuu, I love the sound of that." I was delighted. "You know me. I'm game whatever you say."

"I know, hon. That is what makes me love you so much."

We looked at each other for a while.

"I have always loved you all my life. But I guess the shade or hue of the colour of my love has changed as we have come closer." I said looking into the emptiness. "That's why I think I never really batted an eye for how we have arrived at this moment in our life. For me this is just another colour of my love for you."

"And I was never sure of which colour our love should or meant to be." She said. "I always loved you the way you loved me, but the changing shades and hues kept confusing me." She interpreted my analogy. "Now you know why I was so confused and in two minds about you all this time."

"I guess I never really thought like that." I acknowledged.

"Einstein." She stuck her tongue out.

I looked at her. I caressed her face and cupped her cheek gazing deep in her warm sensual eyes. "I don't know much, but I know I love you. And that may be all I need to know." I softly hummed the lyrics.

"Oh kill me now." She dropped her head burying it in my neck melting at my words. "You are killing me." She waited for a moment and then with blushed red face she raised her eyes and looked at me with deep love. "There is nothing I wouldn't do for you!" she said. "Hug me, kiss me, love me. I just want to melt inside you."

We both slid down in the bed, under the duvet. She rolled on her back and I wrapped my arm under her head hugging her from around her waist with my other arm. I rolled on top of her pressing myself on her, burying her in my arms in the bed. She wrapped her arms pulling me, pressing herself inside my bear hug. I tiled my face and landed my lips on her lips.

As I parted my lips, she took my tongue and we kissed deeply with our passion let loose. Her fingers were running through my hair tenderly, as she pressed her lips with fervour and licked the life out of me. She wrapped her legs around my waist and pulled me closer from every way. We licked and sucked with our kisses for a long while.

"I have been waiting for this day all this time." She gasped pausing for breath. "I'm so going to flood you with love. I hope you don't get overwhelmed."

"Bring it on honey. I want nothing more." I purred in her ear.

"You drive me so wild." She wrapped her arms around my neck and went back to kissing me passionately. "How the hell do you manage to do that so often so easily?" she sighed as she paused for breath.

"Just as you drive me wild." I smiled back at her, touching our noses and kissing her nose gently.

"This is going to be so much better now." She exclaimed with big gleaming eyes.

"I'm glad we finally found each other." I said looking deep into her eyes. "I have got everything in life I ever wanted. You are the best gift I would have ever received."

"Same here. Anything we need to sort out, we will do it together." She sighed looking deep in my eyes.

"Hand in hand." I replied back

"A step at a time."

"Enjoying each day to its fullest."

"In sickness and in health." She stared at me with inquisitive look.

"For richer or poorer." I stared at her back confidently.

"Till death do us part." She gazed at me deep into my eyes.

"I do." I looked at her, with sincere stare.

"I so do too." She kissed me deeply. I returned her love by kissing her deeply.

Chapter 13 – making up

We had decided to spend all day together as we had missed each other on and off during the week. We decided to drive down to the next city so there was less chance of raising any eyebrows in case some acquaintance saw us.

Before we went out, she decided to clear the table in the kitchen from the previous night.

"I've put the food away," I said. "We will clear the rest when we get back. Don't worry. I will help you too." I assured her.

I asked her to pick out what she wanted me to wear. She smiled and got out a nice t-shirt and some pale blue jeans. I chose for her a sleeveless dress with a generous V-neck, and soft frills that stopped just above her knees. She did her hair in a loose thick multiple plats weaving together her hair and letting the rest fall naturally. After she got dressed, she did a twirl for me. I used to be just amazed on how sensual she looked in the simple ways.

While we drove to the shopping mall, I kept gazing her from head to toe, enjoying her beauty. "You are just too easy to please," she caressed my cheek and smiled at me. "Even if I pulled a face, you'd think it was sweet." She giggled.

"You are right." I nodded. "You are just too gorgeous."

"You are just too deeply in love with me." She looked at me. "You see me through rose-tinted glasses."

I just looked at her.

"I am scared of what will happen when those glasses come off eventually." She had said as a matter-of-fact.

"I may be madly in love with you, but I see you as you are." I made sure she realised my conviction.

"I do hope so, hon." She gently squeezed my hand. "I couldn't live without your love, you know that. Not now."

"Neither will I." I looked at her with deep gazing eyes.

When we parked at the mall, we were like two lovebirds without a care in the world. She took my hand in her and we walked in, strolling around the shopping galleries.

As we came to a clothing store, she pulled me to a display and pointed at some dresses on the mannequins. As we stood there close to each other, she let go of my hand and wrapped her hand around my waist pulling me closer. I wrapped my arm around her back pulling her closer to me.

We stood there looking at the dresses and she looked at me. "What do you think?"

"They are nice. But I like that one better." I pointed to one with a V-neck and low back.

She smiled at me and kissed my cheek. "Come on then, let me try it on for you."

We stepped in the store and walked to the area where we could see the dress on the rack. She browsed through and got a size she felt would fit her. Then while we were looking around, I glanced around and saw a few more I liked.

"I have a nice pair of jeans to go with that top," she said looking at one top I selected for her.

As I held on to the hangers, we traipsed around the store looking at some more I liked.

Our clothes shopping had come down to this as usual – she shopped for my clothes and I shopped for her. We both just chose the right size ourselves.

As we looked around, we walked into the lingerie and nightwear section. I saw nightwear and looked at her. She realised what was on my mind.

"See anything you like?" She whispered in my ear softly as we walked hand in hand.

"I know what I like but I ain't seeing it here." I replied looking around.

"What do you like?" she inquired.

"I won't be able to tell you, I can point it to you if I saw it." I said sheepishly.

"That's no good hon. I think we need to educate you in women's nightwear today." She giggled. "Come with me. I will show you some of the hot stuff and see if you catch on." She winked at me.

I paid for our shopping and while carrying the bag in one hand, I held her hand with my other as she led me through the shopping mall.

"Remind me when we get back, we need a joint account now." She smiled at me with warmth in her eyes.

I just cuddled her in my arms and kissed her lovingly.

We entered a shop dedicated to sleepwear and lingerie. I just looked around.

"Heaven." I murmured.

She giggled. "Come on. I will show you some stuff. Now pay attention." She poked me in the stomach.

I saw some nice sensual nightwear for her. "I love this." I exclaimed softly.

"Yeah." She said looking at it and felt the texture. "It is soft."

She took out a hanger for her size. "This is a night dress." She pointed out.

"This is a night vest." She pointed to one on a different rack.

I looked at them. "Night dress is a long t-shirt that ends below the bum." I tried to summarise.

"Usually narrow around the bum. Vest has half sleeves while dress has full." She clarified.

"Which one do you prefer?" I asked her.

"It's your choice that counts, remember?" she gazed at me coyly.

"I want you to feel comfy too." I whispered caringly.

"The dress is good in winter and the vest is good in summer." She pointed out. "Otherwise they are the same."

"I like how it ends up just below your bum." My eyes glowed as she held it against herself. "It makes me wonder if you are wearing any panties."

"That kind of knowledge can be abused." She smiled and flicked her eyebrow.

"Tee is a short version of night vest similar to a normal t-shirt." She added pointing to a rack. "For that reason, you have to wear either a pj or shorts under it."

I just looked at it uninterested, as it did not appeal to my taste. "Too much material on the bottom," I smiled.

"They are good to wear around the house when our parents are around." She said to me looking at my eyes. "If you chose some, at least I would be wearing the ones you like."

"We will see to it later." I just said nonchalantly. "What else?" I looked around.

"These are night shirts." She pointed out.

"It is ordinary full shirt past the bum." I said. "You could be wearing mine if you wanted."

"I have." She smiled at me with gleaming eyes.

"Have you?" I was surprised.

She winked and smiled at me. "Remember your blue one? The one you like? I wore that one for a morning once and slipped it back in your closet." She said. "I had missed you too much the day before."

"You are so naughty." I was surprised. "Now I remember, I smelled your fragrance all over me all day and did not really understand how. I felt so horny all day, I could hardly focus."

"I know." She smiled. "The way you kissed me and squeezed me at night made it worthwhile." She flicked her eyebrow at me with a sly smile.

"You are so naughty." I grabbed her at the waist and hugged her trying to tickle her. She let out a girly squeal and giggled. When we noticed some of the other customers glance at us with smiles we straightened and composed ourselves. She glared at me with a 'behave' expression. I loved the little play-fights we used to have between us. It made me feel so close to her.

As we continued to browse through the store, I pointed out to another nightwear.

"This is a chemise." She whispered. "That one is a slip." She pointed to another in a different rack.

I just looked at them. "Which one feels better?" I was perplexed. "They look the same."

She shook her head in exasperation. "Men." She giggled. "This one fits close to the body and has a better fit for the bust than the slip. That one, the slip, is loose and doesn't really provide support." She gestured at her boobs to indicate supporting them from the bottom.

"At night wouldn't you want to sleep easy?" I questioned. "I would think all the tightness around the bust would feel rather uncomfortable."

She shook her head. "It's not that uncomfortable. In fact, many women like the support. Moreover, it's not all about comfort; we also like to look sexy." She shook her head at my limited understanding about women.

"Forget that." I whispered. "At night I want to feel comfy. Hell if I have to wear something uncomfortable just to look sexy." I rolled my eyes.

"What if I like seeing you sexy?" she said with her sensual eyes.

"I'm just glad you haven't asked me to wear anything like that then." I looked at her.

"I wouldn't ask you to, hon. You are sexy enough for me to rip you naked as it is." She giggled.

"And so are you." I gazed at her sincerely. "I would never ask of you to do anything you aren't comfy about. You know that. Nor should you feel obligated or even enticed into doing something like that just for my sake."

She just looked at me. "And just by saying things like that you make me go weak in my knees and I want to please you even more."

I smiled at her and caressed her cheek. "As long as I have your love, I don't need anything else."

When I was looking at some of these nightwear, she came up by my side and whispered in my ear softly, "the problem with these is I can't wear them in the house usually when mom and dad are around." I looked at her. "They would find this a bit too revealing."

I understood what she meant.

"This is good only when we are together alone. At the moment that is not a lot of times." She gazed at me.

"At the moment?" I was perplexed. "Something you haven't told me yet?" I was expecting some elaboration.

"Well something is cooking, you will see." She smiled. "But I too love them all. I would love to wear them for you." She said with a sensual smile.

"So...," I wanted to know what these were and I pointed to each one at a time as she told me what they were, "Chemise, Slip, Camisole, Babydoll."

I nodded my head. "I like this one." I flicked my eyebrows at her with a glowing smile.

"I can see why." She giggled. "Tell you what, let's buy one of each just for now so you at least get to see me wearing them." She tried to appease me.

My eyes glowed with excitement.

"So easy to please." She caressed my face and planted a quick kiss on my cheek.

I was muttering to myself now as she went to try them out.

'Chemise is a straight top that comes to the thighs and has a 'bra' fitting. Cami is a short chemise ending at waist. Babydoll is similar to chemise but fits more snugly at the bust and ends shorter and flared at the hip. Slip is similar to chemise but without a bra fitting.' I made a mental note to myself.

'No wonder we (men) are so confused.' I thought to myself. 'We have two styles – boxer and brief. End of! Here I have to memorise a whole wardrobe just for nightwear. Damn!'

She came out with a glowing smile looking at me. I looked at her with a query on my face.

"What is this then?" I pointed to something on the rack.

"This is a playsuit or Teddy." She smiled.

"It looks like it can't make its mind up," I smiled. "It's like a slip but is one piece like dungaree and some elastic fit at the waist." I remarked.

She giggled. "Well spotted." She admired my increased vocabulary. "It is for convenience, but I think you won't like it." She shook her head. "You like easy access."

I looked at it as she moved her hand underneath to illustrate her justification.

"Ah." I realised and agreed sheepishly.

She raised her eyebrows at me in gratitude. "I know you well now."

"You are right." I nodded. "No good for my wandering hands."

"They may not be good as nightwear but they make for excellent sensual casual wear for the day." She gleamed her eyes at me. "You can see now what I mean."

I stared at her holding it against her and then turning around holding it against her back.

"I can see what you mean." I tried imagining her in it.

"Particularly with thongs, the bum looks really nice if the dress material is sheer like this." She added indicating the thin material on the teddy she was holding up.

"O man." I became breathless. "That will certainly kill me." I blushed out red in my face.

She giggled at my expressions of desires.

"Come on then. Let's pay for these." She took my hand and handed me the hangers.

When I was paying for them, the girl at the counter smiled at Sam and said softly, "This is a fine treat indeed."

Sam looked at her, hugged me close and said teasingly, "It's a treat for him. And he deserves every bit." She gently kissed me on my cheek pulling me close. I blushed and hugged Sam in response.

After the payment was done, the girl blushed and handed me the bag and the receipt. "Hope you guys enjoy the rest of the day. Thank you for shopping with us."

"Shall I put them in the car for now?" I asked Sam as we stepped out of the store.

Sam nodded. "If you wish."

"Wait here and I will be right back." I suggested after kissing her forehead as we were standing close to each other.

"Na a." She shook her head. "I'm coming too." She took my hand and we started walking to the car.

"I love to hang out with you." She whispered to me pressing herself close to me. "Why would I hang about alone?"

"It is a fair bit of walk to the car and back." I was just softly putting my perspective across. "I did not want you walking unnecessary."

"I'd walk to the ends of the earth with you." She whispered and looked at me.

I just smiled looking at her gleaming eyes. "I love you."

"And so you should...." She was in a very teasing mood. "...for someone who would walk such long distances with you."

After we had walked back, we decided to have some lunch and then catch a nice movie. We chose a nice restaurant and sat in a semi-circular couch. While we were having lunch, we kept glancing into each other's eyes. We were sitting next to each other on the couch. She grinned, played footie under the table and ran her hand on my thigh. We fed each other some spoonfuls of our meals. As we both liked each other's meal choice, we fed each other spoonfuls on and off. As we were sitting close to each other, that came naturally.

When the waiter had taken away our empty dishes, she leaned forward with her elbows on the table and slightly turned toward me and was looking at me. I kept stroking her back gently, following her long hair and feeling its silken caress. Since she had tender curves, I loved feeling her all over when I caressed her.

"I am not a baby." She said to me with a grin on her face slightly tilting her head in a rather girlish way. "You don't need to burp me."

"Shut up." I gently pushed her away for taking the piss out of my gentle caress.

She giggled softly. "I'm sorry." She apologised coming closer and kissing my cheeks. "I'm just pulling your leg hon."

I crossed my arms and held my hands away from her pretending to be cross.

"I'm sorry hon." She stroked my cheek pulling my face toward her. "You know I was just kidding." She smiled. She ran her fingers through my hair on the back of my head and gazed sensually in my eyes.

I looked at her with a pretend sulk. I loved these pretend sulks and her attempts to appease me.

She leaned into me, brought her lips close to me and looking deep into my eyes whispered, "Kiss me."

I could never say no to her anyway, so I leaned and planted a soft long kiss on her lips, parting my lips and letting our tongues lick each other.

"Now that is called a dessert." She said. "Um um." She licked her lips.

"I am so hard right now." I whispered to her.

She reached down and gently ran her hand on the bulge in my jeans. She gently gasped biting her bottom lip gently. "Is it the movie next?" She giggled.

My heart skipped a beat.

We skipped the desserts and went to the movie theatre. She bought the tickets and I got us a 3-scoop ice cream tub. When we entered the cinema, we selected two seats aloof in the back row. When we settled in the seat, she fed each other the ice cream in between kisses.

Then the lights dimmed, the adverts and previews came on. She lifted the hand rest between us and propped it away at the back. Then she turned and scooted into my arms and slouched slightly as I wrapped her in my hug. She sat reclining on my chest with my arm around her tummy. There were hardly any others in the cinema so we had fair bit of privacy for ourselves.

She then pulled her cardigan on top of her, covering my wandering hands. I let my hands wander on her tummy and boobs while gently circling down to her thighs. She parted her legs slightly and let me carry on caressing her. She held my other hand on her boob. This carried on for a while as she enjoyed my caresses.

After a while she whispered, "I want to show you something."

While she pushed her head against me, she raised her bum slightly off her seat, flipped her dress up from the sides, tucked her thumbs up the hem, pulled down her panties to her thighs and sat back down. Then in single sweep, she pulled her panties down her legs as she bent her legs at the knees, pulling them closer to her and slouched back in my hug. Then she handed me the panties and whispered, "I've been dripping wet all day, thanx to you."

I took the panties and felt the moist fabric with her feminine fragrance. My eyes gleamed with pleasure and pride.

She looked at me and looked down to her thighs parting them slightly. "That is what you do to me." She tilted her head, gazed toward her hem and looked at me. I felt her hand on mine and she guided it between her thighs.

I slid my hand gently under her dress. My heart gasped at the wetness I felt on my fingers as I touched her between her thighs. As I slipped my finger, she parted her legs slightly, and I could feel the wetness on the tips as it slipped effortlessly.

When she felt my finger touch her spot, she gasped and threw her head back into my shoulder, and pressed my hand deeper into her thighs. She turned and buried her face under my chin in my neck. "I'm so desperate for you to finger me." She sighed. "I can't take it anymore. Please, make me cum."

Her words lit my fingers like a magic wand. I caressed her arm with my other hand as I slowly and gently rubbed her clit in slow circles. Her breathing got progressively deeper and she buried her face deep in my neck.

I slowly and gently rubbed her clit, sliding past it on her labia, getting little deeper between the wet lips and rubbing my finger all the way as I slid up and down. Occasionally, I slipped it inside just a little to feel her wetness inside. I was being careful not to slide inside too deep; I was aware she was sore from the previous night.

I went back to rubbing and massaging her clit.

As she got nearer to the orgasm, she pulled my lips on hers and kissed me deep to stop her from moaning loudly and she shuddered a few times as she came on my finger.

As she calmed into my hug, she relaxed and then slumped in my arms kissing me passionately on my lips a few times. She looked deep in my eyes. As the previews rolled on, I gazed at her drunken pleasure she had enjoyed at my fingertips.

"You take my breath away, in every sense." She said.

As she settled in my arms she wrapped herself in my hug.

"When you need me, you just let me know." She whispered as she stroked my bulge.

I kissed her. "I will have you in our bed when we get back."

"I can't wait to get back." She turned around and kissed me passionately with hungry licks.

We decided we would enjoy the movie and then head home. When the titles rolled on, we hugged each other and calmed ourselves for the duration.

After the movie ended, as we came out of the movie theatre, we headed to the parking. We went past a jewellery store and she suddenly stopped us.

"I want to get something," she said softly.

"Like what?" I asked.

She just pulled me into the store. "Just come along and I will tell you."

"An engagement ring." She whispered pointing at a collection in the window.

"Why?" I was surprised.

"I don't want any male attention now that I have got yours." She smiled coyly. "It would signal that I am taken."

I was speechless. "Really?" I stopped walking for a moment, pulling her into my arms.

She nodded with a feminine shyness, staring me sensually in my eyes. "I don't want to be bothered by anyone anymore. And anyway, I am yours technically now that we have shared our vows."

I gently planted a quick kiss and stepped inside the store.

"This one's on me." I said. "Just pick one that you like."

"No silly. You need to choose it. It is meant to be your ring and I would be wearing it." She smiled.

"Ok." I smiled. "If you say so."

I looked around and saw a beautiful solitaire gold zircon diamond ring in a classic 6-point clasp. I signalled her to check it out.

"Hon." She gasped. "That is a bit pricy isn't it?"

"Don't worry about that." I pressed her. "Just tell me if you like it."

She nodded with a gleaming smile. The lady at the counter got a ring for Sam's size.

When Sam tried it on, she looked at me with gleaming eyes admiring the ring lovingly.

"It even has facility to engrave it." I smiled.

"What would you like to engrave on it?" she asked me.

I thought about it for a while. 'I AM URS' I said. "How about that? It has 1-2-3 characters in its 3 words"

She paused for a thought. Then she used her fingers to count in her mind.

"How about 'I AM ALL YOURS'?" she suggested. "It has the word ALL in it which I like and it follows the Fibonacci series 1-2-3-5."

"How is that significant?" I asked her reasoning.

"Fibonacci series is encoded in nature everywhere." She elaborated showing off her intelligence. "And I would like to think ALL of me is yours." She said.

"I would wonder if all those words would fit there." I looked at her sceptically.

"Let's ask them." She pointed at the lady behind the counter.

"That would be a little too long." The lady said.

Sam looked at me for a solution. Then she came up with "How about 'I AM HIS'," she suggested.

I took a moment and then just smiled widely. "You are really something."

She looked at the lady and said, "That's it. I would like that ring with the engraving 'I AM HIS' please."

The lady was perplexed about the phrase but we both knew exactly what it meant.

We paid for the ring and as the lady took the ring inside for the engraving, we waited looking around.

"I would like to have something from you too," I whispered to her.

"A ring on your finger would attract a lot of curious looks, hon." She said softly. "We don't want that. Girls wear rings all the time so it can be looked as casual jewellery." She smiled.

"What do you suggest then?" I was keen about it.

"How about a pendant?" she suggested. "A split-heart pendant. You can wear one piece and I will wear the other. So appropriate." She said.

"And we can get it engraved too." I pointed out one design suitable for it.

"What would you like on it?" she said.

I thought for a while. "I was thinking, why don't you create something original and different." I smiled.

I asked the lady for a pen and paper. Then Sam wrote the engraving on it as it was meant to look, including the split in the middle:

When I looked at it, I smiled and hugged her gently. "You are truly something hon." I kissed her softly. "I love it."

I asked the lady about the pendant and she went and checked for us for the engraving.

"Is it ok if we arranged it in a font that would fit the words on each part?" she asked.

We both agreed.

Sam also saw another pendant that she liked. It was a small old key pendant. I was perplexed about it and wanted her to elaborate.

"Only you hold the key to my heart." She said in my ear.

I smiled at her creativity. I purchased that pendant too.

As we waited for the engraving, I went to pay for them.

Sam pulled me back. "I will pay for the pendants. You paid for the ring." She smiled.

I complied with a smile.

When they were ready, we got them packed and left the place. Then we headed home.

Chapter 14 – getting up-close

The drive home was one of the longest. She had held out her hand so I could hold it for the whole journey back. She had been restraining herself from getting too intimate while I drove ever since the accident. I had slowly gotten over it as I had responded to her touch and encouraged her to be tactile like she always had been. After all, I could never keep myself away from her sensual and tender caress.

When we got home, we locked our front door, and ran upstairs. It was late evening and we went straight to her bedroom. I dropped all the shopping in my room.

"Put the ring on my finger." She said excitedly to me when we were in the bedroom.

I smiled and opened the box and slid the ring slowly on her finger. She looked at it and her eyes gleamed with gratitude.

"This says to the world, I'm taken. Now I am all yours." She said sensually looking deep in my eyes. "Only yours."

"And only I hold the key to your heart." I smiled back putting on the key pendant.

Then we split the heart pendant and each of us wore one part.

We hugged and kissed holding each other in a cuddle.

"I would like a bath together." She said looking at me.

"Deal." I smiled back to her. "I'll run the bath."

"I'll get the stereo and the candles." She exclaimed.

I got into the bathroom and let the hot water run in the bath after I plugged it shut. I emptied a generous amount of bath gel in the water.

She came in with the stereo and some candles. She lit them one by one and placed them around. Then she turned off the lights in the bathroom. It was flooded with soft candlelight. She plugged in the stereo.

"Play the list you had on last night for the dinner." I requested her.

She looked at me with a puzzled look.

"This time, I want us to enjoy it without you being tearful." I said softly.

She smiled coyly, set the playlist and pressed play.

I took her in my arms and we kissed each other slowly and deeply. I wrapped her in my arms gently squeezing her, with my arms running all over her back and bum.

"I so want to blend into you right now. Just squeeze into you and become one." She said. "I love your bear hugs. I cannot get enough of it." She kept pulling me tight and pressing herself into my arms.

"I can't get enough of you." I sighed.

As we kissed deep and long, I felt her hands wander and unzip my jeans. They had been locking my erection for all day. Then she loosened the jeans and let it fall to the floor. Then I felt her fingers gently dig in my underwear on my waist and slide it past my hips. I gently moved my hands and unzipped her dress at the back. As she stepped back, she let it slide off her shoulders. Then she unclasped her bra from the back and let it slide off her shoulders. I lifted my t-shirt over my head and let it drop.

We were standing there staring at each other naked. The music was playing in the background. My favourite songs now seem so much better with her smiling all along.

I leaned down and checked the bath temperature. The bubbles had covered the bath all over. When I turned the tap off, I looked at her, stepping in the bath slowly. I lowered myself at one end, leaned back and settled in the bath.

"Oh wow, it's nice and hot." I exclaimed as the water warmed me up.

She held out her hand and I helped her step in the bath. As she turned to sit down, I stretched my legs and parted my knees. Then she lowered herself down between my legs holding on to the bath.

"Ah." She gasped as the hot water warmed her up.

I gently wrapped her in my arms as she settled in my hug and lay on me with her back pressed against my chest. As we settled in, the bathroom filled with the soft music playing in the background.

I slowly ran my hands all over her chest, bosoms and tummy. The soap was sticking all over her face and hair. She placed her hands on mine and stroked them gently to encourage me. She intertwined our fingers together and wrapped herself in my arms tightly. I interlocked our legs and pulled them close, bending them at the knees. I cuddled her in my hug, like a love cocoon.

We lay still for a while. Our passion was surpassing the heat from the water.

She turned around slightly to press her cheek against mine. When I felt her lips so close to mine, I turned her face and landed my lips on her, planting them with deep hunger.

She had melted in my arms a while ago any way, but now she felt limp in my hug as she let me kiss and lick her as I pleased. As I kissed her, I was running my hands all over her, caressing her thighs, her labia, her bosoms and all the while licking and sucking on her lips and tongue. She gasped as she paused for breath. She lay back in my arms as she wrapped herself in my hug. Her face was flush red and she was very drowsy.

"You are killing me with your passion." She sighed. "How the hell are you so good at making me so desperate for you!" She lay there for a while just trying to calm down.

Then when she had composed herself, she turned around and sat facing me. I got her legs over mine and pulled her pelvis slowly toward me. As we bent our knees we could get closer to each other.

The bubbles were sticking all over her chin and cheeks. She looked so cute.

I just stared at her. Then she moved closer to me and kissed me softly on my nose. Then she looked at me and coming closer, kissed me on my eyelids one after the other, gently. Then she kissed my forehead. Then she kissed both of my cheeks. Then she looked at me for a while, with deep desire. Then she guided me to move closer to her.

She wrapped her legs around my waist and propped herself on my lap and asked me to cross my legs. As she settled in between my lap within my crossed legs, she wrapped her legs around my hips, looked at me deeply, slowly wrapped her arms around my neck and lowered her lips on mine, sealing them in a long, gentle kiss. I wrapped her in a tight bear hug, pulling her into my arms, wrapping her waist tightly, running my hands all over her back.

All the while, she was kissing my lips with such hunger that I could feel her lips suck the life out of me. She was running her fingers through my hair, and gently grinding her pelvis on my erection as she kissed and licked my lips and tongue. Her long hair were now wet and stuck to her back. I could feel her boobs press on my chest.

She gasped for breath as she paused her kisses, and while propping herself up on her knees, she wrapped her arms around my neck and she pressed my face on her bosom. I lowered my lips and kissed her boob one by one, licking her nipples and sucking them gently. She moaned and threw her head back as she arched gently. I held onto her waist and let her lean back a little.

"I don't ever want you to stop loving me." She was welling up. "I couldn't live without your love, not now."

I guess the music was making her emotional again.

"I ain't going anywhere." I sighed in her ear. "I'm all yours, to have as you please, when you please."

"Oh god." She moaned. "You are making me so warm inside talking like that."

She broke out of her hug and taking my face in her palms looked deep in my eyes. I could she her eyes were wet.

"I still keep thinking this is a dream and I am going to wake up in a nightmare." She sighed. "I imagined this so many times in my mind that it is hard to believe it is actually happening."

I pinched her slowly on her bum until she groaned softly.

"There." I said with a grin. "This isn't a dream. It is as real as it gets."

"That hurt." She whimpered very sensually. "Caress it better then." She urged me while she kissed me softly.

I ran my fingers on her bum where I had pinched her. Then as she lifted herself from my lap slightly, I ran my hands on her bum, stroked her inner thighs and then ran my fingers between them, closer to her mound.

She realised and parted her thighs to let me caress her more as she wrapped herself in my hug. When she felt my fingers run on her labia, her breath got heavy and she gasped, throwing her head back and moaned deeply, "Oh fuck."

Then she slowly brought her head forward again and looked at me with drunken eyes and shook her head and said, "Take your sweet time."

I slowly ran my fingers on her labia, playing, teasing and spreading them as I rubbed them gently. Her breathing told me she was in a universe of bliss and did not want to leave that place. Surrendering herself in my arms, she couldn't even think straight of kissing me as she just propped herself there moaning and gasping enjoying my touch and caress.

She took my face and again buried it in her bosoms, and kept running her fingers through my hair. All the while she gasped and kept repeating, "I love you."

I felt her spasm a couple of times and I paused while she recovered, but continued to finger her gently and slowly rubbing her clit and labia with my fingers.

She loosened her hug, took my face in her hands and pressed her forehead on mine as she looked at me. I saw her face flushed red from the hot water and orgasms, and she looked drunk from the pleasure I had given her.

"As much as I love you, I need you to stop." She gasped. "I cannot take it anymore."

She collapsed in my arms. "I need some time to recover."

As she lay limp in my arms, I was concerned so I asked her, "You ok?" I had to hold her up as she had lost all strength to prop herself on my lap.

"Just need a minute, hon." She gasped slowly. She looked totally drunk.

I held her in my arms as she lay limp in my hug for a while. She had rested her face on my shoulder as she stayed in my hug. She had her arms around my neck but they dangled loosely on my back. Then I felt her arm gently move to hug my neck and take my head in her arms tenderly. Her cheek was pressed on mine as she had rested her chin on my shoulder.

The music was still rolling in the background as the bathroom was filled with the soft music.

Then she slowly sat up. She slouched in my lap now and I held her in my arms. She looked at me with blissful eyes, drunk with love.

"Never did I ever imagine I would have to tell you to stop pleasuring me." She smiled at me. "But I couldn't take it anymore. I had to stop you." She smiled again.

"So you enjoyed it then." I smiled being pleased about my abilities.

She just grinned with obvious pleasure.

As she regained her composure, she slowly leaned back and floated on the water with her head thrown back. The bubbles circled around her face and I held her waist to prop her head above water. She was still regaining from her intense orgasms.

She slowly regained her composure, sat up slowly, straddled on my lap again as I moved my legs and placed her into my hug. She kept looking at me, inspecting every little detail on my face and gazing deep in my eyes with sensual warmth. I realised she was speechless. Our thoughts had gone telepathic for that moment.

"Can I ask you something?" I decided to break the silence.

She simply nodded slowly.

"Why did you arrange last night the way you did?" I asked her softly. "I still don't understand why you did it that way."

She looked at me for a while, gazing all over my eyes and then kissed me sensually.

After she pulled away, she softly spoke, "Why do you want to know?"

"I want to know." I said persistently. I was still hugging her gently.

"Promise you won't get mad or upset with me?" She said in my ear as she hugged me. "I won't be able to deal with that right now as I am totally drunk with your love at the moment."

"That is not at all why I'm asking you." I assured her. "I won't get upset. I just want to know why you did it the way you did. That's all. We have not talked about it since we had our misunderstanding in the morning. So I want to know the real gist behind all of it."

I caressed her to reassure her.

She looked at me. "Ok then."

She took a deep breath and started speaking.

"As you know we have always been close as twins, but I fell for you over the past few years when I knew I shouldn't had. And I did not know in what way I had fallen either. As you know, we have always had a very grey area between us regarding feelings of love. So I did not know how you felt about me and if you felt the same." She continued speaking slowly. "I did know you loved me. There was no doubt about that. But not if you loved me like I loved you."

"The feelings were bubbling up inside and were killing me because I couldn't share them with you. I did not want to risk messing what we had. I love you more than life itself anyway. On top of that, I had started falling for you, and I mean physically. Now you know in what way." She was feeling emotional.

"I wanted to tell you how I felt. But then I knew there was a big possibility you may have rejected me or worse fallen out with me for thinking I was so perverted." She was welling up.

I held her close. "You weren't perverted. Don't cry. It kills me to see you in tears." I held her reassuringly as she calmed herself.

She composed herself and continued speaking. "I could never have been able to live with myself if I had messed our relation. I imagined all sorts of horrors about me opening up to you. I would lose you, mom and dad. It was just a horrible thought." Tears rolled down her cheeks. I just held her close to soothe her.

"But several times I tried keeping it to myself, and I felt more miserable. You kept loving me deeper and we kept getting closer and I was a complete mess all that time. I felt your love and yet I was not sure if I should tell you how I felt." She was composing herself now as she gasped her breath.

"During my recovery, you took such good care of me, that I felt guiltier of ruining things with you." She welled up again. "You are the most decent man I have ever seen in my whole life." She looked straight in my eyes and her eyes welled up. "I would have never ever forgiven myself if I had done anything to belittle your decency. You are the most perfect gentleman a girl could ever wish for. And all I wanted to do was to open up my heart so I could actually enjoy loving you." Tears were rolling down her cheeks. I tried to brush her tears away gently caressing her back. I was welling up looking at her in tears.

Looking at me she continued speaking softly, "I wanted to tell you about my feelings for you, so IF there was even a slight chance that you even remotely understood my feelings, I would had felt so much better. I wanted to love you, physically, mentally, emotionally, spiritually from the bottom of my heart in every way I could think." She looked at me deep in my eyes. "Not being able to do so was killing me inside." She ran her hands all over my face looking at me as she waited for my response.

"Why did you use the songs and not speak to me outright?" I spoke when she went silent.

She looked at me.

"I thought of a million ways to say it to you. I couldn't find the right words. Every time I thought of saying anything, I imagined it going south and ending up in a messy argument. That is why I decided to let the songs do it for me. They were all your favourite songs anyway so I decided to leave my fate to them." She looked at me. "At least that way you would have heard it from your favourites so there was a chance you wouldn't get so upset with me." She looked at me sheepishly.

"Then when you gave me the voucher...." she smiled, after a long while of being tearful. "...that was like a gift heaven-sent. At least with it, I had some way to make you listen to me before you wanted to say anything. At least then, I could give myself to you as your special gift and take a chance for you not to reject me. And even if you had been cross with me later, I would have given you the gift I was treasuring for you for so long."

She smiled at me. "Before you gave me that voucher, I was a total wreck because all I kept imagining was you falling out with me half way into the dinner or in bed."

When she had stopped speaking, I looked at her and I could feel just how much she loved me and wanted me. "Oh honey, if only you had some confidence in my feelings for you, you would have saved yourself so much heartache." I hugged her tightly. "It kills me knowing you went through so much pain for me."

I looked at her with wet eyes. She was shocked to see me so emotional. She took my face in her palms and slowly wiped my tears away. "Shh. There is no need for this now. We both know how much we love each other. That is all that matters." She kissed my lips caressing my cheeks, brushing my tears away.

We stayed there for a while and felt each other's arms wrap us together in a love hug.

"I think we should get into bed." She whispered to me. "I want to feel you wrap me in your bear hug."

"Ok." I looked at her. "We are like prunes now." I giggled showing her my fingers.

"I wonder which fluids did that." She winked at me.

She kissed me a few times before gently opening her legs from around my waist. I helped her to stand up and step out of the bath.

I pulled the plug and let the water drain out.

"Dry your hair." I said to her. "I don't want you catching a cold."

She grinned at me and kissed me. "You are so thoughtful."

"You know I'm right." I pointed it out to her.

"I never said you weren't." She narrowed her eyes in sarcasm.

As she dried her hair in the towel, we walked into her bedroom. I took the candles into her room. She entered the bedroom with the stereo and plugged it in her surround system. She wrapped me in a towel and started to dry me gently. I stood there looking at her as she enjoyed taking her time running her hands all over me.

She kneeled down, dried my legs and all the while was staring at my erection. She glanced up at me, smiled and then lowered her gaze at my erection again as she continued drying me with the towel. As she ran the towel gently around it, she padded it while cupping it in her hands softly. As she stood up, she dried my hair and handed me the towel to dry it. She then got her hairdryer and started drying her hair. The loud uproar of the drier seemed to shatter the soft sensual trickles of music that had filled the room.

I sat on the bed and watched her dry her long hair. She was standing naked in front of the mirror. From where I was sitting, she had her back to me, and I could see her front in the reflection off the mirror. As she dried her hair, I could feast my eyes on her sensual beauty. She kept glancing at me noticing my hungry eyes devouring her nakedness, her sensuality. After a while, she cocked her head to get me close to her. As I walked to her, she looked at my hair and then started drying it with her hair drier while running her fingers through it.

"If I get to dry my hair, so does my honey." She muttered to herself. "He is just as special."

I held on her waist as I let her dry my hair. The hot air felt tantalising while I was feasting my eyes on her naked bosoms. When her eyes met mine, she blushed slightly and then looked away and continued drying my hair. As she blew the air on the back of my head while standing in front of me, I took the cue and gently hugged her and lay my chin on her shoulder as I wrapped her.

She simply moved into my arms, letting me hug her as she continued running her hand through my hair while blow-drying it with the other hand. I ran my hands all over her naked back, pressing her pelvis on my erection. She sighed when she felt my hardness press on her soft mound. I kissed her neck planting wet kisses and heard her moan softly.

I ran my fingers through her dry and soft hair. It now swayed softly on her back in contrast to when it was wet before. I ran my fingers through it and caressed it running my hands on it all over her back. Feeling my arousal, she turned off the dryer placing it on the table, wrapped her arms and hugged me tightly, pressing herself in my hug against my bare skin. She loved to soak the warm sensual feel of our skins touching and caressing each other.

After we paused for breath from kissing, she sighed, "Take me to bed."

I picked her up in my arms gently and carried her to the bed. As I lowered her, she reached out and flicked away the duvet as I gently laid her in the bed. Then she got under it, and held out her hand to get me in with her.

I slipped under the duvet and she lay on her back, arms stretched out, waiting for me to hug her.

Chapter 15 – pleasing and pleasuring

The music had rolled along. Its sensuality had fuelled our passion and hunger just as deep as last night except tonight we both were enjoying the bliss with full content.

I began kissing her slowly running my hands all over her body. She held my arms and let me kiss her deep in her mouth. Then I lowered my lips on her chin and her neck as she tilted her head back and opened herself to me. I kissed her neck and gently carried down kissing her chest. Then I kissed her bosoms and caressed them in my hand. As I planted soft wet kisses on them, she moaned and ran her fingers through my hair.

Then I sucked on her nipples one by one. She let out a deep moan as she arched her back. As I continued to kiss her on her chest, I planted wet kisses on her tummy. Then she sighed as I caressed her thighs and kissed them as I carried down her legs. She looked at me and could not hold back any longer. She guided me to lie beside her.

As we lay there looking at each other, she gently caressed my face then ran her fingers around my neck and shoulders and then over my arms. She kept grazing her fingers as they caressed and ran down my arms. Then she circled her fingers around my thighs and slowly closed in on my erection. As she touched it, she sighed and dug her face in my chest kissing me in my neck. She put her hand on my erection wrapping it gently, feeling its hardness in her soft genteel hands. It flinched when I felt her warm sensual touch around it and she sighed again as she moved in closer to me for a hug, burying her face in my neck. All the while I was letting her enjoy her desire to touch me, feel me.

She slowly came up to my lips and kissed me deep as she gently rolled me over on my back. As I lay on my back, she lay beside me, propped on her elbow, looking at me deeply, running her fingers slowly around my thighs and my tummy, occasionally brushing against my erection and rolling it on my tummy, letting her hand gently slide down to caress my balls. She kept touching and caressing me casually like that for a while. She was gazing deep in my eyes.

Then she scooted a bit and kissed me on my lips and started travelling her kisses slowly down on to my neck and my chest and then my nipples. She kissed and sucked them gently running her hands on my tummy and caressing my erection occasionally.

As she continued kissing me down my navel, she slowly turned and got on her elbow now facing toward my erection with her legs gently folded next to my hips. As she slowly kissed her way past my navel, I could feel the wetness of her lips get closer to my groin. She sneaked pass the erection and travelled around it, flicking it aside as she kissed her way down the inner thighs and next to my balls. She planted soft kisses on my inner thighs, ignoring my erection. She took her time kissing me all over on my inner thighs. She shifted her bum up toward me as she positioned her mouth close to my erection. I was running my hands on her bum and thighs.

Then while stroking my thighs slowly and kissing them all over, she neared my erection and started caressing my balls. Then I felt her fingers pull my foreskin back slowly and felt her lips plant kisses gently on the head. Then she gazed at the head and stuck her tongue out and licked all around the crown slowly. Then I felt her soft fingers run all over its length, caressing it gently as she opened her lips to take more of it in her mouth.

Then I felt her lips wrap around the crown as she sucked me gently into her mouth. I gasped at her wet warm lips sucking so sensually. I raised my hips to meet her lips. She eased me, gently pressing her hand on my thighs as she continued sucking me, caressing my balls and thighs. Her tongue was now dancing around, flicking me in her mouth as her lips worked wonders on it. She traced her tongue in the groove of the crown, her lips and tongue slurping the erection like a popsicle. She could hear my breathing get rapid and she continued kissing it all over, caressing it and sucking it in turns. All the while, her fingers were caressing and massaging my balls.

As she kept at her sucking, I could feel getting close to my orgasm. "I'm gonna cum hon." I gently stroked her hair and back. She just continued on sucking just as passionately and intently. She ran her hands all over my thighs and caressed my erection and my balls encouraging me to cum.

The thought of her sucking me dry was so arousing that I could not hold back anymore. "I'm gonna cum." I sighed again. At that moment, I felt my orgasm flood and erupt in her mouth, her lips continuing to suck me, licking it while spurting in her mouth. As she felt it in her mouth, she gently pumped my balls and encouraged me to erupt, emptying me of my cream.

As I slowly calmed down, she eased her sucking and then licked my prick all over and kissed it with wet lips. Then she planted kisses all over my crotch and turning around looked at me. She brushed her hair aside as she glanced at me with a smile.

She was licking her lips as she looked at me, her face half covered with her soft hair. As she moved and lay beside me, I gently pushed her hair away from her face and I could see her eyes, warm, full of lust and now bliss. With a sweep of her hand, she flicked her hair at the back.

She reached for the water bottle at the side of her bed and had a gulp. Then she put it back and lay down in my arms hugging me closely.

She gently came close to me and kissed me. Then she looked all over me, deep in my eyes and sighed softly, "That was my first. I hope you enjoyed it."

"I loved it." I sighed, cuddling her tenderly.

She kissed me again gently. "You taste so good." She smiled coyly.

"Really?" I was amazed at her bliss.

She nodded. "It is thick but tastes nice. And it smells so organic; better than any perfume."

We both looked at each other.

"Where did that urge come from?" I asked her.

"I'm sorry." She lowered her gaze for a moment. "I couldn't stop myself. You made me lose my senses with your love. Back in the movie theatre, I pushed you to finger me. I hope you did not feel I had bulldozed you into it. But I was desperate for you and you gave me such an intense orgasm."

"You shouldn't apologise." I nudged her. "I love pleasing you."

She looked at me. "I couldn't stop myself. You make me so desperate for you at times that I lose all of my senses."

"You did not push me." I sighed looking at her. "I like that I have such effect on you."

"I wanted to lick you too. I have waited for so long. I was hesitant because I wasn't sure I would be good at it." She admitted sheepishly.

"I love everything you do." I smiled at her. "Everything. You should not hold back. On the contrary, I would like you to please yourself."

"I intend to." She sighed, laid her face on my chest, and kissed me.

"If we are on about pleasing each other, can I not lick you?" I asked her.

She looked at me with sensual eyes. "I would love you to hon...", she paused for a while and then continued, "...but I want to wake up at your lips licking me." She said. "I've always had that fantasy."

She blushed shyly. "And I cannot believe I'm saying this but you have made me cum so much, I need some rest for now." She blushed and pressed her face on my chest.

"I would love that to no end." I exclaimed. "That is a promise."

"Really?" she was surprised.

"I would love to wake you like that every day!" I whispered.

"Then I would love to fall asleep to that thought so you can wake me up later." She said as she melted in my arms.

As we slept in each other's arms, I felt a new bliss in my heart. We did not just love each other, we loved each other in the same way. We wanted each other in the same way, with same hunger and desire.

In the night, I must have woken up for some reason. I lay there realising how lucky I was to for being loved by someone like Sam. I gazed at her as she lay on my side in my arms. She seemed truly angelic, sleeping so peacefully. She had infused such peace and complacency in my heart and mind by expressing her love for me that I didn't want anything more in life. Seeing her next to me in my arms, sleeping naked and lovingly, sent my heart thumping with bliss and joy.

I had realised how some people spend a lifetime looking for love like this. In movies, I had seen so many tragedies of life and love. Given my failed attempts with some of her friends who had been too eager to 'go out with me', I had realised how difficult it was going to be for me to find true love – the kind that I wanted. For that reason, I felt myself so lucky to have been with someone like Sam who loved me the way she did, the way I liked. I had found true love, finally.

In the night she must had rolled on her back. I stirred up and looked around. She was sleeping peacefully on her back. My hand was still under her pillow so I gently slid it out. She did not stir. She must have been tired. I looked at her sleeping gently like an angel. She was indeed my angel.

As I looked at her feminine tenderness, I couldn't help but think of what she had told me earlier of her fantasy. It was just past 4am. I wanted to make her happy.

I gently moved around and positioned myself in between her thighs. She stirred a bit but drifted back to sleep in no time. Then I slowly started kissing her on her thighs and inner thighs. As I kissed her, instinctively, she moved and opened them up, parting them slightly. I could smell her vulva. She was clean-shaven just as I liked it.

I lowered my lips and planted kisses gently on her labia. As I kissed it, I could feel her legs slowly move and her pelvis react to my lips. I did not stop, I did not want to.

I continued licking her, and I gently parted her labia with my tongue sliding in between them. As I licked her, she started moving her pelvis to my kisses, her breathing got deeper. I gently parted her labia and placed my finger on her clit as I licked and flicked it with my tongue. As I did that for a while, I could feel her pelvis move in response and she was now breathing deep. When I continued licking her clit, and tickled it with my thumb, I could feel her spasms through her pelvis as she came for the first time. She sighed deeply and her hands found my hair on my head, her fingers running through them. She was beginning to stir as she enjoyed my licking. I continued fingering and licking her clit. As I licked her, I darted my tongue and planted wet kisses all over her labia and inner thighs.

Her breathing was now deep and rapid. She was writhing in the bed with pleasure. I slowly extended my left hand and caressed her boob gently as I licked and tickled her clit and vulva. Her moans had become deep and I could feel another wave of orgasm flood through her as she held on my hair and let out deep moans. She pushed her mouth in the pillow, and let out a deep moan.

I knew she was enjoying it very much and I did not want to stop. Now licking and fingering her spots, I kissed and licked her inner thighs. As I kissed and licked her, her moans had become deep and she was in a different world most probably as orgasms rippled through her body one after another. I did not stop, just slowed down for a while between each orgasm, until I felt her relax again and then I would start again.

After a few minutes, she started to sigh "Hon, I can't take it anymore. You got to stop." I took that to be her pleasure summit and continued to lick her. She came one more time again and moaned deeply, closing her thighs and pressing my head between them. She tossed and turned around in bed. I guessed it was a strong and deep one. As she calmed down, she sighed, "Hon please you got to stop." She sighed again begging me.

When she realised I was not going to stop, she lifted herself up propping on her hands, leaned forward, pulled my face in her hands closer to her lips and gently kissed me lowering on my wet lips.

"You got to stop, hon." She gasped under her breathlessness. "I've gone tender now. And I have lost count on the times you have made me cum." She was pleading me to give her time to recover.

As I lay down on her side, she collapsed and caught her breath. As she turned her head and looked at me with sleepy but blissful gaze, she sighed to me, "I don't know why I waited this long to get your lips on mine." She said. "You are one hell of a lover hon." She rolled around, cuddled into my arms and hugged me.

"So you liked that?" I asked her.

"That was beyond my wildest fantasies." She said kissing me on my lips and cheek. "I even dreamed that you were licking me before I woke up just then." She smiled coyly.

"Wow. So it did work." I was pleased.

"It blew my mind." She smiled.

"Well I'm glad to hear that. Have a little sleep and I will love to blow it a few more times before dawn." I whispered to her.

"Oh god." She sighed in deep pleasure. "I'm so in love with you. Don't ever stop loving me because I won't survive without you."

"You are all I think about." I confessed. "I miss you when I don't see you."

"You have no idea how I ache for you." She sighed.

"If you have some sleep, I will wake you again with my lips. How about that?" I whispered.

"May your kisses lull me to sleep for now and wake me in the morning." She said.

We kissed each other softly.

"You have eternity to stop." She said as she wrapped herself in my arms and melted in my hug.

Chapter 16 – the agreement

I wasn't sure if I was dreaming but I felt warm lips around my erection in the early hours of the morning. I was dozing in and out of sleep so the feeling was very erotic although confusing. The lips were very tender yet sucking firmly. They were slow and intense. I didn't feel any other sensation and that was what was tripping me. I could feel them lick and suck for a while as I got closer to my orgasm. I must have been sleepy as I let it spurt out without much worry. By the time I came, I had stirred up and found Sam crawled under the duvet sucking me. When I looked over the duvet all I saw was her legs popped outside the duvet and a bump on the duvet where her head rested between my thighs. As I calmed down, I slid the duvet from my chest down to expose her head.

She was still sucking me tenderly. As I gazed at her from under the sheet, she looked at me with love in her eyes and a sweet smile.

"Good morning angel." She sighed softly. "I hope I didn't disturb your sleep."

"That's ok hon." I smiled. "Waking up to your licks is like waking in heaven."

"Oh good." She blushed. "I wanted to return the favour from the night."

"That was very sweet of you." I smiled and beckoned her to lie next to me.

"Let me freshen up." I whispered as I got out of the bed.

After freshening up, I walked back in the bedroom. I saw her under the duvet wrapped up snug. She was looking at me with a big smile. I knew she had something on her mind.

As I got in under the duvet, she turned and gazed at me with intentional eyes. Then as I lay beside her, she scooted into my arms, pressed herself into my hug and planted her lips on mine. Then she slowly pulled me over her as she rolled on her back. I had slipped one of my hands under her neck as she gently raised her head. When I had wrapped her closely, I felt her melt in my arms as she hugged me pulling me on top of her as we kissed.

I could feel her lips lick and suck my lips with hungry passion. I ran my hands on her thighs, and she parted her legs slowly and let me caress her between them. As I touched her labia, her breathing became deep. She encouraged me and pulled me in her arms.

"I don't think I will ever get enough of you." She sighed as she paused for breath. "I'm sorry."

"Hey." I tried to be stern. "Don't be silly."

She realised she had said something she ought not to. "I'm sorry." She said sheepishly. "I'm just not handling all the excitement of you accepting my love for you." She exclaimed.

"I'm surprised you had doubts." I was sarcastic.

"I couldn't bear the risk of losing you for a mistake I could have made." She whispered.

"Enough of that talk." I tried to stop her. "Don't ever mention it again ok?"

"Ok." She nodded. "I'm just so lucky to have you. I am going to flood you with my love, you will see. I just hope I don't scare you away." She acknowledged with reluctance.

"Bring it on hon." I smiled. "I love the way you love me."

"We are going to have to be so careful around mom and dad now." She spoke softly looking at me.

I had propped myself on my elbow as I rested my head on my hand. "I know. It will kill me to hold back from touching you as and when I miss you or want to."

"You talking about touching?" she exclaimed. "At times I want to devour you." She smiled at me with a feline growl. I looked at her 'feline hunger' and smiled. "In fact now that we can have each other, I would want to rip your clothes and feel you inside me most of the time."

I just braced myself with an 'ok' expression and a smile. "What are we going to do then?"

"We will just have to use one of our cues." She smiled.

"I just hope mom and dad don't catch on it." I smiled.

"That will be bad news." She sighed. "What about when we are at college?" she gasped.

"That is certainly going to kill me." I sighed. "At least at home I can hug and kiss you."

"This is going to be so difficult." She sighed.

"We will find a way." I tried to calm her.

"You better, otherwise don't blame me for ripping your clothes." She giggled.

"mm. I might like the feel of that." I smiled.

"You think this is funny don't you?!" she exclaimed. "Well just you wait and see when you get desperate and then I will recall this conversation."

"Ok ok." I acknowledged. "We will sort something out hon." I kissed her softly.

"Talking of clothes, we have not yet checked out the shopping we got yesterday." She said reminding me. I knew she would jack-jump eventually.

"Also, we will need to clear the house and the kitchen before mom and dad get here." I reminded her.

"Let's check out the shopping first and then we will clear the house together." She gazed at me with warm eyes.

"Ok." I smiled back. "I would love that."

She kissed me gently, got out of the bed and ran into my bedroom.

"How about I model for you each nightwear and you let me know what you think." She yelled out from my bedroom. "You stay in there."

"Ok." I replied.

She walked in wearing the nightdress. It was pink and it ended just below her bum. She twirled around and my heart skipped a bit as I feasted my eyes on her thighs.

"Do you want to guess?" She looked at me gazing at the parting at her thighs. "Am I wearing panties, yes or no?"

She looked at me and grinned ear to ear as I gazed at her. She could see my eyes gleaming from the sheer imagination.

She started giggling after I had not spoken for a moment.

I guessed, "Yes." I looked at her.

She laughed. "Ok." She shrugged her shoulders and walked back into my room to change.

"Hey come on. Tell me was I right?" I protested feebly.

"Next time I will just let you find out for yourself," she yelled back.

"O." I fell back on the bed. "This is torture."

She came back wearing the chemise next.

"I will wear that but on one condition..." she pointed to the nightdress "...on that occasion, you will have to guess if I am wearing any panties. If you get it wrong you can't touch me then." She suggested.

"O come on!" I exclaimed. "You can't do that."

"Surely makes it fun for me to see you squirm." She winked. "ok. What about this?" she posed with the chemise.

"It looks good." I said to her. "I now understand what you said earlier about it being figure hugging." I said ogling at her figure. "You have an excellent one." I was nearly dribbling.

She just smiled. "See, it hugs my bust too." She cupped her boobs. "At night, sometimes, that is good."

"If you say so." I just agreed.

"This is a rather half descent nightwear I could get away wearing it and still hope our parents don't mind. But it would be testing their patience a bit. Now you get me."

Then she left and came back dressed in the slip. As soon as I saw her in it, my eyes light up. "Plenty of access." I smiled. "That is so sexy."

She just blushed, lowering and shaking her head smiling softly. "This is loose, see." She ran her hands over her bust and tugged the material.

"I like that." I said. "Makes me wonder if you are wearing a bra underneath." I smiled.

"That seems like your thing." She pointed out. "You like to let your imagination wander."

"Probably." I smiled coyly.

She looked at me narrowing her eyes, trying to suss my thoughts.

Then she left and came back in the baby doll.

She looked hot and enticing. "This is getting a bit too much to handle now." I gasped with a sigh.

She smiled. "Like it?"

I nodded with a big smile. "Yeah!"

"Too bad I can't wear it in the house normally." She flared the hem to indicate the nakedness. "Now you understand what I meant about wearing it only when we are together."

"I get it now." I agreed. "It is a bit too revealing for wearing it around the house."

I still stared at her. "You look amazing though. I feel like unwrapping you."

"That is the general idea hon." She smiled. "Give me a minute."

She went into my room and came out wearing one of my thin longish shirts. It was buttoned as usual and she walked in without pants or trousers.

"Whoa" I exclaimed with pleasure. She looked hot in it.

"You like this?" she asked me.

"Yeah." I exclaimed. "You look hot."

"More than the night dress?" she questioned looking at herself.

"I would say so." I agreed.

"Why? It's just your shirt." She was perplexed.

"I don't know but on you it is like the most seductive wear." I replied trying to eat her out with my eyes.

Then she started folding the cuffs, just a little above her wrists.

"O man." I gasped.

She smiled realising the rolled cuffs added a bit more sensuality. "Really?"

"What else do I do to make it more appealing?" she asked me.

"Undo one more button on the top." I suggested.

As she did it, the very slight cleavage was visible through the parting, just barely. "Good enough or one more?"

I looked at her with big wide eyes. "That's just perfect."

"Anything more?" she asked becoming more curious and excited.

"Umm. How about pinning your hair up in a loose bun." I suggested with a shy grin.

"All of it?" she confirmed

I nodded.

She looked in the mirror, gathered her hair in a bun and stuck a bobble in it. Turning around she looked at my approval.

"Like this?" Her neck was visible now and the soft loose bun of her hair was sensual enough to make her the temptress that could melt a thousand hearts.

"O man." I fell back on the bed. "kill me now!" I exclaimed throwing my hands wide on the bed.

"Really?" she exclaimed not believing how a simple shirt could get me so turned on. She turned and saw herself in the mirror. "Ok." She made a mental note. "One more weakness I can harness." She turned around and walked toward me and then lay on top of me. "And I have a whole wardrobe full already!" she giggled. "You are so dead mister." She nuzzled her nose on mine and kissed me softly.

I took her into my arms and sighed, "I knew that a long time ago genius," I smirked teasingly. "Since the time when you got dressed to go out with me the first time."

She looked at me trying to recall her first date with me.

"You ruined me for appreciating other girls." I smiled at her. "I could never see any other girl and think of her as being beautiful after I saw your beauty."

She raised herself over me and planted a long deep wet kiss on my lips. "I did that because you had ruined me too." She gazed deep into my eyes.

I wrapped my arms around her back and we hugged each other, her arms around my neck. She kissed me for a long while, our lips licking and sucking gently and sensually.

"You are so mysterious," she sighed. "The more I get to know you the more I realise there is so much more to you."

"I will take that as a compliment." I smiled.

"Of course." She giggled. "I like it that you are such a deep person."

"Well thank you hon." I kissed her. "I love the fact that you love me so much, for who I am."

"For me, you are perfect." She said and laid her head on my shoulder as we hugged.

After a while of warm closeness, I reminded her, "We need to get cracking with the kitchen and the lounge hon."

"I know." She just murmured without making any movements.

Then after a moment, she looked at me, kissed me on the lips and grinned. "I know." She sighed, getting up slowly and standing up straight. She stretched her hands out and helped me pull myself up on my feet from the bed.

As we walked downstairs, I kept glancing at her in my shirt that she was wearing. She looked smoking hot in it. I could not believe just how sexy she looked.

Catching my gaze on her, she kept smiling and blushing sensually, letting me eat her with my eyes.

We cleared the table and started loading the dishwasher. Most of the meal was put anyway. I looked at the lip marks on the glasses and kissed them. She grinned at me watching me kiss it.

"Why don't you play the songs while we clear this." She suggested.

"Ok." I got the stereo from her bedroom and plugged into the main surround system in the lounge. When I pressed play, the bars rolled in and shivers ran down my spine when the memories came rushing in my mind.

"The whole night has been burned in my brain for the rest of my life." I hugged her from the back as she was at the sink clearing up the dishes. "Every moment and every song will stay in my mind forever." I whispered in her ear.

"I think I was lucky all the hard work in planning it finally paid out." She smiled and pressed her cheek against mine. She had gloves on and did not want to hug me with them on. I wrapped my hands around her tummy, squeezed her into my arms and nuzzled my lips on her neck planting kisses under her ear.

"umm." She moaned seductively. She just let me love her, while enjoying the bliss.

Then releasing her from my hug, I went back to the table and continued clearing it.

When I was done with the table, I helped her in the kitchen. We glanced at each other and grinned at the music playing in the background. As we moved in the kitchen, we stopped for kisses and caresses occasionally. We were like a pair of lovebirds, crazy about each other.

After we had cleared the kitchen, I stepped behind her as she was standing at the worktop facing away from me. I pressed my hips on her bum and gently ran my hands over her bum and thighs, raising the hem from the shirt and caressing her cheeks. I had been gazing at her long enough to lose control on my urge.

As she felt my hands on her bum, she paused, pushed her bum back, and pressed it out for me to caress it. I ran my hands all over it, gently caressing her labia through the panties. Her breath got heavy and deep as she felt my fingers graze on her panties in between her thighs.

"I so wish I wasn't still sore, hon." She whispered. "I so want you inside me."

"I can wait." I whispered in her ear. "Just let me know when you are healed."

"It won't be long now." She turned around and looked me in my eyes holding my face in between her hands. "But I know if we rush it, it will take longer."

"I know." I said kissing her. "I don't mean to rush you."

"I know honey." She smiled. "I know how decent you are about that."

"It's just hard to stay away from you now, particularly how you are dressed at the moment." I smiled sheepishly.

"Really?!" she exclaimed. "I need to change then. I don't wish to torture you like this particularly when we can't have each other."

"No you don't have to." I said. "I love to see you in this." I gazed at her beauty.

"But if this is going to turn you on so much, it is not right particularly when you can't have me." She kissed me softly on my lips. "Don't get me wrong, I love the effect I have on you but I wouldn't want to torture you like this, not even tease you. I only like to entice you," she said sensually, "so then you can devour me."

"You are so ...." I was trying hard to find an adjective. "....wonderful." I sheepishly shrugged my shoulders to accept my defeat in finding anything better. "I can't find words anymore to appreciate you." I said apologetically.

"You don't have to say anything hon." She gazed in my eyes with warmth, running her fingers in my hair. "Your eyes do the talking and your actions speak louder than any words can say."

We hugged each other and I squeezed her in my arms gently in a big bear hug. She melted in my arms, as I felt her become limp, and I snaked my arms around her trying to squeeze her into me.

I heard sniffs in my ear and some gasps. I moved out of the hug and looked at her. Tears had rolled down her eyes as she gazed at me.

"What's the matter honey?" I was alarmed. I tried to console her.

She gasped for a moment and then brushed her tears trying to compose herself, breaking out in a soft grin. "I'm sorry."

"What's the matter?" I tried consoling her again. I rubbed her back and caressed her arms.

She spoke softly after composing herself. "For the past 2 days I have had you all to myself, like it was a dream, in fact better than any dream. Now when mom and dad get back, I will have to restrain myself when I miss you or when I want to have you." She acknowledged. "I won't be able to hug you or kiss you like I have done all this weekend and I can't bear the thought of that."

"Honey." I took her into my arms and hugged her. "You will be able to do all that with me. It's just going to be tricky at first but we will find a way." I assured her.

She looked at me as we came out of the hug.

"We will always find a way." I assured her. "You just have to let me know that you need me, and I will be there for you."

"After this weekend, it is just going to get worse." Her tears rolled again. "I can see it. I ain't going to get enough of you." She shook her head.

"That's ok too." I calmed her down with kisses. "As much as you need me. Whenever, wherever."

I caressed her as I hugged her gently. "Hell I am desperate for you a lot too. I just don't show it."

"I want you to tell me." She sighed looking at me with urgency. "It makes me less guilty of feeling so obsessed with you."

"You are not obsessed with me." I tried to shun it off. "It's called love and I am crazy for you too. And I promise to tell you when I miss you." I nodded.

"And tell me if I start to become too clingy or too suffocating for you." She lowered her gaze. "I don't want to lose you now I have had you. I won't be able to bear it."

"Hey silly." I took her in my arms as she sighed with more tears. "You never suffocate me. I love the way you desire me. I wish I had the courage like you to express my hunger for you."

"You should." She thumped me gently in my back with frustration. "You need to show me that you miss me and you want me."

"I will." I said promising her. "I will try to be more open with my desires."

"Not just try." She exclaimed. "I want you to show me openly."

"Honey, you know me. I feel I am mistreating you if I impose my desires on you. I would never live with myself if I know I have upset you like that."

"You have never disrespected or mistreated me." She exclaimed with anger and frustration. "This is all because I told you about that stupid jerk. I should had just kept my mouth shut. Now I can't enjoy your affection; the one person I love the most in the world." She pushed her hand on my chest and shook out of my hug in protest.

"I'm sorry. I do love you immensely. You know that." I tried to reason with her, at the same time explaining her where I was coming from.

"No, that's not enough." She protested loudly. "I want to see the real you, hidden deep inside there," she poked my chest at the heart. "I want you to be yourself and break those stupid restraints down." She looked me in the eyes. "I don't want you to restrain yourself regarding me."

I just stared at her for a moment. I opened my arms to ask for a hug. She seemed so sweet.

"No. Promise me first that you will bring down that wall of restrain and you will show me the real you." She was stern. "I want to see YOU. I am not afraid of what I may see. I love you and I want to see the real you, every detail as it is."

I looked at her. "Ok." I acknowledged with a simple nod and a smile, still holding out my arms.

"Promise?" she was sceptical.

"Promise." I said. "100% raw, uncut and unprocessed." I smiled trying to lighten the mood.

She looked at me for a moment and then grinned slowly. Then she walked into my open arms and hugged me.

"Do I get some time to acclimate myself to this luxury?" I said.

"You have 1 minute." She said without much thought. "I want you to do the first thing that pops in your head. No holds bar." She looked straight at me in my eyes.

As I stared at her, I could see the sincerity of her request she was making.

I grabbed her, ran my hands inside her shirt all over her back, pulled her in my arms and kissed her passionately. As she realised my burst of passionate hunger, she succumbed and melted in my arms, wrapping her legs around my waist as she propped herself while I held her bum. Then I pressed her against the kitchen wall and began kissing her, the tongue licking and sucking her tongue and our lips devouring each other's mouths. Her fingers were running through my hair as I held her firmly in my arms and propped her against the wall, my crotch pressed against hers. The burst of hungry passion surprised her. She was expecting me to take her panties off and she had loosened her legs around my waist.

"As much as I want to, I love you far more to know, you are sore for now. So that is the only reason I am holding back, waiting for you to heal. The next time, I won't hold back when I finally have you."

The words must have come as a surprise as she kissed me with increased fervour.

"I so adore you." She kissed me passionately. "I know it won't work in our favour to push you to have me right now. That's the only reason I will let you off this one time." She looked at me with deep sensual passion. "Next time, there will be fireworks."

I pushed her higher up against the wall as I dug in her neck and parted her shirt to kiss between her cleavage. Then I kissed her neck with wet kisses. She wrapped her arms around my neck running her fingers through my hair encouraging me to kiss her bosom.

"I want you to want me, without any second thoughts." She whispered. "I know we have to be careful, but when we don't, I want you to express all your desires for me unrestricted, unhindered."

"I so love you." I gasped between my kisses.

"I'm all yours. Remember that." She said. "I love you. All of you."

"And stop thinking that you would overwhelm me with your desires. Bring it all on." I whispered.

"Oh baby, make sure you are braced and ready because you will be flooded for sure." She sighed sensually.

We hugged each other for a moment like that and then I slowly eased her down as she let her feet dangle to the ground.

"You will need to pick them soon." She reminded me about mom and dad arriving at the airport.

"I know." I said. "Aren't you coming?" I was a bit perplexed.

"No. You go and pick them up. I will stay here and make sure everything is in order before they arrive." She looked around and smiled. "Plus, I need some time to calm down." She blushed.

I smiled. "OK." I kissed her. "The best birthday I have had." I looked deep in her eyes.

"This is just the beginning." She caressed my cheek. "It will get better each day, you will see." She flicked her eyebrow in a tease and smiled.

"I am so lucky to have found you." I said to her while I hugged her gently in my arms.

"We are lucky to have found each other." She said. "I can't imagine my life without you now."

"You won't need to." I shrugged off her concerns. "I ain't going anywhere, not without you."

"I don't ever wanna lose you." She sighed.

"You will never." I assured her.

As we looked at each other deeply, we sealed our promises with a deep sensual kiss.

We decided to have early lunch as mom and dad would be arriving later in the afternoon anyway. She heated the left over meal from our night, and got my favourite dessert. "I always make plenty more than you need," she said to me. "I know you have big appetite. Mom always taught me to have a generous hand when measuring ingredients."

I just smiled at her. She looked at me with love filled in her eyes as she had her spoonfuls.

"You sure you don't want to come with me to pick mom and dad?" I asked her again.

"No. I will stay behind." She grinned softly.

"You aren't going to be tearful again when I leave are you?" I asked her doubtfully.

She smiled unable to disguise her pretence. "Even if I did, at least you won't be here to witness it."

"Honey." I whinged to express my discontent.

She smiled apologetically. Then she took my hand and curled my fingers in hers. "Listen. You have no idea the rollercoaster of emotions I have gone through in the last 3 days. Even now, even when I am bubbling with so much pleasure and joy being with you through the whole weekend, I have a lot to get out of myself and calm down before mom and dad get here. I need some time alone to do it. I got to do it alone, you can't help me in this. Some battles have to be fought alone." She smiled.

"Don't ever say that." I stared at her with a look of hurt.

"Honey." She scooted close to me. "I did not mean it like that. Come on try to understand what I'm saying, please." She kissed me.

"You know I would never ever leave you to fight any battle alone." I said to her.

"I did not mean it like that honey." She pleaded. "I meant to say, I am feeling like this because of my feelings for you and the wonderful time we have had together. I need to calm down and compose myself and it is going to need me to distract myself. Having you around me ain't going to help will it?!" she smiled. I realised and smiled back at her.

"Now you get me?" she smiled back taking my face in her hands. "When you are around, I lose my mind, do you know that? That's the kind of effect you have on me. You send me loopy!" She giggled.

"Ok." I said. "I get it. But if I realise you have cried alone behind my back, I will sort you out tonight." I pretended to be stern.

"Oo." She cooed. "In that case I might get wet right now!" She giggled.

I just shook my head in complete failure and smiled. "You are just impossible."

"Are you complaining mister?" She poked at me.

I shook my head with a grin as I took my spoonfuls.

Then she reached close to me and hinted me to feed her a spoonful.

"We are both eating the same thing!" I was perplexed.

She pouted with a sad face.

"Ok ok." I tried to console her. "I did not realise you wanted to feel close to me with that pretext."

"You are special." She looked at me with a naughty grin on her face.

It took me a while to realise what she had implied ('thick').

"YOU are special." I pushed her away jokingly.

"Einstein."

"Genius."

Then when we stared at each other with a wicked grin on each other's face for a while, we brought our faces close to each other and planted a soft kiss on the lips.

She gestured with her hands and fingers curled in a heart 'love you'. I gestured back, 'love you 2'

When we had finished our dessert, she urged me to get going. "Otherwise you will be late getting there."

"I want to help you clear this." I said.

"I will take care of it. I need some distraction anyway." She acknowledged. "Now go." She urged me.

I looked at her. I opened my arms for a hug as I stood up.

She stood up and jumped into my arms. As we hugged, I caressed her back and ran my hands on her waist.

"Are you trying to burp me again?" she tried to make a joke.

I slapped her bum gently to be stern.

"Oo." She cooed. "Do it again." She giggled in a tease.

"You are so impossible." I smiled at her.

"Just the way you like it." She brushed her nose against mine and planted a few kisses on my lips. "Now go." She pushed me out of her hug and made me turn around.

"Keep your phone on you." I said to her. "I will message you when I get there."

"Not while you are driving." She spoke sternly. "I am warning you."

"No. I promise. I will only message when I am there waiting for them at the arrivals."

"Ok." She waived at me.

The drive to the airport was unusually long and silent. Usually she was with me when I drove around most of the time. I kept thinking of her and the weekend we had spent.

When I was at the arrival gates, I was going to be waiting what looked like at least 40 minutes. So I decided to message her.

'hi hon. What you doing?'

'just clearing. U at the airport?'

'yes. waiting at the gates.
Flight scheduled to arrive
in next 40 mins.'

'ok. xxx'

'how r u?'

                              'feeling weird without u. =('

'me too =S '

I did not get another message back so I sent her another one:

'loved the time we had this weekend'

                                        'me 2 xxx'

'what was ur fav moment?'

                                        'all of it!'

'come on. I mean really. Which 1?'

I waited for her to reply back. She must have paused to reply.

                              'feeling you slide inside
                              me 4 the first time.'

'I could c in ur eyes.'

                        'it was better than I had imagined xxx'

'how did it feel?'

She waited to reply.

                              'words fail me. it was heavenly'

'I think I know what u mean.
Ur eyes closed slowly
as you took me in.
I could see the bliss in ur eyes.'

                                                    '=)'

There was a moment of silence. Then my phone beeped.

                                        'what about u?'

I thought for a moment and replied,

'when I came inside u'

'really?'

'yep. My first orgasm.'

'was it nice?'

'haha nice is not even
close to what it deserves.'

'what then? =) '

'cant describe – simply heavenly. =)'

'try. I want to know ;) '

I composed the words in my mind and messaged back,

'felt like my life energy
was being sucked
through my penis.'

'=) wow really?'

'yes. Like as though I was
covered with a silk sheet
all over my body and it was
slowly being pulled through
my penis as it slipped
across my whole body.'

'I think I know what u mean'

'it was incredible'

'im glad u think that'

'it will stay in my memories for life'

'xxxxx luv u '

'I cant wait to try it again.'

'me 2 xx'

'I feel so hard right now
just thinking about u.'

                        'oh please stop.
         Im trying to calm down here
           and u ain't helping ;)
              ur making me all
           hot & bothered. xxx '

'sorry. U r a very tasty
irresistible temptation.'

             'u r free to enjoy it anytime u like'

'im glad to have the luxury'

                  'its my hunger xxx'

'now u are making me
hot and bothered'

                   'I need to see proof'

'tonight when we are in bed'

                    'cant wait! xxx'

'got to go. The flight has arrived'

               'c u back here soon xx'

I deleted the conversation and put my phone away as I expected
them to walk out of the arrival gate.

Chapter 17 – the love drug

I waved at our parents as I saw them walk out of the arrival doors. They seemed pleased to see me. I hugged my mom and dad.

"How was the break?" I asked them.

"It was fabulous." Dad exclaimed looking at mom. "I did not want to get back." He looked at mom and she smiled.

"He wants us to go back again." She rolled her eyes with exasperation.

"Well that's not a bad idea" I encouraged her. "Did you not enjoy it?" I inquired.

"I loved it." Mom replied. "But no reason to move there," she laughed.

"You can make it a regular holiday destination." I suggested while pushing the trolley with their bags as we were walking toward the car park.

"Now you talking." Dad said. "Next time we make it a week long holiday." He felt thrilled.

"He has certainly enjoyed it." I looked at mom.

"Oh don't get me started." She exclaimed. "He was like a kid all the while we were there."

"That's nice to hear." I smiled. "Did you not have a good time?"

"Yes love. I did." She smiled. "I had very relaxing 2 days."

"Let's get home then, Sam is waiting for us." I said.

"I must thank her for this gift she gave us." Mom said to me. "It must have cost her dearly."

"You know Sam." I said. "She loves to treat you nice."

"But still." Mom continued. "She shouldn't had."

The drive back home was mixed with conversations of memories they both had and were recalling them sporadically. When we got home, mom entered the house and Sam was waiting for us all. Mom flew her arms open for a hug and Sam ran into mom's arms. "Oh thank you so much dear." Mom exclaimed. "We had a lovely time."

Sam blushed. "I'm glad you enjoyed." She smiled looking at me.

I walked upstairs and laid the bags in their bedroom. I could hear dad still excited from the trip.

"You need to tell me how to book that one for a week next time." He laughed looking at Sam.

"Sure dad. I think it would do you guys good to take a week off somewhere like that." Sam suggested.

"I know." Dad was smiling. "That's why I keep telling her to make plans to take some holiday from work."

"One week is too long for doing nothing." Mom sighed. "And I won't feel happy leaving you two behind here on your own."

"Oh don't worry about us." Sam said hiding the delight in her heart as she held my hand when I stood next to her. "We are old enough to take care of the house on our own." We both nodded.

"I know." Mom caressed our cheeks and hugged us. "You have grown so quickly."

"Get settled in as I have already prepared the dinner for us." Sam said glancing at the table.

"Wow." Mom said softly.

"I am famished." Dad exclaimed. "I'm in the shower first." He went ahead to the room.

"He has been like this throughout the break." Mom looked at Sam.

"It seems like he has enjoyed himself then." Sam smiled.

"Just a tad more than I would wish for." Mom laughed. "Ok sweetheart. I will be as quick as your dad let's me." She headed slowly to their bedroom.

"Take your time." Sam said aloud. "We will wait for you."

When mom and dad had disappeared into their bedroom, I asked Sam, "Do you need a hand with anything?"

She nodded and walking toward the kitchen lent out her hand gesturing me to follow her.

In the kitchen, she turned around, wrapped her arms around my neck and hugged me slowly but firmly. I snaked my arms and hugged her squeezing her in my hug. She planted her lips on mine, tilting her head slightly and we kissed each other for a while.

"I'm sorry but I couldn't hold back any longer." She sighed pausing for breath looking sheepishly at me.

"Don't ever be." I caressed her face and brushed her hair gently with my fingers. "As long as we are ok and not reckless, we will have to take chances when we want." I tried to sympathise with her.

"It is going to be difficult." She sighed.

"We will try and make it easy on both of us." I hugged her again and kissed her cheek. "You just be yourself as usual and let me know when you need me." I smiled.

"That will be most of the time." She sighed and kissed me.

Then we slowly drifted apart holding out our hands letting them slide against each other until they separated in mid-air.

We sat at the table waiting for our parents. While we sat there, I gazed at her warm eyes staring at me. She put her palm gently on my eyes shielding them from her sight. "You hypnotise me with your love soaked eyes." She sighed.

I took her hand and moving it down to my lips kissed her palm with a wet kiss.

She closed her eyes feeling the soft wet lips on her palm and gave out a gentle sigh.

Then she looked at me and ran her fingers gently from my forehead all the way over my closed eyelids and over my cheeks.

"You are like the naughty cupid." She sighed.

"You are Venus." I remarked.

"Oh stop it." She blushed. "Now behave." She said as she heard footsteps coming down the stairs.

Dad was humming his way down to the lounge.

"So kids. How was life without us for 2 days?" he smiled. "I guess you two never missed us."

"Of course we did miss you dad." Sam teased him. "I bet it was nice to get away from all the worries."

"It was sweetheart." He settled in the chair after kissing her head briefly. "I had a lovely time. Too bad it was a short break. But I have convinced your mom, next time we are going away for a week." He looked at us with an intention of secretly kidnapping mom away. "You are welcome to join." He looked at us.

"No dad." Sam said looking at me softly squeezing my hand. "We will let you two enjoy your time together." She smiled. "Anyway, we would probably make our own plans in that case."

"Hmm. You are right." He smiled. "You two are stuck at the hip. I forgot." He then chuckled and we all laughed out.

As we saw mom climb down the stairs he yelled out, "Come on missus. I'm starving here."

"Start then. I will be there in a minute." Mom just yelled back.

"All the weekend, she kept me waiting." Dad leaned and said to us softly.

"No need to lie to them." Mom brazed him off. "This is what he did to me all weekend. Rush bloody rush."

"Come on then. I'm starting." Dad tucked into the meal. Mom sat next to him as we started our dinner. We both just looked at each other at their antics and smiled.

Sam and I went back to our old habits, of staring into each other's eyes while enjoying our spoonfuls. She occasionally grazed her fingers on my thighs, or pressed her knee against my leg, or played footie by slowly caressing my toes with her toes. All the while, we pretended to keep a straight face, the emotions only hidden in our eyes.

"Would you like to help me with my college work tonight?" Sam said looking at me.

"Sure." I replied. "How about after the dinner?"

She nodded.

"I'm hitting the bed." Dad said. "I need to get back to reality by tomorrow morning."

"Quicker the better." Mom giggled.

Sam and me just looked at each other and smiled. We hoped they did not catch on what was in our minds.

After the dinner, Sam served the dessert from our dinner night she had put aside. Mom and dad both loved it.

"When did you make it?" mom asked.

"I cooked him a nice dinner on the Friday." Sam said blushing slightly looking at me. "It was meant to be his birthday gift for this year." She looked at mom.

"Awe. That's nice." Mom cooed. "Did you enjoy it?" she asked me.

I nodded. "It was lovely." I held out my hand and indicated Sam to walk to me. As she came close, I hugged her tenderly and kissed her forehead. "She is an angel." I said looking at her and then at mom.

"I know she is." Mom admired Sam's hospitality.

"Do you have some more of this?" dad asked handing out the empty bowl in his hand.

"Sure." Sam took his bowl for a refill. "I made plenty as I knew you would all like it." She said while filling his bowl up again with a serving.

As she handed it to him, she asked mom, "How about you mom?"

"No I am fine darling."

Then Sam slowly sat down next to me on the couch, reclining on my chest and along my side, resting her head on my shoulder. I caressed her arm from behind her back and circled her waist.

As dad licked his lips finishing the last of his serving, Sam got up and took his bowl away.

"No more." He said with complete satiety. "That was brilliant sweetheart." Sam collected mom's bowl and went into the kitchen.

I got up and started to help her clear the table.

When mom got up to help, I requested her to rest for the evening. "Let us do it for today mom." Sam asked her to relax. "You must be tired."

"Tired of relaxing?" mom said sarcastically. "Or tired from enjoying?" she giggled.

Sam and I laughed with her.

As Sam and I cleared the kitchen, we loaded the dishwasher and then sat on the couch watching TV. Dad had clicked several times to see what was on. "We need to change our cable company." He remarked. "There's nothing to watch on here."

Mom just shook her head in exasperation. We both just giggled at their antics looking at each other every time.

After a few minutes, mom got up and wished us good night. "I'm tired." She sighed. "I think the flight here was long."

"That's because you were getting away from fun." Sam teased her.

Mom just smiled.

"Are you coming?" she looked at dad. "I thought you said you were beat and wanted to lie in early."

"Yes dear." Dad said still looking at the TV. "I just wanted to catch some news. Well I'm coming now."

They both got up and walked slowly upstairs to their bedroom, one after the other. "Goodnight kids." Dad yelled out from the top.

"Good night." We both yelled out together. "Sleep tight. Don't let the bedbugs bite."

When they had disappeared in their room, the lounge was desolate and the TV was flickering its program with little attention from us two.

We sat there, Sam still reclining on my chest. Now she slowly rolled on my chest and pressed her forehead in my neck under my chin. I hugged her with my arm, around her waist. Then I stroked her hair as it cascaded on her back. I planted a kiss on her forehead. I felt her snuggle inside my warm hug as she pressed her face on my neck. We lay there like that for a while, enjoying the bliss. After a long passionate weekend, we were again experiencing the norm, trying to live it and enjoy the simple pleasures it gave for such a long time before.

"Do you want to go upstairs?" I whispered.

"I'm waiting for you." She whispered.

"Come on then." I said softly waiting for her to get up.

As she stood up, she looked at me. I looked at her and smiled. I stood up, turned the TV off and without much indication, bent down and lifted her in my arms.

"Whoa." She was taken aback. "This is a surprise." She threw her arm around my neck and held on to me.

"A princess needs to be carried to her bed." I said in her ear.

"Oo." She cooed. "Bed time just got interesting."

I just grinned at her as I carried her upstairs. "Feel free to make any additions."

"I will." Her eyes glowed with a naughty grin.

Next few days went rough for both of us. We had to take it easy and bear the 'separation' during the day. Occasionally when we had opportunity, we hugged and kissed each other when we were at home. We took excuses to work on our college stuff to stay in our rooms. That way we hugged in bed and felt the closeness we so much craved.

Then I came down with a strong strain of flu. It started as a cold and within a day, it had debilitated me to a leaking mess. Sam was more than loving to care for me. I kept asking her to stay away so as not to pass her the infection. She kept ignoring me as usual.

I could not attend classes on the second day. I stayed in bed all day. I had high fever and chesty cough, had terrible cold and body ache. I warned her not to miss classes for my sake. So when she was done with her classes, she ran into my room, and tended to my illness.

"Please stay away, hon. You are going to catch it too." I kept pleading to her.

"Uh." She ignored me as though I was a 5-year-old child.

She helped me change into new clothes, changed my bed as it was soaked with my sweat. She made me hot soup as I could not taste anything. For the whole day I was not myself so I couldn't really tell her off for getting so close to me.

On the fourth day, I showed the first sign of recovery. She made me some hot meal for me to try. My taste buds were still fried. I just ate it without much appreciation.

"I don't want you catching this infection." I pleaded to her.

"It's viral. If you have got it, there is a high chance we all might get it now. There is very little use you worrying about it. Just get better soon so if I get it, you would be well enough to care for me." She calmly spoke to me. "I would hate to make mom care for both of us."

"I need to go to college tomorrow." I spoke slowly.

"What?" she was shocked. "Why? In your state? Are you mad?"

"I have a test and I need to at least attempt it." I said. "If I miss it, I will have to complete a big report instead. If I pass it, one piece of work is done."

"What if you don't pass it?" she argued.

"Then in any case I will end up completing the report. But if I pass it, I don't have to."

"How can you even contemplate in this state?" she argued again. "How long is it?"

"90 minutes." I said. "I will be ok. I am feeling better today. By tomorrow I will be fine."

"No you are not fine. This infection will relapse if you go out tomorrow in this state. Trust me." She tried to persuade me.

"Hon, I have to at least try. I have prepared for it so let me at least attempt it." I begged her.

"What time is it?"

"10:30 am," I replied.

"And after that you are coming straight here!" she got me to promise her.

I nodded. That is all I could negotiate in my given state.

"Then I will wait outside your class." She claimed. "I don't have any class during that time. I will drive you there, stay there and drive you back."

"You don't have to wait there for me." I suggested.

"Then you ain't going." She looked in a matter-of-fact way.

"Ok." I agreed sheepishly.

She just shook her head at the ludicrous idea of me attending a test in my state.

"Why can't you give it later when you are well enough?" she protested.

"It's an in-class test." I tried to rationalise with her. "Anyone who cannot attend it or doesn't pass it gets to complete the report."

"Get to bed and sleep early tonight." She commanded me. "I don't want you staying up late."

"OK." I agreed.

She seemed pissed off with me.

"I'm not well. Why are you angry at me?" I pleaded with a sheepish voice.

"Because you don't see how this is going to hurt your recovery. This one test is going to set your recovery back for at least a few days." She was trying to get her point across.

"I can't help it." I just said softly. "It's a test. It was scheduled at the start of the module. Don't be mad at me."

"Honey. I am not mad at you." She came close to me and took my head in her arms and pressed it on her bosom. "I just don't want you feeling like this for longer."

"I will recover. I will rest after it and you will see." I agreed.

"I hope so." She caressed my face.

"Don't kiss me please." I begged her.

"OK." She agreed with a protest. "I miss you honey."

"I know." I said. "You are already risking too much by being so close."

"I am taking vitamins and trying to keep it at bay. Don't worry." She tried to assure me.

"Do you want your dinner here or would you like to join us at the table?" She asked me.

"I will have it here." I said. "That way I will contain the infection in my room only. I know it means you need to bring it to me. I'm sorry for the trouble." I acknowledged.

"If you apologise again, I ain't taking you tomorrow." She looked at me with stern eyes.

"Ok." I got her drift. "I love you."

"And you know I do love doing things for you. So stop apologising. I hate it when you do." She was upset.

Sam never liked it when I apologised. In her eyes, as we had gotten closer, there was no need to thank or apologise each other. In her eyes, we were one – we experienced life as one entity.

When Sam returned with the tray, she put it down on my lap while I sat up. She helped me while I had my dinner.

"I would have liked it if you had eaten your dinner with me." I suggested softly.

"I will eat with mom and dad." She said as she caressed my face and played with my hair. "I will have to clear the table later anyway."

I nodded in agreement. She kept gazing at me warmly while I had my meal.

"I'm sure it is lovely but I still cannot taste anything." I commented trying to be complimentary of her cooking.

"I'm glad you are eating it at least. If you want I can spice it up a bit for you the next time." She was stroking my arm and caressing my face running her fingers in my hair.

After I had finished, she took the tray away and I went to the bathroom and freshened up for the night.

Sam brought a glass of hot salty water for me to gargle. "It will help fight the cough and the throat infection."

I took it in the bathroom and gargled. It was difficult at first and I felt the hot liquid burn my throat.

All the while, she kept gazing at me head to toe, sitting on the edge of the bath.

When I had finished, she took the glass as I looked at her.

"I know you are missing me." I said to her trying to grin. "When I get better, I will take you out for a nice date."

She just looked at me, caressed my face and smiled. "I miss you all the time honey. Just get well soon for me."

She helped me into my bed, tucked me in and left me to drift to sleep. "I will wake you up tomorrow in time. Till then I want you to rest. Good night and sweet dreams."

"Sweet dreams hon." I murmured.

She shut the light and left the room with the door ajar.

Next day, I woke up feeling better. My nose was still running, and had a cough but the throat infection had subsided. I had a hot shower and felt good. I got ready. Sam came into my room and stared at me with a stern look. I realised I had woken up earlier than I was meant to. Seeing her, I smiled, showed her two thumbs up to highlight my good spirits. She wasn't impressed.

I went downstairs and waited for her to get ready while I revised from my book.

When she came downstairs, she looked at me.

"I'm ready." I smiled at her.

She looked at me and went to the kitchen. She filled up a bottle with some drinking water, made a flask of hot tea with some ginger in it. She gathered a big box of tissues and some apples and collated all this in a bag.

Then she held out her hand and I followed her holding her hand.

We got to the class on time. She hugged me, handed me the bag with all the stuff for me and hugged me planting a quick kiss on my cheek. "Good luck." She whispered. "I will be here if you need me."

I smiled at her and entered the class. I sat in a corner away from the rest of the class.

The test itself wasn't that difficult as I had prepared for it a few weeks ahead anyway. What was troubling was the illness I had. I went through quite a few tissues. When I got the flask out, I felt good sipping on the hot tea. Sam was so thoughtful. It never occurred to me to prepare for the illness as well – I was only prepared for the test.

When the test had finished, I waited until all the class had left. That gave me time to check my answers too.

As I went outside, Sam was there waiting for me just as she promised. I smiled at her.

"Done?" she questioned.

I nodded. "I just need to visit the restroom. Just give me a minute." I handed her the bag and headed to the toilets. She waited for me in the corridor.

When I came out of the toilet, as I was walking toward her, I heard someone callout for me, "Alex. Hi."

I turned around.

"Hi Jessica. How are you?"

Sam saw her talking to me and stopped, slowing down to maintain some distance to avoid the intrusion.

"Hi. I am ok." I did not get close to Jessica.

"What are you doing here?"

"I had a test. I'm just finished so was going home."

"You don't seem ok." She remarked.

"I'm not well actually. I am recovering from the flu." I acknowledged. By now, Sam was standing a small distance away from us so as not to interject in our conversation.

"Oh." Jessica backed away slightly. "I better stay away then. Don't want to catch your infection." She giggled to make it sound as a joke. I laughed to make light of the remark.

Sam on the other hand wasn't impressed so she walked briskly toward me and stood by me taking my arm and placing it around her shoulder. She hugged my waist and glared at Jessica with a straight face.

Jessica glanced at her and was taken aback with the gesture and the closeness Sam portrayed toward me.

"I better get going." I excused myself. "See you around."

"See you." Jessica replied.

Sam and I walked along the corridor to the exit.

"Feel ok hon?" she caressed my back.

I nodded.

"Who's the bimbo?" she cocked her head indicating Jessica.

"That's Jessica." I chuckled at her sarcasm. "She was in my class last semester. Just an acquaintance."

"Did not want to know you when she realised you were ill." Sam sounded angry.

"I know. That's typical of most of the girls I have known." I shrugged my shoulder. "No one can come even a mile within your league."

Sam just rubbed and caressed my back and hugged me. "When we have each other, we don't need nobody."

When we got home, Sam instructed me to lie on the couch while she got the lunch ready.

"Stay on the couch." She gently pushed me back into the couch when she saw me lingering in the kitchen behind her. "I don't want you walking around. You are not that well enough yet."

She gave me a stern look. "I did what you asked me today. Now you do what I'm asking you to do." She tried to reason with me. "I'm right here. I just want to get our lunch sorted. Then we can have lunch together and then you are going to bed for an afternoon nap."

"OK." I agreed without any choice. "Can I have a quick hug?" I looked sheepishly at her.

"Oh honey. Don't make me feel guilty." She ran into my open arms.

"I love you." I sighed.

"You know I'm looking out for you. I want you to recover fast." She moved out of the hug and caressed my face.

"Now you can lie on the couch and keep me company while I get the lunch ready." She covered me up with a blanket.

When lunch was ready, we sat down to eat it. I could barely taste it.

I kept gazing at her as usual. "I am so going to make up for this time I have lost with you when I get better."

"Good." She smiled. "Then get better soon." She caressed my hand.

"If I get better soon, we could have the weekend for ourselves." I realised.

"Now that would be good wouldn't it?" she exclaimed. "So get some rest and in a day or two we will have so much fun."

"In one day." I spoke softly.

"We will see, hon." She smiled and cupped my face.

After the meal, she handed me a hot cup of ginger tea. "Finish this and then it's time for bed."

She came and sat by me with her mug of tea as we sipped together.

"Why am I drinking so much ginger tea suddenly?" I quizzed her.

"It's good at keeping infections at bay." She said.

After a moment of silence and pause, as I stared at her with glowing eyes, I smiled ear to ear.

"What?!" she exclaimed.

"You would look so hot in a nurse uniform." I smiled shyly.

"Really?!" She couldn't believe her ears. "You have been ill all this time and you imagine that?"

I just looked at her coyly. "You would. So hot." I dimmed my eyes to indicate a sexy look.

"I will remember that for the next time." She giggled shaking her head. "Any particular colour?"

I thought about it. "Nah. Just a short skirt and flared partially buttoned top."

"You are so kinky." She blushed. "I never knew you had such a naughty streak."

"You don't know the half of just how naughty I can be." I flicked my eyebrow at her.

"Get well soon and let's find out." She gazed at me sensually.

After we finished our tea, we walked to my bedroom. Sam tucked me in my bed under the duvet. She closed the curtains and then as she caressed my face and ran her fingers in my hair, she gazed at me with loving smile. "Sleep tight. I am going to close the door so you are not disturbed. I want you to sleep for at least 90 minutes. So do not come out before then. If you sleep past that, I will come and wake you in about 3 hrs just in case you sleep over. Ok?"

I nodded looking deep in her eyes.

"Get well soon. I'm missing you like hell you know." She sighed. "You won't let me kiss you or even near you. It's killing me."

"I promise I will be better soon." I held her hand.

As she got up to leave, she turned on my audio system. After pressing some buttons, she pressed play and then turned down the volume to a gentle level.

"This will help you sleep. I've set it on a sleep timer for about 15 minutes." She smiled at me, blew a kiss and closed the door after stepping out of the room.

I closed my eyes as the room filled with soft music. I think she must have set the Tryptophan playlist. That was my lullaby music.

I don't remember when I zonked off. I remember slowly drifting out of sleep in the afternoon. My door was ajar and the time was past 4pm. I had slept like a log.

Sam popped her head in the room and saw me awake.

She went back and returned with a thermometer. She took a reading and checked my forehead.

"Normal." She smiled. She checked my chest and back.

"No sweats. That's a good sign." She smiled. "My Pooh bear is getting better." She caressed my cheek with her knuckles.

"Want to come down and sit with me?" She ruffled my hair and caressed my face.

I nodded. I was still sleepy.

She chose fresh pair of sleep wear for me and told me to change into them. "I will get your clothes washed when you change. Bring them down with you."

She left the room with my laundry. By the time I walked down, she had loaded the washing machine waiting for my change of clothes. Then dropping them into the washer, she set it on a cycle.

She asked me to lie on the couch for a while. "Stay wrapped under the blanket hon." She advised me.

Then she came out with a bowl full of fruit salad, one for her and one for me – pineapple, apple, banana, strawberry, blueberry and pear.

"I don't want to share yet, as you are still recovering." She clarified.

I smiled at her cautious thoughtfulness. "I know. Not long now." I smiled.

While we ate the fruits, she suggested softly, "Would you like a mug of hot cocoa after?"

I thought about it and nodded. "Why not hot chocolate?"

"Cocoa is better – less sugar, low fat, but all the goodness. In fact I have dark cocoa, even better." She raised her eyebrows.

When I had a sip of the hot cocoa drink, I pulled a face. "It tastes bitter."

She laughed. "O my god. You are such a baby when you are ill. It doesn't taste that bad hon." She giggled. "It's good for you; full of anti-oxidants. I have added some sugar just for you."

"How can this be good?" I looked at her with a surprise.

"Most things that taste bitter are good for you." She explained.

"You aren't bitter." I gazed at her coyly. "Yet you are so good." I cooed. "In fact you are so delicious."

She laughed. "There is always an exception to the rule hon." She caressed my face lovingly. "And not all good things are necessarily bitter."

"You are right about that; you are a complete exception in all respects." I exclaimed.

"You are such a charmer." She gazed at me sensually. "Seems like you are feeling better after all."

I just smiled at her looking all lovey-dovey.

In the evening, we sat on the couch while watching TV. I made her sit an arm's length away from me. However, she wanted to hold my hand and I stretched out lying on the couch so she had placed my legs on her thighs. Since I was covered with a blanket, she ran her hand on my legs and caressed my thighs occasionally.

I had difficulty feeling sleepy that night maybe for a number of factors – nap in the afternoon, magic caresses from Sam all eve, having missed her for all week. Sam suggested she would lie in bed with me until I felt sleepy. As she was not allowed to be close to me, she lay at the feet on my bed and I lay on my side while I chatted to her. I had tucked and folded my legs at the knees, making room for her in the bed to lie across. We chatted for a long while.

After I realised she was nodding off, I fiend feeling sleepy myself and she and I bid each other good night.

When she turned my light off, she left the door ajar.

"Wake me if you need anything." She smiled and blew me a kiss as she walked to her room. She had left her door ajar before settling into her bed and turning the lights off.

After about half an hour of tossing and turning, I still could not sleep. I had missed her closeness too much. I needed to calm my desperation. I stroked myself and while imagining about her sensuality, I had climaxed and ejaculated on my bare tummy. Then I straightened my t-shirt, pulled my shorts up and I drifted to sleep.

I woke up in the early hours and again had to put myself back to sleep. Again, I stroked at the thoughts of being with Sam. The memories of her tenderness, fragrance and sensuality tipped me over to my orgasm in no time.

In the morning, I had slept until 8am. When I sat up in the bed, I felt sleepy but I was not groggy or ill. I felt much better waking up to a new day.

I went into the bathroom and realised Sam was downstairs in the kitchen. She must be preparing breakfast for me. My parents had left for work as usual.

I decided to take a quick hot shower and join her downstairs. I flung my t-shirt and shorts on the bed, and walked to the shower with a fresh clean set. I took my time enjoying the hot water running all over me. It felt really nice. I washed my hair – Sam had not allowed me to wash it in case I caught a cold again while I was recovering. When I stepped out and dried myself, I felt a new person. I put on my antiperspirant, sprayed the eau de toilette and slipped into my clothes.

As I walked out of my bathroom into my room, I saw Sam lying in my bed on her side slightly rolled on her chest. Her one arm was pushed under the pillow and the other tucked around her chest. She had bent her legs at the knees and her face was pressed into the bed. When I walked closer to her I realised she was lying with her eyes closed, her hair cascading all over her shoulders, face and splayed on the bed. I noticed she had my t-shirt in her hand and her face was pressed deep in it. She was in a daze.

When I sat down next to her, she gazed at me slowly opening her eyes. She seemed drunk.

"Did you help yourself last night?" She asked me after a moment with a serene tone.

I was taken aback with the blunt statement. I looked at the t-shirt she was holding in her hand and realised the deep orgasmic fragrance that had ratted me out.

I simply nodded. "I couldn't fall asleep." I tried to explain myself.

"But I saw you get sleepy last night that's why I left." She was puzzled.

"I thought I was. But when you left, I couldn't sleep for a while." I spoke softly as she continued staring at me. She had rolled on her back while she listened to me.

"Then I woke up in the early morning and couldn't fall back to sleep. So..." I paused.

"When was this?" she asked.

"I think after 6am." I replied. "I just kept thinking of you and I have missed you so much."

She just rolled over on to her chest again, pressing her face into the shirt and taking deep breath.

"Oh." She moaned. "Why didn't you call me?"

She rolled on her back after a silent moment. "Why did you not say anything last night?" The despair in her voice was evident.

"You had gone to bed." I said. "I couldn't just call you, could I?"

"Yes you could. If you needed me for anything else you would have. Wouldn't you?" she looked at me bluntly.

"Yes I suppose." I lowered my gaze.

"So how is this different?" She quizzed me.

"I couldn't just ask you...." I trailed that sentence.

"Yes?" She appeared offish now. "What? What can't you just ask me?" she sat up and leaned on her hand placed behind her.

"I haven't been well and I've tried to keep you away from me so you don't catch this infection. I've missed you like hell and I was just trying to get to sleep." I lowered my gaze trying to make an excuse. "I just missed you."

She looked at me. "Bull shit." She said with a sharp tone. "You are making an excuse and a very lame at that."

I glanced at her and lowered my gaze again.

"Look at me." she was stern again.

I looked into her eyes.

"You felt too inhibited to ask me. Right?" She stared straight into my eyes.

I glanced at her briefly and could not say much. "It's not that simple."

"Why does it have to be so complex?" She nearly jumped down my throat while sitting up on the bed now.

I just looked at her. I did not say anything for a while. She gazed at my eyes trying to decipher the thoughts in my mind.

"I couldn't just call you in the night even on a pretext, could I? We are not meant to be close while I'm still recovering."

"There are a lot of things I could have done without getting close." She said calmly.

I thought for a minute. "That seems only sexual rather than sensual." I tried to justify.

"You had to think of that excuse." She looked straight in my eyes. "I can't argue much about it except to say, there are times for love and lust. Both are justified." She stared squarely into my eyes. "And anyway, pleasing you pleases me. How about that?"

We looked at each other. I realised she had got me with my lame excuse. I did not say anything.

"Answer this Einstein. Which of the two would you really enjoy – you doing it yourself or me doing it to you?"

I lowered my gaze as I realised she was going to score a point above me then.

"You know the answer to that. No need to rub it in." I whispered. "But I wouldn't want to bother you just for that. I wouldn't have felt ok making you do it for me."

Sam just looked at me with a piercing glare of hurt and stood up in a split second. I realised she was pissed off. As she started to walk away, I jumped and grabbed her hand and pulled her back. I knew I had upset her.

"Hey." I pulled her back and wrapped her into my arms.

"Let me go. Let me go." She kept trying to free herself pushing me without much serious effort. She was very upset and tearful.

I had wrapped my hands around her waist firmly and in the tussle, we fell on the bed with her pressed down under me in the bed.

As we lay there, I wrapped her in my arms tightly so she couldn't escape. She continued trying to free herself, pushing on my chest, all the while saying, "Let me go."

I buried my face next to her ear and I started whispering repeatedly in her ear as I hugged her tightly, "I love you."

"No you don't." She yelled. Still trying to free herself. She kept punching and pushing on my shoulders, my back and arms with timid force trying to free herself.

I kissed her cheek and neck and continued whispering repeatedly, "I love you."

As she calmed down, I could feel her arms go limp and they fell on my back and shoulder. I hugged her tightly, kissed her repeatedly and continued whispering to her "I love you."

Then I felt her arms move slowly and I felt her hug me. I felt her limp hands squeeze me tenderly.

I moved out of the hug slightly to glance at her. I could see tears in her eyes.

"I love you." I whispered again to her, gazing deep in her eyes.

"No you don't." She yelled at me with wet eyes. "People who truly love each other don't hold back."

I collapsed on top of her, hugging her tightly again. "Oh honey. You know I love you." I kissed her several times with wet kisses.

After a moment of silence, she asked me sternly while I was pressing her down in my arms. "What is it, huh?" She had stopped sobbing now.

"Am I not slutty enough for you?" she blurted.

I froze. I propped myself up on my elbow slowly and moved to look at her. I did not believe what I had just heard her say.

"Don't you EVER say that again." I stressed my words slowly with utmost sternness. "EVER!" I was very angry.

She realised she had said something she should not had.

"Am I too prim and proper for your taste? Is that it?" she rephrased with a calmer voice, but still a straight face and narrowed eyes. She still seemed equally pissed off.

"No." I replied in a controlled voice.

"What is it then?" she asked me calmly. "Why can't you just let go and have me for lust as well?"

I just gazed at her. She gazed at me back. We were both staring deep into each other's eyes. The verbal conversation had now gone telepathic as we tried reading each other's eyes.

Then she ran her hands on my bum and caressed my back slowly and tenderly. Then she wrapped her hands around my neck and pulled me for a kiss. I tried to resist and she just blurted again very sternly, "I don't give a fuck about your infection anymore. Just kiss me."

I knew there was little point arguing with her at that minute so I kissed her back. I could feel her warmth and her boobs pressed against me as I gave into her hug. She was wearing short pants and a thin t-shirt. As she felt me get hard, she moved and undid my shorts, pushing them below my waist. She ran her hands on my bum cheeks holding and caressing them. Then she felt my erection touch and rub against her thighs. She lifted her hips, pushed her pants down and let them slip past her thighs.

"I want you to show me how much you love me." She looked straight in my eyes. She caressed my hair and my face. "I want to feel you inside me. No ifs, no buts." She gazed at me.

I propped myself on an elbow and freed her legs from her shorts. Then I pushed my shorts down and tossed them aside.

Then I lowered myself as she parted her legs taking me in between her thighs. Her lust and passion had changed my instinct and I just wanted to have her right then. Her piercing lusty eyes were gazing deep into my heart for passion and lust. My heart was thumping out of the rib cage. This was the first time I had seen her be this aroused and desperate, while still being so angry.

As I pressed her into the bed, I hugged her burying my face in her neck as I kissed her ear and neck planting wet kisses.

"I love you so much." I kept whispering in her ear.

"Then show me." She ran her fingers through my hair. "Just have me."

As I raised my hip, I positioned my erection on her tender and wet labia. She parted her legs staring deep in my eyes with anticipation mixed in with sheer excitement. Then wrapping my arms around her neck, I slipped them under her pillow. As she felt my erection on her entrance, her breathing became rapid. Then I slowly and gently lowered myself as I pushed inside her. She arched her back in a soft moan and I saw her eyes close like blinds, her pleasure was splashed on her face.

I stopped after a few inches and then I slid out again and pushed back in again feeling the moisture lubricate me. I slid in and out for a few more shallow strokes and then I slid deep inside as I pushed myself inside her. I could hear her gasp as she felt me fill her up inside. She kissed my neck and wrapped her legs around my thighs pulling me closer as I sank deep inside her, into her hug, pressing her in the bed.

As I slowly started to slide inside her, I kissed her lips and felt my passion and lust for her rise. She responded by encouraging me, caressing my face, kissing my lips and neck. I stopped and rose on my knees, tossed my t-shirt away. Then I lifted her top over her head, tossed it aside and then we settled in the bed continuing to enjoy the blissful pleasures. I loved feeling her warm skin caress mine. She kept kissing my chest and neck every time I slid deep inside her. She kept staring at me deep in my eyes.

"Take your sweet time." She said. "You feel so good inside me."

As she felt me slide inside her, she flooded with orgasms one after another. Every time she came, she dug her fingers in my shoulders and back and held on to my arms as she let out deep moans. I slowed while she enjoyed every one of them and then carried on sliding deep.

"I missed you so much." She hissed in my ear. "I so wanted you to have me."

I looked at her in deep lust. "I missed you like crazy." I pressed my lips on her kissing her passionately.

"You should have said." She went through a few more orgasms as I realised I was getting nearer to mine.

"I'm going to cum." I sighed.

"Oh honey, give me your cream." She pulled at me hungrily. "I want you to cum inside me." She flew her arms and hugged me tightly, kissing me with wet hungry lips.

As I plunged inside her a few more times, I felt the rush build inside of me just like last time. I twitched and shuddered. Then I went still as I came inside her. She pulled me tightly into her arms, wrapping her legs around my waist, pulling and locking me inside her as I came several spurts.

When she felt the warm cream inside her, she moaned and came with me one more time.

As I collapsed on her, she wrapped her arms and we lay there gasping. She ran her fingers through my hair tenderly as I gasped in her neck closer to her ear.

"You are such a good fuck." She hissed erotically and hugged me close, quivering all over. She held me in her arms, her hands and fingers running slow and tender along my bare skin. Her fingers running through my hair as she caressed my head lovingly. She hugged me close, softly caressing and pulling me in her arms. She planted kisses on my shoulder as I lay on top of her. I could feel her love pouring out all over me, drenching me with warmth. It felt so good to be loved by her.

After a few moments of silence, I moved gently on her side and lay beside her on my side straddling along her side. I lay my head on the pillow close to her cheek, and I felt her hand run through my hair seductively. She moved back and rolled on her side to look at me.

She gazed at me while caressing my lips and cheeks with her fingers.

After a moment of silence, she spoke, "If you love me so much, why do you hold back, why do you hesitate so much?"

"It's complicated." I gazed with deep sincerity straight into her eyes. "It not easy to explain."

"I have all day today." She touched my hand and kissed it. "I'm all ears. Talk to me. I need to know."

I paused for a moment trying to collect my thoughts.

"You know how you said to me that you keep me on a high pedestal and that I would never come down no matter what?" I looked at her for her response.

She nodded.

"Well, you are not just on a pedestal. You are in the clouds. For me you are an angel – pristine, pure, and hallowed. I am in awe of you and your personality. Everything I have seen and known about you makes me believe you are a gift from heaven. And I constantly wonder what I have done to deserve you."

She moved in closer and kissed me caressing my face gently. "Sorry I just wanted to kiss you. I did not mean to interrupt you. Carry on, I'm listening."

I continued verbalising my thoughts slowly.

"You are gold; nothing will ever change or tarnish you, just like gold is very stable and inert in itself you will never ever change yourself, and there is nothing to compare to your standards. You are 24 carat pure gold. Enough said."

I looked at her and carried verbalising my thoughts. "It's not that I don't feel I don't deserve you. I do love you immensely. And I would think I love you enough to justify me being blessed with you. But I don't just love you. I adore you, I revere you. You might not realise this, but I look up to you. I derive strength from you. I am overwhelmed by the depth of your character, the truthful and trustworthy dependence you offer and the sincerity you have in your heart."

She was gazing at me, her eyes welling up.

"Given all this, it is difficult to relate the human qualities like lust and sex to such heavenly entity as you. I don't have problems with love and pleasure. But when it comes to lust, I feel I would be contaminating you, that I would be belittling you, humiliating you in some way."

She caressed my face and let me continue; tears still rolling from her eyes.

"When we spoke about our new love the other day, I might have appeared to be quite blasé about it. You thought I had handled it well. On the contrary, inside I am overwhelmed. I am clueless. I have known you ever since I can remember. We have grown together like two peas in a pod. Dad is right, we are stuck at the hip. I cannot see myself without you. Over the years, we have just kept getting closer. Our 'love' (I air quoted) for each other has changed so many shades and hues, I don't know whether we can think about colours anymore. I think we need something else – there just aren't enough colours left to describe our love."

I continued. "Not that I don't agree with everything that has happened between us. I love every bit. You know that already. I wouldn't change a thing. But then I don't really know how to define 'us' anymore." I air quoted again.

I looked at her again. She just stared at me waiting for me to continue.

"I don't worry about 'defining' us per say. We are who we are. In fact I know we are very different from any one else and every one will have a tough time understanding us. So I ain't really bothered by that. But because I see you as so many things and in so many ways, particularly something that I revere, it comes hard for me to associate earthy menial animalistic behaviours like lust and sex with you."

I looked at her. She had stopped welling up and she had brushed her tears.

"On top of that I can't seem to forget at times, that you are my sister, my one and only true love of my life. You have no idea how much I love you; what you see is just the tip of the iceberg. You are my soul mate; I live my life for you. You complete me. Without you, I do not want to exist. You can imagine why I would find it difficult to ask you for something raw as sex or just express lust as and when."

I looked at her hoping she understood me and that I was not just rambling on as usual.

Now I waited in silence. I stared at her, raised my eyebrows and shrugged my shoulders in anticipation of a response.

She slowly came close to me, and planted her lips on mine, kissing me softly and gently looking in my eyes all the while, running her fingers through my hair and caressing my face.

Then when she lay down again close to me, she gently caressed my face and spoke softly, "I was correct in that sense." She sighed. "I AM too prim and proper for your own good."

I just looked at her.

Then she spoke carefully verbalising her thoughts. "If I am this angel as you see me, then I need to take a dive and fall to earth, shed my wings and take human form so I can be with you, right?" She stared at me. "But, what if I have already done that, just to be with you? What if I have taken this human form so I could love and be loved by you, like a human, with all its raw, animalistic vice?"

She looked at me. "What if I have already chosen my path? Would you not reciprocate then?"

I just looked at her. Then I nodded slowly. "I could never live knowing I have upset you. I cannot bear to realise I have lost your respect for any reason." I stared at her with tears in my eyes. I could feel my throat choke. "It means a lot to me that you think of me highly, that I never lose your respect."

She came close to me and kissed my lips. Then taking a deep breath, she spoke, "you know you said you adore and revere me. Well shall I tell you something? I worship the ground you walk on."

She stared back with a piercing gaze. "And I'm being truthful and honest about it. I am not just saying it. I know what I am on about. And there is NOTHING that you might say or do that will EVER change it. NOTHING. EVER." I was taken aback with her words.

She stared back at me after a moment of silence. "I think we should just give each other time so that each of us gets to open up at our own pace. I realise, pushing you ain't going to help, nor will feeling upset about it be productive. I realise now. It's not your fault you hold back. You just love me too much just as I love you too much. In time, we will grow to do all the other things too. We just have to wait a while and let our hearts come together."

I nodded. "I am trying."

"I know honey." She crawled into my hug. "It was nice to finally hear your side. Now I know, I would never question you ever again." She kissed me gently. "But would you mind expressing yourself at times when I persuade and encourage you? Gently? Would you object to reciprocate when I want you to?"

I shook my head. "I would love to please you."

"Good. Then we are in agreement."

We kissed again and hugged for a while.

"Good news." She smiled with bright eyes. "Looks like I've healed."

"You did not feel any pain?" I asked with a concerning tone.

"Only pure pleasure." She said. "It was awesome. Out of this world."

"You told me to cum inside you." I voiced my concern.

"It is ok sweetheart. I am using protection." She grinned and caressed my face.

"I would like to think it would be safer if I just withdrew at the time." I suggested.

She just shook her head. "No way. It is the best part of making love when I feel your warm cream inside me." She quivered at the thought of it. "I want every single drop every single time. For me, that is the ultimate sign of love."

"Then at least let me know the days when it is safer." I suggested.

She just shook her head with a smile. "We are not machines. I would like to think we would have each other when we feel like it, not at a set time and date. There would be no spontaneity then."

I just smiled. "We still have to be careful so you don't end up ...." I did not finish the sentence.

"We can use double protection if it worries you so much." She suggested.

I was perplexed. "Condoms?" I was less than keen about them.

"No!" she threw the idea out of the window. "Hell no. I like to feel you when you are inside me. No that ain't happening. But there are lots of options for protection I could use which are non-interfering."

I was curious.

"Woman thing. You don't have to worry about it." She smiled.

"I would like to know." I suggested with sincerity. "I too want to be part of it."

"Really?" she was surprised.

"Why does it surprise you?" I was perplexed.

She just smiled. "You are right. I shouldn't be surprised at all." She shrugged her shoulders. "You have been different from every guy I have known in every other way, all because you have a heart of gold. You are bound to be different even in this matter." She smiled at the obvious.

"So?" I continued to see what she had to say.

"Tell you what, I will make an appointment with the doc and find out all the contraception methods I could have. Then together we will decide which one to go for. How about that?" She cupped my face in her palm.

"I would have liked to come with you." I murmured under my breath.

"I know honey. But we don't want to attract attention, remember?"
She tried to console me.

I nodded.

As we lay there, staring at each other's eyes, she caressed my face
running her fingers on my cheeks, lips and chin.

"I did not know you had such deep bottomless heart. I guess the
fall was worth it after all." She giggled sarcastically.

I just stared at her without being amused.

"Honey, I too am just a human, full of flaws, idiosyncrasies, needs,
desires and hunger for love, lust, passion and pleasure." She said.

"That's after you chose to fall from grace and give up your rightful
place in heaven." I stared at her with warmth.

"O man. You are such a romantic." While rolling on top of me, she
smiled as she came closer, and hugged me tenderly, planting
kisses on my lips.

"If it's any consolation, I did it all for you." She kissed me softly on
my lips.

While we were kissing, I moved around and she felt my erection
on her legs. She slowly traced her hand down my tummy and
circled it gently. As she touched it, it twitched at her warm fingers.

"I would love to have another round." She said.

"Get on top then. I want to see you enjoy it this time."

"I am your plug-in charger." She smiled with a sexy look.

"Really?" I grinned back.

"Um huh." She nodded, lowering her lips and kissing me.

She looked deep in my eyes. "I'm hoping you wouldn't want a
different charger though." Her look was very sombre.

"I am only compatible with this charger." I held her face in my
palms and kissed her deeply. "Don't you ever worry about that. I
love you. Only you."

"You can charge anytime." She grinned. "Just make sure you spill over so I know you are charged fully." She smiled slyly.

"What about you?" I asked. "What if you are charged up and would like to discharge?"

"I am hoping you wouldn't mind taking some of my charge then." She played along with our analogy. "I would hope you wouldn't mind being charged up all the time."

"Sounds good to me." I smiled.

"I'm glad we agree." Her eyes shone with lust.

Her eyes lit up as she straddled my waist and positioned herself on my erection. She lowered her face and planted kisses on my lips. As she licked and sucked my lips, our tongues danced around seductively and sensually. I ran my hands all over her bum and caressed her bum cheeks and inner thighs. Her breathing got rapid very soon.

She raised herself up on her hands and gently let me guide my erection on to her wet labia. With my fingers, I parted her labia as she lowered her bum down slowly. With her eyes closed, her tongue licked her top lip and she bit her bottom lip. Her expressions full of deep intense pleasure were such turn on for me just to watch.

"You enjoy me so much." I sighed.

"Oh you have no idea how much pleasure you give me." She sighed with a deep moan. Her eyes glazed like drunk.

As she started moving her hip, I lay there, letting her decide the rhythm and pace. I watched her awash with carnal bliss wave after wave as she experienced the pleasure.

As she sat up on my crotch, she slowly ground her hips on my erection looking at me with pleasure soaked eyes. Her hair kept dancing on her back as I ran my fingers and hands through it. I slid my hand in front and using my thumb, tickled and rubbed her clit gently as she moved her hips in rhythm.

When she felt me tickle her clit, her moans erupted to a new level and I could feel her spasm and explode with waves of orgasm one after another. I cupped my hands on her breasts and gently massaged them as she tilted her head back. She rested her hands at the back on my thighs and throwing her head back, she arched her bosoms out for me to caress them. This also propped her waist just that much higher for my thumb to tickle her clit. She went through multiple orgasms. I loved to see her eyes closed shut in her carnal bliss.

As she got exhausted from multiple orgasms, she lay on my chest, and slid her arms around my neck under my pillow. I wrapped her back and waist and hugged her tightly. Holding her bum, I rocked her over my erection, thrusting my hips slowly making sure she felt my full length slide all the way out before going in. She was milking me, squeezing and clenching my erection inside her.

She kept kissing me as I slid inside her, licking and sucking my mouth in drunken state. She was limp with pleasure and she was letting me please her. I held on her bum cheeks and bounced her hips on my erection sliding deep and hard inside her, going full length while sliding in and out. I loved the feeling of sliding all the way out before I slid all the way back in again. The wetness inside her was like lighter fluid for me. She kept kissing and caressing me to encourage my pounding.

Her moans were adding fuel to my fiery passion. Her hair was cascading all over her back, seducing my fingertips as I played with it. I could feel her wetness drip on my erection, and she was in heavenly bliss enjoying every moment.

When I could not hold back any longer, I sighed to her that I was going to cum. "Every drop, inside me." That is all she could sigh.

I came inside her deep and intensely. I pulled her tightly as I spurted and she held on to me as she felt the hot cream hit her walls. She came again feeling the warm cream and sighed in my ear. She went limp and rested on my chest trying to catch her breath. I caressed her back and her hair as I calmed from my orgasm.

When we calmed after a few minutes of breathlessness, she raised her head on my chest and placing her chin on her folded arms, sighed sensually, "This is better than any drug."

She looked at me feeling completely spent from all the multiple orgasms. "Now I don't even have words to say anymore. So I'm just going to lie here." She lowered herself and lay on my chest, her bosoms pressed on my chest. I wrapped my arms tenderly around her back and caressed her in my hug.

She relaxed and stretched out her legs still holding me inside her. "Hope you don't mind if I don't move. I like to feel you inside me, although I am so spent and drugged."

"I'm so pleased that I can pleasure you."

She just shook her head. "You have no idea."

Chapter 18 – explorations

Luckily, Sam never caught my infection. After our torrid moment of passion, it was all emotions let loose.

As promised, Sam had visited the doctor and sought advice on appropriate contraception. She had then sat with me one afternoon when we were alone the whole day and gone through all the options. It was a rather eye opening experience for me to say the least. She just could not get enough of how I had shown so much interest in the discussion.

"Hon, usually young males are not so into these things. The girls tend to sort this out themselves, and that too only those who are really conscientious." She had said.

"I am different. I want to know so I can support you if you need me to." I had replied back.

"I know." She caressed my face. "You are so very different; one of a kind."

The whole discussion was rather interesting. "It is nice to know about women stuff you know." I said to her. "There is so much to know."

She just giggled. "What's so interesting about this?"

"Don't you find it interesting?" I was surprised. "I do. There is just so much to think about and so many variables to decide about."

"Hon. It's just a means to an end, the end being more important. Hello." She smirked with sarcasm.

"I know. But this is interesting too." I smiled.

"There is no telling what will get you amused." She smiled shaking her head at a loss. "You are just a naughty and mysterious little kid."

Once we had decided the contraception, she told me that we just needed to be cautious around the ovulation time just to be on the safe side. "And I don't want you to worry or hold back because of it." She warned me pointing her finger and poking me gently in my chest. "It will just be a couple of days in a month."

"I won't know until you tell me." I made a sheepish face.

"Good. Then I won't be telling you."

"Don't do that. Just include me in it too. I want to help too, you know." I pleaded.

"I know hon." She caressed my face and kissed me. "I know you do. Just be yourself and make sure you enjoy me. That is what would be most helpful." She had spoken those words with the sensuality that melted my heart and warmed my blood.

Once the contraception was sorted, Sam had a permanent grin on her face. Her lips with the little tips curved up melting my heart every time I gazed at her. Her eyes drowned me with love and her touch burned my skin. When I touched her, she quivered and moaned with her eyes closed. Especially when we were home alone, we used to fire up all cylinders with our passion and let it loose.

Although she never teased or 'tortured' me by dressing seductively, her need to entice me had increased 10 folds, particularly when we were home alone.

One morning, she came downstairs in one of my shirts and no pants or trousers. She had gathered her hair in a loose bun on top and she had raised the cuffs half way up her arms. She had undone two buttons on the top. I just smiled at her because the sensual invitation to be devoured was oozing out of her.

I was lying on the sofa when I saw her walk down the stairs slowly, taking her time, her eyes locked on mine, gazing at me tracing her figure as she slowly climbed down the stairs.

I just shook my head and let out a loud sigh, "You are such a tease." I could not contain the heavy breathing she had set off in me.

She turned around, with a hand on her hip, swung it on the side seductively, and asked, "Who me? You must me kidding." She gave out a very wicked grin and turned around to work in the kitchen.

I looked at her working away in the kitchen and she stole glances at me making sure I was still staring at her. Every time she locked her eyes on my gaze staring at her, she giggled to herself. Her bum was being veiled just enough that I couldn't see if she was wearing any panties. Her thighs were tender and shapely. The cleavage was slightly open for my gaze as she moved around and the shirt flared ajar just slightly every time.

As she continued pretending to be busy in the kitchen, she spoke to me trying to make small talk. I couldn't resist her seduction anymore. I got off the lounger and walked to her. Expectedly, she turned her face toward me without turning around and sighed, "Yes hon? Need anything?" She smiled coyly.

"Yes. I just wanted to hug this for a while." I slowly snaked my hands around her waist as I got close to her and then pressing my pelvis on her bum, I wrapped her in my hug. I snaked my hands all over her tummy and bosoms. She let out a gentle, warm and sensual sigh that originated deep within and spread out all over her. I felt no bra under the shirt and that made my heart skip a beat or two. She felt it as my breathing got heavy. She placed her hands over mine and continued to enjoy the bliss with her eyes closed, lost in a trance, as I planted wet kisses on her neck and below her ear.

"You are just so gorgeous." I whispered in her ear with a deep sigh. I could smell her sensual fragrance.

She quivered and melted in my arms. "It's all for you to enjoy." She pressed her hands on mine pushing herself inside my hug. I ran my hands all over her tummy and then moved them down to her thighs over her crotch. She threw her hands at the back around my neck and arched back tilting her head back over my shoulder.

I ran my hands on the sides of her waist slowly from the bottom of the thighs. As I traced my fingers slowly up to her bum, I did not feel any panties that I was expecting to tuck my fingers into. She heard my sharp breath as I realised the erotic fact and she felt my fingers run crazy all over her pelvis like a kid in a toyshop. She giggled with a girlish tease. I caressed her labia gently and she moaned as I pressed my crotch into her bum letting her feel my erection growing due to her tease. She ran her hands around my bum tugging on my shorts. She wanted me to take things further.

I let my shorts loose and let them slide past my hips. Then after letting her feel my erection between her thighs, I pressed it and let it slide on her wet labia from behind. She let out gasps as she arched her back pressing her bum on it. I ran my hands over her bosom.

She turned and faced me, throwing her arms around my neck and pressing her pelvis on my erection. I took the cue and raised her legs as she wrapped them around my waist. I propped her holding her bum and I gently pressed her back against the kitchen wall. I watched her eyes glow with anticipation as she remembered the time when I had done the same but had to stop - there were going to be fireworks.

She held on to my neck as I gently pressed her back against the wall and positioned her so I could slide inside her. Feeling her labia with my fingers I positioned myself and gently slid inside slowly, making sure I was lubricated with slow shallow stokes, before I dug deep inside.

I could hear her moan loudly, while she felt me slide inside and go through deep waves of pleasure. I could feel her wetness on my fingers as I held her thighs and bum and slid inside her. I kissed her neck and planted deep wet kisses all over her neck and chest. She ran her fingers through my hair and pressed my face into her bosom.

"You are so deep inside."She moaned deeply. "Oh this feels so good." She locked her legs firmly around my waist while experiencing her orgasms one after another.

As she flooded through her orgasm, I moaned looking deep in her eyes, "I am going to cum."

She locked her legs tightly around my waist, and held on tightly for me to spurt inside her. "Go on. Deep inside me." She sighed.

As I came, I pushed hard inside her. As she felt my warm cream, she came again and I felt her legs tighten around my waist as she sighed with ecstasy. I could feel her fingers run through my hair on my head and squeeze my hair on the back of my head. I had my face pressed on her neck.

As I calmed down she still had her legs around my waist but the grip was beginning to loosen.

"Hold on to me." I whispered to her.

Holding her bum, I slipped my arm under her dangling knees and took her in my arms. Then I carried her to the couch in the lounge. As I gently laid her on the lounger, I lay on top of her. My legs were wobbly, more so with the orgasm than the knee-trembler I just had. She wrapped her arms around my neck and took me into her hug with sensual warmth. We were still gasping from the spontaneous exercise we just had.

"Do you remember I had promised you some fireworks last time we were in the kitchen in the same position?" I reminded her the day after our celebratory dinner.

"Oh I did see some fireworks." She giggled.

"As promised." I smiled at her.

"That was awesome." She quivered at the feelings reflecting on the bliss she had experienced. "So erotic yet sensual. That was what I call lust. That was not demeaning was it?"

I smiled in acknowledgment. "As long as you like it hon."

"I loved it." She exclaimed. "Did you?"

I nodded with a big smile.

Just then we heard a loud clang and a packet of letters dropped on the floor through the mail slot in the door.

We froze. Our hearts had stopped beating.

When we realised it was just the post delivery, we looked at each other and started breathing again.

"Shit. Scared the hell out of me." Sam exclaimed slowly turning from white to warm again. "Stupid post."

"Me too." I gained some strength in my legs. "I wasn't hoping they would be home by now."

"Tell me about it." She breathed a bit more. "I wasn't expecting anyone." She took some deep breaths.

"Phew." I made a sound realising we had a narrow shave.

Then both of us looked at each other and fell about laughing. I was the first to speak, "Your face went white."

"You were like a rabbit in headlights." Sam giggled.

We fell about laughing. "Oh I don't know what we are laughing for. If this had been one of them, we wouldn't be laughing right now" She tried to compose herself through her fit of giggles.

"You are still laughing though." I giggled at her seeing her in that giggling fit.

"That's cause of you." She poked me and continued giggling.

We were on the floor now, rolling in laughter, both naked from waist down. As we gathered our breaths, we looked at each other and calmed down our laughter. Then as we stared at each other, she noticed my erection still glistening with our juices. She slowly rolled and crawled on her fours toward me.

Then she lay down resting her elbow on my side on the carpet, and propped her face close to my chest. She slowly touched my erection as it had gone limp but still trying with difficulty to keep up straight. As she touched it, it seemed to resurrect with life again slowly. I heard her gasp softly.

"Mmm." She moaned. "He recognises me now." She giggled. She stroked it as though it was her pet.

"Would you like to play with my kitty?" She spoke to it with baby babble.

I was just perplexed at her new role-play. I folded my arms under my head and lay there watching her play with my erection. This was turning out very interesting little play. I looked at her for the remark she had made with a perplexed expression.

"What!" she tried to clarify. "Mine is a kitty (pussy) and this has a bone so obviously it is a puppy – dog with bone – so I think it wants to come and play with my kitty." She giggled.

"O man." I exclaimed. "I've fucked your brains out this time."

She just fell about laughing. "No. Stop it. I am trying to be kinky here. Play along." She slapped me teasing on my arm.

Then she went back to my erection and played with it stroking it gently. By now, it was growing slowly and she could feel the hardness in it.

"See it wants to play." She looked at me with big wide eyes. "Ah." She smiled excitedly.

She got on her knees and flung her one leg on the other side, straddling me at my waist. I held her hips and supported her. She positioned herself on my erection and taking it in her soft fingers placed it on her wet labia. "There little puppy. You can have a little play with my kitty now." She was still playing out her kinky role-play.

As she lowered herself on me, I could see her eyes close slowly like blinds and she went into a carnal trance. Then she adjusted her knees and started to move in rhythm. She then unbuttoned her shirt and flung it aside. As she arched herself back she pushed her bosoms out for me to caresses them. With one hand, I caressed her bosom and with the other I was busy tickling her clit. She was in her own sweet place. As the ecstasy on her face was so erotic, it was fuelling my desire to pleasure her without stopping. She moaned many times indicating that she came in waves one after the other.

I slowed down a little to give her a breather after every time she came. Then I asked her to straighten her legs as I sat up. Then holding her by her waist I propped her up and folded and crossed my legs and sat her in my lap. Then she wrapped her legs around my waist and hugged me tightly. I held on her back and while holding her bum I rocked her on my erection. She ran her fingers through my hair and I pressed my face in her bosoms. She then slowly lifted my shirt over my head and then letting it drop aside she pressed her bosoms on my face. When she felt my skin all over hers, she moaned.

I wrapped my hands around her back and waist. I kissed her bosoms and she kissed my forehead. All the time I rocked her hips sliding myself inside her. She lowered her lips and kissed me taking my tongue and licking it all over.

We collapsed slowly as I came inside her again. She held me tightly as she felt me squirt deep inside her. "Oh it feels so warm inside." She exclaimed when she felt me cum inside her. She kissed me a few more time, pulling me close to her bosoms holding me in her arms.

I asked her to hold on to me tightly. While I was still inside her, I slowly got up and laid her down on the lounger and lay on top of her. It was a bit of a twister but I managed it without getting myself out of her.

"Wow. That felt so weird." She smiled. "I love to feel you inside me like this. I am so dilated you wouldn't believe." She quivered with the feeling.

We lay there hugging and kissing. I caressed her face while she looked deep in my eyes.

During the rest of the week, she crept in my bed late in the night and made love to me. She must have missed me so much for her to do that. I loved the sensual and yet erotic nature of that feeling.

Once she had buried her face in my neck and kissed me on my lips to stop her from moaning when she was swathed with waves of multiple orgasms.

On one occasion, she had crept in the bed after we had kissed each other good night. Whenever she would pop into my room to creep under my duvet, it used to make me instantly hard since I knew she was hungry for me. That thought alone would get me aroused. So when she would be next to me, usually all she would need to do is climb on top of me, position herself and take me inside her. We both used to be ready for it – me erect and she wet. We seldom bothered about wasting time trying to take our tops off. In fact that would make it feel so much more erotic.

"You are the most intense addiction I have ever had." She once sighed into my ear when we had collapsed into each other's arms after climaxing. "And it is not just sex with you. Because you love me so deeply, I get to feel everything when I have you – sex, lust, love, pleasure, desire, hunger and an eagerness to please me. That makes it the sweetest drug ever and gets me wilder!"

"I do love to please you hon, and that's because I can see in you how much you enjoy me. That fuels my desires to please you even more." I said to her.

"We are both bad for each other." She admitted. "I think of nothing else these days you know. All the while I just want to have you inside me." She looked at me unashamedly and shrugged her shoulders. "I don't know how I managed before without it."

"I know what you mean." I acknowledged too. "I think of having you all the time. But as you know me now, I feel guilty that I am being shallow and that lust is not the only thing I should be thinking about." I admit sheepishly. "But I know what you mean. It's not just lust or sex with us, although we may be seeking just that at the time. When we do have each other, even I feel everything you just said – love, lust, sex, pleasure, sensuality. Everything rolled into one. That's why I think having you makes it feel so good." I had rambled on.

Chapter 19 – uncertainty

***

One day, Sam was helping Beverly in the kitchen in the afternoon. Sam was trying to learn a new recipe to cook for Alex. When they were sitting at the table sipping on some cocoa and tea, Beverly looked at her and asked, "Can I ask you something?"

"Sure mom." Sam lowered her cup and turned to her.

"Don't take this the wrong way. I am neither prying nor preaching. I just wanted to know."

Sam was a bit anxious and waited for her to speak.

Beverly looked at the ring on the finger that Sam had been wearing ever since Alex had given to her. "Nice ring."

Sam looked at her ring and tried to brush it off. "Yeah. Got it a while ago. It does look nice doesn't it?" She pretended it was just a piece of fake jewellery.

"You haven't taken it off ever since I have seen it when we came back from our weekend break." Beverly spoke softly.

"Yeah. I like it actually. Plus it keeps the lads at college away from bothering me." Sam looked at Beverly and rolled her eyes trying to make some lame excuse. Sam could feel her own breathing getting heavy.

Beverly just looked at her and touched her hand gently. "Does this mean he loves you?"

Sam was taken aback and did not want to recognise what Beverly was asking. Sam made a perplexed expression.

"Does he love you?" Beverly just repeated her question slowly as a matter-of-fact, making sure Sam needed to know that she had realised it. "It is ok honey. I am not going to argue. I just want to know if it's really love or just infatuation."

Sam realised she had been found out. She just rested her cup on the table and from a lowered gaze, glanced straight at Beverly looking in her eyes and said calmly, "He not only loves me, but he adores and reveres me."

"And what about you?" Beverly asked without hesitation.

Sam again looked at her and replied calmly, "I worship the ground he walks on."

Beverly nodded after hearing the response and took a deep breath. She was silent for a while. She avoided eye contact.

Sam took a deep breath. "How long have you known?"

Beverly looked at her. "It doesn't matter now sweetheart. Things will just need to unfold from here on. Although your dad was concerned, I knew there was no way we could have prevented this."

Sam was alarmed. "He knows?"

Beverly looked at Sam and grinned with paternal warmth. "We are your parents, dear. Just because we don't say anything doesn't mean we haven't noticed something, and just because we might not see something, doesn't mean we don't realise anything."

Sam looked at her cup on the table, holding it in between her hands, trying to focus on her fingers playing with it aimlessly. Tears were building up in her eyes and as they ran down her cheeks, she sighed and tried to speak, "I'm sorry mom. I did not intend on it happening. It just snowballed."

"Don't be sweetheart. I know what you two feel for each other." Beverly stroked her hand and caressed it.

"I'm sorry I did not come to you earlier." Sam confessed. "It was hard enough confessing to him. We did not want to upset you two." She burst into a sob.

Mom took her in her arms. "Well what's done is done, unless there is any way it can be undone?"

Sam shook her head and looked at Beverly through tearful eyes. "I love him very much. And I know he loves me just as much."

"Then we will just have to look ahead and see what hurdles we have to face." Beverly just sighed.

"I am sorry to have put you two in this position." Sam sighed. "I did not mean to. You were not meant to know this."

"Sweetheart. As I said, what's done is done. I know you did not mean any harm and it was just innocence." Beverly tried to console her. "Just out of curiosity, are you two aware what you are getting yourself into?"

Sam sat back and brushing off her tears looked at Beverly and just nodded without saying much.

"The road you two have chosen is full of hurdles and problems." Beverly looked at her and stroked her hand. "It is lined with difficulties and deprivation."

Sam lowered her gaze and nodded in acknowledgment. "He has promised me to be by my side."

"I hope so. This ain't something to be taken lightly." Beverly's voice now had caution.

"We won't let anything come to you two." Sam said.

"Oh sweetheart. I am not worried about us. I am scared of what you two will have to put up with to see this through." Beverly sighed.

"Don't worry about us." Sam held her hand and caressed it. "We will sort something out."

"Nor do I want you two falling out with each other over this." Beverly now was very sincere in her voice. "I can't afford to see either of you being hurt in this."

"I promise you that will never happen. We are in this for life." Sam replied her with as much sincerity.

"On such roads, there are always very little options, honey." Beverly caressed her face and sighed. "But you will do what you will do. You both are adults now. You will make your own choices and decisions."

It seemed like Beverly had given up on them.

Sam burst out into tears again, "You can't give up on us."

"No sweetheart. We would never do that. But nor would we be of much help either." Beverly expressed her helplessness. "You will always have us to love you, no matter what. Don't worry about that."

They both had just stayed there at the table silent for a while.

Beverly was the first to get up slowly. "Don't let him see you like this." She cautioned Sam. "I know he looks up to you to sort things out. Come on and let's get some dinner ready. They will be home soon."

Sam brushed her tears and dried her eyes. As she stood up, she hugged Beverly tenderly and started to well up again. "I love you guys so much. Thank you for being so considerate."

"Shh. Now stop that." Beverly tried to calm her down. "You can't keep crying like this. You need to compose yourself." Beverly patted Sam's back.

"What will you tell dad?" Sam asked.

"Don't worry about him. I will talk to him when it's appropriate."

Beverly went upstairs and Sam went into the kitchen.

***

When I had returned home that evening, Sam greeted me with just a smile. There was something different about her. In fact, she did not seem that tactile. I thought she was just being cautious.

At the dinner table, she kept to her meal and barely made small talk, only replying to questions.

After the dinner, she lingered in the kitchen and got us our dessert she had spent time preparing that afternoon.

"What's this?" dad exclaimed as usual. "Treat for your brother?!" he giggled looking at Sam and then mom.

"No. I've made it for everyone." Sam blushed slightly.

"Yeah sure you have." Dad smiled.

"You better like it mister." He looked at me. "At least that way I will get it another time." He winked at me.

"Oh dad. Stop it." Sam tried to make a joke of it.

When we had our first bites, everyone was moaning from the delicious taste. I looked at her and nodded with a raised brow and a smile. Sam just smiled back warmly. She happened to glance at mom briefly.

Once everyone had finished the dessert, Sam spent longer time than usual in the kitchen trying to tidy it up, instead of sitting down with me in the lounger.

I went in and asked if I could help.

"No hon." She smiled. "It's ok. I was just clearing the mess from early on. You go ahead and sit down. I need to go upstairs anyway. Have a few things to sort out."

I looked at her. "Everything ok?" I mimed at her in our code.

She dimmed her eyes to assure me.

"Ok. Let me know if you need anything." I went back and sat in the lounger.

That evening Sam spent time in her room. When I went to kiss her goodnight, she was already in her bed. She was facing away from the door and on her side. She had already changed and was under the duvet. When I entered her bedroom, she did not stir around. I went on the other side of the bed and found her sleeping.

I did not want to disturb her so I just planted a very soft kiss on her cheek and left her room, closing the door behind me.

The next morning, I saw her still in bed past her usual time.

"Hey hon. Everything ok?" I asked her caressing her hair away from her face as I sat beside her in the bed.

She just nodded. She took my hand in her hand to assure me. "Just feel run down that's all."

"Ok. Anything I can do?" I smiled at her suggestively.

She realised my hint and blushed. "No. I will be fine. Thanx hon."

I just nodded in acknowledgement and left her to it. I had early class to attend so I couldn't do much anyway.

The next whole day I did not get to see her much. She spent quite a lot of time in the library.

'I will see you at home. Call me when you need to be picked up.' I messaged her.

'Sure. xxx'

That evening when she sat in the lounger, she was sitting up rather than lying on me as usual. She took my legs on her lap and calmly watched the TV for a while. Then bid us good night and went to her bedroom. "I have a long day tomorrow." She said to me.

"Ok." I just waved her good night.

This did change and Sam came around after a few days. However, she was a bit refrained with her usual hunger for me. Instead of being tactile, she waited for me to initiate and then complied. Once I had shown my desires, she would always go along and comply for us to enjoy together. Although I was not overly concerned, it did make me realise something in her had changed – she seemed to have 'cooled off'.

One day, as I did not have any morning class so I stayed in bed for a while. Sam had changed and left for college. She had wished me good morning but something was not right. I could sense it.

I got up and freshened up. I went in her room and looked around. I got under her duvet and stayed in her bed for a while. It smelled of her sensual fragrance. It was so arousing. It certainly made me think of her instantly and I missed her in that bed. Soon my mind drifted to her current mindset and I was trying to figure out what was going on with her.

As I was leaving her room, I noticed a book on university league tables. It had a list of universities and their information. I was surprised to find it on her desk. She had not mentioned it to me that she was looking in the options to carry on in universities. I did not make much of it so I decided to leave it there.

While I was trying to get ready for my class for later that afternoon, I was trying to find my notebook. I thought maybe she had borrowed it so I looked through her drawers. In one of her drawers, I say a pack of half-opened envelops and letters wrapped in a rubber band. Out of curiosity, I took them out and looked at them without unwrapping the bundle. They were responses she had been receiving for all the applications she had apparently sent out for continuing her studies at universities. I stripped the rubber band and sat down to look through the letters. Apparently, they were all addressed to her in response to her inquiries. All of the universities were away from home, at least a few hours' drive. It would imply she would need to move out – she could never commute over these distances.

My heart sank. It was as if a sword had pierced through me ripping my heart in two.

'Why has she not told me about all this? Why is she keeping it secret?' A question ran through my mind.

'She is trying to move out without telling me.' I thought to myself. 'Why is she doing that?'

'Has she gone off me? Is she bored with me now? Has she reconsidered about us? Has she changed her mind? Does she want to move on? Has she met someone else?'

There were a million questions running through my mind.

'Even if she has, why can't she just tell me? May be she does not want confrontation. After all the promises she made, she feels ashamed of breaking them. She is trying to move away without actually breaking up. She does not want to hurt me. She doesn't want the confrontation.'

My mind filled with anger.

'What the fuck! How could she ever decrease the damage this way, by just leaving me like this?'

I was so angry I had to leave. I put the letters where I had found them and left the house.

I did not know where to go. I just kept driving. My cell phone rang. I looked at the caller ID. It was Sam.

'What the fuck does she want now?' I cancelled the call and threw the phone on the floor of the car.

I sped away in some random direction for a while.

I drove back home late in the night. I slowly and quietly parked the car in the garage. I waited in the car with my head on the steering and breathed for a while. I composed myself and entered the house.

Mom and dad had probably gone upstairs.

"Where have you been?" She turned around and asked with a certain panic in her voice. "I've been trying to call you."

"Sorry I must have missed it. I was out with friends driving and the battery must have run out." I tried to give her the excuse.

"Driving? At this hour? Where?" She was puzzled. It was so not me.

"Yeah. I was just hanging out. What is it that you were after?" I asked her.

"Just wanted to talk that's all." She relaxed on the couch and turned to the TV with nonchalance.

"Ok. Well I'm beat and going to bed. Good night" and I ran upstairs.

I decided I would try to act as normal as I could for the next few days – easier said than done but I had to. If she was planning to break up with me without saying goodbye, then I had to gather my strength to survive the tsunami that would eventually hit me once she leaves.

As I stepped in the bathroom, I stood under the shower. The hot water was making futile attempts to relax my stressed muscles. My head was full of rage and anger of betrayal. 'How could she do this after all I had done for her?' is all I kept thinking in my head.

Then I broke into tears. I couldn't contain them anymore. I tried to keep my voice down through the sobbing. I had to compose myself so I tried to dry my tears, ironic as I was in the shower.

I stepped out of the shower and quickly and quietly dried myself. I made sure her bedroom door was closed. I quickly stepped out of the bathroom and into my bedroom. I closed the door behind me quietly and locked it.

I changed in my sleepwear and quickly got into my bed. I tried to become as motionless as possible so I did not make a sound. I turned and tried to fall sleep.

Sods law says when you want to sleep, you will never fall asleep. I stayed awake for a whole hour. Just staring at the ceiling and the wall that was lit from the streetlight entering through the window. I did not want to toss around either, as I would give away my wakefulness. I did not want to give her excuse to come into my room. I did not want to see her. I did not want to talk to her; I would not have been able to.

Sometime in the night, I must have dozed off. In the morning, I heard a knock on the door.

"Hold on." I realised the door was locked.

I got up, unlocked it, and opened it. It was Sam.

"Good morning." Sam spoke quietly with a perplexed expression.

"Good morning." I tried to be calm.

"You are late waking up. You did not sleep well?" she sounded concerned. As I stayed talking to her at the door she did not know why I was not letting her in.

"Had a rough night, don't know why." I was trying to be casual.

"Everything ok?" she queried very cautiously but sincerely.

"uh huh." I nodded pretending to be still sleepy.

"You were going to drop me at the college, remember?" she reminded me gently. "Will you still be ok or should I get a lift?"

"Give me 5 minutes and I will get ready." I asked her to wait downstairs.

When I walked downstairs, she was waiting in the lounge on the couch.

"Sorry about that. Let's go. I will drop you first and I will sort myself later when I get back."

"You have a class in the afternoon." She reminded me.

"I know." I was trying to be sure of myself.

She did not say anything. We drove to the college with little talk. I turned the radio to kill the silence and conversation. She glanced at me several time in the car but I did not look at her – I just couldn't bring myself to it.

When I dropped her, she wished me a good day.

"Thanx. You too." I replied casually and drove off.

My head was reeling with frustration again. I had to calm down.

I went home and jumped into the shower. I stayed there for a while.

I had visions of her flooding in my mind. I started getting an erection.

'For fuck sake,' I grunted to myself. 'She is leaving you. Stop thinking about her.'

I tried to distract myself out of anger and frustration.

I stepped out of the shower and dried myself. At least I did not have to worry about tiptoeing to my own room again. I got to my room and changed into something casual.

I went into the lounge and tried fixing myself some breakfast. I was famished. I remembered that I did not have dinner the previous night.

I tried to gulp down the cereal. I seemed to have lost appetite too.

'Fucking great,' I thought to myself.

I shoved the cereal down my throat, drank the hot drink, and sat in front of the TV. I tried to distract myself with some TV.

I flicked through some channels. I never realised daytime TV was so crap. 'When was the last time you watched day time TV,' I spoke to myself. 'Thanks to her you have enjoyed her all these days. Well now get used to the normal mundane life', I thought to myself.

Just then my phone rang. I looked at the screen. It was Sam again. I diverted it to voice mail.

As I waited, a notification popped up for a voice mail. I dialled it and heard her voice.

"Hi it's me. Just calling to see if you were in and ok. Talk to you later. Call me. Love you."

My head went spinning again. 'She must be so good at playing this pretence,' I thought to myself. 'I need to play her at her own game,' I thought.

I got up and decided I would go to college early and get distracted. This lounging in an empty house wasn't helping.

At the library, I tried doing some research and homework for my classes. At first, it was a struggle to focus, but then as I distracted myself, I seemed to have lost my anger and eventually focused at my work. Later I had something to eat and attended my afternoon lecture.

Just before I was finishing my class, I got a message. It was from Sam.

"I'm ready and waiting at the library. C u later. xxx"

I had forgotten about taking her home. 'Great. One more journey I have to pretend and try to make conversation'.

When I picked her up, I exchanged normal 'Hi hello'.

The radio was already on.

"Had a good day?" I pretended.

"Yes. Busy but ok. How about you?" She gazed at me.

"Ok. Been busy myself too." I pretended again.

"Probably that is what it is then." She looked away outside the car window.

"What do mean?" I was curious.

"You seem distracted." She pointed out.

"As I said I have a lot on my mind." I tried to push it aside.

"Like what?"

"Just class work. A lot to complete."

"Need any help?" She always wanted to help me out.

"Nah. I will be ok." I tried to be cool. "I'm sure you have plenty on your hands to sort out."

'Oops. Did I just slip there?' I tried to press by lips.

"Ok. If you need me just let me know"

"Sure."

The rest of the journey was relatively quiet.

When we got home, she went ahead first. I took my time getting in the house. She had gone upstairs. I decided to hang around in the lounge. I turned the TV on.

When she came downstairs, she was wearing one of my favourite nightwear.

"I thought you said you had stuff to do." She asked me.

"Yep. Just trying to catch my breath before I start." I switched the TV off and I got up.

"I did not mean it like that." She corrected herself.

"No. I was going to go up anyway." I just played it cool.

I ran upstairs and went into my room.

After a few minutes, I heard footsteps climbing up the stairs. I took a book out and pretended to be working.

As she opened the door, she saw me working.

"Sorry I did not mean to disturb you. What would you like for dinner? I was going to cook since mom will be returning late today." She was trying to be caring.

"Don't mind. Anything easy and I am game."

"How about some pasta?" She suggested.

"Sure. Sounds nice."

"Ok." She looked at me without much to say. "I will give you a shout when it's ready. Dad will be home soon."

"Ok." I tried to fake a smile.

She closed the door and left.

My heart sank. 'Fuck me.' I gasped. 'This is going to kill me,' I thought to myself. 'Few more months of this. Fucking hell'.

I tried to get focused on my work again. 'As if. With her downstairs. Good luck buddy,' my head was taunting me.

I decided I could not stay in. I quickly changed, grabbed the car keys and ran downstairs. "I am popping out for a short while. Need to check out some books at the library before it closes." I made an excuse.

"Ok." She just looked at me.

I dashed out and drove away.

By the time I got back, dad and mom were at the dinner table. Sam was in the lounge sitting on the couch.

"Where have you been?" mom asked as I stepped in. "We waited for you and started eventually."

"That's ok mom. Had to pop to the library for some books."

"At this hour?" dad exclaimed looking at the watch.

"Just before it shut."

"Where are the books?" mom looked at me.

'Oh shit.' I thought looking at my empty hands. "Did not find what I was looking for." I made up an excuse. "I will have to try again tomorrow."

"Come on then. She has been waiting for you." Mom said cocking her head toward Sam.

"You should have started. Why did you wait for me?" I tried to rationalise to Sam.

Sam just looked at me like I had just landed on this planet from outer space.

"You know what she is like." Dad said. "Come on now. Chomp chomp."

I ran upstairs, changed into my nightwear and joined everyone at the table.

Sam had sat down already. I dragged my chair just a tad farther away and sat down, hoping it wasn't too obvious. She just looked at me but chose to ignore.

The rest of the dinner went quietly with only mom and dad making conversations.

I realised that Sam was being quiet tonight.

"You had a good day?" I pretended to be making small talk.

Sam just looked at me. "Uh huh" and nodded without glancing at me.

"How about you love?" mom asked. "How are things going? How time flies," she continued chatting looking at my dad. "Soon they will be completing college and going on to other things."

Dad and mom looked at each other with proud accomplishment. "And just a few years ago they were little kids running around in diapers." They joked.

"So made any plans yet sweetheart?" Dad asked Sam.

My food suddenly choked in my throat and I coughed. She looked at me, waiting to respond.

"Don't know dad. Just looking at options at the moment." She continued eating her meal.

'Wow. Talk about that', I thought to myself.

I couldn't eat anymore. My throat had suddenly closed up. I asked to be excused.

"What about dessert, honey?" Mom asked.

"Nah I will pass on that. I'm full up." Sam never raised her gaze from her meal and did not say a word.

"Ok son. Take it easy." Dad said enjoying his coffee.

As I lay in bed, I was thinking about a lot of things – what my life was going to be like in a few months' time, how I would have to cope without Sam.

'You will have to.' I thought to myself. 'You don't have a choice do you?'

'Oh this sucks big time.' I thought to myself. 'Fucking hell. What an end.' I felt dismayed.

While I lay there trying to sort things out in my head, I heard the dinner being cleared. Mom and dad talking in muffled voices.

Then I heard someone climbing up and down the stairs a couple of times. I was just hoping she did not come in to talk.

While I was lying there with my arm over my eyes, I heard the door click open.

"You ok?" I heard Sam's voice. I lifted my arm to answer her, "Yeah just a headache. I will be fine once I sleep. Don't worry."

"Need a pill?" There was concern and care in her voice.

"No. Once I fall asleep it will be ok. Good night." I lowered my arm on my eyes to shut them.

There was silence for a moment. "Good night." Sam murmured. Then after a brief moment, I heard the door gently click shut.

When I heard her walk into her room, I felt sick in my stomach. 'Fuck me,' I thought to myself. 'Kill me now. I can't take this anymore.' I could not contain my tears. I was overcome with a lot of emotions all at once. The worst part of all this was that I was being so distant and cold to Sam for the first time in my life and that was killing me. All my life, all I had ever done was love her to bits. For the first time now, I was being so distant and short with her. Yet, through the circumstances, I couldn't bring myself to even look her in the eyes. It was killing me either way.

I lay in my bed all night, again trying to get to sleep. I did not sleep for a long time. My back was hurting me very bad through of lack of sleep, tossing and turning. Eventually I fell asleep.

By the time I was awake it was late in the morning. I woke up and washed in the bathroom. When I came downstairs, Sam was in the kitchen clearing up things.

"You don't have a class today?" I inquired.

"I have but I will go a little later."

"I will jump into the shower if you don't need the bathroom."

"Go on." She replied still continuing to work.

'Fuck me. She is being very distant,' I thought.

I went upstairs and got in the shower.

I tried to be there as long as I could.

When I had finished my shower, I went into my room and changed into my clothes. I heard the door click open.

"Can you come to my room after you are done? I need your help with something." Sam was asking for some help.

"Sure. Give me 5 minutes."

She closed the door.

'O fuck. What now'.

I lingered and then opened my door. I looked at Sam's bedroom. I slowly peeped inside and stepped in. I saw Sam sitting at her desk working out something on a pad.

"Have a seat. I need your help." She tipped her head to the bed. "Give me one minute."

As I sat on the beanbag, she looked at me, she put down the pen she was using on the pad and got up. Then she closed her door, pulled up her chair plonking it in front of the door and sat down in it while facing me.

Then staring straight at me, she said, "I want your help to figure out this problem."

"What are you on about?" I pretended to be clueless.

She just looked at me.

"You haven't been yourself for the past 3 days now. You will not talk to me. You will not sit down with me. Hell you will not even look at me. What is the matter?"

"I don't know what you are on about?" I again pretended to be ok. "I have just been busy and stressed about work at college."

"Is that it?" She asked.

"Yep." I nodded trying to give a straight glance.

"Why won't you tell me what it is that is stressing you?"

"It is not important. It will pass." I tried to push it aside. "I'm sure you have your hands full."

"What the fuck!" Sam just sighed helplessly.

I had never heard her swear like this.

"You are killing me do you know that?" Sam looked at me as she spoke softly. "You won't confide in me and the way you have been behaving is killing me inside."

"Really?" I looked at her.

"What do you mean?" she was completely confused. "What the hell is the matter with you? Why are you doing this to me? Have I done something to upset you? Have I said anything? Tell me." She was getting frustrated and dismayed. "Has mom said anything to you?" She looked at me with suspicion.

I just looked at her and shook my head without any clue what she was on about.

"Why don't you just kill me now? If you ain't going to talk to me, I'd rather be dead." She was yelling at me now.

"What have I done wrong, tell me. I can't live without your love, you know that. Why are you doing this to me?"

Her anger was escalating. "Talk to me, Alex." On very seldom occasions has she called me by my name, and only when we were in public.

"Really?" I questioned her. "You cannot live without me? Comes as a little surprise." I muttered under my breath.

Sam just stared at me. "What did you say?"

"I was just making a comment on what you said." I tried to stay calm.

"So what was that?" Sam questioned me. "I am pretending?"

She was fuming. "Why the hell would you think that I was pretending? Pretending about what?"

"That you couldn't live without me." I muttered.

"What?" She was shocked. "Where did you even get that idea from? Why would I pretend?"

"It's ok." I got up to leave.

She slid her chair back against the door blocking my exit. "Where do you think you are going? Sit down. You ain't going anywhere until we have sorted this out. I want you to talk to me and talk to me now." She was being very calm and sincere in her predicament. Basically, she was pissed off with me.

I sat back down as I realised I would had to physically fight my way out otherwise.

"I want you to tell me what's in your mind. Even if I cannot do anything about it, I still would at least like to know what it is that I have done to upset you so much."

"It's you who needs to start talking." I said opening the so-called 'can of worms'.

"Me? About what?" Sam was perplexed.

"Like your plans after college!"

"I haven't decided anything yet. You know that already. I would tell you if there were." She looked perplexed.

"Would you?" I showed doubt.

"What are you on about?" She was perplexed but tried to calm down again. "Can you please tell me what are you on about? What plans?"

"About you going to uni." I confronted her.

"There aren't any plans yet. I am still making inquiries."

"Well then." I asked her. "When were you going to tell me about your confirmation? Would that be just before you left or after you had left?" I questioned her. "Or were you just going to walk out and never said goodbye?" I looked at her.

"Why would I do that?" She looked genuinely clueless.

"May be because you have changed your mind and you want out of here. May be because you don't want to hurt my feelings when you decide to leave."

"Where is this idea even coming from that I would be leaving you?" She wanted to know.

"I'm sorry but I found your application letters for uni."

"And?"

"All of them are far from here so it figures if you are planning to move out it is a good excuse."

"Excuse for what?"

"Moving away from me."

"Really? Is that what you derived from those letters?" I could see her face getting red. "That I am planning some getaway from here, from YOU?"

"Why wouldn't you. Many of my friends have been in the same boat." I tried rationalising. "And if you have changed your mind about us, about me, it figures."

"Really?" Her tone indicated sarcasm. She was being very calm about it now. That showed she was loading up her canons waiting to fire.

"And you thought I was like one of them?" She looked at me with piercing eyes.

"I don't know" I looked away. "People change, they can fall out of love. They have a right to break their promises, take back their word." I shrugged. "There is no crime against that."

"Are you finished?" She calmly asked me.

"Yes." I nodded and looked away.

"Ok. Now listen to me." She looked straight in my eyes with a very sincere look.

"The only thing you have seen is like a tip of the iceberg. The only thing in front of you is some letters of confirmation for applications I have sent out for inquires. And from THAT alone you jump to conclusion about making judgements about ME? How bloody dare you! And for that matters, you aren't even looking at the correct iceberg to consider that analogy! There is NO iceberg. These are just chucks of ice floating around with no significance at the moment."

I just looked at her with little clue. She had learned to ramble, like me.

She was fuming. "I have given my heart and soul to you. I have loved you from the bottom of my heart. And you think I would break up with you? Do you even know me?" She was screaming.

"People change. Do they?! Well sure they do. I am the same kind of person huh?! Wow." She was being sarcastic. "After so many years of dedication that I have shown you, if this is how fragile your trust is in me, then I have certainly failed."

She looked at me with wet eyes. I looked at her.

"You haven't spoken to me in 3 days, it has nearly killed me and you think I could walk away from here leaving you behind? What have you smoked?" She was again shouting, tears running down her cheeks.

"I have loved you with all my heart just as deep." I was shouting back at her now. "It wasn't easy for me to accept that you could had changed your mind about me and decided to leave." Tears were welling up in my eyes. "I could never do anything about it."

"Why not?" She yelled back. "Would you just let me leave?" She looked at me puzzled.

"What can I do if you stopped loving me?" I replied back helplessly. "If you grew distant, if you changed your feelings for me?" I was angry and frustrated.

"Wouldn't you at least try and talk it over?" She calmed down seeing me in a state now.

"What's the use? When someone loses interest, it is the end of the road anyway, isn't it?"

"See there you go again. Accepting defeat lying down." She threw her hands in the air in exasperation. "Is that what you thought? I had lost interest in you?"

"Why else would you want to move away from here alone?" I asked her.

"Hold on. First, let's clarify something. I am not planning to move out and those letters do not prove that. Those are just inquiries and that's all they are." She tried to clarify the main sticky point. "Do you get that?" She looked at me to seek my acknowledgment.

"Ok. So why haven't you told me about it?" I asked her.

"There is nothing to tell. I am still doing preliminary inquiries. Nothing is certain, there are no answers, no solutions yet. I am still finding out options."

"Options for leaving." I calmly implied.

"I swear to you if you bring that point up one more time so help me god." She was trying to reason with me while getting frustrated.

She climbed down from the chair and kneeled down in front of me. She took a deep breath and calmly started speaking looking straight in my eyes, "Honey listen to me. Please listen very carefully. And make sure you trust me when I say this because I seriously don't know any other way I could prove it to you otherwise." She was trying to be very calm and reasonable. "I love you from the bottom of my heart. Leaving you is the ONE thing I will NEVER do. I have been beside myself for the last 3 days just because you haven't been yourself with me. Please understand I was not planning to leave."

"So how do you explain the letters."

"Ok." she calmed down. "I have been thinking." She spoke in a quiet voice. "We need some options after we finish college. And I have been considering looking at some options that will help us stay together while completing uni."

"We?" I was surprised.

"Yes we. You and me?!" she clarified. She had a 'Duh!' expression on her face. "Please. Work with me here! Ok?" She looked at me with a stern face and some exasperation now starting to build.

"But the letters are only addressed to you. They only mention your name for the applications."

"Those are only inquiries hon. I am trying to short list unis that would be suitable for you and me both. That way we could be together AND complete our degrees."

I just looked at her.

"Do you get it?" She wanted my confirmation.

"So what's your plan?" I was still not sure. "What about me? My applications?" I did not know what she had in mind.

"Give me a minute. Stay right here ok. Let me check something." She whispered.

I nodded.

She opened the door, walked downstairs, and after a few minutes I heard her walk up again. She left the door open.

In a very quiet voice she started speaking, "I was thinking we could use the opportunity of our degrees to move out and stay together while we complete our education. What better excuse than that to stay together? No one would mind. It is a legitimate reason. And we would kill two birds in one stone."

I couldn't see the 'birds' or the 'stone' yet. My expressions made her realise the blank spaces waiting to be filled, the spaced out dots waiting to be connected.

"I want us to live together without sacrificing our education. If we moved to the same uni together we would be able to share a place together all the way through to our graduation. Wouldn't that be great?"

"But then you have only applied for yourself. What about my applications?" I asked her.

"Well I thought about it. I wanted to know if I could get any scholarships and a placement in any of the chosen universities and then that would had been my shortlist to ask you to apply to them too. Anyone who offered both of us scholarships and/or a place would be our shortlist to consider."

The penny had dropped.

"There are a lot of factors to consider though. There are a lot of things that need to work out for this to work."

"I know. That is why I said I was still looking for options. I still don't have all the answers." She was glad to be bringing home the point she had been trying to make.

"So you weren't thinking of leaving here alone?" I felt like a fool now.

She moved toward me, knelt on the floor, took my head into her bosoms and hugged me firmly. "Baby if I lost you to death, I would follow you without hesitation." She looked at me. "That's how much I love you. Do you really think I would be able to leave you? I cannot stand being separated from you. Hell I cannot even breathe without you in my thoughts, I feel suffocated otherwise. How could I EVER leave you?" She just looked at me with ridicule in her eyes. "Moreover how could YOU think like that? Don't you know me by now?"

"People change. They cannot be blamed for that. Couples move apart, even after years of marriage." I lowered my gaze sheepishly and muttered.

"I know baby." She took me in her bosoms and hugged me close. "I don't know what the future holds. I am a human too you know. But what I know for now is that you are my life. You are my world. You are everything to me. Without you I don't exist. I would not want to exist. You got to stop worrying about a possibility that may or may not happen."

"I would not be able to live without you." I acknowledged sheepishly. "It would kill me even to lose you, let alone if you break up with me."

"Oh my sweet baby. You cannot be living your life in the shadows of such uncertain nightmares. You don't even know if it will happen. Why ruin your sweet life now for a remote future possibility?" She was kissing me all over my face.

I held on to her tightly. "I love you too much," I whispered. "That is my problem. I am in so deep, if I lost you now, I will just sink and drown."

She stared in my eyes. "And you are my world, my rock. Our love is the source of the strength that we derive to see through any obstacles life may throw at us."

"Without you I would not have that strength." I sighed.

"Me too." She sighed. "Let's not worry about that for now ok?" She kissed me gently on my lips. "For now help me plan how to kill our birds with one stone." She smiled at me. "We would have a lot of fun to look forward then."

"Why move so far away?" I inquired.

"I want us to start living like a couple, or at least see if it would work out like that. Going to a distant place would ensure that no one knows us." She replied. "We cannot stay here for long now that we are close."

The thought of us living together in one place, without any hindrances or prying, judging eyes was so tantalising that it warmed my heart instantly.

"That would certainly be nice." I smiled. "You should have told me about all this before. I would not have gotten the wrong end of the stick then." I apologised feeling foolish.

"Baby I did not want to get your hopes up without anything concrete on paper. I was just beginning to do the window-shopping yet. If things did not pan out, I would have felt really bad to have let you down. Moreover, you give up too easily. You feel defeated and lose hope too quickly. I did not want that to happen. I cannot bear to see you down. I love you and if you are not smiling, I wither inside. You are my rock. I look up to you for strength and you do give me so much strength. You don't realise it but you do."

"You never let me down hon." I smiled. "I rely on you with my life."

"Then trust me when I tell you how much I love you." She smiled warmly. We hugged each other with a soft, gentle and long kiss.

"I know I don't understand hidden agendas very well. I have to have things spelled out to me." I acknowledged my naivety. "If only you had come to me and explained all this, maybe I would have understood it. This misunderstanding happened because I did not know and that scared me. I cannot deal with the unknown very well. If I know what is coming, I am at least prepared. I can deal with any calamity when I am prepared. I do not deal with surprises very well. You know that." I smiled sheepishly.

"I do know." She smiled. "And I am sorry I should have discussed all this with you openly. My bad. I'm very sorry. I can see now why it would have freaked you out." She held my face in her palms as she gazed deep in my eyes warmly.

"It's ok. I'm glad we worked things out." I hugged her.

"We?" she giggled. "I worked it out. You were just going to drop me like a hot tin of soup mister." She said sarcastically. "If it hadn't been for me sitting my ass in front of this door, you were happy to walk out here without even talking to me!" She pointed at the door.

"I'm sorry. But the thought that you had lost interest in me was too much for me to bear."

"You are such a defeatist." She exclaimed. "You are my rock. I rely on you with my life too. If you don't toughen up and fight alongside me, we both will sink eventually. I cannot do this alone you know. I need you beside me." She hugged me squeezing me in her arms.

She spoke softly after a moment of silence, "Let me tell you something today. If EVER I decide to finish with you, if I was saying it over the phone you should know that I was in trouble. Let's agree that to be our code so that you can come and rescue me. Even if I said that to your face, I would expect you not just to fight for our love, but also for you to question my sanity. That day you should say to yourself, 'There is something wrong here. No way would she have ever wanted to do this. There is something else going on and I think she needs my help.' I would want you to fight for me hon. I would want you to slap me and wake me up from my nightmare when I start thinking of finishing with you because that is what it probably would be – a terrible nightmare."

We stared into each other's eyes.

After a long moment of silence, she spoke softly. "Are we ok?" She looked at me.

I nodded sheepishly. "I'm sorry."

"Apology accepted only on one condition."

"You will help me with my window shopping so we can work things out and create a safe and workable plan," she suggested. "And we will find a way. We cannot give up. Deal?"

"It's a deal." I smiled back.

"Great. Now come on downstairs. I have fixed us some breakfast. I know we both are famished. Then we will have a nice shower and then we will complete some work for our college. We still have to graduate college you know." She smiled.

"I know." I smiled. "I am starving. And let's take things one step at a time. It's nice to plan a few steps ahead, but it's never a good idea to run before you walk." I muttered.

"Now explain to me Einstein. If such wisdom is locked in that brain, why isn't there a bit of trust and optimism anywhere to be found?"

"Because love and shit both just happen." I smiled. "Nothing to do with the brain."

"You witty little angel." She lowered herself on my lips and we kissed for a while.

When we were sitting at the dinner table having our breakfast I looked at her with deep gaze.

"What?" She questioned me.

"You know what I said earlier upstairs. That I would die if I lost you." I spoke quietly.

"What about it?" She asked me.

"If you changed your mind in the future about us or me, I won't hold it against you. I want you to stay with me because you want to. Not because of some silly reason to protect me from heartache." I spoke with a serious tone. "I will survive somehow. You wouldn't have to worry about me as long as you just tell me the truth." I sounded sincere.

She dropped her spoon in the plate, folded her arms and gave me a long stare.

"How come an intelligent and wise fella like you happen to be so messed up inside his head?" She was shaking her head in puzzled exasperation.

"I guess too much of anything is never any good." I shrugged my shoulders sheepishly.

"Well then smarty pants. Take a chill pill, finish your damn breakfast and get your delicious ass in my bed before anyone comes back. You owe me 3 days of loving that I have missed because of this palaver." She exclaimed.

"Ok." I smiled sheepishly and continued finishing my breakfast. "I love you." I smiled at her with sincere gaze.

"Definitely not as much as I love you." She stroked my hand and pressed it gently, smiling back at me.

When we were in her bed, I spoke to her softly after a moment of silence and reflection.

"It doesn't explain something." I said to her.

"What are you on about now?" She looked at me anxious.

"A few weeks ago, I noticed a change in you when I came home. You appeared distant and cold. Ever since then, I have noticed that you don't initiate your hunger and desires for me. You wait for me to do that. I thought you had decided to cool off." I spoke at length.

She took a deep breath. Then nuzzled her face in my neck and sighed, "I was hoping you would not had noticed it."

"What's up with that?" I asked being concerned.

"You will not get upset over this. Promise?" She looked me with a very cautious look.

"I won't." I just replied softly.

She buried her face in my neck and spoke slowly, "Mom and I spoke about us that evening before you came home. She knows about us; has known for a long while." She spoke without looking at me.

"Really?" I was shocked. "What did she say? Was she mad?"

"Far from it. She was way more considerate than we both have given them credit."

"Dad knows too?" I exclaimed.

"Duh. They both have known apparently for a while. They just did not say anything to us." She said with helplessness.

I was silent for a while trying to take this in.

"I felt really bad for keeping it from them." She sighed.

"You know we did speak about it and agreed." I reminded her.

"And I did say to you about mom." She looked at me. "I was right."

"How did she broach the subject?" I inquired being curious.

"This gave it away." She pointed her ring at me. "Of course our closeness was probably detected long while before that."

"What did she say?" I asked her while stroking on her back.

"If ours was love or just infatuation."

"And what did you say?" I asked her becoming curious.

"That we adored each other and that it was not going to be undone."

"O man." I sighed. "This makes it so awkward."

"Welcome to my world Einstein." She jumped up on her elbows resting them on my chest and looked at me. "Now you know what I have been going through for the past few weeks, and you thought I had 'cooled off' apparently." She smirked with sarcasm. "And don't you dare act up in front of them now that you know this. I don't want you spilling the beans. I have been trying hard to keep it like normal. This embarrassment is enough. I don't want to have to talk about this to them again."

"Don't worry." I looked at her sheepishly. "Now I get it." I looked at her with apologetic face. "I'm sorry. I did not know did I?" I tried to make excuse.

"You got so many things wrong about me in the past few weeks." She exclaimed. "I cannot believe it."

"I love you." That's all I could say to her.

"Yes. You bloody well should." She growled at me jokingly. "The stuff I put up for you. That is how much I love you."

She lowered her face in my neck and gently slapped my arm. Then she caressed it tenderly.

"I did say to you that I am just a human after all, with all my shortfalls and idiosyncrasies." I whispered sheepishly.

"Yeah, only when it suits you. The rest of the time you are a naughty little angel." She turned around and planted tender kiss on my lips. I took her in my arms and we kissed each other for long while, slowly and tenderly.

She felt my erection build between her thighs. She grinned slightly between the kisses. She undid my shorts and gently tugged on my briefs before she slid them down my legs. Then she shuffled and straddled my legs, lifting her skirt slightly to bare her bum. She wasn't wearing any panties. Then she positioned herself on my erection and let me guide it inside her. We were clothed otherwise and this spontaneity had come to become rather erotic as we had started exploring our carnal desires. I slid inside her slowly and after a few shallow strokes the moisture had lubricated me enough to slide deep inside her.

"You are my drug and my dealer." She grinned with deep sensuality. "I am addicted to you now."

"Anytime, anywhere, anyway." I sighed as I kissed her. "I only have pure gold for you."

My sensual compliance always fuelled her passion. "Oh. You make me so horny." She ground on my erection with deeper thrust. "I need your cream."

We enjoyed each other while we made love. When we collapsed after the orgasms, we kissed each other and stayed in our hug for a while.

"No matter what, I ain't giving you up. Not for anything in the world." I declared to her.

She looked at me with loving eyes. "Me neither. We are in this together, forever."

Chapter 20 – the ghosts from the past

After we had settled into our new pretence, things had become difficult for us. Since we could not be tactile at home that often, we had to find ways to get close and intimate when we were home alone. The time we spent together had decreased. Moreover, the intensity and the hunger in both of us had skyrocketed. Our physical craving for intimacy knew no bounds and particularly when we were home alone, we used to make love until we were exhausted from multiple orgasms.

All this meant we were seeking more time outside to find ways to get close to each other. We used to spend more time at our lake, staying in the car lying on each other in the seats, hugging and kissing each other.

On one such occasion, we had stayed at our lake for longer than usual. It was Sunday and the weekend had proved torturous. Usually mom and dad were at home and that put pressure on us to 'behave'. This meant we could not be ourselves, and enjoy the intimacy we had become addicted to. Over the past few weeks, we had realised that weekends were our biggest downers – little intimacy in the house and little excuse to go out without being obvious. That is why we had lingered a bit longer than we usually did on that day.

"Just a few more minutes." She said. "Once we get home, I won't be able to feel you close to me." She sighed.

I gently caressed and kissed her. As we lay there, the sun had moved toward the horizon and splashed colours on the evening sky that worked like a canvas. Shades of purple, red, maroon, blue and grey had developed like a photograph slowly developing in the trays of a photographer's darkroom. The colours had come alive while the sun slowly faded away, giving back the reins to the oncoming night. As we saw the last of the sun diminish, we lay there, kissing and caressing each other. It felt so good to be so close together in that moment as we had missed each other the whole day.

As the dusk had deepened its shades of grey, we saw headlights flash in our direction. I saw bright lights of a big vehicle driving in our direction to the lake. Usually, we had not seen anyone in this side of the world so seeing the flashes of headlights that night intrigued us.

"Someone is coming this way." Sam rose up and gazed at a distance in the direction of the approaching headlights.

"Who could it be?" I tried to guess. "Some other couple may be."

"Probably." Sam tried to think it through. "We have never seen anyone here before though."

"Hope it's not the police." I said being a bit anxious.

"The headlights seem too high up for a police car." Sam said. "It seems like a truck or something." Now she could see the approaching vehicle as it snaked its way down to the lake.

As the headlights approached our location, I got more concerned and sat up. Sam slid onto the driver side. The vehicle seemed to be coming toward where we were parked. As it approached us, we now realised it was a truck, rather loud and harsh – probably because it had been modified to present itself as a teenage obsession in extravagance. As it screeched to a halt, it stopped a few yards behind where we had parked. I now realised that it was blocking our way for reversing. There was a limited space in the front for us to drive off so unless we did a 5-point turn, we were pretty much boxed in.

I was breathing heavy now as I got a bit anxious. Sam noticed it and she looked at me with concern. I could sense it in her body language.

"Stay calm. Don't panic." I tried to calm her. "We don't know who they are or why they are here."

As we waited and looked over our shoulders, we saw the main headlights had been turned off and only the parking lights were now visible. As our eyes dilated to the lowered luminescence, we watched curiously who had driven and parked so close to us. After a rather long nervous wait, we saw a person climb out of the truck from either side. As they closed their doors slowly, they looked at each other.

"If they know us, I wonder who it could be." I whispered.

As I looked at the side mirrors, I couldn't see the face of the one who was walking to my side.

I saw a face peep into Sam's window. As she looked, he seemed to recognise her.

"It's Sam." He shouted. "Fancy seeing you here." He shouted looking to the other guy who was now standing at my door. I did not recognise him, but I did recognise Billy. He was standing at Sam's door knocking on her window. Sam looked at me with complete puzzlement and lowered the window half way.

"Hey Sam." Billy exclaimed. "How come you are here?" He looked at me. His tone of voice did not seem friendly although he was making feeble attempts.

"Hi." Sam replied with awkwardness in her voice. "Just hanging out." She looked at me.

"Cool." Billy looked at me and giggled. "Sure. Care if we joined?"

"Actually we were about to leave." Sam said looking at me.

"Really?" Billy tried to catch her out. "Seems like you two were in the middle of something. Hope we have not interrupted anything." He giggled at his friend. "I will need to move so you can get out. Why don't we spend time talking and then we will all leave. We just got here, and I've not seen you in ages anyway."

Sam looked at me and tried to play cool. I knew we had to give in as there was no way a protest was going to help us move out of that parking spot. I nodded to Sam. We both opened our doors and stepped outside. We were trying to stay calm and collected. I murmured, 'some time chatting, we will try and make small talk and then make an excuse to get away.'

We walked around at the back of our car and Billy leaned against the front bumper of his truck. His friend stood next to him, not making much conversation. Neither me nor Sam knew him from anywhere.

"It has been so long since I have seen you." Billy tried to make conversations. "You have grown good." He drooled looking at Sam. "Damn you look hot, girl." There was a rather crude rudeness in his tone.

I tried to stay calm and maintain eye contact with Billy and his friend.

Sam was trying to stay calm.

"So what have you been doing these days?" Billy tried to be nosy.

"Just completing college." Sam replied.

"Wow. So you are going to get a diploma and shit huh." Billy looked at his friend and chuckled.

"Yes." Sam acknowledged trying to hold her ground.

"Man. I got fed up with that shit a while ago." Billy replied. "School was more than plenty for me."

I just looked at him. He never had the brains to cope with school, let alone college. It did not come to me as a surprise. I just kept looking at him and his friend.

"So what do you do these days?" Sam tried to make small talk.

"I have just had this bad boy modified." He thumped the hood on the truck. "Chicks dig it you know."

"uh huh." Sam looked at the metal machine with a disenchanted look.

"Don't you know? I have had more lays in this than my bed." Billy was trying to be pompous about his 'victories'. His friend was nodding his head with a stupid smirk on his face.

Sam just tried to ignore his rudeness.

"I thought you were here doing something like that." Billy remarked looking at Sam and then me. "Did not realise it was your brother here. You too are rather close for bro and sis."

"We were just hanging out." Sam tried to create some excuse by playing it down.

"Sure." Billy smirked. "So when did you decide to get physical? Last I saw you, you did not want to know."

"What are you on about?" Sam tried to defend herself. I moved closer to her in protective response.

"Seems to me you were ready to get more than just quiet time today." Billy laughed. "So you have grown up then, from the last time we had met."

Sam did not reply and just looked at him. I moved in closer to her, trying to make sure he was aware of what he was trying to insinuate.

"If you like to go dogging, there are some nice places I know I could show you." Billy laughed looking at his friend.

"Excuse me but I don't think that was necessary." I tried to step in.

"I was just suggesting. If you two want to have some private time together, go ahead. Don't mind us. We won't disturb your quality time." He broke out in a rude laughter.

"I don't think that was called for." I looked at him sternly and indicated Sam to get into the car so I could drive out.

"I wonder how long it took him to make a slut out of you, after you turned this down." Billy looked at Sam and snide a crude remark while holding his crotch. My anger shot up and I was beginning to lose patience.

Sam tried to pull me and gestured me to ignore him.

I continued walking slowly past Sam to the driver side. As I had cornered past the boot, Billy stood up and began walking slowly to us. I stopped and turned facing him. Sam had frozen still on the other corner of the boot.

"What do you say for old time sake?" Billy stood close to Sam. "If you have dropped your panties by now, would you like to give me a joyride?"

Sam was not saying anything anymore. She just glanced at me trying to signal to stay calm and not argue or challenge him.

"I think you need to wash your mouth out." I sounded a bit confrontational.

"And you need to wash your dick." Billy stepped towards me trying to intimidate me. Then he laughed out very crudely.

He was now goading me. "I know her sort of bitches – they like to tease and then pretend butter wouldn't melt. All the time they are dying for a good fuck. Has she flashed her cunt to you yet?"

I was getting very furious now. I tried to move away from them and get going. Looking at Sam, I made a gesture in our code for us to get out of the place quickly.

As I moved to open the door, Billy took hold of Sam and laughed across at me, "Well you can go. She will catch up with you after she has enjoyed her time with us." Billy grabbed her wrist. "What do you say? Would you fancy some cream on your pie?"

Sam tried to shake his grip off from her wrist. As she tried to shake him off, he held on to her more tightly. I sprang into action seeing him get physical with her. "What the hell do you think you are doing? Let me go." Sam started to yell at Billy.

Seeing me make a move, Billy handed Sam over to his friend who held on to Sam and took her arm in his hand. As I came around the boot, Billy charged into me. "Where do you think you are going pimp? Don't you like to share your booty?" Billy grabbed my shirt and punched me in my stomach. I coughed out with pain.

Sam screamed watching me in pain, "Billy let him go. You don't need to do this."

She was trying to free herself from the clutches of the guy who was trying to restrain her. Meanwhile Billy was goading me with many derogatory remarks about Sam. Each one was setting fire inside my brain like torching fuse wire.

Sam was yelling at me to leave him and to not get into a fight. "Alex be careful."

Billy was getting really physical and threatening with me. I realised I had to do something smart or else, something really nasty was going to transpire there soon. I was there alone to protect Sam and I had two thugs on my hands hell bent on creating trouble for us that night.

While Sam was yelling out, Billy shouted out to his friend, "Shut that cunt up."

His friend took Sam and tried to shut her mouth with his palm holding her from the back. Sam was constantly trying to free herself. In the tussle, she seized an opportunity, bit into his fingers and as he loosened his grip on her, she kicked him hard in his crotch. He dropped to the floor on his knees while holding his balls. Then she kicked him hard in his stomach. He was on the floor squirming.

As she ran towards us, Billy saw her charging to him and just when she was at an arm's length from him, in a reflex, he slashed out his arm hard and caught Sam's face with a loud slap. He slapped her hard enough for her to twirl and hit her head on the boot of our car. She dropped down unconscious.

Now I could not hold it together. I swung my hand and lay a punch in his stomach. I had never ever hit anyone in my entire life. In addition, I think I was trying to control my anger. Moreover, Billy was a big guy. Therefore, the punch did not appear to had made much of a dent. Billy swung another punch at me this time in my back. I groaned in pain. Now I realised he was not here to intimidate, he was ready to inflict much more than just pain. I let a punch really rip out of myself as I hit him in the stomach. He stumbled back holding his stomach in pain. I grabbed him and started pushing and shoving him and he kept hitting me in the stomach.

While I was holding on to his neck, trying to shove him back, he drew something from his pocket. It made a 'click' sound and I could not see what it was but I feared it was a knife. I took a bold step of charging him down, as I did not think there was much to hold back if he was going to draw weapon on me. While I held on to his neck at arm's length, I pushed him back with all my strength. I could feel slashes on my chest and realised if I did not put a stop to him, he was going to kill me any minute. Without thinking much, in a reflex, I charged into him with all my strength with a loud burst of cry and I felt him bang against the bumper of his truck as his torso hit the grills. Just then, I felt a sharp pain in my ribs and chest but chose to ignore it. I wanted to put a stop to his intention of striking back at me.

After I had shoved him hard on the grill and held him there for a while I felt him go still. When I saw his face, he had eyes wide filled with shock and pain. I stepped back from him to see him fully as he was not retaliating anymore. He had gone still and limp. As I stepped back slowly, I realised that in the fight I had shoved him against the metal frame grill with a spike embedded in his back. I could see blood on his shirt from the front. Then I came to my senses.

Just then, I looked down on my chest and saw the knife he had stuck in me just when I had shoved him into the bumper. It was then that I had realised how that night had taken a turn for the worst possible scenario. I looked at Billy. His lifeless eyes were staring in the blank darkness, while I was standing there with a knife stuck in my chest through my ribs. The other guy was on his knees trying to recover from the crack in his nuts. Seeing what had transpired, he stumbled to his feet and limped away inconspicuously in a hurry.

In my instinct to keep Sam safe, I had not safeguarded the significance of self-preservation. Having spent all my life loving her, and never ever harmed a single fly so to speak, it had never dawned on me to learn how to defend myself without getting into a cul-de-sac, a check-mate compromise. In the spirit of protecting Sam, I had compromised my own safety. I didn't regret protecting her, but I had realised that I had paid a very hefty and unnecessary price.

I could have dealt with that situation much more favourably had I known how to deal with the darkness in the world without losing my cool. I could have learned to defend myself in a more rational manner and still kept the bad elements at bay; even if I had to stop Billy, I didn't need to endanger myself in the process. I realised then that I had put my life and future with Sam in serious jeopardy.

As I staggered with my darkest realisation, I tried to find my phone in my pocket. I got it out with some degree of urgency but as fast as I could bear it. Every movement I was making was hurting me in my chest. I started thinking logically, trying to buy me some time. I tried to make myself calm, to reduce my heart rate. I knew I had to call for help as soon as I could, as I did not have much time. I dare not touch the knife although it was killing me to leave it in place.

I slowly walked to Sam while dialling the emergency number. I dropped on my knees and lay my head down on her lap. She was lying on the floor still unconscious. I felt her wrist and felt a steady pulse.

"Hello." I spoke calmly to the person on the other side. "My name is Alex. There has been a stabbing by the lake. I need you to send out an ambulance immediately. I have knife stuck in my chest and I think it might have cut my heart. My sister has been knocked unconscious but she has a pulse. Hurry please."

I then carefully gave the location to the person on the other side and tried to hold the phone to my ear as long as I could. I started to feel faint. I looked at Sam, took her hand in mine and whispered to her, "See you on the other side, hon," and then I felt a cold wave come all over me, rising from my feet up to my chest.

***

When Sam came around, she saw Alex with his phone, lying with his head in her lap holding her hand and she screamed at him when she saw the knife stuck in his chest. She shouted out to him "Alex. Oh my god, Alex."

She saw the phone in his hand and took it. It was still connected and she tried to talk in to it.

"Hello." She waited for a response. "Hello."

"Yeah hi. The ambulance is on its way. Ma'm what's your name?"

"Sam."

"Hi. Sam. Was that your brother talking to us before?"

"Yes. Hurry. He is dying. He has a knife stuck in his chest. I think he has been bleeding. I was knocked out so I don't know how long he has been bleeding. Please hurry."

"Don't try to move him ma'm." She cautioned her. "Are you feeling ok?"

"Yes I'm fine but he is not. Hurry." Sam shouted on the phone. "Please hurry."

"Ma'm the dispatch has been already sent to you. It will be there in about 5 minutes I would think. Please stay with me ma'm. I will keep this line connected."

"He doesn't have that long." Sam sighed under her breath realising that it was going to end very badly. She dropped the phone and sat holding him. "Alex. Wake up." She took Alex's hand in her's and caressed it. "Alex please open your eyes baby. Please." She tried stroking his face, caressing it gently.

There was no response from Alex. She tried to check for his pulse and couldn't feel it. She frantically checked on his neck and wrist. She tried to feel his breathing and did not hear him breathe. When she realised his life was slipping away slowly, she took the phone and yelled out one last time, "Hurry. I can't feel his pulse."

Putting the phone aside, she sat by Alex on the ground and gently cushioned his head in her hand. She caressed his face and his hair. "I am right here beside you hon." She spoke to him softly. "You are not alone." Tears were flooded in her eyes. She held his hand. "Alex do you hear me? I'm right her baby. I'm right here with you."

"Honey. Just once, open your eyes so you can see that I am here for you baby. Just once." She pleaded while tears streamed down her cheeks.

She waited for his eyes to show any moments. The faint parking lights left on the truck did little to show her clearly the expressions on his face. All the while, she was caressing his face letting his feeble body feel her touch hoping it would do the trick. She pressed her face on his face and kissed him. "I'm right here beside you." She kept whispering to him while caressing his face. "I'm right her baby. You are with me. Hang in there hon, do it for me please."

She looked up to the night sky and shouted her lungs out, "Take me if you need to, but let him be. Don't take him away from me. Please. I beg you."

"Please. Alex." She caressed his face. She was realising that the moments drifting by were indicating his diminishing lifeline. There was little she could do but see him slip away slowly. She sobbed helplessly and again shouted looking up in the night sky, "Don't take him away from me, please. I cannot live without him." She sobbed her heart out hoping her prayers would be answered, as she looked at the face where she could see the life fading away and while kissing his lips tenderly she whispered softly, "Please save him. I beg of you."

She looked at the sky one last time. "Please. I beg of you. Save him, for me." She pleaded with all her heart and cried out loudly one last time. Then she kissed Alex's lips a few times and laid her face on his as she went silent. She realised she had lost him. She wasn't crying anymore.

When the ambulance arrived, they found her holding Alex in her lap. The knife was still in his chest. Nonetheless, he had bled profusely all this time. The paramedics arrived just before the police. When they tended to Alex, they had tried to check for his brain activity and realised they had been too late. Sam just looked at the paramedic go through the routine as though it was a charade, knowing full well she had lost him a while before. Even if they had been there earlier, they would not have been able to save him – he had a ruptured heart deep inside the rib cage and had bled for all this time. They would not have been able to do anything at that place at that moment. She was not crying or saying anything. Her eyes had gone glassy. She had lost her soul mate, her other half, the only love of her life, and she had realised there was nothing anyone could do to get him back.

Sam was escorted in the police car to the station for reporting the incidence. She had not known the other person who was with Billy so she could only struggle to give his description. He was not around when she had gained consciousness. He had fled after watching Billy and Alex both been stabbed and dead.

All the time in the police station, she was cold and quiet, struggling to answer the impersonal and routine questions. Her mind kept being pushed back to the incidence earlier that night, while the police kept asking her to recount the details. She kept seeing visions and flashes of things she did not want to believe, let alone recall and relive.

"Take your time ma'm, but you do understand we have to get this now while it is fresh in your mind." The police officer taking notes was trying to console Sam.

Sam nodded looking at her. "I'm trying but as I said, I was knocked out. I can only tell you what happened before I was knocked out and after I came around."

Sam had elaborated the history with Billy and where she knew him from. Apparently, there had been reports logged of him assaulting some other girls in the past.

She called home letting her parents know she would be late arriving home. Without alarming her parents, she requested the officers to let her break the news once she was home. One of the female officers drove Sam to her home.

When Sam entered the house, Beverly and Stuart were in the lounge in front of the TV. Seeing the police officer enter behind Sam, they were a bit anxious and nervous. When Sam finally broke the news, Beverly cried out in despair. Stuart sank in the sofa and both cried out with grief. Sam broke out in tears again.

After a while, when all had gathered composure over their grief and despair, they looked at the police officer. The police officer spoke gently explaining the procedures that were going to follow next. She handed her card to Stuart. She quietly took her leave offering her condolences one last time.

When she had left, the shock wave had dissipated across the house. Beverly and Stuart were looking at Sam with tears in their eyes. Beverly took Sam's hand and asked Sam to sit next to her on the sofa.

"Honey, can you please tell us what has actually happened to our Alex?"

"He bled to death ma." Sam said trying to hold back her tears. "He is no longer with us anymore."

Stuart gave out a cry as Beverly sobbed loudly.

"How?" Stuart tried to sound legible. "What happened?"

"Two thugs tried to attack us and Alex was trying to protect me. In the fight, I kicked one guy and Alex ended up killing Billy but it cost him his life." Sam burst out crying. "He ended his life trying to protect me." She broke into tears.

"Billy must have had a knife because he stuck it in Alex's chest before Alex attacked him and ended up killing him." Sam tried to narrate the events as she thought they had happened.

"Is this the same guy you had gone out with a few years ago?" Beverly asked Sam.

Sam nodded. "Billy had knocked me unconscious so I only came around and found Alex on the floor next to me with a knife in his chest. He had already called the ambulance." She sobbed again. "But they couldn't get to him in time to save him and he bled to death in my arms."

"Now he is gone and left me all alone." Sam sobbed her heart out.

Beverly looked at Sam and realised what Sam had said aloud. She gently held Sam and they hugged. Sam let out long bursts of cries as they tried to comfort each other.

"He bled in my lap and I couldn't do anything to save him." Sam cried out sobbing her heart out.

"You can't blame yourself like that. He was just doing what he always did – protect you at all cost." Beverly tried to rationalise Sam's sorrow.

"He protected and saved you in the accident didn't he? And you always stopped him from feeling guilty for being injured. Now you can't blame yourself. He would not like it if he was here now." Beverly tried to reason with Sam.

"He isn't here ma. He will never be here again." Sam cried out, tears running down her eyes. She ran upstairs to her room.

"Sam." Beverly called out to her. Sam did not turn around. Sam slammed her bedroom door as she got into her room. Loud heartfelt crying emanated from her room and then got muffled eventually.

Chapter 21 – the lamentation

The next morning, Sam slowly stirred up from sleep by the soft melancholy sound of the song emanating from Alex's room. As such, she had not had a wink of sleep all night for all kinds of reasons. She had sobbed on and off and her mind was not reasoning well. When she heard the song play, she realised that it was Alex's audio system turning on for the morning alarm – there was no reason she would had remembered to turn it off last night of all the days.

She remembered the tune – 'The first day of spring' by Secret Garden. Coincidently, she had heard this tune before and it had made her very tearful. That day she was hearing it again. As the song rolled on, her emotions got better of her and she instinctively walked into his room and got under his duvet. Tears welled up in her eyes as she continued listening to the song. It was rather an emotional song, and on the best of days would had made anyone well up. That day it was playing in a different sombre context.

Sam realised she missed cuddling him in bed. She realised it was now empty and she would now miss him always and forever. The thought sent shiver down her spine. Her skin craved his touch but all she could do was crave for him while lying in his bed. She hugged his pillows trying to feel his torso. She could not take it anymore so she got up and turned off the stereo. She did not want to be reminded of him, although that seemed too cruel for her to even think about. The ironic nature of the situation was more than she could handle.

Then she remembered something and got up, tossed the covers aside in a hurry and went to her bedroom. She fetched the big teddy bear toy he had given her. Then she squeezed it in her arms. She seemed to melt. She slowly got in her bed, under the duvet and plonking it in the bed and lay on top of it. She dug her hands under the pillow and wrapped it in her hug. She stayed like that for a while. Then she realised the futile attempt of trying to feel his arms around her. It was evident what the toy could not do. Her pathetic attempt to conjure some love for herself made her realise her loss. She was overwhelmed with the sadness, and tears rolled from her eyes. Then she closed them slowly in dismay. She sobbed quietly.

Her mom happened to walk to her room to check on her and entered the room. Seeing her in the state, Beverly started to well up. She sat next to Sam in her bed and stroked her hair and back trying to console her. Beverly struggled to string words of consolation through her welled-up throat. Her mind had nothing sensible to say to Sam. Finally, she spoke something to calm her daughter down because she could not see her in this state anymore.

"We all miss him honey and I know how you feel. But you got to stop crying now." She stroked and caressed Sam's head and tried to console her. Sam continued to sob for a while and then slowly tried to calm down. Sam sat up in bed and tried to control her tears. She looked at her mom who was trying to console her. Beverly was in tears too. They both sat there in silence for a while.

"He saved me twice. And I could not save him even once." Sam said softly and welled up again. "He bled in my arms and I could do nothing." She sobbed again from the depths of her heart. "I don't even know if he knew I was there for him at his side in his last moments."

Sam opened her heart and cried out uncontrollably. Beverly had to hug her and hold her as Sam cried her heart out.

Beverly could not hold back her tears either. "He must have known honey. You were there with him." She tried to calm Sam with her words.

Sam knew very well the futile attempt but chose to respect it nonetheless. Her mom would not know anything; she was not even there when it all happened.

"I do hope so." Sam came out of the hug and looked at her mom.

"You need to stop blaming yourself for this sweetheart. This was not your doing. Please know that." Beverly was being sincere in her assurance.

Sam did not say anything. In her mind, at that moment, it did not matter what the reason was. She had lost Alex forever.

"This is helping no one." Beverly said with some determination. "Get freshened up, come downstairs and we will all have some breakfast. Dad hasn't had any this morning either."

Sam looked at her and gently nodded.

When Sam joined her parents in the lounge, her mom had already laid the breakfast. She asked Sam to sit down at the table. Sam gazed at the three plates laid out and felt the one missing. She slowly sat down in her usual place and instinctively pulled Alex's chair closer to her. Then as she realised what she had done, she shifted in her chair and pretended to be nonchalant.

Her parents tried to ignore it and they all tucked into the breakfast. Sam was famished – she had slept without having anything all night. Basic needs had overcome her grief and she ate hungrily. In between her spoonfuls, she would gaze at the chair next to her, hoping to find Alex to feed a spoonful. Instinctively she ran her hand on the empty seat hoping to caress his thigh. The empty feelings were making her realise the truth. She was hoping to wake up from this nightmare.

"Thanx for that ma." Sam spoke softly after finishing her breakfast. "Dad it is ok if you want to go to work." Sam looked at him. His eyes welled up. Then he tried to control his tears and sat up trying to breathe in deeply. He got up, came over to Sam and hugged her while she was still seated. She wrapped her arms around his waist.

"I'm so sorry sweetheart. However, I know I am going to be worse staying here. I need to get distracted otherwise I will be no good." Stuart welled up in tears as he tried to justify.

"I know dad. You don't have to say anything." Sam hugged him as he kneeled down to hug her. He raised her to her feet and they both hugged for a while. They both were trying to console each other. When he realised he was welling up again, he decided to move out of the hug and kissed Sam goodbye.

Sam sat back down on her seat. "Leave it for me to clear. I just need a moment for myself." She told her mom that she would clear the table. Her mom agreed and left the table.

Sam looked out in the garden. She pulled Alex's chair close to her, crossed her arms and placed them over its backrest. Then placing her cheek on her arm, she stroked the backrest looking at it warmly. She then ran her fingers on the seat. Her eyes wandered on the empty chair trying to find his torso for her to touch.

Beverly came close to Sam from behind and stroked her hair. "This is not going to help." She whispered to Sam.

"Nothing will ma." Sam said without turning around. "I know that. I am just hoping to wake up from this nightmare somehow."

"Why don't we go out somewhere? That will distract you." Her mom suggested.

"No." Sam sat up and looked at her. Then Sam hugged her mom at her waist. "You go to work too ma. There is little reason for you to miss work."

"Only if you promise to go to college." Beverly tried to reason. "I can't have you staying in like this."

Sam looked at her mom and nodded in acceptance.

"And don't try to fool me and come home early." Beverly tried to nudge her in her arms.

"I won't ma." Sam realised she had to attend some classes today even if she did not want to.

When Sam was in her class, she could not focus on the lecture. Her mind kept wandering to Alex. She kept looking at her phone hoping for his message. She looked out of the window aimlessly. When the session was over, she walked slowly toward the library in hope that she could kill some time there skimming through some shelves aimlessly.

On the way to the library, Sam bumped into Jennifer.

"Hey Sam." Jennifer said seeing her sombre. "What is the matter?"

Sam came to her senses and said, "Hi Jen."

"What's the matter?" Jennifer was concerned.

Sam elaborated the events that had unfolded in the previous night. Jennifer was shocked and saddened. She had always fancied Alex. She welled up in tears.

"I'm so sorry." She hugged Sam.

Sam tried to keep a brave face. "Thanx. I know you liked him very much."

"You did?" Jennifer was surprised.

"uh huh." Sam nodded. "I'm sorry it did not work out between the two of you."

"It's ok." Jen said. "At least I had him as a good friend."

Sam tried hiding her feelings.

"Do you want to catch some lunch?" Jennifer asked Sam.

"OK." Sam did not have much planned and this was sure to get her distracted.

They both went to a fast-food joint. At the meal, the girls had a long talk. They had not spent time like this in many months. Ever since Alex had stopped seeing Jennifer, things had become weird between Sam and Jennifer and Sam had not realised how to get back with her. She had been her good friend for years and that is why when Jennifer had asked to go out with Alex few years ago, it had created some awkward moments in Sam's mind. Then later when Alex had stopped seeing Jennifer, Sam felt guilty and shied back from her. This had put a strain on their friendship.

After the meal, the girls hugged each other in condolence and parted their ways. Sam went to the library to kill some time.

When it was afternoon, Sam headed home. A flood of warmth hit her as instinct and she reached to her phone. She used to call Alex when she would be ready to go home and he would meet her and pick her up. Then just as suddenly she had felt the warmth, her heart sank when she saw her phone. She realised there was no one to call. She was driving home alone. A feeling of despair hit her like a cold winter breeze.

When Sam got back home, it was late evening. She had decided to drive around on the sunset roads she and Alex used to go when they wanted to get away for all. When she entered the house, she saw her mom and dad waiting for her to return, sitting in the lounge. The TV was off so they must have been talking.

"I hope you haven't been waiting for long." Sam apologised.

"No darling. We were just talking while we waited for you." Her mom and dad looked at her.

"Give me a minute. I will be right back." Sam rushed to her room to change into her nightwear.

When she returned, they all settled at the table for the evening meal. This time Sam remembered not to pull Alex's chair close to her. It was difficult but she controlled it. Beverly and Stuart seemed pleased about the headway she had managed. There was little small-talk at the table. Sam was quiet through most of the conversations, struggling at her best abilities to keep herself involved. Every time her mind drifted off to Alex, she shook it and focused back to the conversation at the table. It was not that she was trying to get past his memories; rather she was trying to stop herself from the torture of the mourning. She knew that thinking about him would bring back all the grief she had been bottling up all day.

After the meals, she helped her mom clear the table and later her mom and dad sat on the couch. Sam turned the TV on and handed the remote to her dad.

"Put something nice on." She grinned warmly. "We cannot sit here staring at a black screen for long. That is not going to bring him back."

"If you say so sweetheart." Her dad beckoned her for a quick hug.

"Come and sit with us for a while. You will feel better." Her mom suggested.

"Give me a minute." Sam cleared the kitchen, loaded the dishwasher and went upstairs. She came down with her toy teddy bear. Then placing him in the lounger she cuddled next to him. Beverly and Stuart did not say anything. At least she was sitting in the lounge doing something else other than welling up. They were happy just to see her without tears for now.

While Sam watched over the shifting pictures on the TV screen, her mind wandered off. She kept feeling the teddy for a warm cuddle and hugged the pillows on the lounger. About half an hour into the evening, she had dozed off. Her exhaustion had finally caught up with her. Finally, her mind was ready to shut down for the night and get some much-needed rest.

Stuart turned the TV off when it was time to sleep. He looked at Beverly and she looked at him suggesting that he carry Sam to her bed.

"I ain't doing that." He shook his head. "I know what will happen in her given state of mind if she wakes up in my arms. I cannot do that to her."

Beverly realised. She then spread a soft blanket over Sam and they both decided to leave her with a small night light and let her sleep there until she woke up on her own. Beverly and Stuart went to their room quietly.

Sam woke up in the night with some sighs. She must have had a wet dream. Seeing herself in the lounge, it took her a while to figure out what had happened. Then after her heart sank, she gathered herself holding on to the teddy, and climbed to her bedroom. She missed Alex's strong arms to carry her to her bed. Slipping under the duvet, she hugged the teddy and drifted back to sleep.

"I miss you so much." She whispered in her sleepy state.

In the morning, the stereo turned on automatically for the morning alarm again and starting playing. This time the song had a more feminine feel. Although she remembered listening to this one before, she could not recall which one it was ('Lotus' by Secret Garden). She felt consoled. The tune had a rather soothing effect, even though it was still very emotional in composition.

She stirred and rolled over on her side in her bed. She glanced at the kiss mark on her wall. Her heart filled with warmth. Listening to the song, she felt the urge and she got out of bed, touched, and caressed it. Then she kissed it gently in a futile attempt to feel his lips. She let the music continue to roll on from one song to another. It was now making her emotional.

She glanced around her room. She noticed the gift of pearl he had given her. She took it and gazed at it with renewed warmth. She got up and walked over to her desk. She gazed at the crystal cube. The words warmed her heart. She felt the pining in herself rise again. She fetched the cards he had presented her. The picture card with a swan; his first gift that had melted her heart and made her fall for him and the poem he had written for her. She touched them trying to appreciate what she had enjoyed then and was missing it immensely. Soon she was tearful again and decided to shut off the stereo.

Beverly came in and checked up on Sam. Sam looked at her.

"You are going to be ok?" her mom came close and held Sam's hands in her's.

Sam nodded. "I will be ok. Don't worry."

As her mom left for work, Sam walked into Alex's room. She lay down in his bed. Turning on her side, she pressed her chest into the bed. She glanced over his pillow. She took a deep breath pressing her face into his pillow hoping to catch his aroma. She missed his fragrance so she got out of bed and found his bottle of eau de toilette in his cupboard. She sprayed it on herself. Wrapping herself with her arms, she tried to feel him all over her.

She saw the laundry hamper. It was half-full with his clothes ready for washing. Her heart skipped a beat. She dashed to it and pulling his clothes out of it, and clumping them in a ball, she pressed her face against them and breathed in deep. Then she hugged them against her bosom.

Slowly she realised she was slipping back into the nightmare of the emotional tug-of-war between her fond dreams and the nightmarish reality. She welled up and curled on the floor trying to pull her legs and knees into a cocoon with his clothes pressed close to her chest in her arms.

While Sam was lying on the floor, the doorbell rang. She did not believe she had heard it the first time. When she waited for a while, it rang again. She was surprised and perplexed. She cautiously went to the door to figure out who it could be. She looked at the person standing outside.

"Yes?" she called out.

"Delivery for Ms. Sam." The male voice replied in a bland tone. Sam opened the door.

"Are you Sam?" He asked in a routine manner.

"Yes." Sam looked at him in a perplexed glance.

He handed her a pad. "Sign here please." He said in a hurry.

Sam signed her initials and he handed her a big beautiful bouquet of one dozen long stemmed red roses in a water bowl. There was a card attached to it.

"Thanks." He went away nonchalantly.

"Hold on." Sam came to her senses and yelled at him to ask him. "Who are they from?"

"Don't know miss." He shook his head. "I am just delivering them."

"How can I find out?"

"You will have to call the office."

"What is the number?"

He gave out the number and the name of the florist.

Sam carefully took it down. She rushed into the house, picked up the phone and called the number.

"Hi." Sam got on her feet. "I am calling regarding a delivery I just received. I wanted to know who it was from."

"What's your address miss?"

Sam gave out the address. "I just received it now. I wanted to know who sent it."

"We don't have a name miss. It was paid on a card but I cannot divulge that information."

"Give me a minute." Sam ran upstairs to Alex's room. She hurriedly found his wallet and got his card out.

"Can you confirm if the last four digits are these please?" she read out the numbers.

"Yes miss."

Sam's heart sank. She sat down on the bed.

"Hi hello?" Sam continued talking. "Can you tell me when this was paid for?"

"Some time last week. It was booked to be delivered for today at a specific time."

Sam went quiet again.

"Ok thanx." Sam hung up.

A million different thoughts ran across Sam's mind. She took a moment and looked at the bouquet again. It must have cost dearly. It was fabulous. She glanced at the card.

It had a picture on it – with Sam and Alex in arms together looking into each other's eyes lovingly. She remembered it from the photo session they had had a while ago.

Inside were handwritten words:

You are,
my lo♥e,
my life!
X

Sam burst into tears. All this time she had been trying hard to come to grips with his loss. Although she had been craving for his presence and struggling to come to terms with his absence, she had been trying nonetheless. This had suddenly put a big spanner in the works. She would not forget this gift.

Obviously, he must have gone through a lot of planning to make this happen. Sam's mind started working it out. She wanted to, she needed to. She could not let go this message from him no matter how insanely coincidental and ironic it might seem.

'Since the card has our picture, he must have specially ordered it through some website. It has a barcode at the back.' It was definitely not printed on a home printer. It was thick commercial card. 'So he ordered the card first. Then wrote the words himself. Then he must have ordered the flowers and asked for the card to be delivered with the flowers.'

Sam's mind was trying to get inside Alex's brain. He used to be very cryptic at times in the ways he loved to surprise her. She did not want to miss any detail. Her heart was fluttering like a butterfly's wings.

'Why today?' she wondered. That day they did not have any classes. It was one day in the week when they both used to be home alone for the day.

Sam's heart skipped a beat and she suddenly felt warm inside. Her tummy took a turn and she quivered all over realising what he might have planned in his mind for that day. She closed her eyes, wrapped her hands over her chest and pressed her bosom trying to feel his hands all over her. She felt the tingle inside her and suddenly the wetness she felt reminded her about what she had missed all this time.

"Now look what you have done to me." She grinned and pretended to talk to him. She took the flowers in the kitchen and placed them in a vase with water. Then she took them upstairs to her bedroom. Placing them on her desk, she glanced at his photo. She gently touched it as she recalled the occasion when it was taken.

Placing the flowers in front of his picture, she gazed at him for a while.

"Thank you for the gift." She sighed touching his picture. "Wish you were here to give the rest of it."

She welled up in tears and missed his presence in her life. It all came back to haunt her. She walked into the bathroom and decided to take a bath. She ran the bath and when it was ready, she slowly entered the bath and lay in it. This was the first time she was taking a bath alone after a long time. Usually they used to enjoy something like that together, particularly when home alone.

She felt the hot water comforting although it could never come close to his bear hugs. As she lay there with her eyes closed, she tried to feel herself between her thighs, trying to imagine his touch, his desires and his eagerness to please her. However, no matter how hard she tried, she could not feel as aroused as she had felt with his touch. She paused for a moment and filled up with tears at her inability even to pleasure herself in his absence. She decided just to stay there for a while. She washed her hair and conditioned it.

After lying in the bath quietly for a while, she stepped out. She dried herself. Then she blow-dried her hair and did it in a nice French plat. She changed into something he would have loved to see her dressed in. She put on his favourite perfume he had given her and decided to spend time going out to their favourite places. She wanted to honour his desire for the day, in his memory.

There was no way she would know what he had planned for that day. Obviously, he wanted to spend time at home making love to her as they would be alone, but she could not bring herself to think about that. The next closest thing of warmth was spending time in his memories doing things they usually did outdoors.

She window-shopped around the mall. She even bought a nice t-shirt for him and a dress and lingerie for herself that he would have loved. She had lunch at their favourite restaurant and watched a movie with a big drink and two straws and a double scoop ice cream cone. She stopped at the jewellery store where they had shopped for her ring and their love pendants. She welled up at the futility for buying anything now. She glanced at her ring and reminisced the good times they had. With a heavy heart, she continued walking back to her car.

In the evening when she entered the house, her mom and dad were perplexed and a bit concerned looking at her all dressed up. She appeared complacent yet sombre, rather unexpected state of mind.

"Where have you been?" her mom asked her calmly.

"Out on a date." Sam replied grinning slightly. "X had sent me flowers and so I decided to go out with him."

"Flowers?" Her dad was puzzled. "When?"

"Today." Sam smiled. "He apparently had ordered them last week sometime to be delivered today." She grinned.

Stuart tried to voice his concern for the lack of realistic perspective of the current situation. Beverly pressed his hand to shush him.

"Hungry?" She asked Sam.

"Nope. I have had nice lunch." Sam grinned again. "I'm tired and off to bed. Hope you don't mind."

Sam hopped to her room.

Beverly just looked at Stuart. She shook her head with helplessness. "We will need to help her tomorrow when she plummets, because she will surely crash tomorrow." She sighed. "God help us then."

The following day Sam woke up and freshened up. Her stroll was particularly slow and emotionless again that day. It was not clear if that was due to lack of sleep as usual or depression. As she freshened up without any hurry, her expressions on the face were blank. She did not gaze at herself in the mirror all the time she was in the bathroom. Either she seemed to have exhausted herself while pining for him or she had crashed and tumbled from the euphoric dream she had lived the day before.

When she stepped out of the bathroom, she saw her mom in her bedroom. Sam walked to her. She hugged her mom gently without saying much. Then Sam spoke slowly, "He is never coming back, is he?" She continued hugging her mom.

Beverly just shook her head and hugged Sam tenderly.

"I love you very much you know that." Beverly caressed her face. "We all are trying to cope with this tragedy. You are not alone." She tried to console Sam.

"I know ma." Sam hugged her again. Sam had welled up in tears. As she came out of the hug, Sam brushed her own tears from her cheeks.

"I never imagined I would have to bear this pain, you know." Sam's throat had choked up as she welled up in tears.

"Nobody did, sweetheart." Beverly took Sam's face in her palms and tried to console her. "This is painful to us too. Your dad is just trying to pretend to be brave. It has killed him inside."

After looking at Sam, her mom said, "There is very little we can do but carry on living. We will have to find strength to get over this grief and live with the pain for life."

Sam did not say anything and just looked at her mom. Then she hugged her again and said, "Go on now. I will see you in the evening."

Beverly hugged her with warmth and Sam left her room. When Sam saw mom leave, she got back to her room.

Sam recalled the dream she had in the night. She was missing him too much to bear it anymore. She went to his room and turned the stereo to play a song. The stereo started playing and the song 'Belonging' by Secret Garden started to play. As she lay in his bed, the soft music filled the room and her heart with warmth. As the song played along, she started to well up with emotions.

She got up, emptied all his clothes from his wardrobe, piled them on his bed and then lay in the pile trying to drown herself in his aroma. Her addiction for his physical pleasures had pushed her to her acceptable limit and she could not take the cravings anymore. By the end of the song, she burst into a loud cry and sobbed her heart out. She spoke hoping he was around listening to her, "I can't do this alone anymore." Then she sobbed quietly burying her head in the pillow. "I just can't", she gasped softly as her eyes ran dry.

She got up and turned off the stereo. She took off her sleepwear and selected one of his favourite shirts. She put on his shirt, and rolled up the sleeves. She did her hair in a bun and took off her panties. Then she pretended she was going to seduce him while he sat in the lounge like she had done before.

She walked downstairs and went into the kitchen. As she was preparing breakfast, she kept imagining his eyes gazing at her all the time. She felt warm butterflies in her tummy and her heart fluttered as she traipsed around the kitchen. While she stood there with her pelvis pressed against the worktop, she imagined him walking behind her and pressing himself against her bum. She gasped and wished she could feel his arms around her. When she missed them, she turned around and looked at the empty lounger. Her heart sank.

She continued to prepare breakfast and once she was done, she sat at the table. She tried hard to gulp it down, but it proved difficult, as she had welled up too much. After a few more spoonfuls, she put it aside in utter despair and frustration.

She glanced at the lounger. She walked to it and lay down on her chest. Just then, it started to rain outside. As she heard the rumble in the sky, it reminded her of the first time they had kissed on the lounger, while renovating the garden – they had taken a day off due to rains. It brought memories flooding back to her mind. She felt the quiver recalling the time when she had kissed him on his lips. Everything came back to haunt her – his touch, caress, kisses and her hunger for all of them.

Feeling overwhelmed, she burst into tears. She sobbed for a while. Then her sorrow could not be contained any more. She rolled over on her back and gave out a loud cry, full of frustration and anger. "Why couldn't you had taken me with you?" She yelled out. "Why did you leave me behind like this? What for?" She sobbed helplessly. "How am I to carry on without you?" She rolled over on her chest and sobbed into the pillow on the lounger. "You should have taken me with you." As her sobbing calmed down, she seemed to have realised something, something she would want to do.

She got up, composed herself and went upstairs. She cleared his bed of all his clothes that were in the bed. She neatly folded them back into his wardrobe. She cleared her wardrobe and spent time clearing her bedroom. She put all their laundry to wash. She changed the bed covers and cleaned both of their rooms. In the afternoon, she spent time going through her bank account making sure she had paid all the bills on their cards. She drove to the library and made sure she had returned all of their books on loan.

Later in the evening, she sat down with her parents and had the evening meal. She gazed at them fondly. Occasionally tears welled up in her eyes.

"You have been so considerate and supportive to me through all this." She acknowledged their understanding behaviour.

Her mom and dad looked a bit amazed at her remark. "We do love you sweetheart."

At that, she had welled up again. "I know. I hope you know how much I love you two." She said.

"We do sweetheart." Her mom said to her looking a bit perplexed at her behaviour. However, her mom thought this was, most probably, a phase of depression/recovery that Sam was going through again.

"You haven't eaten much today." Her mom asked her.

"I had a heavy brunch in the morning." Sam replied. "I am ok."

In the night, Sam stayed in the lounge with her parents watching TV. When they finally retired for the night, Sam kissed and hugged them tightly and wished them good night.

In the morning, Stuart mentioned about the stereo not playing the songs. "It feels so weird not to hear their music in the morning. Feels like weekend." He mentioned to Beverly.

"The songs remind her of him so I think she has turned it off." Beverly tried to justify. "She has been struggling to cope, you know."

"I can tell. She hasn't gone out or even eaten properly." He was concerned.

"She is pining for him, as you can guess." She said sadly. "Leave her be. She will come around. I will speak to her today before I go to work." Stuart left for work soon after.

Beverly had not seen Sam that morning. Sam's bedroom door was ajar. Beverly went in there, but she did not find Sam in the bedroom. Her bed was made. Their bathroom door was closed. 'Sam has been in the bathroom for a long time today', she thought to herself. As she was about to leave the bedroom, Beverly say a note on the desk. It was handwritten and addressed to 'mom and dad'. Going closer to the desk, she picked it up and read it. Then she hurried to the bathroom and opened the door without knocking.

When Beverly entered the bathroom, she gasped and shrieked with grief at the sight. Sam was in the bathtub in her sleepwear, resting her head against her stuffed teddy bear. Her eyes were closed and her head was drooped against the teddy bear on one side. Approaching the bath closer, Beverly could see Sam submerged in crimson water. Her legs were stretched and her colour was ghostly white. She had earphones in her ears and an audio player was resting on the edge of the bath.

When Beverly came out of the bathroom, she stood there horrified with her eyes closed trying to catch her breath. She slowly walked to her bedroom, picked up the phone and dialled a number.

"Honey, It's me." She spoke softly, trying to hide her panic.

She heard him answer back.

"Can you come home, please, if you can?"

She heard him ask if everything was ok.

"Yes. We just need you right now. Please." Beverly said while trying to hold back her tears. "Just be careful and come home safe. Talk to you when you get here ok?"

After hanging up the phone, Beverly sobbed looking at the paper note again as she sat down in the bed. Her outbursts said it all.

My dearest mom and dad,

Of all the scenarios that you two hoped for us, I am sure this one wasn't in your wildest dreams. You have been the best parents anyone could ask for and I am sorry to bring you this failure. I am sorry about X, and I am very sorry about myself. I hope you find strength and compassion to forgive me for my mistakes and for taking this drastic step.

I can't live without him. I tried, but I just can't, and now I don't wish to either. I can't live in a world in which he doesn't exist. Even if I can't be with him, I definitely can't be without him. He sacrificed his life to keep me safe. To be honest, I died with him when he was taken from me.

With all my love to you both,
Sam

If I could ask you for one last wish - please cremate us together, if you could.

Acknowledgement

If you have enjoyed this novel, your positive feedback, reviews and word-of-mouth recommendations would be greatly appreciated. Please refrain from including any spoilers in your reviews or comments.

I have also adapted this novel into a screenplay accompanied with music soundtrack. I already 'watch' it in my mind while listening to the sound track. It would be nice to share my interpretation/adaptation with you some day as a motion picture.

- K. Loma

www.ingramcontent.com/pod-product-compliance
Lightning Source LLC
Chambersburg PA
CBHW051520250626
47156CB00001B/160